MW01641811

MURDER
short & sweet

Edited by

Paul D. Staudohar

FALL RIVER PRESS

This 2010 edition published by Fall River Press,
by arrangement with Chicago Review Press, Inc.

Interior design: Emily Brackett/Visible Logic
Interior illustrations: Laura D'Argo
Typesetting: Jonathan Hahn

Fall River Press
122 Fifth Avenue
New York, NY 10011

ISBN: 978-1-4351-1966-6

Printed and bound in the United States of America

10 9 8 7 6 5 4 3 2 1

CONTENTS

ACKNOWLEDGMENTS

This is the tenth book in a series that began in 1995 with *Baseball's Best Short Stories*. The other collections of short stories from the publisher and me are on golf, football, boxing, fishing, hunting, a variety of sports (in two volumes), and dogs. Throughout the years publisher Cynthia Sherry has been a valuable source of ideas, inspiration, and advice. The work of former managing editor Gerilee Hundt is also always excellent and greatly appreciated. Project editor Devon Freeny did fine work on this book. Numerous other people gave generously of their knowledge and time to make this book possible, especially Abby Browning and Clare Crowley from Penny Publications, the publisher of *Ellery Queen's Mystery Magazine*, where many of the stories originally appeared; Margery Flax of the Mystery Writers of America; and Craig Tenney of Harold Ober Associates. Many thanks are due to Anna Abreu at Curtis Brown, Ltd.; Kate Ausman at Random House; David Austern at Liza Dawson Associates; Vicky Bijur Literary Agency; Denise Crozier and Barry Zepel at California State University, East Bay; Lawrence Ganem of JackTime (the Ellery Queen Trust); Bette Graber at Alfred A. Knopf; James A. Mangan, professor emeritus at the University of Strathclyde in Scotland; Peter Mason at Sterling Lord Literistic, Inc.; Erin Overbay, librarian at *The New Yorker*; Amanda Pennelly at Watkins/Loomis Agency; Lucie Prinz at the *Atlantic Monthly*; David Schmit at *Playboy*; Maxine Schweitzer at Scott Meredith Literary Agency; Sandie Sorenson from the University of Southern California; and Gwen Stevenson from the University of California, Berkeley.

Kudos also to the talented librarians at California State University, East Bay: Tom Bickley, Todd H. Charles, Dana Edwards, Judith Faust, Paul Maclennan, and Stephen Philibosian.

Paul D. Staudohar

INTRODUCTION

Mystery stories are nearly as old as civilization, dating back at least four thousand years to ancient Egypt. Tales of murder are related in the Bible, as when "Cain rose up against Abel his brother and slew him." It is not uncommon for people to fleetingly contemplate murder. Fortunately, they seldom act on these random impulses. Motives are real enough—hate, jealousy, revenge, greed, or even the thrill of the act—but fear of prosecution is a powerful deterrent. Moreover, homicide may provide its own form of retribution to the murderer, as feelings of remorse inflict intense psychological punishment.

A good story colorfully describes a scenario that leads to an imaginative and often surprising conclusion. Of the twenty-five murder stories in this book, some focus on the intricate plotting that leads to murder. Others deal more with the aftermath of the crime. Many of them also involve detection, either by the police or a private eye. Whatever the particulars, all the murder stories in this book are mysteries, because they pose and resolve a puzzle: whether the act will go unpunished or justice will be served.

The great fun of murder mysteries is pondering this elaborate riddle and seeking to resolve it through the author's clues and one's own powers of ratiocination. The essence of these stories is the ability of the authors to rouse the reader's curiosity. The clever unfolding of suspenseful details of the plot heightens the reader's determination to unravel the solution. Even if one cannot correctly guess the outcome, the attempt to do so is wonderfully entertaining. Also, a vicarious sense of relief may occur, because the villainous act is happening to someone else. One gets to enjoy the excitement of the chase without its inconvenience and dangers.

This anthology draws from three principal sources. One is classic tales from writers like Edgar Allan Poe and A. Conan Doyle. The second source is stories that were widely read and praised in their day but have been long out of print and unavailable to present-day readers. The third source is outstanding stories from contemporary authors.

Although the world has changed dramatically since the days of the early murder classics, fashions in mystery fiction remain much the same. Similar to stories about love, politics, or sports, mystery fiction alters only in details or manner of treatment. Human nature changes only superficially over time, so the tales from the past remain as poignant today as when they were written.

Many of the stories in the book are from the "Golden Age" of mystery fiction, roughly the period from 1925 to 1940. Women writers flourished during this time, including Agatha Christie, Dorothy L. Sayers, Daphne du Maurier, and Margery Allingham. Christie and Sayers, the most famous of the group, are included in this collection. There is also a story from a distinguished successor, Ruth Rendell.

The creator of the first fictional detective was Poe, an American whose pioneering story "The Murders in the Rue Morgue" was written in 1841. However, much of the best mystery fiction after Poe has come from Britain. Therefore, this book is distinctly Anglo-American. About half of the stories are from British writers: Doyle, Christie, Sayers, Rendell, Roald Dahl, Thomas Burke, Anthony Berkeley/Francis Iles, Lord Dunsany, Hugh Walpole, Anthony Gilbert, and C. S. Forester. The rest of the stories are by Americans: Poe, Ellery Queen, Ben Ray Redman, Brendan DuBois, Stanley Ellin, John Updike, Donald E. Westlake, Lawrence Block, Vincent Starrett, James Holding, Clark Howard, and Lawrence Treat.

The Edgar Awards, named after Poe, are presented annually by the Mystery Writers of America for the best short stories and novels, similar to Hollywood's Oscars. The Gold Dagger Award is Britain's version of the Edgar, and the Shamus Awards are presented by the Private Eye Writers of America. The highest honor in the mystery writing field is the Grand Master Edgar

Award, given for lifetime achievement. Seven of the authors in the book have won this coveted prize: Christie, Starrett, Queen, Ellin, Westlake, Block, and Rendell.

Several of the stories originally appeared in first-rate literary outlets like *The New Yorker*, *Harper's*, *Saturday Evening Post*, *Playboy*, and especially *Ellery Queen's Mystery Magazine*. *EQMM* started in 1941, one hundred years after the publication of Poe's first detective story, and remains the gold standard for mystery writers today.

THE BLACK CAT

(1843)

Edgar Allan Poe

This macabre tale blends rationality with madness, as a self-destructive alcoholic with a feline phobia commits vile deeds. Edgar Allan Poe (1809–1849) lived a relatively brief and tragic life during which he produced luminous prose and poetry that are widely read throughout the world today. The psychological symbolism that is threaded through his stories gives them a haunting credibility that lingers in the mind. Among his masterpieces are "The Purloined Letter," "The Mystery of Marie Roget," "The Fall of the House of Usher," "The Masque of the Red Death," "The Pit and the Pendulum," and "The Gold Bug." Poe's "The Raven" is one of the best known of all American poems. He is revered by his hometown, which calls its National Football League team the Baltimore Ravens. "The Black Cat" originally appeared in the *Saturday Evening Post*.

For the most wild yet most homely narrative which I am about to pen, I neither expect nor solicit belief. Mad indeed would I be to expect it, in a case where my very senses reject their own evidence. Yet, mad am I not—and very surely do I not dream. But to-morrow I die, and to-day I would unburden my soul. My immediate purpose is to place before the world, plainly, succinctly, and without comment, a series of mere household events. In their consequences, these events have terrified—have tortured—have destroyed me. Yet I will not attempt to expound them. To me, they have presented little but horror—to many they will seem less terrible than *baroques*. Hereafter, perhaps, some intellect may be found which will reduce my phantasm to the commonplace—some intellect more calm, more logical, and far less excitable than my own, which will perceive, in the circumstances I detail with awe, nothing more than an ordinary succession of very natural causes and effects.

From my infancy I was noted for the docility and humanity of my disposition. My tenderness of heart was even so conspicuous as to make me the jest of my companions. I was especially fond of animals, and was indulged by my parents with a great variety of pets. With these I spent most of my time, and never was so happy as when feeding and caressing them. This peculiarity of character grew with my growth, and, in my manhood, I derived from it one of my principal sources of pleasure. To those who have cherished an affection for a faithful and sagacious dog, I need hardly be at the trouble of explaining the nature or the intensity of the gratification thus derivable. There is something in the unselfish and self-sacrificing love of a brute, which goes directly to the heart of him who has had frequent occasion to test the paltry friendship and gossamer fidelity of mere *Man*.

I married early, and was happy to find in my wife a disposition not uncongenial with my own. Observing my partiality for domestic pets, she lost no opportunity of procuring those of the most agreeable kind. We had birds, gold-fish, a fine dog, rabbits, a small monkey, and a *cat*.

This latter was a remarkably large and beautiful animal, entirely black, and sagacious to an astonishing degree. In speaking of his intelligence, my wife, who at heart was not a little tinctured with superstition, made frequent allusion to the ancient popular notion, which regarded all black cats as witches in disguise. Not that she was ever *serious* upon this point—and I mention the matter at all for no better reason than that it happens, just now, to be remembered.

Pluto—this was the cat's name—was my favorite pet and playmate. I alone fed him, and he attended me wherever I went about the house. It was even with difficulty that I could prevent him from following me through the streets.

Our friendship lasted, in this manner, for several years, during which my general temperament and character—through the instrumentality of the Fiend Intemperance—had (I blush to confess it) experienced a radical alteration for the worse. I grew, day by day, more moody, more irritable, more regardless of the feelings of others. I suffered myself to use intemperate language to my wife. At length, I even offered her personal violence. My pets, of course, were made to feel the change in my disposition. I not only neglected, but ill-used them. For Pluto, however, I still retained sufficient regard to restrain me from maltreating him, as I made no scruple of maltreating the rabbits, the monkey, or even the dog, when, by accident, or through affection, they came in my way. But my disease grew upon me—for what disease is like Alcohol!—and at length even Pluto, who was now becoming old, and consequently somewhat peevish—even Pluto began to experience the effects of my ill temper.

One night, returning home, much intoxicated, from one of my haunts about town, I fancied that the cat avoided my presence. I seized him; when, in his fright at my violence, he inflicted a slight wound upon my hand with his teeth. The fury of a demon instantly possessed me. I knew myself no longer.

My original soul seemed, at once, to take its flight from my body; and a more than fiendish malevolence, gin-nurtured, thrilled every fibre of my frame. I took from my waistcoat-pocket a penknife, opened it, grasped the poor beast by the throat, and deliberately cut one of its eyes from the socket! I blush, I burn, I shudder, while I pen the damnable atrocity.

When reason returned with the morning—when I had slept off the fumes of the night's debauch—I experienced a sentiment half of horror, half of remorse, for the crime of which I had been guilty; but it was, at best, a feeble and equivocal feeling, and the soul remained untouched. I again plunged into excess, and soon drowned in wine all memory of the deed.

In the meantime the cat slowly recovered. The socket of the lost eye presented, it is true, a frightful appearance, but he no longer appeared to suffer any pain. He went about the house as usual, but, as might be expected, fled in extreme terror at my approach. I had so much of my old heart left, as to be at first grieved by this evident dislike on the part of a creature which had once so loved me. But this feeling soon gave place to irritation. And then came, as if to my final and irrevocable overthrow, the spirit of PERVERSENESS. Of this spirit philosophy takes no account. Yet I am not more sure that my soul lives, than I am that perverseness is one of the primitive impulses of the human heart—one of the indivisible primary faculties, or sentiments, which give direction to the character of Man. Who has not, a hundred times, found himself committing a vile or a stupid action, for no other reason than because he knows he should *not?* Have we not a perpetual inclination, in the teeth of our best judgment, to violate that which is *Law*, merely because we understand it to be such? This spirit of perverseness, I say, came to my final overthrow. It was this unfathomable longing of the soul *to vex itself*—to offer violence to its own nature—to do wrong for the wrong's sake only—that urged me to continue and finally to consummate the injury I had inflicted upon the unoffending brute. One morning, in cold blood, I slipped a noose about its neck and hung it to the limb of a tree;—hung it with the tears streaming from my eyes, and with the bitterest remorse at my heart;—hung it *because* I knew that it had loved me, and *because* I felt it had given me no reason of offence;—hung it *because* I knew that in so doing I was committing a sin—a deadly sin that would so jeopardize my immortal soul as to place it—if such a thing were possible—even beyond the reach of the infinite mercy of the Most Merciful and Most Terrible God.

On the night of the day on which this most cruel deed was done, I was aroused from sleep by the cry of fire. The curtains of my bed were in flames. The whole house was blazing. It was with great difficulty that my wife, a servant, and myself, made our escape from the conflagration. The destruction was complete. My entire worldly wealth was swallowed up, and I resigned myself thenceforward to despair.

I am above the weakness of seeking to establish a sequence of cause and effect, between the disaster and the atrocity. But I am detailing a chain of facts—and wish not to leave even a possible link imperfect. On the day succeeding the fire, I visited the ruins. The walls, with one exception, had fallen in. This exception was found in a compartment wall, not very thick, which stood about the middle of the house, and against which had rested the head of my bed. The plastering had here, in great measure, resisted the action of the fire—a fact which I attributed to its having been recently spread. About this wall a dense crowd were collected, and many persons seemed to be examining a particular portion of it with very minute and eager attention. The words "strange!" "singular!" and other similar expressions, excited my curiosity. I approached and saw, as if graven in *bas-relief* upon the white surface, the figure of a gigantic *cat*. The impression was given with an accuracy truly marvelous. There was a rope about the animal's neck.

When I first beheld this apparition—for I could scarcely regard it as less—my wonder and my terror were extreme. But at length reflection came to my aid. The cat, I remembered, had been hung in a garden adjacent to the house. Upon the alarm of fire, this garden had been immediately filled by the crowd—by some one of whom the animal must have been cut from the tree and thrown, through an open window, into my chamber. This had probably been done with the view of arousing me from sleep. The falling of other walls had compressed the victim of my cruelty into the substance of the freshly-spread plaster; the lime of which, with the flames, and the *ammonia* from the carcass, had then accomplished the portraiture as I saw it.

Although I thus readily accounted to my reason, if not altogether to my conscience, for the startling fact just detailed, it did not the less fail to make a deep impression upon my fancy. For months I could not rid myself of the phantasm of the cat; and, during this period, there came back into my spirit a half-sentiment that seemed, but was not, remorse. I went so far as to regret the loss of the animal, and to look about me, among the vile haunts which I now habitually frequented, for another pet of the same species, and of somewhat similar appearance, with which to supply its place.

One night as I sat, half stupefied, in a den of more than infamy, my attention was suddenly drawn to some black object, reposing upon the head of one of the immense hogsheads of gin, or of rum, which constituted the chief furniture of the apartment. I had been looking steadily at the top of this hogshead for some minutes, and what now caused me surprise was the fact that I had not sooner perceived the object thereupon. I approached it, and touched it with my hand. It was a black cat—a very large one—fully as large as Pluto, and closely resembling him in every respect but one. Pluto had not a white hair upon any portion of his body; but this cat had a large, although indefinite splotch of white, covering nearly the whole region of the breast.

Upon my touching him, he immediately arose, purred loudly, rubbed against my hand, and appeared delighted with my notice. This, then, was the very creature of which I was in search. I at once offered to purchase it of the landlord; but this person made no claim to it—knew nothing of it—had never seen it before.

I continued my caresses, and when I prepared to go home, the animal evinced a disposition to accompany me. I permitted it to do so; occasionally stooping and patting it as I proceeded. When it reached the house it domesticated itself at once, and became immediately a great favorite with my wife.

For my own part, I soon found a dislike to it arising within me. This was just the reverse of what I had anticipated; but—I know not how or why it was—its evident fondness for myself rather disgusted and annoyed me. By slow degrees these feelings of disgust and annoyance rose into the bitterness of hatred. I avoided the creature; a certain sense of shame, and the remembrance of my former deed of cruelty, preventing me from physically abusing it. I did not, for some weeks, strike, or otherwise violently ill use it; but gradually—very gradually—I came to look upon it with unutterable loathing, and to flee silently from its odious presence, as from the breath of a pestilence.

What added, no doubt, to my hatred of the beast, was the discovery, on the morning after I brought it home, that, like Pluto, it also had been deprived of one of its eyes. This circumstance, however, only endeared it to my wife, who, as I have already said, possessed, in a high degree, that humanity of feeling which had once been my distinguishing trait, and the source of many of my simplest and purest pleasures.

With my aversion to this cat, however, its partiality for myself seemed to increase. It followed my footsteps with a pertinacity which it would be difficult to make the reader comprehend. Whenever I sat, it would crouch beneath my chair, or spring upon my knees, covering me with its loathsome caresses. If I arose to walk it would get between my feet and thus nearly throw me down, or, fastening its long and sharp claws in my dress, clamber, in this manner, to my breast. At such times, although I longed to destroy it with a blow, I was yet withheld from so doing, partly by a memory of my former crime, but chiefly—let me confess it at once—by absolute *dread* of the beast.

This dread was not exactly a dread of physical evil—and yet I should be at a loss how otherwise to define it. I am almost ashamed to own—yes, even in this felon's cell, I am almost ashamed to own—that the terror and horror with which the animal inspired me, had been heightened by one of the merest chimeras it would be possible to conceive. My wife had called my attention, more than once, to the character of the mark of white hair, of which I have spoken, and which constituted the sole visible difference between the strange beast and the one I had destroyed. The reader will remember that this mark, although large, had been originally very indefinite; but, by slow degrees—degrees nearly imperceptible, and which for a long time my reason struggled to reject as fanciful—it had, at length, assumed a rigorous distinctness of outline. It was now the representation of an object that I shudder to name—and for this, above all, I loathed, and dreaded, and would have rid myself of the monster *had I dared*—it was now, I say, the image of a hideous—of a ghastly thing—of the GALLOWS!—oh, mournful and terrible engine of Horror and of Crime—of Agony and of Death!

And now was I indeed wretched beyond the wretchedness of mere Humanity. And *a brute beast*—whose fellow I had contemptuously destroyed—*a brute beast* to work out for *me*—for me, a man fashioned in the image of the High God—so much of insufferable woe! Alas! neither by day nor by night knew I the blessing of rest any more! During the former the creature left me no moment alone, and in the latter I started hourly from dreams of unutterable fear to find the hot breath of *the thing* upon my face, and its vast weight—an incarnate nightmare that I had no power to shake off—incumbent eternally upon my *heart!*

Beneath the pressure of torments such as these the feeble remnant of the good within me succumbed. Evil thoughts became my sole intimates—the darkest and most evil of thoughts. The moodiness of my usual temper increased to hatred of all things and of all mankind; while from the sudden, frequent, and ungovernable outbursts of a fury to which I now blindly abandoned myself, my uncomplaining wife, alas, was the most usual and the most patient of sufferers.

One day she accompanied me, upon some household errand, into the cellar of the old building which our poverty compelled us to inhabit. The cat followed me down the steep stairs, and, nearly throwing me headlong, exasperated me to madness. Uplifting an axe, and forgetting in my wrath the childish dread which had hitherto stayed my hand, I aimed a blow at the animal, which, of course, would have proved instantly fatal had it descended as

I wished. But this blow was arrested by the hand of my wife. Goaded by the interference into a rage more than demoniacal, I withdrew my arm from her grasp and buried the axe in her brain. She fell dead upon the spot without a groan.

This hideous murder accomplished, I set myself forthwith, and with entire deliberations, to the task of concealing the body. I knew that I could not remove it from the house, either by day or by night, without the risk of being observed by the neighbors. Many projects entered my mind. At one period I thought of cutting the corpse into minute fragments, and destroying them by fire. At another, I resolved to dig a grave for it in the floor of the cellar. Again, I deliberated about casting it in the well in the yard—about packing it in a box, as if merchandise, with the usual arrangements, and so getting a porter to take it from the house. Finally I hit upon what I considered a far better expedient than either of these. I determined to wall it up in the cellar, as the monks of the Middle Ages are recorded to have walled up their victims.

For a purpose such as this the cellar was well adapted. Its walls were loosely constructed, and had lately been plastered throughout with a rough plaster, which the dampness of the atmosphere had prevented from hardening. Moreover, in one of the walls was a projection, caused by a false chimney, or fireplace, that had been filled up and made to resemble the rest of the cellar. I made no doubt that I could readily displace the bricks at this point, insert the corpse, and wall the whole up as before, so that no eye could detect any thing suspicious.

And in this calculation I was not deceived. By means of a crowbar I easily dislodged the bricks, and, having carefully deposited the body against the inner wall, I propped it in that position, while with little trouble I relaid the whole structure as it originally stood. Having procured mortar, sand, and hair, with every possible precaution, I prepared a plaster which could not be distinguished from the old, and with this I very carefully went over the new brick-work. When I had finished, I felt satisfied that all was right. The wall did not present the slightest appearance of having been disturbed. The rubbish on the floor was picked up with the minutest care. I looked around triumphantly, and said to myself: "Here at least, then, my labor has not been in vain."

My next step was to look for the beast which had been the cause of so much wretchedness; for I had, at length, firmly resolved to put it to death. Had I been able to meet with it at the moment, there could have been no doubt of its fate; but it appeared that the crafty animal had been alarmed at the violence of my previous anger, and forbore to present itself in my present mood. It is impossible to describe or to imagine the deep, the blissful sense of relief which the absence of the detested creature occasioned in my bosom. It did not make its appearance during the night; and thus for one night, at least, since its introduction into the house, I soundly and tranquilly slept; aye, *slept* even with the burden of murder upon my soul.

The second and the third day passed, and still my tormentor came not. Once again I breathed as a freeman. The monster, in terror, had fled the premises for ever! I should behold it no more! My happiness was supreme! The guilt of my dark deed disturbed me but little. Some few inquiries had been made, but these had been readily answered. Even a search had been instituted—but of course nothing was to be discovered. I looked upon my future felicity as secured.

Upon the fourth day of the assassination, a party of police came, very unexpectedly, into the house, and proceeded again to make rigorous investigation of the premises. Secure, however, in the inscrutability of my place of concealment, I felt no embarrassment whatever. The officers bade me accompany them in their search. They left no nook or corner unexplored. At length, for the third or fourth time, they descended into the cellar. I quivered not in a muscle. My heart beat calmly as that of one who slumbers in innocence. I walked the cellar from end to end. I folded my arms upon my bosom, and roamed easily to and fro. The police were thoroughly satisfied and prepared to depart. The glee at my heart was too strong to be restrained. I burned to say if but one word, by way of triumph, and to render double sure their assurance of my guiltlessness.

"Gentleman," I said at last, as the party ascended the steps, "I delight to have allayed your suspicions. I wish you all health and a little more courtesy. By the bye, gentlemen, this—this is a very well-constructed house," (in the rabid desire to say something easily, I scarcely knew what I uttered at all),—"I may say an *excellently* well-constructed house. These walls—are you going, gentlemen?—these walls are solidly put together"; and here, through the mere frenzy of bravado, I rapped heavily with a cane which I held in my hand, upon that very portion of the brickwork behind which stood the corpse of the wife of my bosom.

But may God shield and deliver me from the fangs of the Arch-Fiend! No sooner had the reverberation of my blows sunk into silence, than I was answered by a voice from within the tomb!—by a cry, at first muffled and broken, like the sobbing of a child, and then quickly swelling into one long, loud, and continuous scream, utterly anomalous and inhuman—a howl—a wailing shriek, half of horror and half of triumph, such as might have arisen only out of hell, conjointly from the throats of the damned in their agony and of the demons that exult in the damnation.

Of my own thoughts it is folly to speak. Swooning, I staggered to the opposite wall. For one instant the party on the stairs remained motionless, through extremity of terror and awe. In the next a dozen stout arms were toiling at the wall. It fell bodily. The corpse, already greatly decayed and clotted with gore, stood erect before the eyes of the spectators. Upon its head, with red extended mouth and solitary eye of fire, sat the hideous beast whose craft had seduced me into murder, and whose informing voice had consigned me to the hangman. I had walled the monster up within the tomb.

LAMB TO THE SLAUGHTER

(1954)

Roald Dahl

It is hard to imagine a more perfect short story than this one, both in plot and in presentation. Roald Dahl (1916–1990) was born in Wales of Norwegian parents and spent most of his life in England. Most of Dahl's early writing was for adults, and he specialized in bizarre tales with surprise endings and stories from his experiences as a fighter pilot for the Royal Air Force during World War II. He later became famous for children's books. *Charlie and the Chocolate Factory* (1964) has twice been made into a movie, most recently in 2005 with Johnny Depp as the reclusive confectioner Willy Wonka. Five other Dahl books have also been made into movies. In a 2000 survey, British readers named Dahl as their favorite author. Among his books are *Someone Like You* (1954), *James and the Giant Peach* (1961), *Danny, the Champion of the World* (1975), *The Witches* (1983), *Matilda* (1988), and *The Minpins*, published posthumously in 1991.

The room was warm and clean, the curtains drawn, the two table lamps alight—hers and the one by the empty chair opposite. On the sideboard behind her, two tall glasses, soda water, whiskey. Fresh ice cubes in the Thermos bucket.

Mary Maloney was waiting for her husband to come home from work.

Now and again she would glance up at the clock, but without anxiety, merely to please herself with the thought that each minute gone by made it nearer the time when he would come. There was a slow smiling air about her, and about everything she did. The drop of the head as she bent over her sewing was curiously tranquil. Her skin—for this was her sixth month with child—had acquired a wonderful translucent quality, the mouth was soft, and the eyes, with their new placid look, seemed larger, darker than before.

When the clock said ten minutes to five, she began to listen, and a few moments later, punctually as always, she heard the tires on the gravel outside, and the car door slamming, the footsteps passing the window, the key turning in the lock. She laid aside her sewing, stood up, and went forward to kiss him as he came in.

"Hullo darling," she said.

"Hullo," he answered.

She took his coat and hung it in the closet. Then she walked over and made the drinks, a strongish one for him, a weak one for herself; and soon she was back again in her chair with the sewing, and he in the other, opposite, holding the tall glass with both his hands, rocking it so the ice cubes tinkled against the side.

For her, this was always a blissful time of day. She knew he didn't want to speak much until the first drink was finished, and she, on her side, was content to sit quietly, enjoying his company after the long hours alone in the house. She loved to luxuriate in the presence of this man, and to feel—almost as a sunbather feels the sun—that warm male glow that came out of him to her when they were alone together. She loved him for the way he sat loosely in a chair, for the way he came in a door, or moved slowly across the room with long strides. She loved the intent, far look in his eyes when they rested on her, the funny shape of the mouth, and especially the way he remained silent about his tiredness, sitting still with himself until the whiskey had taken some of it away.

"Tired darling?"

"Yes," he said. "I'm tired." And as he spoke, he did an unusual thing. He lifted his glass and drained it in one swallow although there was still half of it, at least half of it left. She wasn't really watching him, but she knew what he had done because she heard the ice cubes falling back against the bottom of the empty glass when he lowered his arm. He paused a moment, leaning forward in the chair, then he got up and went slowly over to fetch himself another.

"I'll get it!" she cried, jumping up.

"Sit down," he said.

When he came back, she noticed that the new drink was dark amber with the quantity of whiskey in it.

"Darling, shall I get your slippers?"

"No."

She watched him as he began to sip the dark yellow drink, and she could see little oily swirls in the liquid because it was so strong.

"I think it's a shame," she said, "that when a policeman gets to be as senior as you, they keep him walking about on his feet all day long."

He didn't answer, so she bent her head again and went on with her sewing; but each time he lifted the drink to his lips, she heard the ice cubes clinking against the side of the glass.

"Darling," she said. "Would you like me to get you some cheese? I haven't made any supper because it's Thursday."

"No," he said.

"If you're too tired to eat out," she went on, "it's still not too late. There's plenty of meat and stuff in the freezer, and you can have it right here and not even move out of the chair."

Her eyes waited on him for an answer, a smile, a little nod, but he made no sign.

"Anyway," she went on, "I'll get you some cheese and crackers first."

"I don't want it," he said.

She moved uneasily in her chair, the large eyes still watching his face. "But you *must* have supper. I can easily do it here. I'd like to do it. We can have lamb chops. Or pork. Anything you want. Everything's in the freezer."

"Forget it," he said.

"But darling, you *must* eat! I'll fix it anyway, and then you can have it or not, as you like."

She stood up and placed her sewing on the table by the lamp.

"Sit down," he said. "Just for a minute, sit down."

It wasn't till then that she began to get frightened.

"Go on," he said. "Sit down."

She lowered herself back slowly into the chair, watching him all the time with those large, bewildered eyes. He had finished the second drink and was staring down into the glass, frowning.

"Listen," he said. "I've got something to tell you."

"What is it, darling?" What's the matter?"

He had now become absolutely motionless, and he kept his head down so that the light from the lamp beside him fell across the upper part of his face, leaving the chin and mouth in shadow. She noticed there was a little muscle moving near the corner of his left eye.

"This is going to be a bit of a shock to you, I'm afraid," he said. "But I've thought about it a good deal and I've decided the only thing to do is tell you right away. I hope you won't blame me too much."

And he told her. It didn't take long, four or five minutes at most, and she sat very still through it all, watching him with a kind of dazed horror as he went further and further away from her with each word.

"So there it is," he added. "And I know it's kind of a bad time to be telling you, but there simply wasn't any other way. Of course I'll give you money and see you're looked after. But there needn't really be any fuss. I hope not anyway. It wouldn't be very good for my job."

Her first instinct was not to believe any of it, to reject it all. It occurred to her that perhaps he hadn't even spoken, that she herself had imagined the whole thing. Maybe, if she went about her business and acted as though she hadn't been listening, then later, when she sort of woke up again, she might find none of it had ever happened.

"I'll get the supper," she managed to whisper, and this time he didn't stop her.

When she walked across the room she couldn't feel her feet touching the floor. She couldn't feel anything at all—except a slight nausea and a desire to vomit. Everything was automatic now—down the steps to the cellar, the light switch, the deep freeze, the hand inside the cabinet taking hold of the first object it met. She lifted it out, and looked at it. It was wrapped in paper, so she took off the paper and looked at it again.

A leg of lamb.

All right then, they would have lamb for supper. She carried it upstairs, holding the thin bone-end of it with both her hands, and as she went through the living-room, she saw him standing over by the window with his back to her, and she stopped.

"For God's sake," he said, hearing her, but not turning round. "Don't make supper for me. I'm going out."

At that point, Mary Maloney simply walked up behind him and without any pause she swung the big frozen leg of lamb high in the air and brought it down as hard as she could on the back of his head.

She might just as well have hit him with a steel club.

She stepped back a pace, waiting, and the funny thing was that he remained standing there for at least four or five seconds, gently swaying. Then he crashed to the carpet.

The violence of the crash, the noise, the small table overturning, helped bring her out of the shock. She came out slowly, feeling cold and surprised, and she stood for a while blinking at the body, still holding the ridiculous piece of meat tight with both hands.

All right, she told herself. So I've killed him.

It was extraordinary, now, how clear her mind became all of a sudden. She began thinking very fast. As the wife of a detective, she knew quite well what the penalty would be. That was fine. It made no difference to her. In fact, it would be a relief. On the other hand, what about the child? What were the laws about murderers with unborn children? Did they kill them both—mother and child? Or did they wait until the tenth month? What did they do?

Mary Maloney didn't know. And she certainly wasn't prepared to take a chance.

She carried the meat into the kitchen, placed it in a pan, turned the oven on high, and shoved it inside. Then she washed her hands and ran upstairs to the bedroom. She sat down before the mirror, tidied her hair, touched up her lips and face. She tried a smile. It came out rather peculiar. She tried again.

"Hullo Sam," she said brightly, aloud.

The voice sounded peculiar too.

"I want some potatoes please, Sam. Yes, and I think a can of peas."

That was better. Both the smile and the voice were coming out better now. She rehearsed it several times more. Then she ran downstairs, took her coat, went out the back door, down the garden, into the street.

It wasn't six o'clock yet and the lights were still on in the grocery shop.

"Hullo Sam," she said brightly, smiling at the man behind the counter.

"Why, good evening, Mrs. Maloney. How're *you*?"

"I want some potatoes please, Sam. Yes, and I think a can of peas."

The man turned and reached up behind him on the shelf for the peas.

"Patrick's decided he's tired and doesn't want to eat out tonight," she told him. "We usually go out Thursdays, you know, and now he's caught me without any vegetables in the house."

"Then how about meat, Mrs. Maloney?"

"No, I've got meat, thanks. I got a nice leg of lamb from the freezer."

"Oh."

"I don't much like cooking it frozen, Sam, but I'm taking a chance on it this time. You think it'll be all right?"

"Personally," the grocer said, "I don't believe it makes any difference. You want these Idaho potatoes?"

"Oh yes, that'll be fine. Two of those."

"Anything else?" The grocer cocked his head on one side, looking at her pleasantly. "How about afterwards? What you going to give him for afterwards?"

"Well—what would you suggest, Sam?"

The man glanced around his shop. "How about a nice big slice of cheesecake? I know he likes that."

"Perfect," she said. "He loves it."

And when it was all wrapped and she had paid, she put on her brightest smile and said, "Thank you, Sam. Goodnight."

"Goodnight, Mrs. Maloney. And thank *you*."

And now, she told herself as she hurried back, all she was doing now, she was returning home to her husband and he was waiting for his supper; and she must cook it good, and make it as tasty as possible because the poor man was tired; and if, when she entered the house, she happened to find anything unusual, or tragic, or terrible, then naturally it would be a shock and she'd become frantic with grief and horror. Mind you, she wasn't *expecting* to find anything. She was just going home with the vegetables. Mrs. Patrick Maloney going home with the vegetables on Thursday evening to cook supper for her husband.

That's the way, she told herself. Do everything right and natural. Keep things absolutely natural and there'll be no need for any acting at all.

Therefore, when she entered the kitchen by the back door, she was humming a little tune to herself and smiling.

"Patrick!" she called. "How are you, darling?"

She put the parcel down on the table and went through into the living room; and when she saw him lying there on the floor with his legs doubled up and one arm twisted back underneath his body, it really was rather a shock. All the old love and longing for him welled up inside her, and she ran over to him, knelt down beside him, and began to cry her heart out. It was easy. No acting was necessary.

A few minutes later she got up and went to the phone. She knew the number of the police station, and when the man at the other end answered, she cried to him, "Quick! Come quick! Patrick's dead!"

"Who's speaking?"

"Mrs. Maloney. Mrs. Patrick Maloney."

"You mean Patrick Maloney's dead?"

"I think so," she sobbed. "He's lying on the floor and I think he's dead."

"Be right over," the man said.

The car came very quickly, and when she opened the front door, two policemen walked in. She knew them both—she knew nearly all the men at that precinct—and she fell right into Jack Noonan's arms, weeping hysterically. He put her gently into a chair, then went over to join the other one, who was called O'Malley, kneeling by the body.

"Is he dead?" she cried.

"I'm afraid he is. What happened?"

Briefly, she told her story about going out to the grocer and coming back to find him on the floor. While she was talking, crying and talking, Noonan discovered a small patch of congealed blood on the dead man's head. He showed it to O'Malley who got up at once and hurried to the phone.

Soon, other men began to come into the house. First a doctor, then two detectives, one of whom she knew by name. Later, a police photographer arrived and took pictures, and a man who knew about fingerprints. There was a great deal of whispering and muttering beside the corpse, and the detectives kept asking her a lot of questions. But they always treated her kindly. She told her story again, this time right from the beginning, when Patrick had come in, and she was sewing, and he was tired, so tired he hadn't wanted to go out for supper. She told how she'd put the meat in the oven—"it's there now, cooking"—and how she'd slipped out to the grocer for vegetables, and come back to find him lying on the floor.

"Which grocer?" one of the detectives asked.

She told him, and he turned and whispered something to the other detective who immediately went outside into the street.

In fifteen minutes he was back with a page of notes, and there was more whispering, and through her sobbing she heard a few of the whispered phrases—" . . . acted quite normal . . . very cheerful . . . wanted to give him a good supper . . . peas . . . cheesecake . . . impossible that she . . ."

After a while, the photographer and the doctor departed and two other men came in and took the corpse away on a stretcher. Then the fingerprint man went away. The two detectives remained, and so did the two policemen. They were exceptionally nice to her, and Jack Noonan asked if she wouldn't rather go somewhere else, to her sister's house perhaps, or to his own wife who would take care of her and put her up for the night.

No, she said. She didn't feel she could move even a yard at the moment. Would they mind awfully if she stayed just where she was until she felt better. She didn't feel too good at the moment, she really didn't.

Then hadn't she better lie down on the bed? Jack Noonan asked.

No, she said. She'd like to stay right where she was, in this chair. A little later perhaps, when she felt better, she would move.

So they left her there while they went about their business, searching the house. Occasionally one of the detectives asked her another question.

Sometimes Jack Noonan spoke at her gently as he passed by. Her husband, he told her, had been killed by a blow on the back of the head administered with a heavy blunt instrument, almost certainly a large piece of metal. They were looking for the weapon. The murderer may have taken it with him, but on the other hand he may've thrown it away or hidden it somewhere on the premises.

"It's the old story," he said. "Get the weapon, and you've got the man."

Later, one of the detectives came up and sat beside her. Did she know, he asked, of anything in the house that could've been used as the weapon? Would she mind having a look around to see if anything was missing—a very big spanner, for example, or a heavy metal vase.

They didn't have any heavy metal vases, she said.

"Or a big spanner?"

She didn't think they had a big spanner. But there might be some things like that in the garage.

The search went on. She knew that there were other policemen in the garden all around the house. She could hear their footsteps on the gravel outside, and sometimes she saw the flash of a torch through a chink in the curtains. It began to get late, nearly nine she noticed by the clock on the mantle. The four men searching the rooms seemed to be growing weary, a trifle exasperated.

"Jack," she said, the next time Sergeant Noonan went by. "Would you mind giving me a drink?"

"Sure I'll give you a drink. You mean this whiskey?"

"Yes, please. But just a small one. It might make me feel better."

He handed her the glass.

"Why don't you have one yourself," she said. "You must be awfully tired. Please do. You've been very good to me."

"Well," he answered. "It's not strictly allowed, but I might take just a drop to keep me going."

One by one the others came in and were persuaded to take a little nip of whiskey. They stood around rather awkwardly with the drinks in their hands, uncomfortable in her presence, trying to say consoling things to her. Sergeant Noonan wandered into the kitchen, came out quickly and said, "Look, Mrs. Maloney. You know that oven of yours is still on, and the meat still inside."

"Oh *dear* me!" she cried. "So it is!"

"I better turn it off for you, hadn't I?"

"Will you do that, Jack. Thank you so much."

When the sergeant returned the second time, she looked at him with her large, dark, tearful eyes. "Jack Noonan," she said.

"Yes?"

"Would you do me a small favour—you and these others?"

"We can try, Mrs. Maloney."

"Well," she said. "Here you all are, and good friends of dear Patrick's too, and helping to catch the man who killed him. You must be terrible hungry by now because it's long past your suppertime, and I know Patrick would never forgive me, God bless his soul, if I allowed you to remain in his house without offering you decent hospitality. Why don't you eat up that lamb that's in the oven. It'll be cooked just right by now."

"Wouldn't dream of it," Sergeant Noonan said.

"Please," she begged. "Please eat it. Personally I couldn't touch a thing, certainly not what's been in the house when he was here. But it's all right for you. It'd be a favour to me if you'd eat it up. Then you can go on with your work again afterwards."

There was a good deal of hesitating among the four policemen, but they were clearly hungry, and in the end they were persuaded to go into the kitchen and help themselves. The woman stayed where she was, listening to them through the open door, and she could hear them speaking among themselves, their voices thick and sloppy because their mouths were full of meat.

"Have some more, Charlie?"

"No. Better not finish it."

"She *wants* us to finish it. She said so. Be doing her a favour."

"Okay then. Give me some more."

"That's the hell of a big club the guy must've used to hit poor Patrick," one of them was saying. "The doc says his skull was smashed all to pieces just like from a sledgehammer."

"That's why it ought to be easy to find."

"Exactly what I say."

"Whoever done it, they're not going to be carrying a thing like that around with them longer than they need."

One of them belched.

"Personally, I think it's right here on the premises."

"Probably right under our very noses. What you think, Jack?"

And in the other room, Mary Maloney began to giggle.

PHILOMEL COTTAGE

(1927)

Agatha Christie

The following story is horrifically suspenseful. A happily married woman has premonitions of danger. But from whom? A jealous former boyfriend? Or is it her husband who is up to no good?

Agatha Christie (1890–1976) created two of the most popular detectives ever: Hercule Poirot and Miss Jane Marple, he a Belgian sleuth who exercises his "little grey cells," and she an Englishwoman with a knack for solving murders from everyday gossip in her village. These characters appear in more than fifty novels and short story collections. In 1954 Christie was honored with the inaugural Grand Master Edgar Award, the highest a mystery writer can achieve. In 1971 she became "Dame Agatha" when she was named a Dame Commander of the Order of the British Empire, the female equivalent of knighthood. Christie's sixty-eight novels include celebrated works like *The Murder of Roger Ackroyd* (1926), *Murder at the Vicarage* (1930), *Death on the Nile* (1938), *The Moving Finger* (1942), *Blood Will Tell* (1951), and *Murder on the Orient Express* (1960).

"Good-bye, darling."

"Good-bye, sweetheart."

Alix Martin stood leaning over the small rustic gate, watching the retreating figure of her husband, as he walked down the road in the direction of the village.

Presently he turned a bend and was lost to sight, but Alix still stayed in the same position, absent-mindedly smoothing a lock of the rich brown hair which had blown across her face, her eyes far away and dreamy.

Alix Martin was not beautiful, nor even, strictly speaking, pretty. But her face, the face of a woman no longer in her first youth, was irradiated and softened until her former colleagues of the old office days would hardly have recognized her. Miss Alix King had been a trim businesslike young woman, efficient, slightly brusque in manner, obviously capable and matter-of-fact. She had made the least, not the most, of her beautiful brown hair. Her mouth, not ungenerous in its lines, had always been severely compressed. Her clothes had been neat and suitable without a hint of coquetry.

Alix had graduated in a hard school. For fifteen years, from the age of eighteen until she was thirty-three, she had kept herself (and for seven years of the time, an invalid mother) by her work as a shorthand typist. It was the struggle for existence which had hardened the soft lines of her girlish face.

True, there had been romance—of a kind. Dick Windyford, a fellow clerk. Very much of a woman at heart, Alix had always known without seeming to know that he cared. Outwardly they had been friends, nothing more. Out of his slender salary, Dick had been hard put to it to provide for the schooling of a younger brother. For the moment, he could not think of marriage. Nevertheless when Alix envisaged the future, it was with the half acknowledged certainty that she would one day be Dick's wife. They cared for one another, so she would have put it, but they were both sensible people. Plenty of time, no need to do anything rash. So the years had gone on.

And then suddenly deliverance from daily toil had come to the girl in the most unexpected manner. A distant cousin had died leaving her money to Alix. A few thousand pounds, enough to bring in a couple of hundred a year. To Alix, it was freedom, life, independence. Now she and Dick need wait no longer.

But Dick reacted unexpectedly. He had never directly spoken of his love to Alix, now he seemed less inclined to do so than ever. He avoided her, became morose and gloomy. Alix was quick to realise the truth. She had become a woman of means. Delicacy and pride stood in the way of Dick's asking her to be his wife.

She liked him none the worse for it and was indeed deliberating as to whether she herself might not take the first step when for the second time the unexpected descended upon her.

She met Gerald Martin at a friend's house. He fell violently in love with her and within a week they were engaged. Alix, who had always considered herself "not the falling-in-love kind," was swept clean off her feet.

Unwittingly she had found the way to arouse her former lover. Dick Windyford had come to her stammering with rage and anger.

"The man's a perfect stranger to you. You know nothing about him."

"I know that I love him."

"How can you know—in a week?"

"It doesn't take everyone eleven years to find out that they're in love with a girl," cried Alix angrily.

His face went white.

"I've cared for you ever since I met you. I thought that you cared also."

Alix was truthful.

"I thought so too," she admitted. "But that was because I didn't know what love was."

Then Dick had burst out again. Prayers, entreaties, even threats. Threats against the man who had supplanted him. It was amazing to Alix to see the volcano that existed beneath the reserved exterior of the man she had thought she knew so well. Also, it frightened her a little . . . Dick, of course, couldn't possibly mean the things he was saying, the threats of vengeance against Gerald Martin. He was angry, that was all . . .

Her thoughts had gone back to that interview now, on this sunny morning, as she leant on the gate of the cottage. She had been married a month, and she was idyllically happy. Yet, in the momentary absence of the husband who was everything to her, a tinge of anxiety invaded her perfect happiness, and the cause of that anxiety was Dick Windyford.

Three times since her marriage she had dreamed the same dream. The environment differed, but the main facts were always the same. She saw her husband lying dead and Dick Windyford standing over him, and she knew clearly and distinctly that his was the hand which had dealt the fatal blow.

But horrible though that was, there was something more horrible still—horrible, that was, on awakening, for in the dream it seemed perfectly natural and inevitable. *She, Alix Martin, was glad that her husband was dead*—she stretched out her grateful hands to the murderer, sometimes she thanked him. The dream always ended the same way, with herself clasped in Dick Windyford's arms.

She had said nothing of this dream to her husband, but secretly it had perturbed her more than she liked to admit. Was it a warning—a warning against Dick Windyford? Had he some secret power which he was trying to establish over her at a distance? She did not know much about hypnotism, but surely she had always heard that persons could not be hypnotized against their will.

Alix was roused from her thoughts by the sharp ringing of the telephone bell from within the house. She entered the cottage, and picked up the receiver. Suddenly she swayed, and put out a hand to keep herself from falling.

"Who did you say was speaking?"

"Why, Alix, what's the matter with your voice? I wouldn't have known it. It's Dick."

"Oh!" said Alix—"Oh! Where—where are you?"

"At the Traveller's Arms—that's the right name, isn't it? Or don't you even know of the existence of your village pub? I'm on my holiday—doing a bit of fishing here. Any objection to my looking you two good people up this evening after dinner?"

"No," said Alix sharply. "You mustn't come."

There was a pause, and Dick's voice, with a subtle alteration in it, spoke again.

"I beg your pardon," he said formally. "Of course I won't bother you——"

Alix broke in hastily. Of course he must think her behaviour too extraordinary. It was extraordinary. Her nerves must be all to pieces. It wasn't Dick's fault that she had these dreams.

"I only meant that we were—engaged to-night," she explained, trying to make her voice sound as natural as possible. "Won't you—won't you come to dinner to-morrow night?"

But Dick evidently noticed the lack of cordiality in her tone.

"Thanks very much," he said, in the same formal voice. "But I may be moving on any time. Depends upon whether a pal of mine turns up or not. Good-bye, Alix." He paused, and then added hastily, in a different tone, "Best of luck to you, my dear."

Alix hung up the receiver with a feeling of relief.

"He mustn't come here," she repeated to herself. "He mustn't come here. Oh! what a fool I am! To imagine myself into a state like this. All the same, I'm glad he's not coming."

She caught up a rustic rush hat from a table, and passed out into the garden again, pausing to look up at the name carved over the porch, Philomel Cottage.

"Isn't it a very fanciful name?" she had said to Gerald once before they were married. He had laughed.

"You little Cockney," he had said, affectionately. "I don't believe you have ever heard a nightingale. I'm glad you haven't. Nightingales should sing only for lovers. We'll hear them together on a summer's evening outside our own home."

And at the remembrance of how they had indeed heard them, Alix, standing in the doorway of her home, blushed happily.

It was Gerald who had found Philomel Cottage. He had come to Alix bursting with excitement. He had found the very spot for them—unique—a gem—the chance of a lifetime. And when Alix had seen it, she too was captivated. It was true that the situation was rather lonely—they were two miles from the nearest village—but the cottage itself was so exquisite with its old-world appearance, and its solid comfort of bathrooms, hot-water system, electric light and telephone, that she fell a victim to its charm immediately. And then a hitch occurred. The owner, a rich man who had made it his whim, declined to rent it. He would only sell.

Gerald Martin, though possessed of a good income, was unable to touch his capital. He could raise at most a thousand pounds. The owner was asking three. But Alix, who had set her heart on the place, came to the rescue. Her own capital was easily realised, being in bearer bonds. She would contribute half of it to the purchase of the home. So Philomel Cottage became their very own, and never for a minute had Alix regretted the choice. It was true that servants did not appreciate the rural solitude—indeed at the moment they had none at all—but Alix, who had been starved of domestic life, thoroughly enjoyed cooking dainty little meals and looking after the house.

The garden which was magnificently stocked with flowers was attended to by an old man from the village who came twice a week, and Gerald Martin, who was keen on gardening, spent most of his time there.

As she rounded the corner of the house, Alix was surprised to see the old gardener in question busy over the flower beds. She was surprised because his days for work were Monday and Fridays, and to-day was Wednesday.

"Why, George, what are you doing here?" she asked, as she came towards him.

The old man straightened up with a chuckle, touching the brim of an aged cap.

"I thought as how you'd be surprised, Ma'am. But 'tis this way. There be a Fête over to Squire's on Friday, and I sez to myself, I sez, neith Mr. Martin nor yet his good lady won't take it amiss if I comes for once on a Wednesday instead of a Friday."

"That's quite all right," said Alix, "I hope you'll enjoy yourself at the Fête."

"I reckon to," said George simply. "It's a fine thing to be able to eat your fill and know all the time as it's not you as is paying for it. Squire allus has a proper sit-down tea for 'is tenants. Then I thought too, Ma'am, as I might as well see you before you goes away so as to learn your wishes for the borders. You'll have no idea when you'll be back, Ma'am, I suppose."

"But I'm not going away."

George stared at her.

"Bain't you going to Lunnon to-morrow?"

"No. What put such an idea into your head?"

George jerked his head over his shoulder.

"Met Maister down to village yesterday. He told me you was both going away to Lunnon to-morrow, and it was uncertain when you'd be back again."

"Nonsense," said Alix, laughing. "You must have misunderstood him."

All the same, she wondered exactly what it could have been that Gerald had said to lead the old man into such a curious mistake. Going to London? She never wanted to go to London again.

"I hate London," she said suddenly and harshly.

"Ah!" said George placidly. "I must have been mistook somehow, and yet he said it plain enough it seemed to me. I'm glad you're stopping on here—I don't hold with all this gallivanting about, and I don't think nothing of Lunnon. I've never needed to go there. Too many moty cars—that's the trouble nowadays. Once people have got a moty car, blessed if they can stay still anywheres. Mr. Ames, wot used to have this house—nice peaceful sort of gentleman he was until he bought one of them things. Hadn't 'ad it a month before he put up this cottage for sale. A tidy lot he'd spent on it, too, with taps in all the bedrooms, and the electric light and all. 'You'll never see your money back,' I sez to him. 'It's not everyone as'll have your fad for washing themselves in every room in the house, in a manner of speaking.' But 'George,' he sez to me, 'I'll get every penny of two thousand pounds for this house.' And sure enough, he did."

"He got three thousand," said Alix, smiling.

"Two thousand," repeated George. "The sum he was asking was talked of at the time. And a very high figure it was thought to be."

"It really was three thousand," said Alix.

"Women never understand figures," said George, unconvinced. "You'll not tell me that Mr. Ames had the face to stand up to you, and say three thousand brazen like in a loud voice."

"He didn't say it to me," said Alix. "He said it to my husband."

George stooped again to his flower bed.

"The price was two thousand," he said obstinately.

Alix did not trouble to argue with him. Moving to one of the further beds, she began to pick an armful of flowers. The sunshine, the scent of the flowers, the faint hum of hurrying bees, all conspired to make the day a perfect thing.

As she moved with her fragrant posy towards the house, Alix noticed a small dark-green object, peeping from between some leaves in one of the beds. She stooped and picked it up, recognising it for her husband's pocket diary. It must have fallen from his pocket when he was weeding.

She opened it, scanning the entries with some amusement. Almost from the beginning of their married life, she had realised that the impulsive and emotional Gerald had the uncharacteristic virtues of neatness and method. He was extremely fussy about meals being punctual, and always planned his day ahead with the accuracy of a time-table. This morning, for instance, he had announced that he should start for the village after breakfast—at 10:15. And at 10:15 to the minute he had left the house.

Looking through the diary, she was amused to notice the entry on the date of May 14th. "Marry Alix St. Peter's 2:30."

"The big silly," murmured Alix to herself, turning the pages.

Suddenly she stopped.

"Wednesday, June 18th—why that's to-day."

In the space for that day was written in Gerald's neat precise hand: "*9 p.m.*" Nothing else. What had Gerald planned to do at 9 p.m.? Alix wondered. She smiled to herself as she realized that had this been a story, like those she had so often read, the diary would doubtless have furnished her with some sensational revelation. It would have had in it for certain the name of another woman. She fluttered the back pages idly. There were dates, appointments, cryptic references to business deals, but only one woman's name—her own.

Yet as she slipped the book into her pocket and went on with her flowers to the house, she was aware of a vague uneasiness. Those words of Dick Windyford's recurred to her, almost as though he had been at her elbow repeating them: "The man's a perfect stranger to you. You know nothing about him."

It was true. What did she know about him? After all, Gerald was forty. In forty years there must have been women in his life. . . .

Alix shook herself impatiently. She must not give way to these thoughts. She had a far more instant preoccupation to deal with. Should she, or should she not, tell her husband that Dick Windyford had rung her up?

There was the possibility to be considered that Gerald might have already run across him in the village. But in that case he would be sure to mention it to her immediately upon his return and matters would be taken out of her hands. Otherwise—what? Alix was aware of a distinct desire to say nothing about it. Gerald had always shown himself kindly disposed towards the other. "Poor devil," he had said once, "I believe he's just as keen on you as I am. Hard luck on him to be shelved." He had had no doubts of Alix's own feelings.

If she told him, he was sure to suggest asking Dick Windyford to Philomel Cottage. Then she would have to explain that Dick had proposed it himself, and that she had made an excuse to prevent his coming. And when he asked her why she had done so, what could she say? Tell him her dream? But he would only laugh—or worse see that she attached an importance to it which he did not. Then he would think—oh! he might think anything!

In the end, rather shamefacedly, Alix decided to say nothing. It was the first secret she had ever kept from her husband, and the consciousness of it made her feel ill at ease.

When she heard Gerald returning from the village shortly before lunch, she hurried into the kitchen and pretended to be busy with the cooking so as to hide her confusion.

It was evident at once that Gerald had seen nothing of Dick Windyford. Alix felt at once relieved and embarrassed. She was definitely committed now to a policy of concealment. For the rest of the day she was nervous and absent-minded, starting at every sound, but her husband seemed to notice nothing. He himself seemed to have his thoughts far away, and once or twice she had to speak a second time before he answered some trivial remark of hers.

It was not until after their simple evening meal, when they were sitting in the oak-beamed living room with the windows thrown open to let in the sweet night air scented with the perfume of the mauve and white stocks that grew outside, that Alix remembered the pocket diary, and seized upon it gladly to distract her thoughts from their doubt and perplexity.

"Here's something you've been watering the flowers with," she said, and threw it into his lap.

"Dropped it in the border, did I?"

"Yes, I know all your secrets now."

"Not guilty," said Gerald, shaking his head.

"What about your assignation at nine o'clock to-night?"

"Oh! that—" he seemed taken aback for a moment, then he smiled as though something afforded him particular amusement. "It's an assignation with a particularly nice girl, Alix. She's got brown hair and blue eyes and she's particularly like you."

"I don't understand," said Alix, with mock severity. "You're evading the point."

"No, I'm not. As a matter of fact, that's a reminder that I'm going to develop some negatives to-night, and I want you to help me."

Gerald Martin was an enthusiastic photographer. He had a somewhat old-fashioned camera, but with an excellent lens, and he developed his own plates in a small cellar which he had had fitted up as a dark room. He was never tired of posing Alix in different positions.

"And it must be done at nine o'clock precisely," said Alix teasingly.

Gerald looked a little vexed.

"My dear girl," he said with a shade of testiness in his manner. "One should always plan a thing for a definite time. Then one gets through one's work properly."

Alix sat for a minute or two in silence watching her husband as he lay in his chair smoking, his dark head flung back and the clear-cut lines of his clean-shaven face showing up against the somber background. And suddenly, from some unknown source, a wave of panic surged over her, so that she cried out before she could stop herself. "Oh! Gerald, I wish I knew more about you."

Her husband turned an astonished face upon her.

"But, my dear Alix, you do know all about me. I've told you of my boyhood in Northumberland, of my life in South Africa, and these last ten years in Canada which have brought me success."

"Oh! business!"

Gerald laughed suddenly.

"I know what you mean—love affairs. You women are all the same. Nothing interests you but the personal element."

Alix felt her throat go dry, as she muttered indistinctly: "Well, but there must have been—love affairs. I mean—If I only knew——"

There was silence again for a minute or two. Gerald Martin was frowning, a look of indecision on his face. When he spoke, it was gravely, without a trace of his former bantering manner.

"Do you think it wise, Alix—this—Bluebeard's chamber business? There have been women in my life, yes. I don't deny it. You wouldn't believe me if I did deny it. But I can swear to you truthfully that not one of them meant anything to me."

There was a ring of sincerity in his voice which comforted the listening wife.

"Satisfied, Alix?" he asked, with a smile. Then he looked at her with a shade of curiosity.

"What has turned your mind onto these unpleasant subjects to-night of all nights? You never mentioned them before."

Alix got up and began to walk about restlessly.

"Oh! I don't know," she said. "I've been nervy all day."

"That's odd," said Gerald, in a low voice, as though speaking to himself. "That's very odd."

"Why is it odd?"

"Oh! my dear girl, don't flash out at me so. I only said it was odd because as a rule you're so sweet and serene."

Alix forced a smile.

"Everything's conspired to annoy me to-day," she confessed. "Even old George had got some ridiculous idea into his head that we were going away to London. He said you had told him so."

"Where did you see him?" asked Gerald sharply.

"He came to work to-day instead of Friday."

"The old fool," said Gerald angrily.

Alix stared in surprise. Her husband's face was convulsed with rage. She had never seen him so angry. Seeing her astonishment, Gerald made an effort to regain control of himself.

"Well, he *is* a stupid fool," he protested.

"What can you have said to make him think that?"

"I? I never said anything. At least—oh! yes, I remember, I made some weak joke about being 'off to London in the morning' and I suppose he took it seriously. Or else he didn't hear properly. You undeceived him, of course?"

He waited anxiously for her reply.

"Of course, but he's the sort of old man who if once he gets an idea in his head—well, it isn't so easy to get it out again."

Then she told him of the gardener's insistence on the sum asked for the cottage.

Gerald was silent for a minute or two, then he said slowly:

"Ames was willing to take two thousand in cash and the remaining thousand on mortgage. That's the origin of that mistake, I fancy."

"Very likely," agreed Alix.

Then she looked up at the clock, and pointed to it with a mischievous finger.

"We ought to be getting down to it, Gerald. Five minutes behind schedule."

A very peculiar smile came over Gerald Martin's face.

"I've changed my mind," he said quietly. "I shall not do any photography to-night."

A woman's mind is a curious thing. When she went to bed that Wednesday night, Alix's mind was contented and at rest. Her momentarily assailed happiness reasserted itself, triumphant as of yore.

But by the evening of the following day, she realised that some subtle forces were at work undermining it. Dick Windyford had not rung up again, nevertheless she felt what she supposed to be his influence at work. Again and again those words of his recurred to her. "The man's a perfect stranger. You know nothing about him." And with them came the memory of her husband's face, photographed clearly on her brain as he said: "Do you think it wise, Alix, this—Bluebeard's chamber business?" Why had he said that? What had he meant by those words?

There had been warning in them—a hint of menace. It was as though he had said in effect—"You had better not pry into my life, Alix. You may get a nasty shock if you do." True, a few minutes later, he had sworn to her that there had been no woman in his life that mattered—but Alix tried in vain to recapture her sense of his sincerity. Was he not bound to swear that?

By Friday morning, Alix had convinced herself that there had been a woman in Gerald's life—a Bluebeard's chamber that he had sedulously sought to conceal from her. Her jealousy, slow to awaken, was now rampant.

Was it a woman he had been going to meet that night, at 9 p.m.? Was his story of photographs to develop a lie invented upon the spur of the moment? With a queer sense of shock Alix realized that ever since she had found that pocket diary she had been in torment. And there had been nothing in it. That was the irony of the whole thing.

Three days ago she would have sworn that she knew her husband through and through. Now it seemed to her that he was a stranger of whom she knew nothing. She remembered his unreasonable anger against old George, so at variance with his usual good-tempered manner. A small thing, perhaps, but it showed her that she did not really know the man who was her husband.

There were several little things required on Friday from the village to carry them over the week-end. In the afternoon Alix suggested that she should go for them whilst Gerald remained in the garden, but somewhat to her surprise he opposed this plan vehemently, and insisted on going himself whilst she remained at home. Alix was forced to give way to him, but his insistence surprised and alarmed her. Why was he so anxious to prevent her going to the village?

Suddenly an explanation suggested itself to her which made the whole thing clear. Was it not possible that, whilst saying nothing to her, Gerald had indeed come across Dick Windyford? Her own jealousy, entirely dormant at the time of their marriage, had only developed afterwards. Might it not be the same with Gerald? Might he not be anxious to prevent her seeing Dick Windyford again? This explanation was so consistent with the facts, and so comforting to Alix's perturbed mind, that she embraced it eagerly.

Yet when tea time had come and past, she was restless and ill at ease. She was struggling with a temptation that had assailed her ever since Gerald's departure. Finally, pacifying her conscience with the assurance that the room did need a thorough tidying, she went upstairs to her husband's dressing room. She took a duster with her to keep up the pretense of housewifery.

"If I were only sure," she repeated to herself. "If I could only be sure."

In vain she told herself that anything compromising would have been destroyed ages ago. Against that she argued that men do sometimes keep the most damning piece of evidence through an exaggerated sentimentality.

In the end Alix succumbed. Her cheeks burning with the shame of her action, she hunted breathlessly through packets of letters and documents, turned out the drawers, even went through the pockets of her husband's clothes. Only two drawers eluded her, the lower drawer of the chest of drawers, and the small right-hand drawer of the writing desk were both locked. But Alix was by now lost to all shame. In one of those drawers she was convinced that she would find evidence of this imaginary woman of the past who obsessed her.

She remembered that Gerald had left his keys lying carelessly on the sideboard downstairs. She fetched them and tried them one by one. The third key fitted the writing table drawer. Alix pulled it open eagerly. There was a cheque book, and a wallet well stuffed with notes, and at the back of the drawer a packet of letters tied up with a piece of tape.

Her breath coming unevenly, Alix untied the tape. Then a deep burning blush overspread her face, and she dropped the letters back into the drawer, closing and relocking it. For the letters were her own, written to Gerald Martin before she married him.

She turned now to the chest of drawers, more with a wish to feel that she had left nothing undone than from any expectation of finding what she sought. She was shamed and almost convinced of the madness of her obsession.

To her annoyance none of the keys on Gerald's bunch fitted the drawer in question. Not to be defeated, Alix went into the other rooms and brought back a selection of keys with her. To her satisfaction, the key of the spare room wardrobe also fitted the chest of drawers. She unlocked the drawer and pulled it open. But there was nothing in it but a roll of newspaper clippings already dirty and discoloured with age.

Alix breathed a sigh of relief. Nevertheless she glanced at the clippings, curious to know what subject had interested Gerald so much that he had taken the trouble to keep the dusty roll. They were nearly all American papers, dated some seven years ago, and dealing with the trial of the notorious swindler and bigamist, Charles LeMaitre. LeMaitre had been suspected of doing away with his women victims. A skeleton had been found beneath the floor of one of the houses he had rented, and most of the women he had "married" had never been heard of again.

He had defended himself from the charge with consummate skill, aided by some of the best legal talent in the United States. The Scottish verdict of "Non proven" might perhaps have stated the case best. In its absence, he was found Not Guilty on the capital charge, though sentenced to a long term of imprisonment on the other charges preferred against him.

Alix remembered the excitement caused by the case at the time, and also the sensation aroused by the escape of LeMaitre some three years later. He had never been recaptured. The personality of the man and his extraordinary power over women had been discussed at great length in the English papers at this time, together with an account of his excitability in court, his passionate protestations, and his occasional sudden physical collapses, due to the fact that he had a weak heart, though the ignorant accredited it to his dramatic powers.

There was a picture of him in one of the clippings Alix held, and she studied it with some interest—a long-bearded scholarly-looking gentleman. It reminded her of someone, but for the moment she could not tell who that someone was. She had never known that Gerald took an interest in crime and famous trials, though she knew that it was a hobby with many men.

Who was it the face reminded her of? Suddenly, with a shock, she realised that it was Gerald himself. The eye and brow bore a strong resemblance to him. Perhaps he had kept the cutting for that reason. Her eyes went on to the paragraph beside the picture. Certain dates, it seemed, had been entered in the accused's pocket book, and it was contended that these were dates when he had done away with his victims. Then a woman gave evidence and identified the prisoner positively by the fact that he had a mole on his left wrist, just below the palm of the left hand.

Alix dropped the papers from a nerveless hand, and swayed as she stood. *On his left wrist, just below the palm, Gerald had a small scar. . . .*

The room whirled round her. . . . Afterwards it struck her as strange that she should have leaped at once to such absolute certainty. Gerald Martin was Charles LeMaitre! She knew it and accepted it in a flash. Disjointed fragments whirled through her brain, like pieces of a jig-saw puzzle fitting into place.

The money paid for the house—her money—her money only. The bearer bonds she had entrusted to his keeping. Even her dream appeared in its true significance. Deep down in her, her subconscious self had always feared Gerald Martin and wished to escape from him. And it was to Dick Windyford this self of hers had looked for help. That, too, was why she was able to accept the truth so easily, without doubt or hesitation. She was to have been another of LeMaitre's victims. Very soon, perhaps.

A half cry escaped her as she remembered something. Wednesday 9 p.m. The cellar, with the flagstones that were so easily raised. Once before, he had buried one of his victims in a cellar. It had been all planned for Wednesday night. But to write it down beforehand in that methodical manner—insanity! No, it was logical. Gerald always made a memorandum of his engagements—murder was, to him, a business proposition like any other.

But what had saved her? What could possibly have saved her? Had he relented at the last minute? No—in a flash the answer came to her. Old George. She understood now her husband's uncontrollable anger. Doubtless he had paved the way by telling everyone he met that they were going to London the next day. Then George had come to work unexpectedly, had mentioned London to her, and she had contradicted the story. Too risky to do away with her that night, with old George repeating that conversation. But what an escape! If she had not happened to mention that trivial matter—Alix shuddered.

But there was no time to be lost. She must get away at once—before he came back. For nothing on earth would she spend another night under the same roof with him. She hurriedly replaced the roll of clippings in the drawer, shut it to and locked it.

And then she stayed motionless as though frozen to stone. She had heard the creak of the gate into the road. Her husband had returned.

For a moment Alix stayed as though petrified, then she crept on tiptoe to the window, looking out from behind the shelter of the curtain.

Yes, it was her husband. He was smiling to himself and humming a little tune. In his hand he held an object which almost made the terrified girl's heart stop beating. It was a brand new spade.

Alix leaped to a knowledge born of instinct. *It was to be tonight. . . .*

But there was still a chance. Gerald, still humming his little tune, went round to the back of the house.

"He's going to put it in the cellar—ready," thought Alix with a shiver.

Without hesitating a moment, she ran down the stairs and out of the cottage. But just as she emerged from the door, her husband came round the other side of the house.

"Hullo," he said. "Where are you running off to in such a hurry?"

Alix strove desperately to appear calm and as usual. Her chance was gone for the moment, but if she was careful not to arouse his suspicions, it would come again later. Even now, perhaps. . . .

"I was going to walk to the end of the lane and back," she said, in a voice that sounded weak and uncertain to her own ears.

"Right," said Gerald, "I'll come with you."

"No—please, Gerald. I'm—nervy, headachy—I'd rather go alone."

He looked at her attentively. She fancied a momentary suspicion gleamed in his eye.

"What's the matter with you, Alix? You're pale—trembling."

"Nothing," she forced herself to be brusque—smiling. "I've got a headache, that's all. A walk will do me good."

"Well, it's no good your saying you don't want me," declared Gerald with his easy laugh. "I'm coming whether you want me or not."

She dared not protest further. If he suspected that she *knew*——

With an effort she managed to regain something of her normal manner. Yet she had an uneasy feeling that he looked at her sideways every now and then, as though not quite satisfied. She felt that his suspicions were not completely allayed.

When they returned to the house, he insisted on her lying down, and brought some eau de cologne to bathe her temples. He was, as ever, the devoted husband, yet Alix felt herself as helpless as though bound hand and foot in a trap.

Not for a minute would he leave her alone. He went with her into the kitchen and helped her to bring in the simple cold dishes she had already prepared. Supper was a meal that choked her, yet she forced herself to eat, and even to appear gay and natural. She knew now that she was fighting for her life. She was alone with this man, miles from help, absolutely at his mercy. Her only chance was so to lull his suspicions that he would leave her alone for a few moments—long enough for her to get to the telephone in the hall and summon assistance. That was her only hope now. He would overtake her if she took to flight long before she could reach assistance.

A momentary hope flashed over her as she remembered how he had abandoned his plan before. Suppose she told him that Dick Windyford was coming up to see them that evening?

The words trembled on her lips—then she rejected them hastily. This man would not be baulked at a second time. There was a determination, an elation underneath his calm bearing that sickened her. She would only precipitate the crime. He would murder her there and then, and calmly ring up Dick Windyford with a tale of having been suddenly called away. Oh! if only Dick Windyford were coming to the house this evening. If Dick——

A sudden idea flashed into her mind. She looked sharply sideways at her husband as though she feared that he might read her mind. With the forming of a plan, her courage was reinforced. She became so completely natural in manner that she marveled at herself. She felt that Gerald now was completely reassured.

She made the coffee and took it out to the porch where they often sat on fine evenings.

"By the way," said Gerald suddenly. "We'll do those photographs later."

Alix felt a shiver run through her, but she replied nonchalantly:

"Can't you manage alone? I'm rather tired to-night."

"It won't take long." He smiled to himself. "And I can promise you you won't be tired afterwards."

The words seemed to amuse him. Alix shuddered. Now or never was the time to carry out her plan.

She rose to her feet.

"I'm just going to telephone to the butcher," she announced nonchalantly. "Don't you bother to move."

"To the butcher? At this time of night?"

"His shop's shut, of course, silly. But he's in his house all right. And to-morrow's Saturday, and I want him to bring me some veal cutlets early, before someone else grabs them from him. The old dear will do anything for me."

She passed quickly into the house, closing the door behind her. She heard Gerald say, "Don't shut the door," and was quick with her light reply. "It keeps the moths out. I hate moths. Are you afraid I'm going to make love to the butcher, silly?"

Once inside she snatched down the telephone receiver and gave the number of the Traveller's Arms. She was put through at once.

"Mr. Windyford? Is he still there? May I speak to him?"

Then her heart gave a sickening thump. The door was pushed open and her husband came into the hall.

"Do go away, Gerald," she said pettishly. "I hate anyone listening when I'm telephoning."

He merely laughed and threw himself into a chair.

"Sure it really is the butcher you're telephoning to?" he quizzed.

Alix was in despair. Her plan had failed. In a minute Dick Windyford would come to the phone. Should she risk all and cry out an appeal for help? Would he grasp what she meant before Gerald wrenched her away from the phone? Or would he merely treat it as a practical joke?

And then as she nervously depressed and released the little key in the receiver she was holding, which permits the voice to be heard or not heard at the other end, another plan flashed into her head.

"It will be difficult," she thought. "It means keeping my head, and thinking of the right words, and not faltering for a moment, but I believe I could do it. I *must* do it."

And at that minute she heard Dick Windyford's voice at the other end of the phone.

Alix drew a deep breath. Then she depressed the key firmly and spoke.

"Mrs. Martin speaking—from Philomel Cottage. *Please come* (she released the key) to-morrow morning with six nice veal cutlets (she depressed the key again). *It's very important* (she released the key). Thank you so much, Mr. Hexworthy, you don't mind my ringing you up so late, I hope, but those veal cutlets are really a matter of (she depressed the key again) *life or death* . . . (she released it). Very well—to-morrow morning—(she depressed it) *as soon as possible* . . ."

She replaced the receiver on the hook and turned to face her husband, breathing hard.

"So that's how you talk to your butcher, is it?" said Gerald.

"It's the feminine touch," said Alix lightly.

She was simmering with excitement. He had suspected nothing. Surely Dick, even if he didn't understand, would come.

She passed into the sitting room and switched on the electric light. Gerald followed her.

"You seem very full of spirits now," he said, watching her curiously.

"Yes," said Alix. "My headache's gone."

She sat down in her usual seat and smiled at her husband, as he sank into his own chair opposite her. She was saved. It was only five and twenty past eight. Long before nine o'clock Dick would have arrived.

"I didn't think much of that coffee you gave me," complained Gerald. "It tasted very bitter."

"It's a new kind I was trying. We won't have it again if you don't like it, dear."

Alix took up a piece of needlework and began to stitch. She felt complete confidence in her own ability to keep up the part of the devoted wife. Gerald read a few pages of his book. Then he glanced up at the clock and tossed the book away.

"Half past eight. Time to go down to the cellar and start work."

The work slipped from Alix's fingers.

"Oh! not yet. Let us wait until nine o'clock."

"No, my girl, half past eight. That's the time I fixed. You'll be able to get to bed all the earlier."

"But I'd rather wait until nine."

"Half past eight," said Gerald obstinately. "You know when I fix a time, I always stick to it. Come along, Alix. I'm not going to wait a minute longer."

Alix looked up at him, and in spite of herself she felt a wave of terror slide over her. The mask had been lifted; Gerald's hands were twitching; his eyes were shining with excitement; he was continually passing his tongue over his dry lips. He no longer cared to conceal his excitement.

Alix thought: "It's true—*he can't wait*—he's like a madman."

He strode over to her, and jerked her onto her feet with a hand on her shoulder.

"Come on, my girl—or I'll carry you there."

His tone was gay, but there was an undisguised ferocity behind it that appalled her. With a supreme effort she jerked herself free and clung cowering against the wall. She was powerless. She couldn't get away—she couldn't do anything—and he was coming towards her.

"Now, Alix——"

"No—no."

She screamed, her hand held out impotently to ward him off.

"Gerald—stop—I've got something to tell you, something to confess . . ."

He did stop.

"To confess?" he said curiously.

"Yes, to confess." She went on desperately, seeking to hold his arrested attention. "Something I ought to have told you before."

A look of contempt swept over his face. The spell was broken.

"A former lover, I suppose," he sneered.

"No," said Alix. "Something else. You'd call it, I expect—yes, you'd call it a crime."

And at once she saw that she had struck the right note. Again his attention was arrested, held. Seeing that, her nerve came back to her. She felt mistress of the situation once more.

"You had better sit down again," she said quietly.

She herself crossed the room to her old chair and sat down. She even stooped and picked up her needlework. But behind her calmness she was thinking and inventing feverishly. For the story she invented must hold his interest until help arrived.

"I told you," she said, "that I had been a shorthand typist for fifteen years. That was not entirely true. There were two intervals. The first occurred when I was twenty-two. I came across a man, an elderly man with a little property. He fell in love with me and asked me to marry him. I accepted. We were married." She paused. "I induced him to insure his life in my favor."

She saw a sudden keen interest spring up in her husband's face, and went on with renewed assurance.

"During the war I worked for a time in a Hospital Dispensary. There I had the handling of all kinds of rare drugs and poisons. Yes, poisons."

She paused reflectively. He was keenly interested now, not a doubt of it. The murderer is bound to have an interest in murder. She had gambled on that, and succeeded. She stole a glance at the clock. It was five and twenty to nine.

"There is one poison—it is a little white powder. A pinch of it means death. You know something about poisons, perhaps?"

She put the question in some trepidation. If he did, she would have to be careful.

"No," said Gerald. "I know very little about them."

She drew a breath of relief. This made her task easier.

"You have heard of hyoscine, of course. This is a drug that acts much the same way, but it is absolutely untraceable. Any doctor would give a certificate of heart failure. I stole a small quantity of this drug and kept it by me."

She paused, marshalling her forces.

"Go on," said Gerald.

"No. I'm afraid. I can't tell you. Another time."

"Now," he said impatiently. "I want to hear."

"We had been married a month. I was very good to my elderly husband, very kind and devoted. He spoke in praise of me to all the neighbours. Everyone knew what a devoted wife I was. I always made his coffee myself every evening. One evening, when we were alone together, I put a pinch of the deadly alkaloid in his cup."

Alix paused, and carefully rethreaded her needle. She, who had never acted in her life, rivaled the greatest actress in the world at this moment. She was actually living the part of the cold-blooded poisoner.

"It was very peaceful. I sat watching him. Once he gasped a little and asked for air. I opened the window. Then he said he could not move from his chair. Presently he died."

She stopped, smiling. It was a quarter to nine. Surely they would come soon.

"How much," said Gerald, "was the insurance money?"

"About two thousand pounds. I speculated with it, and lost it. I went back to my office work. But I never meant to remain there long. Then I met another man. I had stuck to my maiden name at the office. He didn't know I had been married before. He was a younger man, rather good-looking, and quite well off. We were married quietly in Sussex. He didn't want to insure his life, but of course he made a will in my favour. He liked me to make his coffee myself also, just as my first husband had done."

Alix smiled reflectively, and added simply:

"I make very good coffee."

Then she went on.

"I had several friends in the village where we were living. They were very sorry for me, with my husband dying suddenly of heart failure one evening after dinner. I didn't quite like the doctor. I don't think he suspected me, but he was certainly very surprised at my husband's sudden death. I don't know why I drifted back to the office again. Habit, I suppose. My second husband left about four thousand pounds. I didn't speculate with it this time. I invested it. Then, you see——"

But she was interrupted. Gerald Martin, his face suffused with blood, half choking, was pointing a shaking forefinger at her.

"The coffee—My God! the coffee!"

She stared at him.

"I understand now why it was bitter. You devil. You've poisoned me."

His hands gripped the arms of his chair. He was ready to spring upon her.

"You've poisoned me."

Alix had retreated from him to the fireplace. Now, terrified, she opened her lips to deny—and then paused. In another minute he would spring upon her. She summoned all her strength. Her eyes held his steadily, compellingly.

"Yes," she said. "I poisoned you. Already the poison is working. At this minute you can't move from your chair—you can't move——"

If she could keep him there—even a few minutes——

Ah! what was that? Footsteps on the road. The creak of the gate. Then footsteps on the path outside. The door of the hall opened——

"You can't move," she began again.

Then she slipped past him and fled headlong from the room to fall half fainting into Dick Windyford's arms.

"My God! Alix!" he cried.

Then he turned to the man with him, a tall stalwart figure in policeman's uniform.

"Go and see what's been happening in that room."

He laid Alix carefully down on a couch and bent over her.

"My little girl," he murmured. "My poor little girl. What have they been doing to you?"

Her eyelids fluttered and her lips just murmured his name.

Dick was aroused from tumultuous thoughts by the policeman's touching him on the arm.

"There's nothing in that room, sir, but a man sitting in a chair. Looks as though he'd had some kind of bad fright, and——"

"Yes?"

"Well, sir, he's—dead."

They were startled by hearing Alix's voice. She spoke as though in some kind of dream.

"And presently," she said, almost as though she were quoting from something, "he died. . . ."

THE ADVENTURE OF THE SPECKLED BAND

(1905)

A. Conan Doyle

Sherlock Holmes is not only the world's most popular detective, but probably the most familiar figure in all of modern fiction. The original author wrote sixty Sherlock Holmes stories, which have been translated into 234 languages. The first of the two stories chosen for this book, "The Adventure of the Speckled Band," was the author's own favorite.

Arthur Conan Doyle (1859–1930) was a medical doctor by training who based his highly eccentric hero on his old mentor at Edinburgh University, Dr. Joseph Bell. Although writing short fiction started out as just a hobby with Doyle, he soon became the toast of Victorian England. What is distinctive about his stories is that, in a style similar to that created by Poe, they present a series of seemingly unrelated facts and circumstances from which a reader could seek to deduce the outcome. To use one of Holmes's catchphrases, "the plot thickens" as the reader puzzles over the answer to the literary riddle. In the story below, Holmes and his good friend and narrator, Dr. Watson, are on the trail of a diabolically clever murderer.

"The Adventure of the Speckled Band" was first published in *Strand Magazine*.

In glancing over my notes of the seventy odd cases in which I have during the last eight years studied the methods of my friend Sherlock Holmes, I find many tragic, some comic, a large number merely strange, but none commonplace; for, working as he did rather for the love of his art than for the acquirement of wealth, he refused to associate himself with any investigation which did not tend towards the unusual, and even the fantastic. Of all these varied cases, however, I cannot recall any which presented more singular features than that which was associated with the well-known Surrey family of the Roylotts of Stoke Moran. The events in question occurred in the early days of my association with Holmes, when we were sharing rooms as bachelors, in Baker-street. It is possible that I might have placed them upon record before, but a promise of secrecy was made at the time, from which I have only been freed during the last month by the untimely death of the lady to whom the pledge was given. It is perhaps as well that the facts should now come to light, for I have reasons to know that there are widespread rumours as to the death of Dr. Grimesby Roylott which tend to make the matter even more terrible than the truth.

It was early in April in the year '83 that I woke one morning to find Sherlock Holmes standing, fully dressed, by the side of my bed. He was a late riser as a rule, and, as the clock on the mantelpiece showed me that it was only a quarter past seven, I blinked up at him in some surprise, and perhaps just a little resentment, for I was myself regular in my habits.

"Very sorry to knock you up, Watson," said he, "but it's the common lot this morning. Mrs. Hudson has been knocked up, she retorted upon me, and I on you."

"What is it, then? A fire?"

"No, a client. It seems that a young lady has arrived in a considerable state of excitement, who insists upon seeing me. She is waiting now in the sitting-room. Now, when young ladies wander about the Metropolis at this hour of the morning, and knock sleepy people up out of their beds, I presume that it is something very pressing which they have to communicate. Should it prove to be an interesting case, you would, I am sure, wish to follow it from the outset. I thought at any rate that I should call you, and give you the chance."

"My dear fellow, I would not miss it for anything."

I had no keener pleasure than in following Holmes in his professional investigations, and in admiring the rapid deductions, as swift as intuitions, and yet always founded on a logical basis, with which he unraveled the problems which were submitted to him. I rapidly threw on my clothes, and was ready in a few minutes to accompany my friend down to the sitting-room. A lady dressed in black and heavily veiled, who had been sitting in the window, rose as we entered.

"Good morning, madam," said Holmes, cheerily. "My name is Sherlock Holmes. This is my intimate friend and associate, Dr. Watson, before whom you can speak as freely as before myself. Ha, I am glad to see that Mrs. Hudson has had the good sense to light the fire. Pray draw up to it, and I shall order you a cup of hot coffee, for I observe that you are shivering."

"It is not cold which makes me shiver," said the woman in a low voice, changing her seat as requested.

"What then?"

"It is fear, Mr. Holmes. It is terror." She raised her veil as she spoke, and we could see that she was indeed in a pitiable state of agitation, her face all drawn and grey, with restless, frightened eyes, like those of some hunted animal. Her features and figure were those of a woman of thirty, but her hair was shot with premature grey, and her expression was weary and haggard. Sherlock Holmes ran her over with one of his quick, all-comprehensive glances.

"You must not fear," said he, soothingly, bending forward and patting her forearm. "We shall soon set matters right, I have no doubt. You have come in by train this morning, I see."

"You know me, then?"

"No, but I observe the second half of a return ticket in the palm of your left glove. You must have started early, and yet you had a good drive in a dog-cart, along heavy roads, before you reached the station."

The lady gave a violent start, and stared in bewilderment at my companion.

"There is no mystery, my dear madam," said he, smiling. "The left arm of your jacket is spattered with mud in no less than seven places. The marks are perfectly fresh. There is no vehicle save a dog-cart which throws up mud in that way, and then only when you sit on the left hand side of the driver."

"Whatever your reasons may be, you are perfectly correct," said she. "I started from home before six, reached Leatherhead at twenty past, and came in by the first train to Waterloo. Sir, I can stand this strain no longer, I shall go mad if it continues. I have no one to turn to—none, save only one, who cares for me, and he, poor fellow, can be of little aid. I have heard of you, Mr. Holmes; I have heard of you from Mrs. Farintosh, whom you helped in the hour of her sore need. It was from her that I had your address. Oh, sir do you not think that you could help me too, and at least throw a little light through the dense darkness which surrounds me? At present it is out of my power to reward you for your services, but in a month or six weeks I shall be married, with the control of my own income, and then at least you shall not find me ungrateful."

Holmes turned to his desk, and unlocking it, drew out a small case-book which he consulted.

"Farintosh," said he. "Ah, yes, I recall the case; it was concerned with an opal tiara. I think it was before your time, Watson. I can only say, madam, that I shall be happy to devote the same care to your case as I did to that of your friend. As to reward, my profession is its own reward; but you are at liberty to defray whatever expenses I may be put to, at the time which suits you best. And now I beg that you will lay before us everything that may help us in forming an opinion upon the matter."

"Alas!" replied our visitor. "The very horror of my situation lies in the fact that my fears are so vague, and my suspicions depend so entirely upon small points, which might seem trivial to another, that even he to whom of all others I have a right to look for help and advice looks upon all that I tell him about it as the fancies of a nervous woman. He does not say so, but I can read it from his soothing answers and averted eyes. But I have heard, Mr. Holmes, that you can see deeply into the manifold wickedness of the human heart. You may advise me how to walk amid the dangers which encompass me."

"I am all attention, madam."

"My name is Helen Stoner, and I am living with my stepfather, who is the last survivor of one of the oldest Saxon families in England, the Roylatts of Stoke Moran, on the western border of Surrey."

Holmes nodded his head. "The name is familiar to me," said he.

"The family was at one time among the richest in England, and the estates extended over the borders into Berkshire in the north, and Hampshire in the west. In the last century, however, four successive heirs were of a dissolute and wasteful disposition, and the family ruin was eventually completed by a gambler in the days of the Regency. Nothing was left save a few acres of ground, and the two-hundred-year-old house, which is itself crushed under a heavy mortgage. The last squire dragged out his existence there, living the horrible life of an aristocratic pauper; but his only son, my stepfather, seeing that he must adapt himself to the new conditions, obtained an advance from a relative, which enabled him to take a medical degree, and went out to Calcutta, where, by his professional skill and his force of character, he established a large practice. In a fit of anger, however, caused by some robberies which had been perpetrated in the house, he beat his native butler to death, and narrowly escaped a capital sentence. As it was, he suffered a long term of imprisonment, and afterwards returned to England a morose and disappointed man.

"When Dr. Roylott was in India he married my mother, Mrs. Stoner, the young widow of Major-General Stoner, of the Bengal Artillery. My sister Julia and I were twins, and we were only two years old at the time of my mother's remarriage. She had a considerable sum of money, not less than a thousand a year, and this she bequeathed to Dr. Roylott entirely whilst we resided with him, with a provision that a certain annual sum should be allowed to each of us in the event of our marriage. Shortly after our return to England my mother died—she was killed eight years ago in a railway accident near Crewe. Dr. Roylott then abandoned his attempts to establish himself in practice in London, and took us to live with him in the old ancestral house at Stoke Moran. The money which my mother had left was enough for all our wants, and there seemed to be no obstacle to our happiness.

"But a terrible change came over our stepfather about this time. Instead of making friends and exchanging visits with our neighbors, who had at first been overjoyed to see a Roylott of Stoke Moran back in the old family seat, he shut himself up in his house, and seldom came out save to indulge in ferocious quarrels with whoever might cross his path. Violence of temper approaching to mania has been hereditary in the men of the family, and in my stepfather's case it had, I believe, been intensified by his long residence in the tropics. A series of disgraceful brawls took place, two of which ended in the police-court, until at last he became the terror of the village, and the folks would fly at his approach, for he is a man of immense strength, and absolutely uncontrollable in his anger.

"Last week he hurled the local blacksmith over a parapet into a stream, and it was only by paying over all the money which I could gather together that I was able to avert another public exposure. He had no friends at all save the wandering gipsies, and he would give these vagabonds leave to encamp upon the few acres of bramble-covered land which represent the family estate, and would accept in return the hospitality of their tents, wandering away with them sometimes for weeks on end. He has a passion also for Indian animals, which are sent over to him by a correspondent, and he has at this moment a cheetah and a baboon, which wander freely over his grounds, and are feared by the villagers almost as much as their master.

"You can imagine from what I say that my poor sister Julia and I had no great pleasure in out lives. No servant would stay with us, and for a long time we did all the work of the house. She was but thirty at the time of her death, and yet her hair had already begun to whiten, even as mine has."

"Your sister is dead, then?"

"She died just two years ago, and it is of her death that I wish to speak to you. You can understand that, living the life which I have described, we were little likely to see anyone of our own age and position. We had, however, an aunt, my mother's maiden sister, Miss Honoria Westphail, who lives near Harrow, and we were occasionally allowed to pay short visits at this lady's house. Julia went there at Christmas two years ago, and met there a half-pay Major of Marines, to whom she became engaged. My stepfather learned of the engagement when my sister returned, and offered no objection to the marriage; but within a fortnight of the day which had been fixed for the wedding, the terrible event occurred which has deprived me of my only companion."

Sherlock Holmes had been leaning back in his chair with his eyes closed, and his head sunk in a cushion, but he half opened his lids now, and glanced across at his visitor.

"Pray be precise as to details," said he.

"It is easy for me to be so, for every event of that dreadful time is seared into my memory. The manor house is, as I have already said, very old, and only one wing is now inhabited. The bedrooms in this wing are on the ground floor, the sitting-rooms being in the central block of the buildings. Of these bedrooms the first is Dr. Roylott's, the second my sister's, and the third my own. There is no communication between them, but they all open out into the same corridor. Do I make myself plain?"

"Perfectly so."

"The windows of the three rooms open out upon the lawn. That fatal night Dr. Roylott had gone to his room early, though we knew that he had not retired to rest, for my sister was troubled by the smell of the strong Indian cigars which it was his custom to smoke. She left her room, therefore, and came into mine, where she sat for some time, chatting about her approaching wedding. At eleven o'clock she rose to leave me, but she paused at the door and looked back.

"'Tell me, Helen,' said she, 'have you ever heard anyone whistle in the dead of the night?'

"'Never,' said I.

"'I suppose that you could not possibly whistle yourself in your sleep?'

"'Certainly not. But why?'

"'Because during the last few nights I have always, about three in the morning, heard a low clear whistle. I am a light sleeper, and it has awakened me. I cannot tell where it came from—perhaps from the next room, perhaps from the lawn. I thought that I would just ask you whether you had heard it.'

"'No, I have not. It must be those wretched gipsies in the plantation.'

"'Very likely. And yet if it were on the lawn I wonder that you did not hear it also.'

"'Ah, but I sleep more heavily than you.'

"'Well, it is of no great consequence at any rate,' she smiled back at me, closed my door, and a few moments later I heard her key turn in the lock."

"Indeed," said Holmes. "Was it your custom always to lock yourselves in at night?"

"Always."

"And why?"

"I think that I mentioned to you that the Doctor kept a cheetah and a baboon. We had no feeling of security unless our doors were locked."

"Quite so. Pray proceed with your statement."

"I could not sleep that night. A vague feeling of impending misfortune impressed me. My sister and I, you will recollect, were twins, and you know how subtle are the links which bind two souls which are so closely allied. It was a wild night. The wind was howling outside, and the rain was beating and splashing against the windows. Suddenly, amidst all the hubbub of the gale, there burst forth the wild scream of a terrified woman. I knew that it was my sister's voice. I sprang from my bed, wrapped a shawl round me, and rushed into the corridor. As I opened my door I seemed to hear a low whistle, such as my sister described, and a few moments later a clanging sound, as if a mass of metal had fallen. As I ran down the passage my sister's door was unlocked, and revolved slowly upon its hinges. I stared at it horror-stricken, not knowing what was about to issue from it. By the light of the corridor lamp I saw my sister appear at the opening, her face blanched with terror, her hands groping for help, her whole figure swaying to and fro like that of a drunkard. I ran to her and threw my arms round her, but at that moment her knees seemed to give way and she fell to the ground. She writhed as one who is in terrible pain, and her limbs were dreadfully convulsed. At first I thought that she had not recognized me, but as I bent over her she suddenly shrieked out in a voice which I shall never forget, 'Oh, my God! Helen! It was the band! The speckled band!' There was something else which she would fain have said, and she stabbed with her finger into the air in the direction of the Doctor's room, but a fresh convulsion seized her and choked her words. I rushed out, calling loudly for my stepfather, and I met him hastening from his room in his dressing-gown. When he reached my sister's side she was unconscious, and though he poured brandy down her throat, and sent for medical aid from the village, all efforts were in vain, for she slowly sank and died without having recovered her consciousness. Such was the dreadful end of my beloved sister."

"One moment," said Holmes; "are you sure about this whistle and metallic sound? Could you swear to it?"

"That was what the county coroner asked me at the inquiry. It is my strong impression that I heard it, and yet among the crash of the gale, and the creaking of an old house, I may possibly have been deceived."

"Was your sister dressed?"

"No, she was in her nightdress. In her right hand was found the charred stump of a match, and in her left a matchbox."

"Showing that she had struck a light and looked about her when the alarm took place. That is important. And what conclusions did the coroner come to?"

"He investigated the case with great care, for Dr. Roylott's conduct had long been notorious in the county, but he was unable to find any satisfactory cause of death. My evidence showed that the door had been fastened upon the inner side, and the windows were blocked by old-fashioned shutters with broad iron bars, which were secured every night. The walls were carefully sounded, and were shown to be quite solid all round, and the flooring was also thoroughly examined, with the same result. The chimney is wide, but is barred up by four large staples. It is certain, therefore, that my sister was quite alone when she met her end. Besides, there were no marks of any violence upon her."

"How about poison?"

"The doctors examined her for it, but without success."

"What do you think that this unfortunate lady died of, then?"

"It is my belief that she died of pure fear and nervous shock, though what it was which frightened her I cannot imagine."

"Were there gipsies in the plantation at the time?"

"Yes, there are nearly always some there."

"Ah, and what did you gather from this allusion to a band—a speckled band?"

"Sometimes I have thought that it was merely the wild talk of delirium, sometimes that it may have referred to some band of people, perhaps to these very gipsies in the plantation. I do not know whether the spotted handkerchiefs which so many of them wear over their heads might have suggested the strange adjective which she used."

Holmes shook his head like a man who is far from being satisfied.

"These are very deep waters," said he; "pray go on with your narrative."

"Two years have passed since then, and my life has been until lately lonelier than ever. A month ago, however, a dear friend, whom I have known for many years, has done me the honour to ask my hand in marriage. His name is Armitage—Percy Armitage—the second son of Mr. Armitage, of Crane Water, near Reading. My stepfather has offered no opposition to the match, and we are to be married in the course of the spring. Two days ago some repairs were started in the west wing of the building, and my bedroom wall has been pierced, so that I have had to move into the chamber in which my sister died, and to sleep in the very bed in which she slept. Imagine, then, my thrill of terror when last night, as I lay awake, thinking over her terrible fate, I suddenly heard in the silence of the night the low whistle which had been the herald of her own death. I sprang up and lit the lamp, but nothing was to be seen in the room. I was too shaken to go to bed again, however, so I dressed, and as soon as it was daylight I slipped down, got a dogcart at the 'Crown' inn, which is opposite, and drove to Leatherhead, from whence I have come on this morning with the one object of seeing you and asking your advice."

"You have done wisely," said my friend. "But have you told me all?"

"Yes, all."

"Miss Roylott, you have not. You are screening your stepfather."

"Why, what do you mean?"

For answer Holmes pushed back the frill of black lace which fringed the hand that lay upon our visitor's knee. Five little livid spots, the marks of four fingers and thumb, were printed upon the white wrist.

"You have been cruelly used," said Holmes.

The lady coloured deeply and covered over her injured wrist. "He is a hard man," she said, "and perhaps he hardly knows his own strength."

There was a long silence, during which Holmes leaned his chin upon his hands and stared into the crackling fire.

"This is a very deep business," he said at last. "There are a thousand details which I should desire to know before I decide upon our course of action. Yet we have not a moment to lose. If we were to come to Stoke Moran to-day, would it be possible for us to see over these rooms without the knowledge of your stepfather?"

"As it happens, he spoke of coming into town to-day upon some most important business. It is probable that he will be away all day, and that there would be nothing to disturb you. We have a housekeeper now, but she is old and foolish, and I could easily get her out of the way."

"Excellent. You are not averse to this trip, Watson?"

"By no means."

"Then we shall both come. What are you going to do yourself?"

"I have one or two things which I would wish to do now that I am in town. But I shall return by the twelve o'clock train, so as to be there in time for your coming."

"And you may expect us early in the afternoon. I have myself some small business matters to attend to. Will you not wait and breakfast?"

"No, I must go. My heart is lightened already since I have confided my trouble to you. I shall look forward to seeing you again this afternoon." She dropped her thick black veil over her face, and glided from the room.

"And what do you think of it all, Watson?" asked Sherlock Holmes, leaning back in his chair.

"It seems to me to be a most dark and sinister business."

"Dark enough, and sinister enough."

"Yet if the lady is correct in saying that the flooring and walls are sound, and that the door, window, and the chimney are impassable, then her sister must have been undoubtedly alone when she met her mysterious end."

"What becomes, then, of these nocturnal whistles, and what of the very peculiar words of the dying woman?"

"I cannot think."

"When you combine the ideas of whistles at night, the presence of a band of gipsies who are on intimate terms with this old Doctor, the fact that we have every reason to believe that the Doctor has an interest in preventing his stepdaughter's marriage, the dying allusion of a band, and finally, the fact that Miss Helen Stoner heard a metallic clang, which might have been caused by one of those metal bars which secured the shutters falling back into their place, I think that there is good ground to think that the mystery may be cleared along those lines."

"But what, then, did the gipsies do?"

"I cannot imagine."

"I see many objections to any such theory."

"And so do I. It is precisely for that reason that we are going to Stoke Moran this day. I want to see whether the objections are fatal, or if they may be explained away. But what, in the name of the devil!"

The ejaculation had been drawn from my companion by the fact that our door had been suddenly dashed open, and that a huge man had framed himself in the aperture. His costume was a peculiar mixture of the professional and of the agricultural, having a black top hat, a long frock coat, and a pair of high gaiters, with a hunting crop swinging in his hand. So tall was he that his hat actually brushed the cross bar of the doorway, and his breadth seemed to span it across from side to side. A large face, seared with a thousand wrinkles, burned yellow with the sun, and marked with every evil passion, was turned from one to the other of us, while his deep-set, bileshot eyes, and his high thin fleshless nose, gave him somewhat the resemblance to a fierce old bird of prey.

"Which of you is Holmes?" asked this apparition.

"My name, sir, but you have the advantage of me," said my companion, quietly.

"I am Dr. Grimesby Roylott, of Stoke Moran."

"Indeed, Doctor," said Holmes, blandly. "Pray take a seat."

"I will do nothing of the kind. My stepdaughter has been here. I have traced her. What has she been saying to you?"

"It is a little cold for the time of the year," said Holmes.

"What has she been saying to you?" screamed the old man furiously.

"But I have heard that the crocuses promise well," continued my companion imperturbably.

"Ha! You put me off, do you?" said our new visitor, taking a step forward, and shaking his hunting crop. "I know you, you scoundrel! I have heard of you before. You are Holmes the meddler."

My friend smiled.

"Holmes the busybody!"

His smile broadened.

"Holmes the Scotland-yard Jack-in-office!"

Holmes chuckled heartily. "Your conversation is most entertaining," said he. "When you go out close the door, for there is a decided draught."

"I will go when I have said my say. Don't you dare to meddle with my affairs. I know that Miss Stoner has been here—I traced her! I am a dangerous man to fall foul of! See here." He stepped swiftly forward, seized the poker, and bent it into a curve with his huge brown hands.

"See that you keep yourself out of my grip," he snarled, and hurling the twisted poker into the fireplace, he strode out of the room.

"He seems a very amiable person," said Holmes, laughing. "I am not quite so bulky, but if he had remained I might have shown him that my grip was not much more feeble than his own." As he spoke he picked up the steel poker, and with a sudden effort straightened it out again.

"Fancy his having the insolence to confound me with the official detective force! This incident gives zest to our investigation, however, and I only trust that our little friend will not suffer from her imprudence in allowing this brute to trace her. And now, Watson, we shall order breakfast, and afterwards I shall walk down to Doctors' Commons, where I hope to get some data which may help us in this matter."

It was nearly one o'clock when Sherlock Holmes returned from his excursion. He held in his hand a sheet of blue paper, scrawled over with notes and figures.

"I have seen the will of the deceased wife," said he. "To determine its exact meaning I have been obliged to work out the present prices of the investments with which it is concerned. The total income, which at the time of the wife's death was little short of £1,100, is now through the fall in agricultural prices not more than £750. Each daughter can claim an income of £250, in case of marriage. It is evident, therefore, that if both girls had married this beauty would have had a mere pittance, while even one of them would cripple him to a very serious extent. My morning's work has not been wasted, since it has proved that he has the very strongest motives for standing in the way of anything of the sort. And now, Watson, this is too serious for dawdling, especially as the old man is aware that we are interesting ourselves in his affairs, so if you are ready we shall call a cab and drive to Waterloo. I should be very much obliged if you would slip your revolver into your pocket. An Eley's No. 2 is an excellent argument with gentlemen who can twist steel pokers into knots. That and a tooth-brush are, I think, all that we need."

At Waterloo we were fortunate in catching a train for Leatherhead, where we hired a trap at the station inn, and drove for four or five miles through the lovely Surrey lanes. It was a perfect day, with a bright sun and a few fleecy clouds in the heavens. The trees and wayside hedges were just throwing out their first green shoots, and the air was full of the pleasant smell of the moist earth. To me at least there was strange contrast between the sweet promise of the spring and this sinister quest upon which we were engaged. My companion sat in the front of the trap, his arms folded, his hat pulled down over his eyes, and his chin sunk upon his breast, buried in the deepest thought. Suddenly, however, he started, tapped me on the shoulder, and pointed over the meadows.

"Look there!" said he.

A heavily-timbered park stretched up in a gentle slope, thickening into a grove at the highest point. From amidst the branches there jutted out the grey gables and high roof-tree of a very old mansion.

"Stoke Moran?" said he.

"Yes, sir, that be the house of Dr. Grimesby Roylott," remarked the driver.

"There is some building going on there," said Holmes; "that is where we are going."

"There's the village," said the driver, pointing to a cluster of roofs some distance to the left; "but if you want to get to the house, you'll find it shorter to get over this stile, and so by the footpath over the fields. There it is, where the lady is walking."

"And the lady, I fancy, is Miss Stoner," observed Holmes, shading his eyes. "Yes, I think we had better do as you suggest."

We got off, paid our fare, and the trap rattled back on its way to Leatherhead.

"I thought it as well," said Holmes, as we climbed the stile, "that this fellow should think we had come here as architects, or on some definite business. It may stop his gossip. Good afternoon, Miss Stoner. You see that we have been as good as our word."

Our client of the morning had hurried forward to meet us with a face which spoke her joy. "I have been waiting so eagerly for you," she cried, shaking hands with us warmly. "All has turned out splendidly. Dr. Roylott has gone to town, and it is unlikely that he will be back before evening."

"We have had the pleasure of making the Doctor's acquaintance," said Holmes, and in a few words he sketched out what had occurred. Miss Stoner turned white to the lips as she listened.

"Good heavens!" she cried, "he has followed me, then."

"So it appears."

"He is so cunning that I never know when I am safe from him. What will he say when he returns?"

"He must guard himself, for he may find that there is someone more cunning than himself upon his track. You must lock yourself up from him tonight. If he is violent, we shall take you away to your aunt's at Harrow. Now, we must make the best use of our time, so kindly take us at once to the rooms which we are to examine."

The building was of grey, lichen-blotched stone, with a high central portion, and two curving wings, like the claws of a crab, thrown out on each side. In one of these wings the windows were broken, and blocked with wooden boards, while the roof was partly caved in, a picture of ruin. The central portion was in little better repair, but the right-hand block was comparatively modern, and the blinds in the windows, with the blue smoke curling up from the chimneys, showed that this was where the family resided. Some scaffolding had been erected against the end wall, and the stonework had been broken into, but there were no signs of any workmen at the moment of our visit. Holmes walked slowly up and down the ill-trimmed lawn, and examined with deep attention the outsides of the windows.

"This, I take it, belongs to the room in which you used to sleep, the centre one to your sister's, and the one next to the main building to Dr. Roylott's chamber?"

"Exactly so. But I am now sleeping in the middle one."

"Pending the alterations, as I understand. By the way, there does not seem to be any very pressing need for repairs at that end wall."

"There were none. I believe that it was an excuse to move me from my room."

"Ah! that is suggestive. Now, on the other side of this narrow wing runs the corridor from which these three rooms open. There are windows in it, of course?"

"Yes, but very small ones. Too narrow for anyone to pass through."

"As you both locked your doors at night your rooms were unapproachable from that side. Now, would you have the kindness to go into your room, and to bar your shutters."

Miss Stoner did so, and Holmes, after a careful examination through the open window, endeavoured in every way to force the shutter open, but without success. There was no slit through which a knife could be passed to raise the bar. Then with his lens he tested the hinges, but they were of solid iron, built firmly into the massive masonry. "Hum!" said he, scratching his chin in some perplexity, "my theory certainly presents some difficulties. No one could pass these shutters if they were bolted. Well, we shall see if the inside throws any light upon the matter."

A small side door led into the whitewashed corridor from which the three bedrooms opened. Holmes refused to examine the third chamber, so we passed at once to the second, that in which Miss Stoner was now sleeping, and in which her sister had met with her fate. It was a homely little room, with a low ceiling and a gaping fireplace, after the fashion of old country houses. A brown chest of drawers stood in one corner, a narrow white-counterpaned bed in another, and a dressing-table on the left-hand side of the window. These articles, with two small wickerwork chairs, made up all the furniture in the room, save for a square of Wilton carpet in the centre. The boards round and the paneling of the walls were of brown, worm-eaten oak, so old and discoloured that it may have dated from the original building of the house. Holmes drew one of the chairs into a corner and sat silent, while his eyes traveled round and round and up and down, taking in every detail of the apartment.

"Where does that bell communicate with?" he asked at last, pointing to a thick bell-rope which hung down beside the bed, the tassel actually lying upon the pillow.

"It goes to the housekeeper's room."

"It looks newer than the other things?"

"Yes, it was only put there a couple of years ago."

"Your sister asked for it, I suppose?"

"No, I never heard of her using it. We used always to get what we wanted for ourselves."

"Indeed, it seems unnecessary to put so nice a bell-pull there. You will excuse me for a few minutes while I satisfy myself as to this floor." He threw himself down upon his face with his lens in his hand, and crawled swiftly backwards and forwards, examining minutely the cracks between the boards. Then he did the same with the woodwork with which the chamber was paneled. Finally he walked over to the bed and spent some time in staring at it, and in running his eye up and down the wall. Finally he took the bell-rope in his hand and gave it a brisk tug.

"Why, it's a dummy," said he.

"Won't it ring?"

"No, it is not even attached to a wire. This is very interesting. You can see now that it is fastened to a hook just above where the little opening for the ventilator is."

"How very absurd! I never noticed that before."

"Very strange!" muttered Holmes, pulling at the rope. "There are one or two very singular points about this room. For example, what a fool a builder must be to open a ventilator into another room, when, with the same trouble, he might have communicated with the outside air!"

"That is also quite modern," said the lady.

"Done about the same time as the bell-rope?" remarked Holmes.

"Yes, there were several little changes carried out about that time."

"They seem to have been of a most interesting character—dummy bell-ropes, and ventilators which do not ventilate. With your permission, Miss Stoner, we shall now carry our researches into the inner apartment."

Dr. Grimesby Roylott's chamber was larger than that of his step-daughter, but was as plainly furnished. A camp bed, a small wooden shelf full of books, mostly of a technical character, an armchair beside the bed, a plain wooden chair against the wall, a round table, and a large iron safe were the principal things which met the eye. Holmes walked slowly round and examined each and all of them with the keenest interest.

"What's in here?" he asked, tapping the safe.

"My step-father's business papers."

"Oh! you have seen inside, then?"

"Only once, some years ago. I remember that it was full of papers."

"There isn't a cat in it, for example?"

"No. What a strange idea!"

"Well, look at this!" He took up a small saucer of milk which stood on the top of it.

"No; we don't keep a cat. But there is a cheetah and a baboon."

"Ah, yes, of course! Well, a cheetah is just a big cat, and yet a saucer of milk does not go very far in satisfying its wants, I daresay. There is one point which

I should wish to determine." He squatted down in front of the wooden chair, and examined the seat of it with the greatest attention.

"Thank you. That is quite settled," said he, rising and putting his lens in his pocket. "Hullo! here is something interesting!"

The object which had caught his eye was a small dog lash hung on one corner of the bed. The lash, however, was curled upon itself, and tied so as to make a loop of whipcord.

"What do you make of that, Watson?"

"It's a common enough lash. But I don't know why it should be tied."

"That is not quite so common, is it? Ah, me! it's a wicked world, and when a clever man turns his brains to crime it is the worst of all. I think that I have seen enough now, Miss Stoner, and, with your permission, we shall walk out upon the lawn."

I had never seen my friend's face so grim, or his brow so dark, as it was when we turned from the scene of this investigation. We had walked several times up and down the lawn, neither Miss Stoner nor myself liking to break in upon his thoughts, before he roused himself from his reverie.

"It is very essential, Miss Stoner," said he, "that you should absolutely follow my advice in every respect."

"I shall most certainly do so."

"The matter is too serious for any hesitation. Your life may depend upon your compliance."

"I assure that I am in your hands."

"In the first place, both my friend and I must spend the night in your room."

Both Miss Stoner and I gazed at him in astonishment.

"Yes, it must be so. Let me explain. I believe that that is the village inn over there?"

"Yes, that is the 'Crown.'"

"Very good. Your windows would be visible from there?"

"Certainly."

"You must confine yourself to your room, on pretence of a headache, when your stepfather comes back. Then when you hear him retire for the night, you must open the shutters of your window, undo the hasp, put your lamp there as a signal to us, and then withdraw quietly with everything which you are likely to want into the room which you used to occupy. I have no doubt that, in spite of the repairs, you could manage there for one night."

"Oh, yes, easily."

"The rest you will leave in our hands."

"But what will you do?"

"We shall spend the night in your room, and we shall investigate the cause of this noise which has disturbed you."

"I believe, Mr. Holmes, that you have already made up your mind," said Miss Stoner, laying her hand upon my companion's sleeve.

"Perhaps I have."

"Then for pity's sake tell me what was the cause of my sister's death."

"I should prefer to have clearer proofs before I speak."

"You can at least tell me whether my own thought is correct, and if she died from some sudden fright."

"No, I do not think so. I think that there was probably some more tangible cause. And, now, Miss Stoner, we must leave you, for if Dr. Roylott returned and saw us, our journey would be in vain. Good-bye, and be brave, for if you will do what I have told you, you may rest assured that we shall soon drive away the dangers that threaten you."

Sherlock Holmes and I had no difficulty in engaging a bedroom and sitting-room at the "Crown" Inn. They were on the upper floor, and from our window we could command a view of the avenue gate, and of the inhabited wing of Stoke Moran Manor House. At dusk we saw Dr. Grimesby Roylott drive past, his huge form looming up beside the little figure of the lad who drove him. The boy had some slight difficulty in undoing the heavy iron gates, and we heard the hoarse roar of the doctor's voice, and saw the fury with which he shook his clenched fists at him. The trap drove on, and a few minutes later we saw a sudden light spring up among the trees as the lamp was lit in one of the sitting-rooms.

"Do you know, Watson," said Holmes, as we sat together in the gathering darkness, "I have really some scruples as to taking you to-night. There is a distinct element of danger."

"Can I be of assistance?"

"Your presence might be invaluable."

"Then I shall certainly come."

"It is very kind of you."

"You speak of danger. You have evidently seen more in these rooms than was visible to me."

"No, but I fancy that I many have deduced a little more. I imagine that you saw all that I did."

"I saw nothing remarkable save the bell rope, and what purpose that could answer I confess is more than I can imagine."

"You saw the ventilator, too?"

"Yes, but I do not think that it is very unusual thing to have a small opening between two rooms. It was so small that a rat could hardly pass through."

"I knew that we should find a ventilator before ever we came to Stoke Moran."

"My dear Holmes!"

"Oh, yes, I did. You remember in her statement she said that her sister could smell Dr. Roylott's cigar. Now, of course that suggested at once that there must be a communication between the two rooms. It could only be a small one, or it would have been remarked upon at the Coroner's inquiry. I deduced a ventilator."

"But what harm can there be in that?"

"Well, there is at least a curious coincidence of dates. A ventilator is made, a cord is hung, and a lady who sleeps in the bed dies. Does not that strike you?"

"I cannot as yet see any connection."

"Did you observe anything very peculiar about that bed?"

"No."

"It was clamped to the floor. Did you ever see a bed fastened like that before?"

"I cannot say that I have."

"The lady could not move her bed. It must always be in the same relative position to the ventilator and to the rope—for so we may call it, since it was clearly never meant for a bell-pull."

"Holmes," I cried, "I seem to see dimly what you are hinting at. We are only just in time to prevent some subtle and horrible crime."

"Subtle enough, and horrible enough. When a doctor does go wrong, he is the first of criminals. He has nerve and he has knowledge. Palmer and Pritchard were among the heads of their profession. This man strikes even deeper, but I think, Watson, that we shall be able to strike deeper still. But we shall have horrors enough before the night is over; for goodness' sake let us have a quiet pipe, and turn our minds for a few hours to something more cheerful."

About nine o'clock the light among the trees was extinguished, and all was dark in the direction of the Manor House. Two hours passed slowly away, and then, suddenly, just at the stroke of eleven, a single bright light shone out right in front of us.

"That is our signal," said Holmes, springing to his feet; "it comes from the middle window."

As we passed out he exchanged a few words with the landlord, explaining that we were going on a late visit to an acquaintance, and that it was possible that we might spend the night there. A moment later we were out on the dark road, a chill wind blowing in our faces, and one yellow light twinkling in front of us through the gloom to guide us on our sombre errand.

There was little difficulty in entering the grounds, for unrepaired breaches gaped in the old park wall. Making our way among the trees, we reached the lawn, crossed it, and were about to enter through the window, when out from a clump of laurel bushes there darted what seemed to be a hideous and distorted child, who threw itself upon the grass with writhing limbs, and then ran swiftly across the lawn into the darkness.

"My God!" I whispered; "did you see it?"

Holmes was for the moment as startled as I. His hand closed like a vice upon my wrist in his agitation. Then he broke into a low laugh, and put his lips to my ear.

"It is a nice household," he murmured. "That is the baboon."

I had forgotten the strange pets which the Doctor affected. There was a cheetah, too; perhaps we might find it upon our shoulders at any moment. I confess that I felt easier in my mind when, after following Holmes' example and slipping off my shoes, I found myself inside the bedroom. My companion noiselessly closed the shutters, moved the lamp on to the table, and cast his eyes round the room. All was as we had seen it in the day-time. Then creeping up to me and making a trumpet of his hand, he whispered into my ear again so gently that it was all that I could do to distinguish the words.

"The least sound would be fatal to our plans."

I nodded to show that I had heard.

"We must sit without light. He would see it through the ventilator."

I nodded again.

"Do not go asleep; your very life may depend upon it. Have your pistol ready in case we should need it. I will sit on the side of the bed, and you in that chair."

I took out my revolver and laid it on the corner of the table.

Holmes had brought up a long thin cane, and this he placed upon the bed beside him. By it he laid the box of matches and the stump of a candle. Then he turned down the lamp, and we were left in darkness.

How shall I ever forget that dreadful vigil? I could not hear a sound, not even the drawing of a breath, and yet I knew that my companion sat open-eyed, within a few feet of me, in the same state of nervous tension in which I was myself. The shutters cut off the least ray of light, and we waited in absolute darkness. From outside came the occasional cry of a night bird, and once at our very window a long drawn, cat-like whine, which told us that the cheetah was indeed at liberty. Far away we could hear the deep tones of the parish clock, which boomed out every quarter of an hour. How long they seemed, those quarters! Twelve struck, and one, and two, and three, and still we sat waiting silently for whatever might befall.

Suddenly there was the momentary gleam of a light up in the direction of the ventilator, which vanished immediately, but was succeeded by a strong smell of burning oil and heated metal. Someone in the next room had lit a dark lantern. I heard a gentle sound of movement, and then all was silent once more, though the smell grew stronger. For half an hour I sat with straining ears. Then suddenly another sound became audible—a very gently, soothing sound, like that of a small jet of steam escaping continually from a kettle. The instant that we heard it, Holmes sprang from the bed, struck a match, and lashed furiously with his cane at the bell-pull.

"You see it, Watson?" he yelled. "You see it?"

But I saw nothing. At the moment when Holmes struck the light I heard a low, clear whistle, but the sudden glare flashing into my weary eyes made it impossible for me to tell what it was at which my friend lashed so savagely. I could, however, see that his face was deadly pale, and filled with horror and loathing.

He had ceased to strike, and was gazing up at the ventilator, when suddenly there broke from the silence of the night the most horrible cry to which I have ever listened. It swelled up louder and louder, a hoarse yell of pain and fear and anger all mingled in the one dreadful shriek. They say that away down in the village, and even in the distant parsonage, that cry raised the sleepers from their beds. It struck cold to our hearts, and I stood gazing at Holmes, and he at me, until the last echoes of it had died away into the silence from which it rose.

"What can it mean?" I gasped.

"It means that it is all over," Holmes answered. "And perhaps, after all, it is for the best. Take your pistol, and we shall enter Dr. Roylott's room."

With a grave face he lit the lamp, and led the way down the corridor. Twice he struck at the chamber door without any reply from within. Then he turned the handle and entered, I at his heels, with the cocked pistol in my hand.

It was a singular sight which met our eyes. On the table stood a dark lantern with the shutter half open, throwing a brilliant beam of light upon the iron safe, the door of which was ajar. Beside this table, on the wooden chair, sat Dr. Grimesby Roylott, clad in a long grey dressing-gown, his bare ankles protruding beneath, and his feet thrust into red heelless Turkish slippers. Across his lap lay the short stock with the long lash which we had noticed during the day. His chin was cocked upwards, and his eyes were fixed in a dreadful rigid stare at the corner of the ceiling. Round his brow he had a peculiar yellow band, with brownish speckles, which seemed to be bound tightly round his head. As we entered he made neither sound nor motion.

"The band! the speckled band!" whispered Holmes.

I took a step forward. In an instant his strange headgear began to move, and there reared itself from among his hair the squat diamond-shaped head and puffed neck of a loathsome serpent.

"It is a swamp adder!" cried Holmes—"the deadliest snake in India. He has died within ten seconds of being bitten. Violence does, in truth, recoil upon the violent, and the schemer falls into the pit which he digs for another. Let us thrust this creature back into its den, and we can then remove Miss Stoner to some place of shelter, and let the county police know what has happened."

As he spoke he drew the dog whip swiftly from the dead man's lap, and throwing the noose round the reptile's neck, he drew it from its horrid perch, and, carrying it at arm's length threw it into the iron safe, which he closed upon it.

Such are the true facts of the death of Dr. Grimesby Roylott, of Stoke Moran. It is not necessary that I should prolong a narrative which has already run to too great a length, by telling how we broke the sad news to the terrified girl, how we conveyed her by the morning train to the care of her good aunt at Harrow, of how the slow process of official inquiry came to the conclusion that the Doctor met his fate while indiscreetly playing with a dangerous pet. The little which I had yet to learn of the case was told me by Sherlock Holmes as we travelled back next day.

"I had," said he, "come to an entirely erroneous conclusion, which shows, my dear Watson, how dangerous it always is to reason from insufficient data. The presence of the gipsies, and the use of the word 'band' which was used by the poor girl, no doubt, to explain the appearance which she had caught a hurried glimpse of by the light of her match, were sufficient to put me upon an entirely wrong scent. I can only claim the merit that I instantly reconsidered my position when, however, it became clear to me that whatever danger threatened an occupant of the room could not come either from the window or the door. My attention was speedily drawn, as I have already remarked to you, to this ventilator, and to the bell rope which hung down to the bed. The discovery that this was a dummy, and that the bed was clamped to the floor, instantly gave rise to the suspicion that the rope was there as a bridge for something passing through the hole, and coming to the bed. The idea of a snake instantly occurred to me, and when I coupled it with my knowledge that the Doctor was furnished with a supply of creatures from India, I felt that I was probably on the right track. The idea of using a form of poison which could not possibly be discovered by any chemical test was just such a one as would occur to a clever and ruthless man who had had an Eastern training. The rapidity with which such a poison would take effect would also, from his point of view, be an advantage. It would be a sharp-eyed coroner indeed who could distinguish the two little dark punctures which would show where the poison fangs had done their work. Then I thought of the whistle. Of course, he must recall the snake before the morning light revealed it to the victim. He had trained it, probably by the use of the milk which we saw, to return to him when summoned. He would put it through this ventilator at the hour that he thought best, with the certainty that it would crawl down the rope, and land on the bed. It might or might not bite the occupant, perhaps she might escape every night for a week, but sooner or later she must fall a victim.

"I had come to these conclusions before ever I had entered his room. An inspection of his chair showed me that he had been in the habit of standing on it, which, of course, would be necessary in order that he should reach the ventilator. The sight of the safe, the saucer of milk, and the loop of whipcord were enough to finally dispel any doubts which may have remained. The metallic clang heard by Miss Stoner was obviously caused by her father hastily closing the door of his safe upon its terrible occupant. Having once made up my mind, you know the steps which I took in order to put the matter to the proof. I heard the creature hiss, as I have no doubt that you did also, and I instantly lit the light and attacked it."

"With the result of driving it through the ventilator."

"And also with the result of causing it to turn upon its master at the other side. Some of the blows of my cane came home, and roused its snakish temper, so that it flew upon the first person it saw. In this way I am no doubt indirectly responsible for Dr. Grimesby Roylott's death, and I cannot say that it is likely to weigh very heavily upon my conscience."

THE HANDS OF MR. OTTERMOLE

(1931)

Thomas Burke

While not as well known as some of his fellow English mystery writers of the 1920s and 1930s, Thomas Burke (1887–1945) has penned a story that is as good as any in the book. Indeed, Ellery Queen has noted that "no finer crime story has ever been written, period." A psychopathic strangler is on the loose, committing random and motiveless murders in foggy London town. Burke is the author of books including *East of Mansion House* (1926), *The Flower of Life* (1931), and *The Beauty of England* (1934). It is in his book *A Tea Shop in Limehouse* (1931) that this story appears.

At six o'clock of a January evening Mr. Whybrow was walking home through the cobweb alleys of London's East End. He had left the golden clamour of the great High Street to which the tram had brought him from the river and his daily work, and was now in the chessboard of byways that is called Mallon End. None of the rush and gleam of the High Street trickled into these byways. A few paces south—a flood tide of life, foaming and beating. Here—only slow-shuffling figures and muffled pulses. He was in the sink of London, the last refuge of European vagrants.

As though in tune with the street's spirit, he too walked slowly, with head down. It seemed that he was pondering some pressing trouble, but he was not. He had no trouble. He was walking slowly because he had been on his feet all day, and he was bent in abstraction because he was wondering whether the Missis would have herrings for his tea, or haddock; and he was trying to decide which would be the more tasty on a night like this. A wretched night it was, of damp and mist, and the mist wandered into his throat and his eyes, and the damp had settled on pavement and roadway, and where the sparse lamplight fell it sent up a greasy sparkle that chilled one to look at. By contrast it made his speculations more agreeable, and made him ready for that tea—whether herring or haddock. His eye turned from the glum bricks that made his horizon, and went forward half a mile. He saw a gas-lit kitchen, a flamy fire and a spread tea table. There was toast in the hearth and a singing kettle on the side and a piquant effusion of herrings, or maybe of haddock, or perhaps sausages. The vision gave his aching feet a throb of energy. He shook imperceptible damp from his shoulders, and hastened towards its reality.

But Mr. Whybrow wasn't going to get any tea that evening—or any other evening. Mr. Whybrow was going to die. Somewhere within a hundred yards of him another man was walking: a man much like Mr. Whybrow and much like any other man, but without the only quality that enables mankind to live peaceably together and not as madmen in a jungle. A man with a dead heart eating into itself and bringing forth the foul organisms that arise from death and corruption. And that thing in man's shape, on a whim or a settled idea—one cannot know—had said within himself that Mr. Whybrow should never taste another herring. Not that Mr. Whybrow had injured him. Not that he had any dislike of Mr. Whybrow. Indeed, he knew nothing of him save as a familiar figure about the streets. But, moved by a force that had taken possession of his empty cells, he had picked on Mr. Whybrow with that blind choice that makes us pick one restaurant table that has nothing to mark it from four or five other tables, or one apple from a dish of half a dozen equal apples; or that drives Nature to send a cyclone upon one corner of this planet, and destroy five hundred lives in that corner, and leave another five hundred in the same corner unharmed. So this man had picked on Mr. Whybrow, as he might have picked on you or me, had we been within his daily observation; and even now he was creeping through the blue-toned streets, nursing his large white hands, moving ever closer to Mr. Whybrow's tea table, and so closer to Mr. Whybrow himself.

He wasn't, this man, a bad man. Indeed, he had many of the social and amiable qualities, and passed as a respectable man, as most successful criminals do. But the thought had come into his mouldering mind that he would like to murder somebody, and, as he held no fear of God or man, he was going to do it, and would then go home to *his* tea. I don't say that flippantly, but as a statement of fact. Strange as it may seem to the humane, murderers must and do sit down to meals after a murder. There is no reason why they shouldn't, and many reasons why they should. For one thing, they need to keep their physical and mental vitality at full beat for the business of covering their crime. For another, the strain of their effort makes them hungry, and satisfaction at the accomplishment of a desired thing brings a feeling of relaxation towards human pleasures. It is accepted among non-murderers that the murderer is always overcome by fear for his safety and horror at his act; but this type is rare. His own safety is, of course, his immediate concern, but vanity is a marked quality of most murderers, and that, together with the thrill of conquest, makes him confident that he can secure it, and when he has restored his strength with food he goes about securing it as a young hostess goes about the arranging of her first big dinner—a little anxious, but no more. Criminologists and detectives tell us that *every* murderer, however intelligent or cunning, always makes one slip in his tactics—one little slip that brings the affair home to him. But that is only half true. It is true only of the murderers who are caught. Scores of murderers are not caught: therefore scores of murderers do not make any mistake at all. This man didn't.

As for horror or remorse, prison chaplains, doctors and lawyers have told us that of murderers they have interviewed under condemnation and the shadow of death, only one here and there has expressed any contrition for his act, or shown any sign of mental misery. Most of them display only exasperation at having been caught when so many have gone undiscovered, or indignation at being condemned for a perfectly reasonable act. However normal and humane they may have been before the murder, they are utterly without conscience after it. For what is conscience? Simply a polite nickname for superstition, which is a polite nickname for fear. Those who associate remorse with murder are, no doubt, basing their ideas on the world legend of the remorse of Cain, or are projecting their own frail minds into the mind of the murderer, and getting false reactions. Peaceable folk cannot hope to make contact with this mind, for they are not merely different in mental type from the murderer: they are different in their personal chemistry and construction. Some men can and do kill, not one man, but two or three, and go calmly about their daily affairs. Other men could not, under the most agonizing provocation, bring themselves even to wound. It is men of this sort who imagine the murderer in torments of remorse and fear of the law, whereas he is actually sitting down to his tea.

The man with the large white hands was as ready for his tea as Mr. Whybrow was, but he had something to do before he went to it. When he had done that something, and made no mistake about it, he would be even more ready for it, and would go to it as comfortably as he went to it the day before, when his hands were stainless.

Walk on, then, Mr. Whybrow, walk on; and as you walk, look your last upon the familiar features of your nightly journey. Follow your jack-o'-lantern tea table. Look well upon its warmth and colour and kindness; feed your eyes with it, and tease your nose with its gentle domestic odours; for you will never sit down to it. Within ten minutes' pacing of you a pursuing phantom has spoken in his heart, and you are doomed. There you go—you and phantom—two nebulous dabs of mortality, moving through green air along pavements of powder blue, the one to kill, the other to be killed. Walk on. Don't annoy your burning feet by hurrying, for the more slowly you walk, the longer you will breathe the green air of this January dusk, and see the dreamy lamplight and the little shops, and hear the agreeable commerce of the London crowd and the haunting pathos of the street organ. These things are dear to you, Mr. Whybrow. You don't know it now, but in fifteen minutes you will have two seconds in which to realise how inexpressibly dear they are.

Walk on, then, across this crazy chessboard. You are in Lagos Street now, among the tents of the wanderers of Eastern Europe. A minute or so, and you are in Loyal Lane, among the lodging houses that shelter the useless and the beaten of London's camp followers. The lane holds the smell of them, and its soft darkness seems heavy with the wail of the futile. But you are not sensitive to impalpable things, and you plod through it, unseeing, as you do every evening, and come to Blean Street, and plod through that. From basement to sky rise the tenements of an alien colony. Their windows slot the ebony of their walls with lemon. Behind those windows strange life is moving, dressed with forms that are not of London or of England, yet, in essence, the same agreeable life that you have been living, and to-night will live no more. From high above you comes a voice crooning *The Song of Katta*. Through a window you see a family keeping a religious rite. Through another you see a woman pouring out tea for her husband. You see a man mending a pair of boots; a mother er baby. You have seen all these things before, and never noticed do not notice them now, but if you knew that you were never going to see them again, you would notice them. You never *will* see them again, not because your life has run its natural course, but because a man whom you have often passed in the street has at his own solitary pleasure decided to usurp the awful authority of nature, and destroy you. So perhaps it's as well that you don't notice them, for your part in them is ended. No more for you these pretty moments of our earthly travail: only one moment of terror, and then a plunging darkness.

Closer to you this shadow of massacre moves, and now he is twenty yards behind you. You can hear his footfall, but you do not turn your head. You are familiar with footfalls. You are in London, in the easy security of your daily territory, and footfalls behind you, your instinct tells you, are no more than a message of human company.

But can't you hear something in these footfalls—something that goes with a widdershins beat? Something that says: *Look out, look out. Beware, beware.* Can't you hear the very syllables of *mur-der-er, mur-der-er?* No; there is nothing in footfalls. They are neutral. The foot of villainy falls with the same quiet note as the foot of honesty. But those footfalls, Mr. Whybrow, are bearing on to you a pair of hands, and there *is* something in hands. Behind you that pair of hands is even now stretching its muscles in preparation for your end. Every minute of your days you have been seeing human hands. Have you ever realised the sheer horror of hands—those appendages that are a symbol for our moments of trust and affection and salutation? Have you thought of the sickening potentialities that lie within the scope of that five-tentacled member? No, you never have; for all the human hands that you have seen have been stretched to you in kindness or fellowship. Yet, though the eyes can hate, and the lips can sting, it is only that dangling member that can gather the accumulated essence of evil, and electrify it into currents of destruction. Satan may enter into man by many doors, but in the hands alone can he find the servants of his will.

Another minute, Mr. Whybrow, and you will know all about the horror of human hands.

You are nearly home now. You have turned into your street—Caspar Street—and you are in the centre of the chessboard. You can see the front window of your little four-roomed house. The street is dark, and its three lamps give only a smut of light that is more confusing than darkness. It is dark—empty, too. Nobody about; no lights in the front parlours of the houses, for the families are at tea in their kitchens; and only a random glow in a few upper rooms occupied by lodgers. Nobody about but you and your following companion, and you don't notice him. You see him so often that he is never seen. Even if you turned your head and saw him, you would only say "Good-evening" to him, and walk on. A suggestion that he was a possible murderer would not even make you laugh. It would be too silly.

And now you are at your gate. And now you have found your door key. And now you are in, and hanging up your hat and coat. The Missis has just called a greeting from the kitchen, whose smell is an echo of that greeting (herrings!) and you have answered it, when the door shakes under a sharp knock.

Go away, Mr. Whybrow. Go away from that door. Don't touch it. Get right away from it. Get out of the house. Run with the Missis to the back garden, and over the fence. Or call the neighbours. But don't touch that door. Don't, Mr. Whybrow, don't open . . .

Mr. Whybrow opened the door.

That was the beginning of what became known as London's Strangling Horrors. Horrors they were called because they were something more than murders: they were motiveless, and there was an air of black magic about them. Each murder was committed at a time when the street where the bodies were found was empty of any perceptible or possible murderer. There would be an empty alley. There would be a policeman at its end. He would turn his back on the empty alley for less than a minute. Then he would look round and run into the night with news of another strangling. And in any direction he looked nobody to be seen and no report to be had of anybody being seen. Or he would be on duty in a long quiet street, and suddenly be called to a house of dead people whom a few seconds earlier he had seen alive. And, again, whichever way he looked nobody to be seen; and although police whistles put an immediate cordon around the area, and searched all houses, no possible murderer to be found.

The first news of the murder of Mr. and Mrs. Whybrow was brought by the station sergeant. He had been walking through Caspar Street on his way to the station for duty, when he noticed the open door of No. 98. Glancing in, he saw by the gaslight of the passage a motionless body on the floor. After a second look he blew his whistle, and when the constables answered him he took one to join him in a search of the house, and sent others to watch all neighbouring streets, and make inquiries at adjoining houses. But neither in the house nor in the streets was anything found to indicate the murderer. Neighbours on either side, and opposite, were questioned, but they had seen nobody about, and had heard nothing. One had heard Mr. Whybrow come home—the scrape of his latchkey in the door was so regular an evening sound, he said, that you could set your watch by it for half past six—but he had heard nothing more than the sound of the opening door until the sergeant's whistle. Nobody had been seen to enter the house or leave it, by front or back, and the necks of the dead people carried no finger prints or other traces. A nephew was called in to go over the house, but he could find nothing missing; and anyway his uncle possessed nothing worth stealing. The little money in the house was untouched, and there were no signs of any disturbance of the property, or even of struggle. No signs of anything but brutal and wanton murder.

Mr. Whybrow was known to neighbours and workmates as a quiet, likeable, home-loving man; such a man as could not have any enemies. But, then, murdered men seldom have. A relentless enemy who hates a man to the point of wanting to hurt him seldom wants to murder him, since to do that puts him beyond suffering. So the police were left with an impossible situation: no clue to the murderer and no motive for the murders; only the fact that they had been done.

The first news of the affair sent a tremor through London generally, and an electric thrill through all Mallon End. Here was a murder of two inoffensive people, not for gain and not for revenge; and the murderer, to whom, apparently, killing was a casual impulse, was at large. He had left no traces, and, provided he had no companions, there seemed no reason why he should not remain at large. Any clear-headed man who stands alone, and has no fear of God or man, can, if he chooses, hold a city, even a nation, in subjection; but your everyday criminal is seldom clear-headed, and dislikes being lonely. He needs, if not the support of confederates, at least somebody to talk to; his vanity needs the satisfaction of perceiving at first hand the effect of his work. For this he will frequent bars and coffee shops and other public places. Then, sooner or later, in a glow of comradeship, he will utter the one word too much and the nark, who is everywhere, has an easy job.

But though the doss houses and saloons and other places were "combed" and set with watches, and it was made known by whispers that good money and protection were assured to those with information, nothing attaching to the Whybrow case could be found. The murderer clearly had no friends and kept no company. Known men of this type were called up and questioned, but each was able to give a good account of himself; and in a few days the police were at a dead end. Against the constant public gibe that the thing had been done almost under their noses, they became restive, and for four days each man of the force was working his daily beat under a strain. On the fifth day they became still more restive.

It was the season of annual teas and entertainments for the children of the Sunday Schools, and on an evening of fog, when London was a world of groping phantoms, a small girl, in the bravery of best Sunday frock and shoes, shining face and new-washed hair, set out from Logan Passage for St. Michael's Parish Hall. She never got there. She was not actually dead until half past six, but she was as good as dead from the moment she left her mother's door. Somebody like a man, pacing the street from which the Passage led, saw her come out; and from that moment she was dead. Through the fog somebody's large white hands reached after her, and in fifteen minutes they were about her.

At half past six a whistle screamed trouble, and those answering it found the body of little Nellie Vrinoff in a warehouse entry in Minnow Street. The sergeant was first among them, and he posted his men to useful points, ordering them here and there in the tart tones of repressed rage, and berating the officer whose beat the street was. "I saw you, Magson, at the end of the lane. What were you up to there? You were there ten minutes before you turned." Magson began an explanation about keeping an eye on a suspicious-looking character at that end, but the sergeant cut him short: "Suspicious characters be damned. You don't want to look for suspicious characters. You want to look for *murderers*. Messing about . . . and then this happens right where you ought to be. Now think what they'll say."

With the speed of ill news came the crowd, pale and perturbed; and on the story that the unknown monster had appeared again, and this time to a child, their faces streaked the fog with spots of hate and horror. But then came the ambulance and more police, and swiftly they broke up the crowd; and as it broke the sergeant's thought was thickened into words, and from all sides came low murmurs of "Right under their noses." Later inquiries showed that four people of the district, above suspicion, had passed that entry at intervals of seconds before the murder, and seen nothing and heard nothing. None of them had passed the child alive or seen her dead. None of them had seen anybody in the street except themselves. Again the police were left with no motive and with no clue.

And now the district, as you will remember, was given over, not to panic, for the London public never yields to that, but to apprehension and dismay. If these things were happening in their familiar streets, then anything might happen. Wherever people met—in the streets, the markets and the shops—

they debated the one topic. Women took to bolting their windows and doors at the first fall of dusk. They kept their children closely under their eye. They did their shopping before dark, and watched anxiously, while pretending they weren't watching, for the return of their husbands from work. Under the Cockney's semi-humorous resignation to disaster, they hid an hourly foreboding. By the whim of one man with a pair of hands the structure and tenor of their daily life were shaken, as they always can be shaken by any man contemptuous of humanity and fearless of its laws. They began to realise that the pillars that supported the peaceable society in which they lived were mere straws that anybody could snap; that laws were powerful only so long as they were obeyed; that the police were potent only so long as they were feared. By the power of his hands this one man had made a whole community do something new: he had made it think, and left it gasping at the obvious.

And then, while it was yet gasping under his first two strokes, he made his third. Conscious of the horror that his hands had created, and hungry as an actor who has once tasted the thrill of the multitude, he made fresh advertisement of his presence; and on Wednesday morning, three days after the murder of the child, the papers carried to the breakfast tables of England the story of a still more shocking outrage.

At 9:32 on Tuesday night a constable was on duty in Jarnigan Road, and at that time spoke to a fellow officer named Petersen at the top of Clemming Street. He had seen this officer walk down that street. He could swear that the street was empty at that time, except for a lame bootblack whom he knew by sight, and who passed him and entered a tenement on the side opposite that on which his fellow officer was walking. He had the habit, as all constables had just then, of looking constantly behind him and around him, whichever way he was walking, and he was certain that the street was empty. He passed his sergeant at 9:33, saluted him, and answered his inquiry for anything seen. He reported that he had seen nothing, and passed on. His beat ended at a short distance from Clemming Street, and, having paced it, he turned and came again at 9:34 to the top of the street. He had scarcely reached it before he heard the hoarse voice of the sergeant: "Gregory! You there? Quick. Here's another. My God, it's Petersen! Garotted. Quick, call 'em up!"

That was the third of the Strangling Horrors, of which there were to be a fourth and a fifth; and the five horrors were to pass into the unknown and unknowable. That is, unknown as far as authority and the public were concerned. The identity of the murderer *was* known, but to two men only. One was the murderer himself; the other was a young journalist.

This young man, who was covering the affairs for his paper, the *Daily Torch*, was no smarter than the other zealous newspaper men who were hanging about these byways in the hope of a sudden story. But he was patient, and he hung a little closer to the case than the other fellows, and by continually staring at it he at last raised the figure of the murderer like a genie from the stones on which he had stood to do his murders.

After the first few days the men had given up any attempt at exclusive stories, for there was none to be had. They met regularly at the police station, and what little information there was they shared. The officials were agreeable to them, but no more. The sergeant discussed with them the details of each murder; suggested possible explanations of the man's methods; recalled from the past those cases that had some similarity; and on the matter of motive reminded them of the motiveless Neil Cream and the wanton John Williams, and hinted that work was being done which would soon bring the business to an end; but about that work he would not say a word. The Inspector, too, was gracefully garrulous on the thesis of Murder, but whenever one of the party edged the talk towards what was being done in this immediate matter, he glided past it. Whatever the officials knew, they were not giving it to newspaper men. The business had fallen heavily upon them, and only by a capture made by their own efforts could they rehabilitate themselves in official and public esteem. Scotland Yard, of course, was at work, and had all the station's material; but the station's hope was that they themselves would have the honour of settling the affair; and however useful the cooperation of the

Press might be in other cases, they did not want to risk a defeat by a premature disclosure of their theories and plans.

So the sergeant talked at large, and propounded one interesting theory after another, all of which the newspaper men had thought of themselves.

The young man soon gave up these morning lectures on the Philosophy of Crime, and took to wandering about the streets and making bright stories out of the effect of the murders on the normal life of the people. A melancholy job made more melancholy by the district. The littered roadways, the crestfallen houses, the bleared windows—all held the acid misery that evokes no sympathy: the misery of the frustrated poet. The misery was the creation of the aliens, who were living in this makeshift fashion because they had no settled homes, and would neither take the trouble to make a home where they *could* settle, nor get on with their wandering.

There was little to be picked up. All he saw and heard were indignant faces, and wild conjectures of the murderer's identity and of the secret of his trick of appearing and disappearing unseen. Since a policeman himself had fallen a victim, denunciations of the force had ceased, and the unknown was now invested with a cloak of legend. Men eyed other men, as though thinking: It might be *him*. It might be *him*. They were no longer looking for a man who had the air of a Madame Tussaud murderer; they were looking for a man, or perhaps some harridan woman, who had done these particular murders. Their thoughts ran mainly on the foreign set. Such ruffianism could scarcely belong to England, nor could the bewildering cleverness of the thing. So they turned to Roumanian gipsies and Turkish carpet sellers. There, clearly, would be found the "warm" spot. These Eastern fellows—they knew all sorts of tricks, and they had no real religion—nothing to hold them within bounds. Sailors returning from those parts had told tales of conjurors who made themselves invisible; and there were tales of Egyptian and Arab potions that were used for abysmally queer purposes. Perhaps it *was* possible to them; you never knew. They were so slick and cunning, and they had such gliding movements; no Englishman could melt away as they could. Almost certainly the murderer would be found to be one of that sort—with some dark trick of his own—and just because they were sure that he *was* a magician, they felt that it was useless to look for him. He was a power, able to hold them in subjection and to hold himself untouchable. Superstition, which so easily cracks the frail shell of reason, had got into them. He could do anything he chose: he would never be discovered. These two points they settled, and they went about the streets in a mood of resentful fatalism.

They talked of their ideas to the journalist in half tones, looking right and left, as though *HE* might overhear them and visit them. And though all the district was thinking of him and ready to pounce upon him, yet, so strongly had he worked upon them, that if any man in the street—say, a small man of commonplace features and form—had cried "*I* am the Monster!" would their stifled fury have broken into flood and have borne him down and engulfed him? Or would they not suddenly have seen something unearthly in that everyday face and figure, something unearthly in his everyday boots, something unearthly about his hat, something that marked him as one whom none of their weapons could alarm or pierce? And would they not momentarily have fallen back from this devil, as the devil fell back from the Cross made by the sword of Faust, and so have given him time to escape? I do not know; but so fixed was their belief in his invincibility that it is at least likely that they would have made this hesitation, had such an occasion arisen. But it never did. To-day this commonplace fellow, his murder lust glutted, is still seen and observed among them as he was seen and observed all the time; but because nobody then dreamt, or now dreams, that he was what he was, they observed him then, and observe him now, as people observe a lamp-post.

Almost was their belief in his invincibility justified; for, five days after the murder of the policeman Petersen, when the experience and inspiration of the whole detective force of London were turned towards his identification and capture, he made his fourth and fifth strokes.

At nine o'clock that evening, the young newspaper man, who hung about every night until his paper was away, was strolling along Richards Lane.

Richards Lane is a narrow street, partly a stall market, and partly residential. The young man was in the residential section, which carries on one side small working-class cottages, and on the other the wall of a railway goods yard. The great wall hung a blanket of shadow over the lane, and the shadow and the cadaverous outline of the now deserted market stalls gave it the appearance of a living lane that had been turned to frost in the moment between breath and death. The very lamps, that elsewhere were nimbuses of gold, had here the rigidity of gems. The journalist, feeling this message of frozen eternity, was telling himself that he was tired of the whole thing, when in one stroke the frost was broken. In the moment between one pace and another silence and darkness were racked by a high scream and through the scream a voice: "Help! help! *He's here!*"

Before he could think what movement to make, the lane came to life. As though its invisible populace had been waiting on that cry, the door of every cottage was flung open, and from them and from the alleys poured shadowy figures bent in question mark form. For a second or so they stood as rigid as the lamps; then a police whistle gave them direction, and the flock of shadows sloped up the street. The journalist followed them, and others followed him. From the main street and from surrounding streets they came, some risen from unfinished suppers, some disturbed in their ease of slippers and shirt sleeves, some stumbling on infirm limbs, and some upright, and armed with pokers or the tools of their trade. Here and there above the wavering cloud of heads moved the bold helmets of policemen. In one dim mass they surged upon a cottage whose doorway was marked by the sergeant and two constables; and voices of those behind urged them on with "Get in! Find him! Run round the back! Over the wall!" and those in front cried: "Keep back! Keep back!"

And now the fury of a mob held in thrall by unknown peril broke loose. He was here—on the spot. Surely this time he *could not* escape. All minds were bent upon the cottage; all energies thrust towards its doors and windows and roof; all thought was turned upon one unknown man and his extermination.

So that no one man saw any other man. No man saw the narrow, packed lane and the mass of struggling shadows, and all forgot to look among themselves for the monster who never lingered upon his victims. All forgot, indeed, that they, by their mass crusade of vengeance, were affording him the perfect hiding place. They saw only the house, and they heard only the rending of woodwork and the smash of glass at back and front, and the police giving orders or crying with the chase; and they pressed on.

But they found no murderer. All they found was news of murder and a glimpse of the ambulance, and for their fury there was no other object than the police themselves, who fought against this hampering of their work.

The journalist managed to struggle through to the cottage door, and to get the story from the constable stationed there. The cottage was the home of a pensioned sailor and his wife and daughter. They had been at supper, and at first it appeared that some noxious gas had smitten all three in mid-action. The daughter lay dead on the hearthrug, with a piece of bread and butter in her hand. The father had fallen sideways from his chair, leaving on his plate a filled spoon of rice pudding. The mother lay half under the table, her lap filled with the pieces of a broken cup and splashes of cocoa. But in three seconds the idea of gas was dismissed. One glance at their necks showed that this was the Strangler again; and the police stood and looked at the room and momentarily shared the fatalism of the public. They were helpless.

This was his fourth visit, making seven murders in all. He was to do, as you know, one more—and to do it that night; and then he was to pass into history as the unknown London horror, and return to the decent life that he had always led, remembering little of what he had done, and worried not at all by the memory. Why did he stop? Impossible to say. Why did he begin? Impossible again. It just happened like that; and if he thinks at all of those days and nights, I surmise that he thinks of them as we think of foolish or dirty little sins that we committed in childhood. We say that they were not really sins, because we were not then consciously ourselves: we had not come to realisation; and we look back at that foolish little creature that we once were, and forgive him because he didn't know. So, I think, with this man.

There are plenty like him. Eugene Aram, after the murder of Daniel Clarke, lived a quiet, contented life for fourteen years, unhaunted by his crime and unshaken in his self-esteem. Dr. Crippen murdered his wife, and then lived pleasantly with his mistress in the house under whose floor he had buried the wife. Constance Kent, found Not Guilty of the murder of her young brother, led a peaceful life for five years before she confessed. George Joseph Smith and William Palmer lived amiably among their fellows untroubled by fear or by remorse for their poisonings and drownings. Charles Peace, at the time he made his one unfortunate essay, had settled down into a respectable citizen with an interest in antiques. It happened that, after a lapse of time, these men were discovered, but more murderers than we guess are living decent lives to-day, and will die in decency, undiscovered and unsuspected. As this man will.

But he had a narrow escape, and it was perhaps this narrow escape that brought him to a stop. The escape was due to an error of judgment on the part of the journalist.

As soon as he had the full story of the affair, which took some time, he spent fifteen minutes on the telephone, sending the story through, and at the end of the fifteen minutes, when the stimulus of the business had left him, he felt physically tired and mentally dishevelled. He was not yet free to go home; the paper would not go away for another hour; so he turned into a bar for a drink and some sandwiches.

It was then, when he had dismissed the whole business from his mind, and was looking about the bar and admiring the landlord's taste in watch chains and his air of domination, and was thinking that the landlord of a well-conducted tavern had a more comfortable life than a newspaper man, that his mind received from nowhere a spark of light. He was not thinking about the Strangling Horrors; his mind was on this sandwich. As a public-house sandwich, it was a curiosity. The bread had been thinly cut, it was buttered, and the ham was not two months stale; it was ham as it should be. His mind turned to the inventor of this refreshment, the Earl of Sandwich, and then to George the Fourth, and then to the Georges, and to the legend of that George who was worried to know how the apple got into the apple dumpling. He wondered whether George would have been equally puzzled to know how the ham got into the ham sandwich, and how long it would have been before it occurred to him that the ham could not have got there unless somebody had put it there. He got up to order another sandwich, and in that moment a little active corner of his mind settled the affair. If there was ham in his sandwich, somebody must have put it there. If seven people had been murdered, somebody must have been there to murder them. There was no aeroplane or automobile that would go into a man's pocket; therefore that somebody must have escaped either by running away or standing still; and again therefore——

He was visualising the front-page story that his paper would carry if his theory were correct, and if—a matter of conjecture—his editor had the necessary nerve to make a bold stroke, when a cry of "Time, gentlemen, please! All out!" reminded him of the hour. He got up and went out into a world of mist, broken by the ragged discs of roadside puddles and the streaming lightning of motor buses. He was certain that he had *the* story, but, even if it were proved, he was doubtful whether the policy of his paper would permit him to print it. It had one great fault. It was truth, but it was impossible truth. It rocked the foundations of everything that newspaper readers believed and that newspaper editors helped them to believe. They might believe that Turkish carpet sellers had the gift of making themselves invisible. They would not believe this.

As it happened, they were not asked to, for the story was never written. As his paper had by now gone away, and as he was nourished by his refreshment and stimulated by his theory, he thought he might put in an extra half hour by testing that theory. So he began to look about for the man he had in mind—a man with white hair, and large white hands; otherwise an everyday figure whom nobody would look twice at. He wanted to spring his idea on this man without warning, and he was going to place himself within reach of a man armoured in legends of dreadfulness and grue. This might appear to be an act of supreme courage—that one man, with no hope of immediate outside support, should place himself at the mercy of one who was holding a whole parish in terror. But it wasn't. He didn't think about the risk. He didn't think about his duty to his employers or loyalty to his paper. He was moved simply by an instinct to follow a story to its end.

He walked slowly from the tavern and crossed into Fingal Street, making for Deever Market, where he had hope of finding his man. But his journey was shortened. At the corner of Lotus Street he saw him—or a man who looked like him. This street was poorly lit, and he could see little of the man: but he *could* see white hands. For some twenty paces he stalked him; then drew level with him; and at a point where the arch of a railway crossed the street, he saw that this was his man. He approached him with the current conversational phrase of the district: "Well, seen anything of the murderer?" The man stopped to look sharply at him; then, satisfied that the journalist was not the murderer, said:

"Eh? No, nor's anybody else, curse it. Doubt if they ever will."

"I don't know. I've been thinking about them, and I've got an idea."

"So?"

"Yes. Came to me all of a sudden. Quarter of an hour ago. And I'd felt that we'd all been blind. It's been staring us in the face."

The man turned again to look at him, and the look and the movement held suspicion of this man who seemed to know so much. "Oh? Has it? Well, if you're so sure, why not give us the benefit of it?"

"I'm going to." They walked level, and were nearly at the end of the little street where it meets Deever Market, when the journalist turned casually to the man. He put a finger on his arm. "Yes, it seems to me quite simple now. But there's still one point I don't understand. One little thing I'd like to clear up. I mean the motive. Now, as man to man, tell me, Sergeant Ottermole, just *why* did you kill all those inoffensive people?"

The sergeant stopped, and the journalist stopped. There was just enough light from the sky, which held the reflected light of the continent of London, to give him a sight of the sergeant's face, and the sergeant's face was turned to him with a wide smile of such urbanity and charm that the journalist's eyes were frozen as they met it. The smile stayed for some seconds. Then said the sergeant: "Well, to tell you the truth, Mr. Newspaper Man, I don't know. I really don't know. In fact, I've been worried about it myself. But I've got an idea—just like you. Everybody knows that we can't control the workings of our minds. Don't they? Ideas come into our minds without asking. But everybody's supposed to be able to control his body. Why? Eh? We get our minds from lord-knows-where—from people who were dead hundreds of years before we were born. Mayn't we get our bodies in the same way? Our faces—our legs—our heads—they aren't completely ours. We don't make 'em. They come to us. And couldn't ideas come into our bodies like ideas come into our minds? Eh? Can't ideas live in nerve and muscle as well as in brain? Couldn't it be that parts of our bodies aren't really us, and couldn't ideas come into those parts all of a sudden, like ideas come into—into" he shot his arms out, showing the great white-gloved hands and hairy wrists; shot them out so swiftly to the journalist's throat that his eyes never saw them—"into *my hands!*"

THE PERFECT CRIME
(1928)
Ben Ray Redman

In this story "the world's greatest detective" and a prominent criminal lawyer have an intellectual discussion about what constitutes a perfect murder. Their dissection of the key elements provides an interesting lesson in "how to do it."

Ben Ray Redman (1896–1961) wrote poetry and comedy, and did a book column for the *New York Herald Tribune*. He was also on the movie production staff at Universal Pictures. Under the pseudonym Jeremy Lord, he authored two mystery novels: *The Bannerman Case* (1935) and *Sixty-Nine Diamonds* (1940). "The Perfect Crime" was originally published in *Harper's Monthly Magazine*.

The world's greatest detective complacently sipped a port some years older than himself and intently gazed across the table at his most intimate acquaintance; for many years the detective had not permitted himself the luxury of friends. Gregory Hare looked back at him, waiting, listening.

"There is no doubt about it," Trevor reiterated, putting down his glass, "the perfect crime is a possibility; it requires only the perfect criminal."

"Naturally," assented Hare with a shrug, "but the perfect criminal . . ."

"You mean he is a mythical fellow, not apt to be met with in the flesh?"

"Exactly," said Hare, nodding his big head.

Trevor sighed, sipped again, and adjusted the eyeglasses on his thin, sharp nose. "No, I admit I haven't encountered him as yet, but I am always hopeful."

"Hoping to be done in the eye, eh?"

"No, hoping to see the perfect methods of detection tested to the limits of their possibilities. You know, a gifted detector of crime is something more than an inspired policeman with a little bloodhound blood in his veins, something more than a precise scientist; he's an art critic as well, and no art critic likes to be condemned to a steady diet of second-rate stuff."

"Quite."

"Second-rate stuff is bad enough, but it's not the worst. Think of the third, fourth, fifth, and heaven-knows-what-rate crimes that come along every day! And even the masterpieces, the 'classics,' are pretty poor daubs when you look at them closely: a bad tone here and a wrong line there; something false, something botched."

"Most murderers are rather foolish," interjected Hare.

"Foolish! Of course they are. You should know, man, you've defended enough of them. The trouble is that murder almost never evokes the best efforts of the best minds. As a rule it is the work of an inferior mind, cunningly striving towards a perfection that is beyond its reach, or of a superior mind so blinded by passion that its faculties are temporarily impaired. Of course, there are your homicidal maniacs, and they are often clever, but they lack imagination and variety; sooner or later their inability to do anything but repeat themselves brings them up with a sharp jerk."

"Repetition is dullness," murmured Hare, "and dullness, as somebody has remarked, is the one unforgivable sin."

"Right," agreed Trevor. "It is, and plenty of murderers have suffered for it. But they have suffered from vanity almost as often. Practically every murderer, unless he has been accidentally impelled to crime, is an egregious egotist. You know that as well as I do. His sense of power is tremendous, and as a rule he can't keep his mouth shut."

Dr. Harrison Trevor's glasses shone brightly, and he plucked continually at the black cord depending from them as he jerked out his sentences with rapidity and precision. He was on his own ground, and he knew what he was talking about. For twenty years criminals had been his specialty and his legitimate prey. He had hunted them through all lands, and he hunted them successfully. Upstairs, in a chiffonier drawer in his bedroom, there was a large red-leather box holding visible symbols of that success: small decorations of gold and silver and bright ribbons bore mute witness to the gratitude that various European governments had felt, on notable occasions, towards the greatest man hunter of his generation. If Trevor was a dogmatist on murder he was entitled to be one.

Hare, on the other hand, was a good and respectful listener, but, being a criminal lawyer of long experience, he was a man with ideas of his own; and he always expressed them when there was no legal advantage to be gained by withholding them. He expressed one now, when he drawled softly, "All murderers are great egotists, are they? How about great detectives?"

Trevor blinked, then smiled coldly, clutching at his black cord. "Most detectives are asses, I grant you, complete asses and vain as peacocks; very few of them are great. I know only three. One of them is now in Vienna, the second is in Paris, and the third is . . ."

Hare raised his hand in interruption and said, "The third, or rather the first, is in this room."

The greatest detective in the world nodded briskly. "Of course. There's no point in false modesty, is there?"

"None at all. And it might be a little difficult to maintain such an attitude so soon after the Harrington case. The poor chap was put out of his misery week before last, wasn't he?"

Trevor snorted. "Yes, if you want to call him a poor chap; he was a deliberate murderer. But let's get back to that perfect crime of ours."

"Of yours, you mean," Hare corrected him politely. "I haven't subscribed to the possibility of it as yet. And how would you know about a perfect crime if it ever were committed? The criminal would never be discovered."

"If he had any artistic pride, he would leave a full account of it to be published after his death. Besides, you are forgetting the perfect methods of detection."

Hare whistled softly. "There's a pretty theoretical problem for you. What would happen when the perfect detector set out to catch the perfect criminal? Rather like the immovable object and the irresistible force business, and just about as sensible. The fly in the ointment, of course, is that there is no such thing as perfection."

Dr. Trevor sat up rigidly and glared at the speaker. "There is perfection in the detection of crime."

"Well, perhaps there is." Hare laughed amiably, "You should know, Trevor. But I think what you really mean is that there is a perfect method for detecting imperfect crimes."

The doctor's rigidity had vanished, and now he was smiling with as much geniality as he ever displayed. "Perhaps that is what I do mean, perhaps it is. But there is a little experiment that I should like to try, just the same."

"And that is?"

"And that is, or rather would be, the experiment of exercising all my intelligence in the commission of a crime, then, forgetting every detail of it utterly, using my skill and knowledge to solve the riddle of my own creation. Should I catch myself, or should I escape myself? That's the question."

"It would be a nice sporting event," agreed Hare, "but I'm afraid it's one that can't be pulled off. The little trifle of forgetting is the difficulty. But it would be interesting to see the outcome."

"Yes, it would," said the other, speaking rather more dreamily than was his habit, "but we can never see quite as far as we should like to. My Japanese man, Tanaka, has a saying that he resorts to whenever he is asked a difficult question. He simply smiles and answers, '*Fuji san ni nobottara sazo tōku made miemashō.*' It means, I believe, that if one were to ascend Mount Fuji one could see far. The trouble is that, as in the case of so many problems, we can't climb the mountain."

"Wise Tanaka. But tell me, Trevor, what is your conception of a perfect crime?"

"I'm afraid it isn't precisely formulated; but I have a rough outline in my mind, and I'll give it to you as I can. First, though, let's go up to the library; we shall be more comfortable there, and it will give Tanaka a chance to clear the table. Bring your cigar, and come along."

Together the two men climbed the narrow staircase, the host leading. Dr. Trevor's house was a compact, brick building in the East Fifties, not far from Madison Avenue. Its picturesqueness was rather uncharacteristic of its owner, but its neatness was entirely like him. It was not a large house according to the standards of wealthy New York, but it was a perfect appointed one, and considerably more spacious than it looked from the street, for the doctor had built on an addition that completely covered the plot which had once been the back yard; and this new section, as well as housing the kitchen and servants' quarters below, held a laboratory and workroom two stories high. An industrial or research chemist might have coveted the equipment of that room; and the filing cases that completely lined the encircling gallery would have furnished any newspaper with a complete reference department. A door opened from the library into the laboratory, and the library itself came close to being the ideal chamber of every student. Dr. Harrison Trevor's house was, in short, and ideal bachelor's establishment, and he had never been tempted to transform it into anything else. More than one male visitor had found reason to remark, "Old Trevor does well for himself."

The same idea flitted across Hare's mind as he puffed at his host's excellent cigar and tasted the liqueur that Tanaka had placed on the table beside his chair. He, too, enjoyed the pleasures of bachelorhood, but he had never learned the knack of enjoying them quite so thoroughly. He would make a few improvements in the routine of his life; he could afford them.

"The perfect crime must, of course, be a murder." Trevor's voice broke the silence that had followed their entrance into the library.

Hare shifted his bulk a little and inquired, "Yes? Why?"

"Because it is, according to our accepted standards, the most reprehensible of all crimes and, therefore, according to my interests, the best. Human life is what we prize most and do our best to protect; to take human life with an art that eludes all detection is unquestionably the ideal criminal action. In it there is a degree of beauty possible in no other crime."

"Humph!" grunted Hare, "you make it sound pleasant."

"I am speaking at once as an amateur and as a professor of crime. You have heard surgeons talk of 'beautiful cases.' Well, that is my attitude precisely; and in my cases invariably, as in most of theirs, the patient dies."

"I see."

Trevor blinked, tugged at his eyeglass cord, and then continued. "The crime must be murder, and it must be murder of a particular kind, the purest kind. Now what is the 'purest' kind? Let us see. The *crime passionel* can be ruled out at once, for it is almost impossible that it should be perfect. Passion does not make for art; hot blood begets innumerable blunders. What about the murder for gain? Murderers of this kind make murder a means, not an end in itself; they kill not for the sake of eliminating the victim but in order to profit by the victim's death. No, we can't look to murder for profit as the type that might produce our perfect crime."

The sharp-nosed doctor paused and held his cigar for a moment between his thin lips. Hare studied his face curiously; the man's complete lack of emotion in discussing such matters was not wholly pleasant, he reflected.

Trevor put down his cigar. "Now, how about political and religious murders? They can be counted out almost immediately, for the simple reason that the murderer in such cases is always convinced that he is either serving the public or serving God and, therefore, seldom makes any attempt to conceal his guilt. But there is another class to be considered—those who kill for the sheer joy of killing, those who are dominated by the blood lust. Offhand you would think that their killing would be of the purest type. But as I have said before, the maniac invariably repeats himself, and his repetition leads to his discovery. And even more important is the consideration that the artist must possess the faculty of choice, and that the born killer has no choice. His actions are not willed by himself, they are compelled; whereas the perfect crime must be a work of art, not of necessity."

"You seem to have written off all the possibilities pretty well," remarked Hare.

The doctor shook his head quickly. "Not all. There is one type of murder left, and it is the kind we are looking for: the murder of elimination, the murder in which the sole and pure object is to remove the victim from the world, to get rid of a person whose continued existence is not desirable to the murderer."

"But that brings you back to your *crime passionel*, doesn't it? Practically all murders of jealousy, for example, are murders of elimination, aren't they?"

"In a sense, yes, but not in the purest sense. And, as I have said before, passion can never produce the perfect crime. It must be studied, carefully meditated, and performed in absolutely cold blood. Otherwise it is sure to be imperfect."

"You do go at this in a rather fish-blooded way," remarked the good listener as the doctor paused for a moment.

"Of course I do, and that is the only way the perfect crime could be committed. Now I can imagine a pure murder of elimination that would be ideal so far as motives and circumstances were concerned. Suppose you had spent fifteen years establishing a certain reading of a dubious passage in one of Pindar's odes."

"Ha, ha!" interrupted Hare jocosely. "Suppose I had."

"And suppose," continued Dr. Harrison Trevor, not noticing the interruption, "that another scholar had managed to build up an argument which completely invalidated your interpretation. Suppose, further, that he communicated his proofs to you, and that he had as yet mentioned them to no one else. There you would have a perfect motive and a perfect set of circumstances; only the method of the murder would remain to be worked out."

Gregory Hare sat bolt upright. "Good God, man! What do you mean, 'the method of the murder'?"

The doctor blinked. "Why, don't you understand? You would have excellent reasons for eliminating your rival and thereby saving your own interpretation of the text from confutation; and no one, once your victim was dead and the proofs destroyed, could suspect that you had any such motive. You could work with perfect freedom, you could concentrate on two essentials: the method of the murder and, of course, the disposition of the body."

"The disposition of the body?" Hare seemed to echo the speaker's last words involuntarily.

"To be sure; that is a very important item, most important in fact. But I flatter myself," and here the doctor chuckled softly, "that I have done some very valuable research work along that line."

"You have, eh?" murmured Hare. "And what have you found out?"

"I'll tell you later," Trevor assured him, "and I don't think I would tell any other man alive, because it's really too simple and too dangerous. But at the moment I want to impress on you that the disposition of the body is perhaps the most important step of all in the commission of the perfect crime. The absence of a *corpus delicti* is curiously troublesome to the police. Harrington should really have managed to get rid of West's body, although it probably wouldn't have kept him from sitting in the electric chair two weeks ago. He was too careless."

Hare again sat up sharply and exclaimed. "Was he? Speaking of that, it was the Harrington case that I chiefly wanted to talk to you about tonight."

"Oh, was it? Well, we can get around to that in a minute. And, by the way, that came pretty close to being a murder of elimination, if you like; but the money element figured in it, big money, and gold is apt to have a fairly strong smell when it is mixed up with crime. Harrington's motive was easily traced, but his position made it impossible to touch him until we had our case absolutely water-tight."

"Water-tight, eh? That's what I want to hear about. You see I was abroad until last week, and didn't even know Harrington had been arrested until just before I sailed. The North African newspapers aren't so informative. I was particularly interested, you see, because I knew both men fairly well, and West's wife even better."

"Oh, yes, his wife, gorgeous woman. They were separated, and she's been in Europe for the last two and a half years."

"Yes, I know she has—most of the time."

"All the time. She hasn't been in the United States during that period."

"Hasn't she? Well, I last saw her at Monte Carlo, but that's not important at the moment. I want to hear how you tracked down Harrington."

Dr. Harrison Trevor smiled complacently, adjusted his eyeglasses, and then launched forth in his characteristic manner. "It was really simplicity itself. The only flaw was that Harrington finally confessed. That rather annoyed me, for we didn't need a confession; the circumstantial evidence was complete."

"Circumstantial?"

"Of course. You know as well as I do that most convictions for murder are based on circumstantial evidence. One doesn't send out invitations for a killing."

"No, of course not. Sorry."

"Well, as you probably know, Ernest West, Wall Street operator and multimillionaire (as the papers had it), was found shot through the heart one night a little more than a year ago. He had a shack down on Long Island, near Smithtown, that he used as a base for duck shooting and fishing. The only servant he kept there was an old housekeeper, a local inhabitant; he liked to lead the simple life when he could. Never even used to take a chauffeur down with him. The evening he was killed the housekeeper was absent, spending the night with a sick daughter of hers in Jamaica. She testified that West had sent her off, saying that he could pick up a light supper and breakfast for himself. She turned up the next morning, and nearly died of the shock. West was shot in what was a kind of gun room where he kept all his gear and a few books—cosy sort of place and the best room in the house. There was no sign of a struggle. He was sitting slumped in a big armchair. The bullet that killed him was a .25 caliber. Furst, of the Homicide Bureau, called me up as soon as the regulars failed to locate any scent, and I went down there immediately. West was an important man, you know." The doctor tugged self-consciously at his black cord. "I went down there at once, and I discovered various things. First of all, the house was isolated, and there was no one in the neighborhood who could give any useful evidence whatsoever. The body had been discovered by a messenger boy with a telegram at about seven-thirty; medical examination indicated that the murder had been committed about an hour before. Inside the house I found only one item that I thought useful. After going over the dust and so forth which I swept up from the gun-room floor, I had several tiny thread ends that had pretty obviously come from a tweed suit; and those threads could not be matched in West's wardrobe. But they might have been months old, so I didn't concentrate on them at first. Outside the house there was more to go on. The ground was damp, and two sets of footprints were visible: a man's and a woman's . . ."

"A woman's?" Hare was all attention now.

"Yes, the housekeeper's, of course."

"Oh, yes, the housekeeper's."

"Certainly. But it was difficult to identify them, for the reason that the man, apparently through nervousness, had walked up and down the lane leading to the road several times before finally leaving the scene of his crime, and he had trampled over almost every one of the woman's footprints, scarcely leaving one intact."

"That was odd, wasn't it?"

"Very, at first glance, but really simple enough when you think it over. The murderer had hurried out of the house after firing the fatal shot; then he hesitated. He was flurried and couldn't make up his mind as to his next step, even though he had an automobile waiting for him at the end of the lane. So he walked up and down for a few minutes, to calm his nerves and collect his ideas. It was a narrow lane, and the obliteration of the other tracks was at once accidental and inevitable."

"He had a car waiting?"

"Yes, a heavy touring car. Its tire marks were plain, as were those of the public hack that West had ordered for his housekeeper that afternoon. And there was one interesting feature about the marks. There was a big, hard blister on one of the shoes, and it left a perfectly defined indentation in the mud every time it came around."

"I see. And both sets of footprints ended at the same spot?"

"Naturally. The hack stopped for the woman just where the murderer later parked his car."

"Hum." Hare had now lighted a new cigar, and he puffed at it reflectively before asking. "And you are quite sure the woman did not get into the car with the man?"

Trevor stared at the speaker blankly and exclaimed, "You must be wool gathering, Hare. The woman was the housekeeper, and she went off in a public hack at least two hours before the crime was committed. In any event,

Harrington confirmed the correctness of all my deductions when he finally confessed." Dr. Harrison Trevor was obviously nettled.

"Oh, yes, of course he did; I'd forgotten. Sorry. Let's hear how you nabbed him."

For a moment the detective looked at his companion doubtfully, as though he feared the other might be baiting him; for Hare's questions had not been of the sort that his alert mind usually asked. He seemed to have something up his sleeve. But Trevor thrust his suspicions aside and returned to the pleasant task of describing his triumph.

"With the bullet, the footprints, the tire marks, and the threads, I had considerable to go on. All I had to do was to relate them unmistakably to one man, and I had my murderer. But the trail soon let into quarters where we had to move cautiously. With my material evidence in front of me, I set out to fasten upon some individual who might have had a motive for killing West. So far as anyone could say, he had no enemies; but on the other hand he had few friends. He believed in the maxim that he travels fastest who travels alone. However, he had nipped some men pretty badly in the Street; and it was upon his financial operations that I soon concentrated my attention. There, with the facilities for investigation at my command, I discovered some very interesting facts. During the three weeks prior to West's death the common stock of Elliott Light and Power had risen fifty-seven points; four days after he had been shot it had dropped back no less than sixty-three points. Investigation showed that on the day West was murdered Harrington was short one hundred and thirty-odd thousand shares of that particular stock. He had been selling it short all the way up, and West had been buying all that was offered. Harrington's resources, great as they were, weren't equal to his rival's. He knew that unless he could break Elliott Common wide open he was a ruined man, and he took the one sure way to do it that he could think of. He eliminated West. It was murder for millions."

Trevor paused impressively; Hare did not say a word.

"That's about all there is to the story; the rest of it was routine sleuthing. One of my men found four tires, three in perfect condition, which had been taken from Harrington's touring car and replaced on the day following the murder. They had been put in a loft of the garage on Harrington's country place. Three perfect tires, mind you; and on the fourth there was a large, hard blister. Harrington's shoes fitted the footprints in West's lane, and the thread ends matched the threads in one of Harrington's suits. And, to top it all off, after the man was arrested, we found a .25, pearl-handled revolver in his wall safe. One shot had been fired, and the weapon hadn't been cleaned since. Harrington's chauffeur testified that his master had taken out the big touring car alone on the afternoon of the murder: the man remembered the date because it had been his wife's birthday. It was all very simple, and even such elements of interest as it possessed were lessened by Harrington's confession. The press made much too much of a stir about my part in the affair." The doctor smiled deprecatingly. "It was really no mystery at all, and if the men involved had not been so rich and so prominent the case would have been virtually ignored. But we nailed him just in time; he was sailing for Europe the following week."

"What kind of a revolver did you say it was?" Hare asked the question so abruptly that Trevor started before answering.

"Why, it was a .25, pearl-handled and nickel-finished. Rather a dainty weapon altogether; Harrington was a bit apologetic about owning such a toy."

"I should think he might have been. Was the handle slightly chipped on the right side?"

Trevor leaned forward suddenly. "Yes, it was. How the devil did you know?"

"Why it got chipped when Alice dropped it on a rock at Davos. The four of us were target shooting back of the hotel."

"Alice!" exclaimed Trevor. "What Alice? And what do you mean by the four of you?"

Hare answered quietly, "Alice West, my dear fellow. You see, it was her gun. And the four of us were West, Alice, Harrington, and myself; we were all staying at the same hotel in Switzerland four years ago."

"Her gun?" The doctor was speaking excitedly now. "You mean she gave it to him?"

"I doubt it, much as she loved him," drawled Hare. "He probably took it away from her, too late."

"You're talking in riddles," snapped the detective. "What do you mean?"

"Simply that that little weapon helped to execute the wrong man," said Hare wearily.

"The wrong man."

"Well, that's one way of putting it; but in this case I am very much afraid that the right 'man' was a woman."

Trevor's apparent excitement had vanished abruptly, and now he was as calm as a sphinx. "Tell me exactly what you mean," he demanded.

Hare put aside the butt of his cigar. "It all began back in Davos, four years ago. Harrington fell in love with Alice West, and she fell in love with him. West played dog in the manger: he wouldn't let his wife divorce him and he wouldn't divorce her. They separated, of course, but that didn't help Alice and Harrington towards getting married. I was on the inside of the affair from the first, you see; accidentally to begin with, and afterwards because they all made me their confidant in various degrees. West behaved like a swine, because he really didn't love the woman any more. He simply had made up his mind that no other man was going to have her, legally at least. And he stuck to it—until she killed him."

"She killed him?" The great detective spoke softly.

"I'm as sure of it as though I had seen her do it. To begin with, it was her revolver that fired the shot, as you have proved to me. I've seen it a hundred times when we were firing at bottles and what not for fun. There was no reason for Harrington to borrow it; he had a nice little armory of his own, hadn't he?"

"Yes, we did find a couple of heavy service revolvers and an automatic."

"Exactly. He never would have used a toy like that in a thousand years; and besides he would never have committed a murder. He was too level-headed. Alice, on the other hand, is an extremely hysterical type; I've seen her go completely off her head with anger. Beautiful, Lord, yes! But dangerous, and in the last analysis a coward. She's proved that. I never did envy Harrington."

"But she was in Europe, man, when the murder was committed."

"She was not, Trevor. She was in Montreal that very month, to my certain knowledge, and Montreal isn't so far from Long Island. Harry Sands ran into her at the Ritz there; they were reminiscing about it at Monte Carlo the last time I saw her. She was in Europe before and after the murder, but she wasn't there when it happened. Anyway, that's not the whole story."

"Well, what is it?" Trevor's mouth was grim.

Hare's fingers were playing with a silver match box, and he hesitated a minute before answering. Then he spoke quickly and to the point.

"The rest of it is this. As I told you, Alice is hysterical, and during the past few years drink and dope haven't helped her any. Well, one night at Monte, just before I left, she went off the deep end. We had been talking about her husband's death, and I had been speculating as to who could have done it. Harrington hadn't been arrested then. And I'd been asking her, too, if she and Harrington weren't going to get married soon. She dodged that question, obviously embarrassed. Then suddenly she burst out into a wild tirade against the dead man, called him every name under heaven, and finally dived into her evening bag and fished out a letter. It was addressed to her, and the post mark was more than a year old; it was almost broken at the creases from having been read over and over again. She shoved it at me, and insisted that I read it. It was from West, and it was a cruel letter if I've ever read one. It was the letter of a cat to a mouse, of a jailer to his prisoner: West had her where he wanted her, and he intended to keep her there. He didn't miss a trick when it came to rubbing it in. It was so bad that I didn't want to finish it, but she made me. When I gave it back to her her eyes were blazing; and she grabbed my hand and cried, 'What would you do to a man like that?' I hemmed and hawed for a minute, and she answered herself by exclaiming, 'Kill him! Kill him! Wouldn't you?' As calmly as I could I pointed out to her that someone had already done just that; and she burst into a fit of the wickedest laughter I've ever heard. Then she calmed down, powdered her nose, and said quietly, 'It's funny that you can shoot the heads off all the innocent bottles you like and no one says a word, but if you kill a human snake they hang you for it. And I don't want to hang, thank you very much.'"

Hare paused as though he were very tired, and then he added, "That's about all there was to it; it wasn't very nice. I left for Africa the next day, and I scarcely ever saw the papers there. But I hadn't any doubts as to who had bumped off Ernest West."

While the minute hand on the mantel clock jumped three times there was silence in the book-lined room. Then Trevor spoke, and his voice was strained. "So you think I made a mistake?"

Hare looked him straight in the eye. "What do you think?"

The detective took refuge in another question. "Have you any theory as to what really happened?"

"It's hard to say exactly, but I'm sure she did it. Her reference to the bottles showed that she knew what weapon had been used; she must have done in a thousand bottles with it at various times. My guess is that she and Harrington went down to see West together, to see if they couldn't make him change his mind after all, and that they failed. Then she pulled out that little toy of hers. She always carried it around in her bag. I use to tell her it was a bad habit. She shot West before he could move; she was a better shot than Harrington, he could never have found the man's heart. Then they left the house and drove off in Harrington's car; but first of all he went back and thoughtfully trampled out every one of her footprints and, just to make sure he wasn't missing any, he walked over the housekeeper's as well. There were three sets of tracks there, Trevor, not two; I'll bet on that. Then Harrington took the gun away from her—if he hadn't taken it before—and drove her to wherever she wanted to go. She left him; she left him to stand the gaff if he was suspected, and it was like him to do what he did. He loved her if any man ever loved a woman; and she loved him in her own way, but it wasn't the best way in the world. She loved her own white neck considerably more." Hare smiled a wry smile. "She had forgotten that New York State doesn't go in for hanging. Altogether it is not a pretty tale. But Harrington, poor devil, wanted to save the woman even if she wasn't worth it. You see, to him she was."

"It's impossible!" Trevor snapped out the words as if despite himself.

"What is?"

"That I made a mistake."

"We all make mistakes, my dear fellow."

"I don't." The tight mouth was tighter than ever.

"Well, it's a shame, but what's done is done." Hare shrugged his shoulders.

Trevor looked at him with cold eyes. "Obviously you do not understand. My reputation does not permit of mistakes. I simply can't make them. That's all."

Hare mustered a genial smile; he was genuinely sorry that Trevor was so distressed and he sought to reassure him. "But your reputation isn't going to suffer. The facts won't come out. Alice West will be dead of dope inside of two years, if I'm any judge, and no one else knows."

"You do."

"Yes, I do; but we can forget about that."

Trevor nodded nervously. "Yes, we must. Do you understand, Hare, we *must*."

Hare studied him quizzically. "Don't worry, old chap, your reputation's safe with me; I'll keep my mouth shut."

Trevor nodded again, more nervously and more emphatically. "Yes, yes, I know you will, of course. I know you will."

"And how about a drink?" Hare swung himself out of his chair.

"On the table there. Help yourself. I'm going into the laboratory for a minute."

The doctor disappeared through the low door, and Hare busied himself with the decanters and the bottles in a preoccupied manner. He was sorry that Trevor was so upset; but what colossal egotism! Perhaps he should have held his tongue; nothing had been gained. He would never mention the subject again. It was a stiff drink of brandy that Hare finally poured himself, and he held it up to the light studying it, with his back to the laboratory door. But he never drank it; for he dropped the glass as he felt the lean fingers at his throat and the chloroform pad smothering his mouth and nostrils. He managed to say only the two words, "My God . . ."

About fifteen minutes later, Dr. Harrison Trevor peered cautiously over the banister of his own stairway. There was no one below, and he descended swiftly. In the kitchen Tanaka heard the front door slam, and almost immediately afterwards his master's voice calling him from the first-floor landing. Tanaka responded briskly.

"Mr. Hare has just left," said the doctor, "and he forgot his cigarette case. Run after him, he may still be in sight."

Tanaka sped upon his errand. Yes, there on the corner was a tall man, obviously Hare *san*; but he was getting into a taxi. Tanaka ran, but before he was half way down the block Hare *san* had driven off. Tanaka returned to report failure.

"Too bad," said his master, who met him on the landing. "But it doesn't really matter. Telephone Mr. Hare's apartment and tell his man that Mr. Hare left his case here, and that he is not to worry about it. You can take it to him in the morning."

Tanaka went downstairs to obey orders; and his master was left to wonder at the coincidence of the man who looked like Hare getting into the taxi. The accidental evidence might prove useful, but it was quite unnecessary, quite unnecessary; he had no need of accidental aid. At the door of his library the detective paused and surveyed the scene with a critical eye: everything was in place, comfortably, conventionally, indisputably in place. There were no fragments of the broken tumbler on the floor; only a dark, wet spot on the carpet that was drying rapidly. Brandy and soda would leave no stain. Dr. Harrison Trevor smiled a chilly smile and then walked resolutely toward the laboratory where his task awaited him. Once the door had been locked behind him, his first act was to switch on the electric ventilator fan which carried off all obnoxious odors through a concealed flue. After that he worked on into the morning hours.

The disappearance of Mr. Gregory Hare, eminent criminal lawyer, within a week after his return from abroad, furnished the front pages of the newspapers with rather more than a nine days' wonder. It was Dr. Trevor who was the first to insist upon foul play; and it was Dr. Trevor who worked fervently upon the case, with all the assistance that the police could give him. Naturally he was deeply concerned, for Hare had been an intimate acquaintance, and he had been among the last to see the man alive; but the body was never found, and there was no evidence to go on with. Tanaka repeated what he knew, reiterating the story of the taxi; and a patrolman on fixed post confirmed the Japanese's testimony. The tall gentleman had come from the direction of Dr. Trevor's house, and had driven off just as the servant had come running after him. All of which helped not at all. A certain "Limping" Louie, whom Hare, years before when he was District Attorney, had sent up for a long term, was dragged in by the police net; but he had a perfect alibi. The mystery remained a mystery.

Dr. Trevor and Inspector Furst were discussing the case one afternoon, long after it had been abandoned. Furst still toyed with the idea that it might not have been murder, but the doctor was positive.

"I'm absolutely sure of it, Furst, absolutely sure. Hare was killed."

"Well," said the inspector, "if you are so sure, I'm inclined to agree. You've never made a mistake."

THE AVENGING CHANCE

(1925)

Anthony Berkeley

We now turn from the "perfect murder" to the "nearly perfect murder." Readers interested in short story technique will appreciate the way the author weaves together his intricate plot. Detective Roger Sheringham, investigating a case of death by poisoned chocolates, quite by chance finds a clue to the perpetrator.

Mystery writers sometimes use pseudonyms or pen names. Anthony Berkeley's real name was Anthony Berkeley Cox, or A. B. Cox (1893–1971). Cox also wrote under the pen name Francis Iles. A story by Iles appears later in this book. Whatever name he uses, the author is one of the great English mystery writers of novels and short stories. Among his novels are *The Piccadilly Murder* (1930), *Malice Aforethought* (1931), and *Death in the House* (1939). Berkeley/Iles/Cox was the founder of the Detection Club of London.

Roger Sheringham was inclined to think afterwards that the Poisoned Chocolates Case, as the papers called it, was perhaps the most perfectly planned murder he had ever encountered. The motive was so obvious, when you knew where to look for it—but you didn't know; the method was so significant when you had grasped its real essentials—but you didn't grasp them; the traces were so thinly covered, when you had realised what was covering them—but you didn't realise. But for a piece of the merest bad luck, which the murderer could not possibly have foreseen, the crime must have been added to the classical list of great mysteries.

This is the gist of the case, as Chief Inspector Moresby told it one evening to Roger in the latter's rooms in the Albany a week or so after it happened:—

On the past Friday morning, the fifteenth of November, at half past ten o'clock, in accordance with his invariable custom, Sir William Anstruther walked into his club in Piccadilly, the very exclusive Rainbow Club, and asked for his letters. The porter handed him three and a small parcel. Sir William walked over to the fireplace in the big lounge hall to open them.

A few minutes later another member entered the club, a Mr. Graham Beresford. There were a letter and a couple of circulars for him, and he also strolled over to the fireplace, nodding to Sir William, but not speaking to him. The two men only knew each other very slightly, and had probably never exchanged more than a dozen words in all.

Having glanced through his letters, Sir William opened the parcel and, after a moment, snorted with disgust. Beresford looked at him, and with a grunt Sir William thrust out a letter which had been enclosed in the parcel. Concealing a smile (Sir William's ways were a matter of some amusement to his fellow members), Beresford read the letter. It was from a big firm of chocolate manufacturers, Mason & Sons, and set forth that they were putting on the market a new brand of liqueur chocolates designed especially to appeal to men; would Sir William do them the honour of accepting the enclosed two-pound box and letting the firm have his candid opinion on them?

"Do they think I'm a blank chorus girl?" fumed Sir William. "Write 'em testimonials about their blank chocolates, indeed! Blank 'em! I'll complain to the blank committee. That sort of blank thing can't blank well be allowed here."

"Well, it's an ill wind so far as I'm concerned," Beresford soothed him. "It's reminded me of something. My wife and I had a box at the Imperial last night. I bet her a box of chocolates to a hundred cigarettes that she wouldn't spot the villain by the end of the second act. She won. I must remember to get them. Have you seen it—*The Creaking Skull*? Not a bad show."

Sir William had not seen it, and said so with force.

"Want a box of chocolates, did you say?" he added, more mildly. "Well, take this blank one. I don't want it."

For a moment Beresford demurred politely and then, more unfortunately for himself, accepted. The money so saved meant nothing to him for he was a wealthy man; but trouble was always worth saving.

By an extraordinarily lucky chance neither the outer wrapper of the box nor its covering letter were thrown into the fire, and this was the more fortunate in that both men had tossed the envelopes of their letters into the flames. Sir William did, indeed, make a bundle of the wrapper, letter and string, but he handed it over to Beresford, and the latter simply dropped it inside the fender. This bundle the porter subsequently extracted and, being a man of orderly habits, put it tidily away in the waste paper basket, whence it was retrieved later by the police.

Of the three unconscious protagonists in the impending tragedy, Sir William was without doubt the most remarkable. Still a year or two under fifty, he looked, with his flaming red face and thickset figure, a typical country squire of the old school, and both his manners and his language were in accordance with tradition. His habits, especially as regards women, were also in accordance with tradition—the tradition of the bold, bad baronet which he undoubtedly was.

In comparison with him, Beresford was rather an ordinary man, a tall, dark, not handsome fellow of two-and-thirty, quiet and reserved. His father had left him a rich man, but idleness did not appeal to him, and he had a finger in a good many business pies.

Money attracts money. Graham Beresford had inherited it, he made it, and, inevitably, he had married it, too. The daughter of a late shipowner in Liverpool, with not far off half a million in her own right. But the money was incidental, for he needed her and would have married her just as inevitably (said his friends) if she had not had a farthing. A tall, rather serious-minded, highly cultured girl, not so young that her character had not had time to form (she was twenty-five when Beresford married her, three years ago), she was the ideal wife for him. A bit of a Puritan perhaps in some ways, but Beresford, whose wild oats, though duly sown, had been a sparse crop, was ready enough to be a Puritan himself by that time if she was. To make no bones about it, the Beresfords succeeded in achieving that eighth wonder of the modern world, a happy marriage.

And into the middle of it there dropped with irretrievable tragedy, the box of chocolates.

Beresford gave them to her after lunch as they sat over their coffee, with some jesting remark about paying his honourable debts, and she opened the box at once. The top layer, she noticed, seemed to consist only of kirsch and maraschino. Beresford, who did not believe in spoiling good coffee, refused when she offered him the box, and his wife ate the first one alone. As she did so she exclaimed in surprise that the filling seemed exceedingly strong and positively burnt her mouth.

Beresford explained that they were samples of a new brand and then, made curious by what his wife had said, took one too. A burning taste, not intolerable but much too strong to be pleasant, followed the release of the liquid, and the almond flavouring seemed quite excessive.

"By Jove," he said, "they are strong. They must be filled with neat alcohol."

"Oh, they wouldn't do that, surely," said his wife, taking another. "But they are very strong. I think I rather like them, though."

Beresford ate another, and disliked it still more. "I don't," he said with decision. "They make my tongue feel quite numb. I shouldn't eat any more of them if I were you. I think there's something wrong with them."

"Well, they're only an experiment, I suppose," she said. "But they do burn. I'm not sure whether I like them or not."

A few minutes later Beresford went out to keep a business appointment in the City. He left her still trying to make up her mind whether she liked them, and still eating them to decide. Beresford remembered that scrap of conversation afterwards very vividly, because it was the last time he saw his wife alive.

That was roughly half past two. At a quarter to four Beresford arrived at his club from the City in a taxi, in a state of collapse. He was helped into the building by the driver and the porter, and both described him subsequently as pale to the point of ghastliness, with staring eyes and livid lips, and his skin damp and clammy. His mind seemed unaffected, however, and when they had got him up the steps he was able to walk, with the porter's help, into the lounge.

The porter, thoroughly alarmed, wanted to send for a doctor at once, but Beresford, who was the last man in the world to make a fuss, refused to let him, saying that it must be indigestion and he would be all right in a few minutes. To Sir William Anstruther, however, who was in the lounge at the time, he added after the porter had gone:

"Yes, and I believe it was those infernal chocolates you gave me, now I come to think of it. I thought there was something funny about them at the time. I'd better go and find out if my wife—" He broke off abruptly. His body, which had been leaning back limply in his chair, suddenly heaved rigidly upright; his jaws locked together, the livid lips drawn back in a horrible grin, and his hands clenched on the arms of his chair. At the same time Sir William became aware of an unmistakable smell of bitter almonds.

Thoroughly alarmed, believing indeed that the man was dying under his eyes, Sir William raised a shout for the porter and a doctor. The other occupants of the lounge hurried up, and between them they got the convulsed body of the unconscious man into a more comfortable position. Before the doctor could arrive a telephone message was received at the club from an agitated butler asking if Mr. Beresford was there, and if so would he come home at once as Mrs. Beresford had been taken seriously ill. As a matter of fact she was already dead.

Beresford did not die. He had taken less of the poison than his wife, who after his departure must have eaten at least three more of the chocolates, so that its action was less rapid and the doctor had time to save him. As a matter of fact it turned out afterwards that he had not had a fatal dose. By about eight o'clock that night he was conscious; the next day he was practically convalescent.

As for the unfortunate Mrs. Beresford, the doctor had arrived too late to save her, and she passed away very rapidly in a deep coma.

The police had taken the matter in hand as soon as Mrs. Beresford's death was reported to them and the fact of poison established, and it was only a very short time before things had become narrowed down to the chocolates as the active agent.

Sir William was interrogated, the letter and wrapper were recovered from the waste paper basket, and, even before the sick man was out of danger, a detective inspector was asking for an interview with the managing director of Mason & Sons. Scotland Yard moves quickly.

It was the police theory at this stage, based on what Sir William and the two doctors had been able to tell them, that by an act of criminal carelessness on the part of one of Mason's employees, an excessive amount of oil of bitter almonds had been included in the filling mixture of the chocolates, for that was what the doctor had decided must be the poisoning ingredient. However, the managing director quashed this idea at once: oil of bitter almonds, he asserted, was never used by Mason's.

He had more interesting news still. Having read with undisguised astonishment the covering letter, he at once declared that it was a forgery. No such letter, no such samples had been sent out by the firm at all; a new variety of liqueur chocolates had never even been mooted. The fatal chocolates were their ordinary brand.

Unwrapping and examining one more closely, he called the Inspector's attention to a mark on the underside, which he suggested was the remains of a small hole drilled in the case, through which the liquid could have been extracted and the fatal filling inserted, the hole afterwards being stopped up with softened chocolate, a perfectly simple operation.

He examined it under a magnifying glass and the Inspector agreed. It was now clear to him that somebody had been trying deliberately to murder Sir William Anstruther.

Scotland Yard doubled its activities. The chocolates were sent for analysis, Sir William was interviewed again, and so was the now conscious Beresford. From the latter the doctor insisted that the news of his wife's death must be kept till the next day, as in his weakened condition the shock might be fatal, so that nothing very helpful was obtained from him.

Nor could Sir William throw any light on the mystery or produce a single person who might have any grounds for trying to kill him. He was living apart from his wife, who was the principal beneficiary in his will, but she was in the South of France, as the French police subsequently confirmed. His estate in Worcestershire, heavily mortgaged, was entailed and went to a nephew; but as the rent he got for it barely covered the interest on the mortgage, and the nephew was considerably better off than Sir William himself, there was no motive there. The police were at a dead end.

The analysis brought one or two interesting facts to light. Not oil of bitter almonds but nitrobenzene, a kindred substance, chiefly used in the manufacture of aniline dyes, was the somewhat surprising poison employed. Each chocolate in the upper layer contained exactly six minims of it, in a mixture of kirsch and maraschino. The chocolates in the other layers were harmless.

As to the other clues, they seemed equally useless. The sheet of Mason's note paper was identified by Merton's, the printers, as of their work, but there was nothing to show how it had got into the murderer's possession. All that could be said was that, the edges being distinctly yellowed, it must be an old piece. The machine on which the letter had been typed, of course, could not be traced. From the wrapper, a piece of ordinary brown paper with Sir William's address hand-printed on it in large capitals, there was nothing to be learnt at all beyond that the parcel had been posted at the office in Southampton Street between the hours of 8:30 and 9:30 on the previous evening.

Only one thing was quite clear. Whoever had coveted Sir William's life had no intention of paying for it with his or her own.

"And now you know as much as we do, Mr. Sheringham," concluded Chief Inspector Moresby; "and if you can say who sent those chocolates to Sir William, you'll know a good deal more."

Roger nodded thoughtfully.

"It's a brute of a case. I met a man only yesterday who was at school with Beresford. He didn't know him very well because Beresford was on the modern side and my friend was a classical bird, but they were in the same house. He says Beresford's absolutely knocked over by his wife's death. I wish you could find out who sent those chocolates, Moresby."

"So do I, Mr. Sheringham," said Moresby gloomily.

"It might have been anyone in the whole world," Roger mused. "What about feminine jealousy, for instance? Sir William's private life doesn't seem to be immaculate. I dare say there's a good deal of off with the old light-o'-love and on with the new."

"Why, that's just what I've been looking into, Mr. Sheringham, sir," retorted Chief Inspector Moresby reproachfully. "That was the first thing that came to me. Because if anything does stand out about this business it is that it's a woman's crime. Nobody but a woman would send poisoned chocolates to a man. Another man would send a poisoned sample of whiskey, or something like that."

"That's a very sound point, Moresby," Roger meditated. "Very sound indeed. And Sir William couldn't help you?"

"Couldn't," said Moresby, not without a trace of resentment, "or wouldn't. I was inclined to believe at first that he might have his suspicions and was shielding some woman. But I don't think so now."

"Humph!" Roger did not seem quite so sure. "It's reminiscent, this case, isn't it? Didn't some lunatic once send poisoned chocolates to the Commissioner of Police himself? A good crime always gets imitated, as you know."

Moresby brightened.

"It's funny you should say that, Mr. Sheringham, because that's the very conclusion I've come to. I've tested every other theory, and so far as I know there's not a soul with an interest in Sir William's death, whether from motives of gain, revenge, or what you like, whom I haven't had to rule quite out of it. In fact, I've pretty well made up my mind that the person who sent those chocolates was some irresponsible lunatic of a woman, a social or religious fanatic who's probably never even seen him. And if that's the case," Moresby sighed, "a fat chance I have of ever laying hands on her."

"Unless Chance steps in, as it so often does," said Roger brightly, "and helps you. A tremendous lot of cases get solved by a stroke of sheer luck, don't they? *Chance the Avenger*. It would make an excellent film title. But there's a lot of truth in it. If I were superstitious, which I'm not, I should say it wasn't chance at all, but Providence avenging the victim."

"Well, Mr. Sheringham," said Moresby, who was not superstitious either, "to tell the truth, I don't mind what it is, so long as it lets me get my hands on the right person."

If Moresby had paid his visit to Roger Sheringham with any hope of tapping that gentleman's brains, he went away disappointed.

To tell the truth, Roger was inclined to agree with the Chief Inspector's conclusion, that the attempt on the life of Sir William Anstruther and the actual murder of the unfortunate Mrs. Beresford must be the work of some unknown criminal lunatic. For this reason, although he thought about it a good deal during the next few days, he made no attempt to take the case in hand. It was the sort of affair, necessitating endless inquiries that a private person would have neither the time nor the authority to carry out, which can be handled only by the official police. Roger's interest in it was purely academic.

It was hazard, a chance encounter nearly a week later, which translated this interest from the academic into the personal.

Roger was in Bond Street, about to go through the distressing ordeal of buying a new hat. Along the pavement he suddenly saw bearing down on him Mrs. Verreker-le-Flemming. Mrs. Verreker-le-Flemming was small, exquisite, rich, and a widow, and she sat at Roger's feet whenever he gave her the opportunity. But she talked. She talked, in fact, and talked, and talked. And Roger, who rather liked talking himself, could not bear it. He tried to dart across the road, but there was no opening in the traffic stream. He was cornered.

Mrs. Verreker-le-Flemming fastened on him gladly.

"Oh, Mr. Sheringham! *Just* the person I wanted to see. Mr. Sheringham, *do* tell me. In confidence. *Are* you taking up this dreadful business of poor Joan Beresford's death?"

Roger, the frozen and imbecile grin of civilised intercourse on his face, tried to get a word in; without result.

"I was horrified when I heard of it—simple horrified. You see, Joan and I were such *very* close friends. Quite intimate. And the awful thing, the truly *terrible* thing is that Joan brought the whole business on herself. Isn't that *appalling?*"

Roger no longer wanted to escape.

"What did you say?" he managed to insert incredulously.

"I suppose it's what they call tragic irony," Mrs. Verreker-le-Flemming chattered on. "Certainly it was tragic enough, and I've never heard anything so terribly ironical. You know about that bet she made with her husband, of course, so that he had to get her a box of chocolates, and if he hadn't Sir William would never have given him the poisoned ones and he'd have eaten them and died himself and good riddance? Well, Mr. Sheringham——" Mrs. Verreker-le-Flemming lowered her voice to a conspirator's whisper and glanced about her in the approved manner. "I've never told anybody else this, but I'm telling you because I know you'll appreciate it. *Joan wasn't playing fair!*"

"How do you mean?" Roger asked, bewildered.

Mrs. Verreker-le-Flemming was artlessly pleased with her sensation.

"Why, she'd seen the play before. We went together, the very first week it was on. She *knew* who the villain was all the time."

"By Jove!" Roger was as impressed as Mrs. Verreker-le-Flemming could have wished. "Chance the Avenger! We're none of us immune from it."

"Poetic justice, you mean?" twittered Mrs. Verreker-le-Flemming, to whom these remarks had been somewhat obscure. "Yes, but Joan Beresford of all people! That's the extraordinary thing. I should never have thought Joan *would* do a thing like that. She was such a *nice* girl. A little close with money, of course, considering how well-off they are, but that isn't anything. Of course it was only fun, and pulling her husband's leg, but I always used to think Joan was such a *serious girl*, Mr. Sheringham. I mean, ordinary people don't talk about honour, and truth, and playing the game, and all those things one takes for granted. But Joan did. She was always saying that this wasn't honourable, or that wouldn't be playing the game. Well, she paid herself for not playing the game, poor girl, didn't she? Still, it all goes to show the truth of the old saying, doesn't it?"

"What old saying?" said Roger, hypnotized by this flow.

"Why, that still waters run deep. Joan must have been deep, I'm afraid." Mrs. Verreker-le-Flemming sighed. It was evidently a social error to be deep. "I mean, she certainly took me in. She can't have been quite so honourable and truthful as she was always pretending, can she? And I can't help wondering whether a girl who'd deceive her husband in a little thing like that might not—oh, well, I don't want to say anything against poor Joan now she's dead, poor darling, but she can't have been *quite* such a plaster saint after all, can she? I mean," said

Mrs. Verreker-le-Flemming, in hasty extenuation of these suggestions, "I do think psychology is so very interesting, don't you, Mr. Sheringham?"

"Sometimes, very," Roger agreed gravely. "But you mentioned Sir William Anstruther just now. Do you know him, too?"

"I used to," Mrs. Verreker-le-Flemming replied, without particular interest. "Horrible man! Always running after some woman or other. And when he's tired of her, just drops her—biff!—like that. At least," added Mrs. Verreker-le-Flemming somewhat hastily, "so I've heard."

"And what happens if she refuses to be dropped?"

"Oh, dear, I'm sure I don't know. I suppose you've heard the latest."

Mrs. Verreker-le-Flemming hurried on, perhaps a trifle more pink than the delicate aids to nature on her cheeks would have warranted.

"He's taken up with the Bryce woman now. You know, the wife of the oil man, or petrol, or whatever he made his money in. It began about three weeks ago. You'd have thought that dreadful business of being responsible, in a way, for poor Joan Beresford's death would have sobered him up a little, wouldn't you? But not a bit of it; he——"

Roger was following another line of thought.

"What a pity you weren't at the Imperial with the Beresfords that evening. She'd never have made that bet if you had been." Roger looked extremely innocent. "You weren't, I suppose."

"I?" queried Mrs. Verreker-le-Flemming in surprise. "Good gracious, no. I was at the new revue at the Pavilion. Lady Gavelstoke had a box and asked me to join her party."

"Oh, yes. Good show, isn't it? I thought that sketch *The Sempiternal Triangle* very clever. Didn't you?"

"*The Sempiternal Triangle*?" wavered Mrs. Verreker-le-Flemming.

"Yes, in the first half."

"Oh! Then I didn't see it. I got there disgracefully late, I'm afraid. But then," said Mrs. Verreker-le-Flemming with pathos, "I always do seem to be late for simply everything."

Roger kept the rest of the conversation resolutely upon theatres. But before he left her he had ascertained that she had photographs of both Mrs. Beresford and Sir William Anstruther, and had obtained permission to borrow them some time. As soon as she was out of view he hailed a taxi and gave Mrs. Verreker-le-Flemming's address. He thought it better to take advantage of her permission at a time when he would not have to pay for it a second time over.

The parlourmaid seemed to think there was nothing odd in his mission, and took him up to the drawing-room at once. A corner of the room was devoted to the silver-framed photographs of Mrs. Verreker-le-Flemming's friends, and there were many of them. Roger examined them with interest, and finally took away with him not two photographs but six, those of Sir William, Mrs. Beresford, Beresford, two strange males who appeared to belong to the Sir William period, and, lastly, a likeness of Mrs. Verreker-le-Flemming herself. Roger liked confusing his trail.

For the rest of the day he was very busy.

His activities would have no doubt seemed to Mrs. Verreker-le-Flemming not merely baffling but pointless. He paid a visit to a public library, for instance, and consulted a work of reference, after which he took a taxi and drove to the offices of the Anglo-Eastern Perfumery Company, where he inquired for a certain Mr. Joseph Lea Hardwick and seemed much put out on hearing that no such gentleman was known to the firm and was certainly not employed in any of their branches. Many questions had to be put about the firm and its branches before he consented to abandon the quest.

After that he drove to Messrs. Weall and Wilson, the well-known institution which protects the trade interests of individuals and advises its subscribers regarding investments. Here he entered his name as a subscriber, and explaining that he had a large sum of money to invest, filled in one of the special inquiry forms which are headed Strictly Confidential.

Then he went to the Rainbow Club, in Piccadilly.

Introducing himself to the porter without a blush as connected with Scotland Yard, he asked the man a number of questions, more or less trivial, concerning the tragedy.

"Sir William, I understand," he said finally, as if by the way, "did not dine here the evening before."

There it appeared that Roger was wrong. Sir William had dined in the club, as he did about three times a week.

"But I quite understood he wasn't here that evening," Roger said plaintively.

The porter was emphatic. He remembered quite well. So did a waiter, whom the porter summoned to corroborate him. Sir William had dined, rather late, and had not left the dining-room till about nine o'clock. He spent the evening there, too, the waiter knew, or at least some of it, for he himself had taken him a whisky and soda in the lounge not less than half an hour later.

Roger retired.

He retired to Merton's, in a taxi.

It seemed that he wanted some new note paper printed, of a very special kind, and to the young woman behind the counter he specified at great length and in wearisome detail exactly what he did want. The young woman handed him the books of specimen pieces and asked him to see if there was any style there which would suit him. Roger glanced through them, remarking garrulously to the young woman that he had been recommended to Merton's by a very dear friend, whose photograph he happened to have on him at that moment. Wasn't that a curious coincidence? The young woman agreed that it was.

"About a fortnight ago, I think, my friend was in here last," said Roger, producing the photograph. "Recognise this?"

The young woman took the photograph, without apparent interest.

"Oh, yes, I remember. About some note paper, too, wasn't it? So that's your friend. Well, it's a small world. Now this is a line we're selling a good deal of just now."

Roger went back to his rooms to dine. Afterwards, feeling restless, he wandered out of the Albany and turned up Piccadilly. He wandered round the Circus, thinking hard, and paused for a moment out of habit to inspect the photographs of the new revue hung outside the Pavilion. The next thing he realised was that he had got as far as Jermyn Street and was standing outside the Imperial Theatre. Glancing at the advertisements of *The Creaking Skull*, he saw that it began at half past eight. Glancing at his watch, he saw that the time was twenty-nine minutes past the hour. He had an evening to get through somehow. He went inside.

The next morning, very early for Roger, he called on Moresby at Scotland Yard.

"Moresby," he said without preamble, "I want you to do something for me. Can you find me a taximan who took a fare from Piccadilly Circus or its neighbourhood at about ten past nine on the evening before the Beresford crime to the Strand somewhere near the bottom of Southampton Street, and another who took a fare back between those points? I'm not sure about the first. Or one taxi might have been used for the double journey, but I doubt that. Anyhow, try to find out for me, will you?"

"What are you up to now, Mr. Sheringham?" Moresby asked suspiciously.

"Breaking down an interesting alibi," replied Roger serenely. "By the way, I know who sent those chocolates to Sir William. I'm just building up a nice structure of evidence for you. Ring up my rooms when you've got those taximen."

He strolled out, leaving Moresby positively gaping after him.

The rest of the day he spent apparently trying to buy a second-hand typewriter. He was very particular that it should be a Hamilton No. 4. When the shop people tried to induce him to consider other makes he refused to look at them, saying that he had had the Hamilton No. 4 so strongly recommended to him by a friend who had bought one about three weeks ago. Perhaps it was at this very shop? No? They hadn't sold a Hamilton No. 4 for the last three months? How odd.

But at one shop they had sold a Hamilton No. 4 within the last month, and that was odder still.

At half past four Roger got back to his rooms to await the telephone message from Moresby. At half past five it came.

"There are fourteen taxidrivers here, littering up my office," said Moresby offensively. "What do you want me to do with 'em?"

"Keep them till I come, Chief Inspector," returned Roger with dignity.

The interview with the fourteen was brief enough, however. To each man in turn Roger showed a photograph, holding it so that Moresby could not see it, and asked if he could recognise his fare. The ninth man did so, without hesitation.

At a nod from Roger, Moresby dismissed them, then sat at his table and tried to look official. Roger seated himself on the table, looking most unofficial, and swung his legs. As he did so, a photograph fell unnoticed out of his pocket and fluttered, face downwards, under the table. Moresby eyed it but did not pick it up.

"And now, Mr. Sheringham, sir," he said, "perhaps you'll tell me what you've been doing?"

"Certainly, Moresby," said Roger blandly. "Your work for you. I really have solved the thing, you know. Here's your evidence." He took from his notecase an old letter and handed it to the Chief Inspector. "Was that typed on the same machine as the forged letter from Mason's, or was it not?"

Moresby studied it for a moment, then drew the forged letter from a drawer of his table and compared the two minutely.

"Mr. Sheringham," he said soberly, "where did you get hold of this?"

"In a secondhand typewriter shop in St. Martin's Lane. The machine was sold to an unknown customer about a month ago. They identified the customer from that same photograph. As it happened, this machine had been used for a time in the office after it was repaired, to see that it was O.K., and I easily got hold of that specimen of its work."

"And where is the machine now?"

"Oh, at the bottom of the Thames, I expect," Roger smiled. "I tell you, this criminal takes no unnecessary chances. But that doesn't matter. There's your evidence."

"Humph! It's all right so far as it goes," conceded Moresby. "But what about Mason's paper?"

"That," said Roger calmly, "was extracted from Merton's book of sample note papers, as I'd guessed from the very yellowed edges might be the case. I can prove contact of the criminal with the book, and there is a gap which will certainly turn out to have been filled by that piece of paper."

"That's fine," Moresby said more heartily.

"As for the taximan, the criminal had an alibi. You've heard it broken down. Between ten past nine and twenty-five past, in fact during the time when the parcel must have been posted, the murderer took a hurried journey to that neighbourhood, going probably by bus or Underground, but returning, as I expected, by taxi, because time would be getting short."

"And the murderer, Mr. Sheringham?"

"The person whose photograph is in my pocket," Roger said unkindly. "By the way, do you remember what I was saying the other day about Chance the Avenger, my excellent film title? Well, it's worked again. By a chance meeting in Bond Street with a silly woman I was put, by the merest accident, in possession of a piece of information which showed me then and there who had sent those chocolates addressed to Sir William. There were other possibilities, of course, and I tested them, but then and there on the pavement I saw the whole thing, from first to last."

"Who was the murderer, then, Mr. Sheringham?" repeated Moresby.

"It was so beautifully planned," Roger went on dreamily. "We never grasped for one moment that we were making the fundamental mistake that the murderer all along intended us to make."

"And what was that?" asked Moresby.

"Why, that the plan had miscarried. That the wrong person had been killed. That was just the beauty of it. The plan had *not* miscarried. It had been brilliantly successful. The wrong person was *not* killed. Very much the right person was."

Moresby gasped.

"Why, how on earth do you make that out, sir?"

"Mrs. Beresford was the objective all the time. That's why the plot was so ingenious. Everything was anticipated. It was perfectly natural that Sir William should hand the chocolates over to Beresford. It was foreseen that we should look for the criminal among Sir William's associates and not the dead woman's. It was probably even foreseen that the crime would be considered the work of a woman!"

Moresby, unable to wait any longer, snatched up the photograph.

"Good heavens! But Mr. Sheringham, you don't mean to tell me that . . . Sir William himself!"

"He wanted to get rid of Mrs. Beresford," Roger continued. "He had liked her well enough at the beginning, no doubt, though it was her money he was after all that time.

"But the real trouble was that she was too close with her money. He wanted it, or some of it, pretty badly; and she wouldn't part. There's no doubt about the motive. I made a list of the firms he's interested in and got a report on them. They're all rocky, every one. He'd got through all his own money, and he had to get more.

"As for the nitrobenzene which puzzled us so much, that was simple enough. I looked it up and found that beside the uses you told me, it's used largely in perfumery. And he's got a perfumery business. The Anglo-Eastern Perfumery Company. That's how he'd know about it being poisonous, of course. But I shouldn't think he got his supply from there. He'd be cleverer than that. He probably made the stuff himself. Any schoolboy knows how to treat benzol with nitric acid to get nitrobenzene."

"But," stammered Moresby, "but Sir William . . . He was at Eton."

"Sir William?" said Roger sharply. "Who's talking about Sir William? I told you the photograph of the murderer was in my pocket." He whipped out the photograph in question and confronted the astounded Chief Inspector with it. "Beresford, man! Beresford's the murderer of his own wife.

"Beresford, who still had hankerings after a gay life," he went on more mildly, "didn't want his wife but did want her money. He contrived this plot, providing as he thought against every contingency that could possibly arise. He established a mild alibi, if suspicion ever should arise, by taking his wife to the Imperial, and slipped out of the theatre at the first interval. (I sat through the first act of the dreadful thing myself last night to see when the interval came.) Then he hurried down to the Strand, posted his parcel, and took a taxi back. He had ten minutes, but nobody would notice if he got back to the box a minute late.

"And the rest simply followed. He knew Sir William came to the club every morning at ten thirty, as regularly as clockwork; he knew that for a psychological certainty he could get the chocolates handed over to him if he hinted for them; he knew that the police would go chasing after all sorts of false trails starting from Sir William. And as for the wrapper and the forged letter, he carefully didn't destroy them because they were calculated not only to divert suspicion but actually to point away from him to some anonymous lunatic."

"Well, it's very smart of you, Mr. Sheringham," Moresby said, with a little sigh, but quite ungrudgingly. "Very smart indeed. What was it the lady told you that showed you the whole thing in a flash?"

"Why, it wasn't so much what she actually told me as what I heard between her words, so to speak. What she told me was that Mrs. Beresford knew the answer to that bet; what I deduced was that, being the sort of person she was, it was quite incredible that she should have made a bet to which she knew the answer. *Ergo*, she didn't. *Ergo*, there never was such a bet. *Ergo*, Beresford was lying. *Ergo*, Beresford wanted to get hold of those chocolates for some reason other than he stated. After all, we only had Beresford's word for the bet, hadn't we?

"Of course he wouldn't have left her that afternoon till he'd seen her take, or somehow made her take, at least six of the chocolates, more than a lethal dose. That's why the stuff was in those meticulous six-minim doses. And so that he could take a couple himself, of course. A clever stroke, that."

Moresby rose to his feet.

"Well, Mr. Sheringham, I'm much obliged to you, sir. And now I shall have to get busy myself." He scratched his head. "Chance the Avenger, eh? Well, I can tell you one pretty big thing Beresford left to Chance the Avenger, Mr. Sheringham. Suppose Sir William hadn't handed over the chocolates after all? Supposing he'd kept 'em, to give to one of his own ladies?"

Roger positively snorted. He felt a personal pride in Beresford by this time.

"Really, Moresby! It wouldn't have had any serious results if Sir William had. Do give my man credit for being what he is. You don't imagine he sent the poisoned ones to Sir William, do you? Of course not! He'd send harmless ones, and exchange them for the others on his way home. Dash it all, he wouldn't go right out of his way to present opportunities to Chance.

"If," added Roger, "Chance really is the right word."

THE DARK SNOW

(1996)

Brendan DuBois

A former military man, seeking peace and quiet, retires to a lakeside home but is hounded by boorish neighbors with loud motorboats and snowmobiles. This tale of revenge may fire emotions in the reader of anger, sadness, or spitefulness. It is arguably the most evocative story in the book.

Brendan DuBois, a lifelong resident of New Hampshire, is the author of six books in the Lewis Cole mystery series. Among his novels are *Resurrection Day* (1999), *Betrayed* (2003), *Primary Storm* (2006), *Twilight* (2007), and *Final Winter* (2008). His short stories have been honored with three Edgar Award nominations and he has twice won the Shamus Award for best short story of the year. "The Dark Snow" first appeared in *Playboy*.

When I get to the steps of my lakeside home, the door is open. I slowly walk in, my hand reaching for the phantom weapon at my side, everything about me extended and tingling as I enter the strange place that used to be mine. I step through the small kitchen, my boots crunching the broken glassware and dishes on the tile floor. Inside the living room with its cathedral ceiling the furniture has been upended, as if an earthquake had struck.

I pause for a second, looking out the large windows and past the enclosed porch, down to the frozen waters of Lake Marie. Off in the distance are the snow-covered peaks of the White Mountains. I wait, trembling, my hand still curving for that elusive weapon. They are gone, but their handiwork remains. The living room is a jumble of furniture, torn books and magazines, shattered pictures and frames. On one clear white plaster wall, next to the fireplace, two words have been written in what looks to be ketchup: GO HOME.

This is my home. I turn over a chair and drag it to the windows. I sit and look out at the crisp winter landscape, my legs stretched out, holding both hands still in my lap, which is quite a feat.

For my hands at that moment want to be wrapped around someone's throat.

After a long time wandering, I came to Nansen, New Hampshire, in the late summer and purchased a house along the shoreline of Lake Marie. I didn't waste much time, and I didn't bargain. I made an offer that was about a thousand dollars below the asking price, and in less than a month it belonged to me.

At first I didn't know what to do with it. I had never had a residence that was actually mine. Everything before this had been apartments, hotel rooms, or temporary officer's quarters. The first few nights I couldn't sleep inside. I would go outside to the long dock that extends into the deep blue waters of the lake, bundle myself up in a sleeping bag over a thin foam mattress, and stare up at the stars, listening to the loons getting ready for their long winter trip. The loons didn't necessarily fly south; the ones here go out to the cold Atlantic and float with the waves and currents, not once touching land the entire winter.

As I snuggled in my bag I thought it was a good analogy for what I'd been doing. I had drifted too long. It was time to come back to dry land.

After getting the power and other utilities up and running and moving in the few boxes of stuff that belonged to me, I checked the bulky folder that had accompanied my retirement and pulled out an envelope with a doctor's name on it. Inside were official papers that directed me to talk to him, and I shrugged and decided it was better than sitting in an empty house getting drunk. I phoned and got an appointment for the next day.

His name was Ron Longley and he worked in Manchester, the state's largest city and about an hour's drive south of Lake Marie. His office was in a refurbished brick building along the banks of the Merrimack River. I imagined I could still smell the sweat and toil of the French Canadians who had worked here for so many years in the shoe, textile, and leather mills until their distant cousins in Georgia and Alabama took their jobs away.

I wasn't too sure what to make of Ron during our first session. He showed me some documents that made him a Department of Defense contractor and gave his current classification level, and then, after signing the usual insurance nonsense, we got down to it. He was about ten years younger than I, with a mustache and not much hair on top. He wore jeans, a light blue shirt, and a tie that looked as if about six tubes of paint had been squirted onto it, and he said, "Well, here we are."

"That we are," I said. "And would you believe I've already forgotten if you're a psychologist or a psychiatrist?"

That made for a good laugh. With a casual wave of his hand, he said, "Makes no difference. What would you like to talk about?"

"What should I talk about?"

A shrug, one of many I would eventually see. "Whatever's on your mind."

"Really?" I said, not bothering to hide the challenge in my voice. "Try this one on then, doc. I'm wondering what I'm doing here. And another thing I'm wondering about is paperwork. Are you going to be making a report down south on how I do? You working under some deadline, some pressure?"

His hands were on his belly and he smiled. "Nope."

"Not at all?"

"Not at all," he said. "If you want to come in here and talk baseball for fifty minutes, that's fine with me."

I looked at him and those eyes. Maybe it's my change of view since retirement, but there was something trustworthy about him. I said, "You know what's really on my mind?"

"No, but I'd like to know."

"My new house," I said. "It's great. It's on a big lake and there aren't any close neighbors, and I can sit on the dock at night and see stars I haven't seen in a long time. But I've been having problems sleeping."

"Why's that?" he asked, and I was glad he wasn't one of those stereotypical head docs, the ones who take a lot of notes.

"Weapons."

"Weapons?"

I nodded. "Yeah, I miss my weapons." A deep breath. "Look, you've seen my files, you know the places Uncle Sam has sent me and the jobs I've done. All those years, I had pistols or rifles or heavy weapons, always at my side, under my bed or in a closet. But when I moved into that house, well, I don't have them anymore."

"How does that make you feel?" Even though the question was friendly, I knew it was a real doc question and not a from-the-next-barstool type of question.

I rubbed my hands. "I really feel like I'm changing my ways. But damn it . . ."

"Yes?"

I smiled. "I sure could use a good night's sleep."

As I drove back home, I thought, Hell, it's only a little white lie.

The fact is, I did have my weapons.

They were locked up in the basement, in strongboxes with heavy combination locks. I couldn't get to them quickly, but I certainly hadn't tossed them away.

I hadn't been lying when I told Ron I couldn't sleep. That part was entirely true.

I thought, as I drove up the dirt road to my house, scaring a possum that scuttled along the side of the gravel, that the real problem with living in my new home was so slight that I was embarrassed to bring it up to Ron.

It was the noise.

I was living in a rural paradise, with clean air, clean water, and views of the woods and lake and mountains that almost broke my heart each time I climbed out of bed, stiff with old dreams and old scars. The long days were filled with work and activities I'd never had time for. Cutting old brush and trimming dead branches. Planting annuals. Clearing my tiny beach of leaves and other debris. Filling bird feeders. And during the long evenings on the front porch or on the dock, I tackled thick history books.

But one night after dinner—I surprised myself at how much I enjoyed cooking—I was out on the dock, sitting in a fifties-era web lawn chair, a glass of red wine in my hand and a history of the Apollo space program in my lap. Along the shoreline of Lake Marie, I could see the lights of the cottages and other homes. Every night there were fewer and fewer lights, as more of the summer people boarded up their places and headed back to suburbia.

I was enjoying my wine and the book and the slight breeze, but there was also a distraction: three high-powered speedboats, racing around on the lake and tossing up great spray and noise. They were dragging people along in inner tubes, and it was hard to concentrate on my book. After a while the engines slowed and I was hoping the boats would head back to their docks, but they drifted together and ropes were exchanged, and soon they became a large raft. A couple of grills were set up and there were more hoots and yells, and then a sound system kicked in, with rock music and a heavy bass that echoed among the hills.

It was then too dark to read and I'd lost interest in the wine. I was sitting there, arms folded tight against my chest, trying hard to breathe. The noise got louder and I gave up and retreated into the house, where the heavy *thump-thump* of the bass followed me in. If I'd had a boat I could have gone out and asked them politely to turn it down, but that would have meant talking with people and putting myself in the way, and I didn't want to do that.

Instead, I went upstairs to my bedroom and shut the door and windows. Still, that *thump-thump* shook the beams of the house. I lay down with a pillow wrapped about my head and tried not to think of what was in the basement.

Later that night I got up for a drink of water, and there was still noise and music. I walked out onto the porch and could see movement on the lake and hear laughter. On a tree near the dock was a spotlight that the previous owners had installed and which I had rarely used. I flipped on the switch. Some shouts and shrieks. Two powerboats, tied together, had drifted close to my shore. The light caught a young muscular man with a fierce black mustache standing on the stern of his powerboat and urinating into the lake. His half dozen companions, male and female, yelled and cursed in my direction. The boats started up and two men and a young woman stumbled to the side of one and dropped their bathing suits, exposing their buttocks. A couple others gave me a one-fingered salute, and there was a shower of bottles and cans tossed over the side as they sped away.

I spent the next hour on the porch, staring into the darkness.

The next day I made two phone calls, to the town hall and the police department of Nansen. I made gentle and polite inquiries and got the same answers from each office. There was no local or state law about boats coming to within a certain distance of shore. There was no law forbidding boats from mooring together. Nansen being such a small town, there was also no noise ordinance.

Home sweet home.

On my next visit Ron was wearing a bow tie, and we discussed necktie fashions before we got into the business at hand. He said, "Still having sleeping problems?"

I smiled. "No, not at all."

"Really?"

"It's fall," I said. "The tourists have gone home, most of the cottages along the lake have been boarded up and nobody takes out boats anymore. It's so quiet at night I can hear the house creak and settle."

"That's good, that's really good," Ron said, and I changed the subject. A half-hour later, I was heading back to Nansen, thinking about my latest white lie. Well, it wasn't really a lie. More of an oversight.

I hadn't told Ron about the hang-up phone calls. Or how trash had twice been dumped in my driveway. Or how a week ago, when I was shopping, I had come back to find a bullet hole through one of my windows. Maybe it had been a hunting accident. Hunting season hadn't started, but I knew that for some of the workingmen in this town, it didn't matter when the state allowed them to do their shooting.

I had cleaned up the driveway, shrugged off the phone calls, and cut away brush and saplings around the house, to eliminate any hiding spots for . . . hunters.

Still, I could sit out on the dock, a blanket around my legs and a mug of tea in my hand, watching the sun set in the distance, the reddish pink highlighting the strong yellows, oranges, and reds of the fall foliage. The water was a slate gray, and though I missed the loons, the smell of the leaves and the tang of woodsmoke from my chimney seemed to settle in just fine.

As it grew colder, I began to go into town for breakfast every few days. The center of Nansen could be featured in a documentary on New Hampshire small towns. Around the green common with its Civil War statue are a bank, a real estate office, a hardware store, two gas stations, a general store, and a small strip of service places with everything from a plumber to video rentals and Gretchen's Kitchen. At Gretchen's I read the paper while letting the mornings drift by. I listened to the old-timers at the counter pontificate on the ills of the state, nation, and world, and watched harried workers fly in to grab a quick meal. Eventually, a waitress named Sandy took some interest in me.

She was about twenty years younger than I, with raven hair, a wide smile, and a pleasing body that filled out her regulation pink uniform. After a couple weeks of flirting and generous tips on my part, I asked her out, and when she said yes, I went to my pickup truck and burst out laughing. A real date. I couldn't remember the last time I had had a real date.

The first date was dinner a couple of towns over, in Montcalm, the second was dinner and a movie outside Manchester, and the third was dinner at my house, which was supposed to end with a rented movie in the living room but instead ended up in the bedroom. Along the way I learned that Sandy had always lived in Nansen, was divorced with two young boys, and was saving her money so she could go back to school and become a legal aide. "If you think I'm going to keep slinging hash and waiting for Billy to send his support check, then you're a damn fool," she said on our first date.

After a bedroom interlude that surprised me with its intensity, we sat on the enclosed porch. I opened a window for Sandy, who needed a smoke. The house was warm and I had on a pair of shorts; she had wrapped a towel around her torso. I sprawled in an easy chair while she sat on the couch, feet in my lap. Both of us had glasses of wine and I felt comfortable and tingling. Sandy glanced at me as she worked on her cigarette. I'd left the lights off and lit a couple of candles, and in the hazy yellow light, I could see the small tattoo of a unicorn on her right shoulder.

Sandy looked at me and asked, "What were you doing when you was in the government?"

"Traveled a lot and ate bad food."

"No, really," she said. "I want a straight answer."

Well, I thought, as straight as I can be, I said, "I was a consultant, to foreign armies. Sometimes they need help with certain weapons or training techniques. That was my job."

"Were you good?"

Too good, I thought. "I did all right."

"You've got a few scars there."

"That I do."

She shrugged, took a lazy puff off her cigarette. "I've seen worse."

I wasn't sure where this was headed. Then she said, "When are you going to be leaving?"

Confused, I asked her, "You mean, tonight?"

"No," she said. "I mean, when are you leaving Nansen and going back home?"

I looked around the porch and said, "This is my home."

She gave me a slight smile, like a teacher correcting a fumbling but eager student. "No, it's not. This place was built by the Gerrish family. It's the Gerrish place. You're from away, and this ain't your home."

I tried to smile, though my mood was slipping, "Well, I beg to disagree."

She said nothing for a moment, just studied the trail of smoke from her cigarette. Then she said, "Some people in town don't like you. They think you're uppity, a guy that don't belong here."

I began to find it quite cool on the porch. "What kind of people?"

"The Garr brothers. Jerry Tompkins. Kit Broderick. A few others. Guys in town. They don't particularly like you."

"I don't particularly care," I shot back.

A small shrug as she stubbed out her cigarette. "You will."

The night crumbled some more after that, and the next morning, while sitting in the corner at Gretchen's, I was ignored by Sandy. One of the older waitresses served me, and my coffee arrived in a cup stained with lipstick, the bacon was charred black, and the eggs were cold. I got the message. I started making breakfast at home, sitting alone on the porch, watching the leaves fall and days grow shorter.

I wondered if Sandy was on her own or if she had been scouting out enemy territory on someone's behalf.

At my December visit, I surprised myself by telling Ron about something that had been bothering me.

"It's the snow," I said, leaning forward, hands clasped between my legs. "It's going to start snowing soon. And I've always hated the snow, especially since . . ."

"Since when?"

"Since something I did once," I said. "In Serbia."

"Go on," he said, fingers making a tent in front of his face.

"I'm not sure I can."

Ron tilted his head quizzically. "You know I have the clearances."

I cleared my throat, my eyes burning a bit. "I know. It's just that it's . . . Ever see blood on snow, at night?"

I had his attention. "No," he said, "no, I haven't."

"It steams at first, since it's so warm," I said. "And then it gets real dark, almost black. Dark snow, if you can believe it. It's something that stays with you, always."

He looked steadily at me for a moment, then said, "Do you want to talk about it some more?"

"No."

I spent all of one gray afternoon in my office cubbyhole, trying to get a new computer up and running. When at last I went downstairs for a quick drink, I looked outside and there they were, big snowflakes lazily drifting to the ground. Forgetting about the drink, I went out to the porch and looked at the pure whiteness of everything, of the snow covering the bare limbs, the shrubbery, and the frozen lake, I stood there and hugged myself, admiring the softly accumulating blanket of white and feeling lucky.

Two days after the snowstorm, I was out on the frozen waters of Lake Marie, breathing hard and sweating and enjoying every second of it. The day before I had driven into Manchester to a sporting goods store and had come out with a pair of cross-country skis. The air was crisp and still, and the sky was a blue so deep I half-expected to see brushstrokes. From the lake, I looked back at my home and liked what I saw. The white paint and plain construction made me smile for no particular reason. I heard not a single sound, except for the faint drone of a distant airplane. Before me someone had placed signs and orange ropes in the snow, covering an oval area at the center of the lake. Each sign said the same thing: DANGER! THIN ICE! I remembered the old-timers at Gretchen's Kitchen telling a story about a hidden spring coming up through the lake bottom, or some damn thing, that made ice at the center of the lake thin, even in the coldest weather. I got cold and it was time to go home.

About halfway back to the house is where it happened.

At first it was a quiet sound, and I thought that it was another airplane. Then the noise got louder and louder, and separated, becoming distinct. Snowmobiles, several of them. I turned and they came speeding out of the woods, tossing up great rooster tails of snow and ice. They were headed straight for me. I turned away and kept up a steady pace, trying to ignore the growing loudness of the approaching engines. An itchy feeling crawled up my spine to the base of my head, and the noise exploded in pitch as they raced by me.

Even over the loudness of the engines I could make out the yells as the snowmobiles roared by, hurling snow in my direction. There were two people to each machine and they didn't look human. Each was dressed in a bulky jump suit, heavy boots, and a padded helmet. They raced by and, sure enough, circled around and came back at me. This time I flinched. This time, too, a couple of empty beer cans were thrown my way.

By the third pass, I was getting closer to my house. I thought it was almost over when one of the snowmobiles broke free from the pack and raced across about fifty feet in front of me. The driver turned so that the machine was blocking me and sat there, racing the throttle. Then he pulled off his helmet, showing an angry face and thick mustache, and I recognized him as the man on the powerboat a few months earlier. He handed his helmet to his passenger, stepped off the snowmobile, and unzipped his jump suit. It took only a moment as he marked the snow in a long, steaming stream, and there was laughter from the others as he got back on the machine and sped away. I skied over the soiled snow and took my time climbing up the snow-covered shore. I entered my home, carrying my skis and poles like weapons over my shoulder.

That night, and every night afterward, they came back, breaking the winter stillness with the throbbing sounds of engines, laughter, drunken shouts, and music from portable stereos. Each morning I cleared away their debris and scuffed fresh snow over the stains. In the quiet of my house, I found myself constantly on edge, listening, waiting for the noise to suddenly return and break up the day. Phone calls to the police department and town hall confirmed what I already knew: Except for maybe littering, no ordinances or laws were being broken.

On one particularly loud night, I broke a promise to myself and went to the tiny, damp cellar to unlock the green metal case holding a pistol-shaped device. I went back upstairs to the enclosed porch, and with the lights off, I switched on the night-vision scope and looked at the scene below me. Six snowmobiles were parked in a circle on the snow-covered ice, and in the center, a fire had been made. Figures stumbled around in the snow, talking and laughing. Stereos had been set up on the seats of two of the snowmobiles, and the loud music with its bass *thump-thump-thump* echoed across the flat ice. Lake Marie is one of the largest bodies of water in this part of the country, but the camp was set up right below my windows.

I watched for a while as they partied. Two of the black-suited figures started wrestling in the snow. More shouts and laughter, and then the fight broke up and someone turned the stereos even louder. *Thump-thump-thump.*

I switched off the nightscope, returned it to its case in the cellar, and went to bed. Even with foam rubber plugs in my ears, the bass noise reverberated inside my skull. I put the pillow across my face and tried to ignore the sure knowledge that this would continue all winter, the noise and the littering and the aggravation, and when the spring came, they would turn in their snowmobiles for boats, and they'd be back, all summer long.

Thump-thump-thump.

At the next session with Ron, we talked about the weather until he pierced me with his gaze and said, "Tell me what's wrong."

I went through half a dozen rehearsals of what to tell him, and then skated to the edge of the truth and said, "I'm having a hard time adjusting, that's all."

"Adjusting to what?"

"To my home," I said, my hands clasped before me. "I never thought I would say this, but I'm really beginning to get settled, for the first time in my life. You ever been in the military, Ron?"

"No, but I know—"

I held up my hand. "Yes, I know what you're going to say. You've worked as a consultant, but you've never been one of us, Ron. Never. You can't know what it's like, constantly being ordered to uproot yourself and go halfway across the world to a new place with a different language, customs, and weather, all within a week. You never settle in, never really get into a place you call home."

He swiveled a bit in his black leather chair. "But that's different now?"

"It sure is," I said.

There was a pause as we looked at each other, and Ron said, "But something is going on."

"Something is."

"Tell me."

And then I knew I wouldn't. A fire wall had already been set up between Ron and the details of what was going on back at my home. If I let him know what was really happening, I knew that he would make a report, and within a week I'd be ordered to go somewhere else. If I'd been younger and not so dependent on a monthly check, I would have put up a fight.

But now, no more fighting. I looked past Ron and said, "An adjustment problem, I guess."

"Adjusting to civilian life?"

"More than that," I said. "Adjusting to Nansen. It's a great little town, but . . . I feel like an outsider."

"That's to be expected."

"Sure, but I still don't like it. I know it will take some time, but . . . well, I get the odd looks, the quiet little comments, the cold shoulders."

Ron seemed to choose his words carefully. "Is that proving to be a serious problem?"

Not even a moment of hesitation as I lied: "No, not at all."

"And what do you plan on doing?"

An innocent shrug. "Not much. Just try to fit in, try to be a good neighbor."

"That's all?"

I nodded firmly. "That's all."

It took a bit of research, but eventually I managed to put a name to the face of the mustached man who had pissed on my territory. Jerry Tompkins. Floor supervisor for a computer firm outside Manchester, married with three kids, an avid boater, snowmobiler, hunter, and all-around guy. His family had been in Nansen for generations, and his dad was one of the three selectmen who ran the town. Using a couple of old skills, I tracked him down one dark afternoon and pulled my truck next to his in the snowy parking lot of a tavern on the outskirts of Nansen. The tavern was called Peter's Pub and its windows were barred and blacked out.

I stepped out of my truck and called to him as he walked to the entrance of the pub. He turned and glared at me. "What?"

"You're Jerry Tompkins, aren't you."

"Sure am," he said, hands in the pockets of his dark-green parka. "and you're the fella that's living up in the old Gerrish place."

"Yes, and I'd like to talk with you for a second."

His face was rough, like he had spent a lot of time outdoors in the wind and rain and an equal amount indoors, with cigarette smoke and loud country music. He rocked back on his heels with a little smile and said, "Go ahead. You got your second."

"Thanks, "I said. "Tell you what, Jerry, I'm looking for something."

"And what's that?"

"I'm looking for a treaty."

He nodded, squinting his eyes. "What kind of treaty?"

"A peace treaty. Let's cut out the snowmobile parties on the lake by my place and the trash dumped in the driveway and the hang-up calls. Let's start fresh and just stay out of each other's way. What do you say? Then, this summer, you can all come over to my place for a cookout. I'll even supply the beer."

He rubbed at the bristles along his chin. "Seems like a one-sided deal. Not too sure what I get out of it."

"What's the point in what you're doing now?"

A furtive smile. "It suits me."

I felt like I was beginning to lose it. "You agree with the treaty, we all win."

"Still don't see what I get out of it," he said.

"That's the purpose of a peace treaty," I said. "You get peace."

"Feel pretty peaceful right now."

"That might change," I said, instantly regretting the words.

His eyes darkened. "Are you threatening me?"

A retreat, recalling my promise to myself when I'd come here. "No, not a threat, Jerry. What do you say?"

He turned and walked away, moving his head to keep me in view. "Your second got used up a long time ago, pal. And you better be out of this lot in another minute, or I'm going inside and coming out with a bunch of my friends. You won't like that."

No, I wouldn't, and it wouldn't be for the reason Jerry believed. If they did come out I'd be forced into old habits and old actions, and I'd promised myself I wouldn't do that. I couldn't.

"You got it," I said, backing away. "But remember, Jerry. Always."

"What's that?"

"The peace treaty," I said, going to the door of my pickup truck. "I offered."

Another visit to Ron, on a snowy day. The conversation meandered along, and I don't know what got into me, but I looked out the old mill windows and said, "What do people expect, anyway?"

"What do you mean?" he asked.

"You take a tough teenager from a small Ohio town, and you train him and train him and train him. You turn him into a very efficient hunter, a meat eater. Then, after twenty or thirty years, you say thank you very much and send him back to the world of quiet vegetarians, and you expect him to start eating cabbages and carrots with no fuss or muss. A hell of a thing, thinking you can expect him to put away his tools and skills."

"Maybe that's why we're here," he suggested.

"Oh, please," I said. "Do you think this makes a difference?"

"Does it make a difference to you?"

I kept looking out the window. "Too soon to tell, I'd say. Truth is, I wonder if this is meant to work, or is just meant to make some people feel less guilty. The people who did the hiring, training, and discharging."

"What do you think?"

I turned to him. "I think for the amount of money you charge Uncle Sam, you ask too many damn questions."

•

Another night at two A.M. I was back outside, beside the porch, again with the nightscope in my hands. They were back, and if anything, the music and the engines blared even louder. A fire burned merrily among the snowmobiles, and as the revelers pranced and hollered, I wondered if some base part of their brains was remembering thousand-year-old rituals. As I looked at their dancing and drinking figures, I kept thinking of the long case at the other end of the cellar. Nice heavy-duty assault rifle with another night-vision scope, this one with crosshairs. Scan and track. Put a crosshair across each one's chest. Feel the weight of a fully loaded clip in your hand. Know that with a silencer on the end of the rifle, you could quietly take out that crew in a fistful of seconds. Get your mind back into the realm of possibilities, of cartridges and windage and grains and velocities. How long could it take between the time you said go and the time you could say mission accomplished? Not long at all.

"No," I whispered, switching off the scope.

I stayed on the porch for another hour, and as my eyes adjusted, I saw more movements. I picked up the scope. A couple of snow machines moved in, each with shapes on the seats behind the drivers. They pulled up to the snowy bank and the people moved quickly, intent on their work. Trash bags were tossed on my land, about eight or nine, and to add a bit more fun, each bag had been slit several times with a knife so it could burst open and spew its contents when it hit the ground. A few more hoots and hollers and the snowmobiles growled away, leaving trash and the flickering fire behind. I watched the lights as the snowmobiles roared across the lake and finally disappeared, though their sound did not.

The nightscope went back onto my lap. The rifle, I thought, could have stopped the fun right there with a couple of rounds through the engines. Highly illegal, but it would get their attention, right?

Right.

In my next session with Ron, I got to the point. "What kind of reports are you sending south?"

I think I might have surprised him. "Reports?"

"How I'm adjusting, that sort of thing."

He paused for a moment, and I knew there must be a lot of figuring going on behind those smiling eyes. "Just the usual things, that's all. That you're doing fine."

"Am I?"

"Seems so to me."

"Good." I waited for a moment, letting the words twist about on my tongue. "Then you can send them this message. I haven't been a hundred percent with you during these sessions, Ron. Guess it's not in my nature to be so open. But you can count on this. I won't lose it. I won't go into a gun shop and then take down a bunch of civilians. I'm not going to start hanging around 1600 Pennsylvania Avenue. I'm going to be all right."

He smiled. "I have never had any doubt."

"Sure you've had doubts," I said, smiling back. "But it's awfully polite of you to say otherwise."

On a bright Saturday, I tracked down the police chief of Nansen at one of the two service stations in town, Glen's Gas & Repair. His cruiser, ordinarily a dark blue, was now a ghostly shade of white from the salt used to keep the roads clear. I parked at the side of the garage, and walking by the service bays, I could sense that I was being watched. I saw three cars with their hoods up, and I also saw a familiar uniform: black snowmobile jump suits.

The chief was overweight and wearing a heavy blue jacket with a black Navy watch cap. His face was open and friendly, and he nodded in all the right places as I told him my story.

"Not much I can do, I'm afraid," he said, leaning against the door of his cruiser, one of two in the entire town. "I'd have to catch 'em in the act of trashing your place, and that means surveillance, and that means overtime hours, which I don't have."

"Surveillance would be a waste of time anyway," I replied. "These guys, they aren't thugs, right? For lack of a better phrase, they're good old boys, and they know everything that's going on in Nansen, and they'd know if you were setting up surveillance. And then they wouldn't show."

"You might think you're insulting me, but you're not," he said gently. "That's just the way things are done here. It's a good town and most of us get along, and I'm not kept that busy, not at all."

"I appreciate that, but you should also appreciate my problem," I said. "I live here and pay taxes, and people are harassing me. I'm looking for some assistance, that's all, and a suggestion of what I can do."

"You could move," the chief said, raising his coffee cup.

"Hell of a suggestion."

"Best one I can come up with. Look, friend, you're new here, you've got no family, no ties. You're asking me to take on some prominent families just because you don't get along with them. So why don't you move on? Find someplace smaller, hell, even someplace bigger, where you don't stand out so much. But face it, it's not going to get any easier."

"Real nice folks," I said, letting an edge of bitterness into my voice.

That didn't seem to bother the chief. "That they are. They work hard and play hard, and they pay taxes, too, and they look out for one another. I know they look like hell-raisers to you, but they're more than that. They're part of the community. Why, just next week, a bunch of them are going on a midnight snow run across the lake and into the mountains, raising money for the children's camp up at Lake Montcalm. People who don't care wouldn't do that."

"I just wish they didn't care so much about me."

He shrugged and said, "Look, I'll see what I can do . . ." but the tone of his voice made it clear he wasn't going to do a damn thing.

The chief clambered into his cruiser and drove off, and as I walked past the bays of the service station, I heard snickers. I went around to my pickup truck and saw the source of the merriment.

My truck was resting heavily on four flat tires.

At night I woke up from cold and bloody dreams and let my thoughts drift into fantasies. By now I knew who all of them were, where all of them lived. I could go to their houses, every one of them, and bring them back and bind them in the basement of my home. I could tell them who I was and what I've done and what I can do, and I would ask them to leave me alone. That's it. Just give me peace and solitude and everything will be all right.

And they would hear me out and nod and agree, but I would know that I had to convince them. So I would go to Jerry Tompkins, the mustached one who enjoyed marking my territory, and to make my point, break a couple of his fingers, the popping noise echoing in the dark confines of the tiny basement.

Nice fantasies.

I asked Ron, "What's the point?"

He was comfortable in his chair, hands clasped over his little potbelly. "I'm sorry?"

"The point of our sessions?"

His eyes were unflinching. "To help you adjust."

"Adjust to what?"

"To civilian life."

I shifted on the couch. "Let me get this. I work my entire life for this country, doing service for its civilians. I expose myself to death and injury every week, earning about a third of what I could be making in the private sector. And when I'm through, I have to adjust, I have to make allowances for civilians. But civilians, they don't have to do a damn thing. Is that right?"

"I'm afraid so."

"Hell of a deal."

He continued a steady gaze. "Only one you've got."

So here I am, in the smelly rubble that used to be my home. I make a few half-hearted attempts to turn the furniture back over and do some cleanup work, but I'm not in the mood. Old feelings and emotions are coursing through me, taking control. I take a few deep breaths and then I'm in the cellar, switching on the single lightbulb that hangs down from the rafters by a frayed black cord. As I maneuver among the packing cases, undoing combination locks, my shoulder strikes the lightbulb, causing it to swing back and forth, casting crazy shadows on the stone walls.

The night air is cool and crisp, and I shuffle through the snow around the house as I load the pickup truck, making three trips in all. I drive under the speed limit and halt completely at all top signs as I go through the center of town. I drive around, wasting minutes and hours, listening to the radio. This late at night and being so far north, a lot of the stations that I can pick up are from Quebec, and there's a joyous lilt to the French-Canadian music and words that makes something inside me ache with longing.

When it's almost a new day, I drive down a street called Mast Road. Most towns around here have a Mast Road, where colonial surveyors marked tall pines that would eventually become masts for the Royal Navy. Tonight there are no surveyors, just the night air and darkness and a skinny rabbit racing across the cracked asphalt. When I'm near the target, I switch off the lights and engine and let the truck glide the last few hundred feet or so. I pull up across from a darkened house. A pickup truck and a Subaru station wagon are in the driveway. Gray smoke is wafting up from the chimney.

I roll down the window, the cold air washing over me like a wave of water. I pause, remembering what has gone on these past weeks, and then I get to work.

The nightscope comes up and clicks into action, and the name on the mailbox is clear enough in the sharp green light. TOMPKINS, in silver and black stick-on letters. I scan the two-story Cape Cod, checking out the surroundings. There's an attached garage to the right and a sunroom to the left. There is a front door and two other doors in a breezeway that runs from the garage to the house. There are no rear doors.

I let the nightscope rest on my lap as I reach toward my weapons. The first is a grenade launcher, with a handful of white phosphorus rounds clustered on the seat next to it like a gathering of metal eggs. Next to the grenade launcher is a 9mm Uzi, with an extended wooden stock for easier use. Another night-vision scope with crosshairs is attached to the Uzi.

Another series of deep breaths. Easy enough plan. Pop a white phosphorus round into the breezeway and another into the sunroom. In a minute or two both ends of the house are on fire. Our snowmobiler friend and his family wake up and, groggy from sleep and the fire and the noise, stumble out the front door onto the snow-covered lawn.

With the Uzi in my hand and the crosshairs on a certain face, a face with a mustache, I take care of business and drive to the next house.

I pick up the grenade launcher and rest the barrel on the open window. It's cold. I rub my legs together and look outside at the stars. The wind comes up and snow blows across the road. I hear the low *hoo-hoo-hoo* of an owl.

I bring the grenade launcher up, resting the stock against my cheek. I aim. I wait.

It's very cold.

The weapon begins trembling in my hands and I let it drop to the front seat.

I sit on my hands, trying to warm them while the cold breeze blows. Idiot. Do this and how long before you're in jail, and then on trial before a jury of friends or relatives of those fine citizens you gun down tonight?

I start up the truck and let the heater sigh itself on, and then I roll up the window and slowly drive away, lights still off.

"Fool," I say to myself, "remember who you are." And with the truck's lights now on, I drive home. To what's left of it.

Days later, there's a fresh smell to the air in my house, for I've done a lot of cleaning and painting, trying not only to bring everything back to where it was but also spruce up the place. The only real problem has been in the main room, where the words GO HOME were marked in bright red on the white plaster wall. It took me three coats to cover that up, and of course I ended up doing the entire room.

The house is dark and it's late. I'm waiting on the porch with a glass of wine in my hand, watching a light snow fall on Lake Marie. Every light in the house is off and the only illumination comes from the fireplace, which needs more wood.

But I'm content to dawdle. I'm finally at peace after these difficult weeks in Nansen. Finally, I'm beginning to remember who I really am.

I sip my wine, waiting, and then comes the sound of the snowmobiles. I see their wavering dots of light racing across the lake, doing their bit for charity. How wonderful. I raise my glass in salute, the noise of the snowmobiles getting louder as they head across the lake in a straight line.

I put the wineglass down, walk into the living room, and toss the last few pieces of wood into the fire. The sudden heat warms my face in a pleasant glow. The wood isn't firewood, though. It's been shaped and painted by a man, and as the flames leap up and devour the lumber, I see the letters begin to fade: DANGER! THIN ICE!

I stroll back to the porch, pick up the wineglass, and wait.

Below me, on the peaceful ice of Lake Marie, my new home for my new life, the headlights go by.

And then, one by one, they blink out, and the silence is wonderful.

THE SPECIALTY OF THE HOUSE

(1948)

Stanley Ellin

The reader will likely never forget this story, the most famous ever written by one of the world's most distinguished short story writers. Brooklyn-based Stanley Ellin (1916–1986) won three Edgar Awards, plus the prestigious Grand Master Edgar for lifetime achievement in 1980. His early short stories are collected in *Mystery Stories* (1956), which Julian Symons calls "the finest collection of stories in the crime form published in the past half century." Among Ellin's other books are the brilliant *The Key to Nicholas Street* (1953), the private eye novel *The Eighth Circle* (1958), and *The Specialty of the House and Other Stories* (1979). This story was originally published in *Ellery Queen's Mystery Magazine*.

"And this," said Laffler, "is Sbirro's." Costain saw a square brownstone façade identical with the others that extended from either side into the clammy darkness of the deserted street. From the barred windows of the basement at his feet, a glimmer of light showed behind heavy curtains.

"Lord," he observed, "it's a dismal hole, isn't it?"

"I beg you to understand," said Laffler stiffly, "that Sbirro's is the restaurant without pretensions. Besieged by these ghastly, neurotic times, it has refused to compromise. It is perhaps the last important establishment in this city lit by gas jets. Here you will find the same honest furnishings, the same magnificent Sheffield service, and possibly, in a far corner, the very same spider webs that were remarked by the patrons of a half century ago!"

"A doubtful recommendation," said Costain, "and hardly sanitary."

"When you enter," Laffler continued, "you leave the insanity of this year, this day, and this hour, and you find yourself for a brief span restored in spirit, not by opulence, but by dignity, which is the lost quality of our time."

Costain laughed uncomfortably. "You make it sound more like a cathedral than a restaurant," he said.

In the pale reflection of the street lamp overhead, Laffler peered at his companion's face. "I wonder," he said abruptly, "whether I have not made a mistake in extending this invitation to you."

Costain was hurt. Despite an impressive title and large salary, he was no more than a clerk to this pompous little man, but he was impelled to make some display of his feelings. "If you wish," he said coldly, "I can make other plans for my evening with no trouble."

With his large, cowlike eyes turned up to Costain, the mist drifting into the ruddy, full moon of his face, Laffler seemed strangely ill at ease. Then "No, no," he said at last, "absolutely not. It's important that you dine at Sbirro's with me." He grasped Costain's arm firmly and led the way to the wrought-iron gate of the basement. "You see, you're the sole person in my office who seems to know anything at all about good food. And on my part, knowing about Sbirro's but not having some appreciative friend to share it is like having a unique piece of art locked in a room where no one else can enjoy it."

Costain was considerably mollified by this. "I understand there are a great many people who relish that situation."

"I'm not one of that kind!" Laffler said sharply. "And having the secret of Sbirro's locked in myself for years has finally become unendurable." He fumbled at the side of the gate and from within could be heard the small, discordant jangle of an ancient pull-bell. An interior door opened with a groan, and Costain found himself peering into a dark face whose only discernible feature was a row of gleaming teeth.

"Sair?" said the face.

"Mr. Laffler and a guest."

"Sair," the face said again, this time in what was clearly an invitation. It moved aside and Costain stumbled down a single step behind his host. The door and gate creaked behind him, and he stood blinking in a small foyer. It took him a moment to realize that the figure he now stared at was his own reflection in a gigantic pier glass that extended from floor to ceiling. "Atmosphere," he said under his breath and chuckled as he followed his guide to a seat.

He faced Laffler across a small table for two and peered curiously around the dining room. It was no size at all, but the half-dozen guttering gas jets which provided the only illumination threw such a deceptive light that the walls flickered and faded into uncertain distance.

There were no more than eight or ten tables about, arranged to insure the maximum privacy. All were occupied, and the few waiters serving them moved with quiet efficiency. In the air were a soft clash and scrape of cutlery and a soothing murmur of talk. Costain nodded appreciatively.

Laffler breathed an audible sigh of gratification. "I knew you would share my enthusiasm," he said. "Have you noticed, by the way, that there are no women present?"

Costain raised inquiring eyebrows.

"Sbirro," said Laffler, "does not encourage members of the fair sex to enter the premises. And, I can tell you, his method is decidedly effective. I had the experience of seeing a woman get a taste of it not long ago. She sat at a table for not less than an hour waiting for service which was never forthcoming."

"Didn't she make a scene?"

"She did." Laffler smiled at the recollection. "She succeeded in annoying the customers, embarrassing her partner, and nothing more."

"And what about Mr. Sbirro?"

"He did not make an appearance. Whether he directed affairs from behind the scenes, or was not even present during the episode, I don't know. Whichever it was, he won a complete victory. The woman never reappeared nor, for the matter, did the witless gentleman who by bringing her was really the cause of the entire contretemps."

"A fair warning to all present," laughed Costain.

A waiter now appeared at the table. The chocolate-dark skin, the thin, beautifully molded nose and lips, the large liquid eyes, heavily lashed, and the silver white hair so heavy and silken that it lay on the skull like a cap, all marked him definitely as an East Indian of some sort, Costain decided. The man arranged the stiff table linen, filled two tumblers from a huge, cut-glass pitcher, and set them in their proper places.

"Tell me," Laffler said eagerly, "is the special being served this evening?"

The waiter smiled regretfully and showed teeth as spectacular as those of the majordomo. "I am so sorry, sair. There is no special this evening."

Laffler's face fell into lines of heavy disappointment. "After waiting so long. It's been a month already, and I hoped to show my friend here . . ."

"You understand the difficulties, sair."

"Of course, of course." Laffler looked at Costain sadly and shrugged. "You see, I had in mind to introduce you to the greatest treat that Sbirro's offers, but unfortunately it isn't on the menu this evening."

The waiter said, "Do you wish to be served now, sair?" and Laffler nodded. To Costain's surprise the waiter made his way off without waiting for any instructions.

"Have you ordered in advance?" he asked.

"Ah," said Laffler, "I really should have explained. Sbirro's offers no choice whatsoever. You will eat the same meal as everyone else in this room. Tomorrow evening you would eat an entirely different meal, but again without designating a single preference."

"Very unusual," said Costain, "and certainly unsatisfactory at times. What if one doesn't have a taste for the particular dish set before him?"

"On that score," said Laffler solemnly, "you need have no fears. I give you my word that no matter how exacting your tastes, you will relish every mouthful you eat at Sbirro's."

Costain looked doubtful, and Laffler smiled. "And consider the subtle advantages of the system," he said. "When you pick up the menu of a popular restaurant, you find yourself confronted with innumerable choices. You are forced to weigh, to evaluate, to make uneasy decisions which you may instantly regret. The effect of all this is a tension which, however slight, must make for discomfort.

"And consider the mechanics of the process. Instead of a hurly-burly of sweating cooks rushing about a kitchen in a frenzy to prepare a hundred varying items, we have a chef who stands serenely alone, bringing all his talents to bear on one task, with all assurance of a complete triumph!"

"Then you have seen the kitchen?"

"Unfortunately, no," said Laffler sadly. "The picture I offer is hypothetical, made of conversational fragments I have pieced together over the years. I must admit, though, that my desire to see the functioning of the kitchen here comes very close to being my sole obsession nowadays."

"But have you mentioned this to Sbirro?"

"A dozen times. He shrugs the suggestion away."

"Isn't that a rather curious foible on his part?"

"No, no," Laffler said hastily, "a master artist is never under the compulsion of petty courtesies. Still," he sighed, "I have never given up hope."

The waiter now reappeared bearing two soup bowls which he set in place with mathematical exactitude and a small tureen from which he slowly ladled a measure of clear, thin broth. Costain dipped his spoon into the broth and tasted it with some curiosity. It was delicately flavored, bland to the verge of tastelessness. Costain frowned, tentatively reached for the salt and pepper cellars, and discovered there were none on the table. He looked up, saw Laffler's eyes on him, and although unwilling to compromise with his own tastes, he hesitated to act as a damper on Laffler's enthusiasm. Therefore he smiled and indicated the broth.

"Excellent," he said.

Laffler returned his smile. "You do not find it excellent at all," he said coolly. "You find it flat and badly in need of condiments. I know this," he continued as Costain's eyebrows shot upward, "because it was my own reaction many years ago, and because like yourself I found myself reaching for salt and pepper after the first mouthful. I also learned with surprise that condiments are not available in Sbirro's.

Costain was shocked. "Not even salt!" he exclaimed.

"Not even salt. The very fact that you require it for your soup stands as evidence that your taste is unduly jaded. I am confident that you will now make the same discovery that I did: by the time you have nearly finished your soup, your desire for salt will be nonexistent."

Laffler was right; before Costain had reached the bottom of his plate, he was relishing the nuances of the broth with steadily increasing delight. Laffler thrust aside his own empty bowl and rested his elbows on the table. "Do you agree with me now?"

"To my surprise," said Costain, "I do."

As the waiter busied himself clearing the table, Laffler lowered his voice significantly. "You will find," he said, "that the absence of condiments is but one of several noteworthy characteristics which mark Sbirro's. I may as well prepare you for these. For example, no alcoholic beverages of any sort are served here, nor for that matter any beverage except clear, cold water, the first and only drink necessary for a human being."

"Outside of mother's milk," suggested Costain dryly.

"I can answer that in like vein by pointing out that the average patron of Sbirro's has passed that primal stage of his development."

Costain laughed. "Granted," he said.

"Very well. There is also a ban on the use of tobacco in any form."

"But, good heavens," said Costain, "doesn't that make Sbirro's more a teetotaler's retreat than a gourmet's sanctuary?"

"I fear," said Laffler solemnly, "that you confuse the words, *gourmet* and *gourmand*. The gourmand, through glutting himself, requires a wider and wider latitude of experience to stir his surfeited senses, but the very nature of the gourmet is simplicity. The ancient Greek in his coarse chiton savoring the ripe olive; the Japanese in his bare room contemplating the curves of a single flower stem—these are the true gourmets."

"But an occasional drop of brandy or pipeful of tobacco," said Costain dubiously, "are hardly overindulgence."

"By alternating stimulant and narcotic," said Laffler, "you see-saw the delicate balance of your taste so violently that it loses its most precious quality: the appreciation of fine food. During my years as a patron of Sbirro's, I have proved this to my satisfaction."

"May I ask," said Costain, "why you regard the ban on these things as having such deep esthetic motives? What about such mundane reasons as the high cost of a liquor license, or the possibility that patrons would object to the smell of tobacco in such confined quarters?"

Laffler shook his head violently. "If and when you meet Sbirro," he said, "you will understand at once that he is not the man to make decisions on a mundane basis. As a matter of fact, it was Sbirro himself who first made me cognizant of what you call 'esthetic' motives."

"An amazing man," said Costain as the waiter prepared to serve the entrée.

Laffler's next words were not spoken until he had savored and swallowed a large portion of meat. "I hesitate to use superlatives," he said, "but to my way of thinking, Sbirro represents man at the apex of his civilization!"

Costain cocked an eyebrow and applied himself to his roast which rested in a pool of stiff gravy ungarnished by green or vegetable. The thin steam rising from it carried to his nostrils a subtle, tantalizing odor which made his mouth water. He chewed a piece as slowly and thoughtfully as if he were analyzing the intricacies of a Mozart symphony. The range of taste he discovered was really extraordinary, from the pungent nip of the crisp outer edge to the peculiarly flat, yet soul-satisfying ooze of blood which the pressure of his jaws forced from the half-raw interior.

Upon swallowing he found himself ferociously hungry for another piece, and then another, and it was only with an effort that he prevented himself from wolfing down all his share of the meat and gravy without waiting to get the full voluptuous satisfaction from each mouthful. When he had scraped his platter clean, he realized that both he and Laffler had completed the entire course without exchanging a single word. He commented on this, and Laffler said, "Can you see any need for words in the presence of such food?"

Costain looked around at the shabby, dimly lit room, the quiet diners, with a new perception. "No," he said humbly, "I cannot. For any doubts I had I apologize unreservedly. In all your praise of Sbirro's there was not a single word of exaggeration."

"Ah," said Laffler delightedly. "And that is only part of the story. You heard me mention the special which unfortunately was not on the menu tonight. What you have just eaten is as nothing when compared to the absolute delights of that special!"

"Good Lord!" cried Costain. "What is that? Nightingale's tongues? Filet of unicorn?"

"Neither," said Laffler. "It is lamb."

"Lamb?"

Laffler remained lost in thought for a minute. "If," he said at last, "I were to give you in my own unstinted words my opinion of this dish, you would judge me completely insane. That is how deeply the mere thought of it affects me. It is neither the fatty chop, nor the too solid leg; it is, instead, a select portion of the rarest sheep in existence and is named after the species—lamb Amirstan."

Costain knit his brow. "Amirstan?"

"A fragment of desolation almost lost on the border which separates Afghanistan and Russia. From chance remarks dropped by Sbirro, I gather it is no more than a plateau which grazes the pitiful remnants of a flock of superb sheep. Sbirro, through some means or other, obtained rights to the traffic in this flock and is, therefore, the sole restauranteur ever to have lamb Amirstan on his bill of fare. I can tell you that the appearance of this dish is a rare occurrence indeed, and luck is the only guide in determining for the clientele the exact date when it will be served."

"But surely," said Costain, "Sbirro could provide some advance knowledge of this event."

"The objection to that is simply stated," said Laffler. "There exists in this city a huge number of professional gluttons. Should advance information slip out, it is quite likely that they will, out of curiosity, become familiar with the dish and thenceforth supplant the regular patrons at these tables."

"But you don't mean to say," objected Costain, "that these few people present are they only ones in the entire city, or for that matter, in the whole wide world, who know of the existence of Sbirro's!"

"Very nearly. There may be one or two regular patrons who, for some reason, are not present at the moment."

"That's incredible."

"It is done," said Laffler, the slightest shade of menace in his voice, "by every patron making it his solemn obligation to keep the secret. By accepting my invitation this evening you automatically assume that obligation. I hope you can be trusted with it."

Costain flushed. "My position in your employ should vouch for me. I only question the wisdom of a policy which keeps such magnificent food away from so many who would enjoy it."

"Do you know the inevitable result of the policy *you* favor?" asked Laffler bitterly. "An influx of idiots who would nightly complain that they are never served roast duck with chocolate sauce. Is that picture tolerable to you?"

"No," admitted Costain, "I am forced to agree with you."

Laffler leaned back in his chair wearily and passed his hand over his eyes in an uncertain gesture. "I am a solitary man," he said quietly, "and not by choice alone. It may sound strange to you, it may border on eccentricity, but I feel to my depths that this restaurant, this warm haven in a coldly insane world, is both family and friend to me."

And Costain, who to this moment had never viewed his companion as other than tyrannical employer or officious host, now felt an overwhelming pity twist inside his comfortably expanded stomach.

By the end of two weeks the invitations to join Laffler at Sbirro's had become something of a ritual. Every day, at a few minutes after five, Costain would step out into the office corridor and lock his cubicle behind him; he would drape his overcoat neatly over his left arm, and peer into the glass of the door to make sure his Homburg was set at the proper angle. At one time he would have followed this by lighting a cigarette, but under Laffler's prodding he had decided to give abstinence a fair trial. Then he would start down the corridor, and Laffler would fall in step at his elbow, clearing his throat. "Ah, Costain. No plans for this evening, I hope."

"No," Costain would say, "I'm footloose and fancy-free," or "At your service," or something equally inane. He wondered at times whether it would not be more tactful to vary the ritual with an occasional refusal, but the glow with which Laffler received his answer, and the rough friendliness of Laffler's grip on his arm, forestalled him.

Among the treacherous crags of the business world, reflected Costain, what better way to secure your footing than friendship with one's employer. Already, a secretary close to the workings of the inner office had commented publicly on Laffler's highly favorable opinion of Costain. That was all to the good.

And the food! The incomparable food at Sbirro's! For the first time in his life, Costain, ordinarily a lean and bony man, noted with gratification that he was certainly gaining weight; within two weeks his bones had disappeared under a layer of sleek, firm flesh, and here and there were even signs of incipient plumpness. It struck Costain one night, while surveying himself in his bath, that the rotund Laffler, himself, might have been a spare and bony man before discovering Sbirro's.

So there was obviously everything to be gained and nothing to be lost by accepting Laffler's invitations. Perhaps after testing the heralded wonders of lamb Amirstan and meeting Sbirro, who thus far had not made an appearance, a refusal or two might be in order. But certainly not until then.

That evening, two weeks to a day after his first visit to Sbirro's, Costain had both desires fulfilled: he dined on lamb Amirstan, and he met Sbirro. Both exceeded all his expectations.

When the waiter leaned over their table immediately after seating them and gravely announced: "Tonight is special, sair," Costain was shocked to find his heart pounding with expectation. On the table before him he saw Laffler's hands trembling violently. But it isn't natural, he thought suddenly. Two full grown men, presumably intelligent and in the full possession of their senses, as jumpy as a pair of cats waiting to have their meat flung at them!

"This is it!" Laffler's voice startled him so that he almost leaped from his seat. "The culinary triumph of all times! And faced by it you are embarrassed by the very emotion it distills."

"How did you know that?" Costain asked faintly.

"How? Because a decade ago I underwent your embarrassment. Add to that your air of revulsion and it's easy to see how affronted you are by the knowledge that man has not yet forgotten how to slaver over his meat."

"And these others," whispered Costain, "do they all feel the same thing?"

"Judge for yourself."

Costain looked furtively around at the nearby tables. "You are right," he finally said. "At any rate, there's comfort in numbers."

Laffler inclined his head slightly to the side. "One of the numbers," he remarked, "appears to be in for a disappointment."

Costain followed the gesture. At the table indicated a gray-haired man sat conspicuously alone, and Costain frowned at the empty chair opposite him.

"Why, yes," he recalled, "that very stout, bald man, isn't it? I believe it's the first dinner he's missed here in two weeks."

"The entire decade more likely," said Laffler sympathetically. "Rain or shine, crisis or calamity, I don't think he's missed an evening at Sbirro's since the first time I dined here. Imagine his expression when he's told that, on his very first defection, lamb Amirstan was the *plat de jour*."

Costain looked at the empty chair again with a dim discomfort. "His very first?" he murmured.

"Mr. Laffler! And friend! I am so pleased. So very, very pleased. No, do not stand; I will have a place made." Miraculously a seat appeared under the figure standing there at the table. "The lamb Amirstan will be an unqualified success, hurr? I myself have been stewing in the miserable kitchen all the day, prodding the foolish chef to do everything just so. The just so is the important part, hurr? But I see your friend does not know me. An introduction, perhaps?"

The words ran in a smooth, fluid eddy. They rippled, they purred, they hypnotized Costain so that he could do no more than stare. The mouth that uncoiled this sinuous monologue was alarmingly wide, with thin mobile lips that curled and twisted with every syllable. There was a flat nose with a straggling line of hair under it; wide-set eyes, almost oriental in appearance, that glittered in the unsteady flare of gaslight; and the long, sleek hair that swept back from high on the unwrinkled forehead—hair so pale that it might have been bleached of all color. An amazing face surely, and the sight of it tortured Costain with the conviction that it was somehow familiar. His brain twitched and prodded but could not stir up any solid recollection.

Laffler's voice jerked Costain out of his study. "Mr. Sbirro. Mr. Costain, a good friend and associate." Costain rose and shook the proffered hand. It was warm and dry, flint-hard against his palm.

"I am so very pleased, Mr. Costain. So very, very pleased," purred the voice. "You like my little establishment, hurr? You have a great treat in store, I assure you."

Laffler chuckled. "Oh, Costain's been dining here regularly for two weeks," he said. "He's by way of becoming a great admirer of yours, Sbirro."

The eyes were turned on Costain. "A very great compliment. You compliment me with your presence and I return same with my food, hurr? But the lamb Amirstan is far superior to anything of your past experience, I assure you. All the trouble of obtaining it, all the difficulty of preparation, is truly merited."

Costain strove to put aside the exasperating problem of that face. "I have wondered," he said, "why with all these difficulties you mention, you even bother to present lamb Amirstan to the public. Surely your other dishes are excellent enough to uphold your reputation."

Sbirro smiled so broadly that his face became perfectly round. "Perhaps it is a matter of the psychology, hurr? Someone discovers a wonder and must share it with others. He must fill his cup to the brim, perhaps, by observing the so evident pleasure of those who explore it with him. Or," he shrugged, "perhaps it is just a matter of good business."

"Then in the light of all this," Costain persisted, "and considering all the conventions you have imposed on your customers, why do you open the restaurant to the public instead of operating it as a private club?"

The eyes abruptly glinted into Costain's, then turned away. "So perspicacious, hurr? Then I will tell you. Because there is more privacy in a public eating place than in the most exclusive club in existence! Here no one inquires of your affairs; no one desires to know the intimacies of your life. Here the business is eating. We are not curious about names and addresses or the reasons for the coming and going of our guests. We welcome you when you are here; we have no regrets when you are here no longer. That is the answer, hurr?"

Costain was startled by this vehemence. "I had no intention of prying," he stammered.

Sbirro ran the tip of his tongue over his thin lips. "No, no," he reassured, "you are not prying. Do not let me give you that impression. On the contrary, I invite your questions."

"Oh, come, Costain," said Laffler. "Don't let Sbirro intimidate you. I've know him for years and I guarantee that his bark is worse than his bite. Before you know it, he'll be showing you all the privileges of the house—outside of inviting you to visit his precious kitchen, of course."

"Ah," smiled Sbirro, "for that, Mr. Costain may have to wait a little while. For everything else I am at his beck and call."

Laffler slapped his hand jovially on the table. "What did I tell you!" he said. "Now let's have the truth, Sbirro. Has anyone, outside of your staff, ever stepped into the sanctum sanctorum?"

Sbirro looked up. "You see on the wall above you," he said earnestly, "the portrait of one to whom I did the honor. A very dear friend and a patron of most long standing, he is evidence that my kitchen is not inviolate."

Costain studied the picture and started with recognition. "Why," he said excitedly, "that's the famous writer—you know the one, Laffler—he used to do such wonderful short stories and cynical bits and then suddenly took himself off and disappeared in Mexico!"

"Of course!" cried Laffler, "and to think I've been sitting under his portrait for years without even realizing it!" He turned to Sbirro. "A dear friend, you say? His disappearance must have been a blow to you."

Sbirro's face lengthened. "It was, it was, I assure you. But think of it this way, gentlemen: he was probably greater in his death than in his life, hurr? A most tragic man, he often told me that his only happy hours were spent here at this very table. Pathetic, is it not? And to think the only favor I could ever show him was to let him witness the mysteries of my kitchen, which is, when all is said and done, no more than a plain, ordinary kitchen."

"You seem very certain of his death," commented Costain. "After all, no evidence has ever turned up to substantiate it."

Sbirro contemplated the picture. "None at all," he said softly. "Remarkable, hurr?"

With the arrival of the entrée Sbirro leaped to his feet and set about serving them himself. With his eyes alight he lifted the casserole from the tray and sniffed at the fragrance from within with sensual relish. Then, taking great care not to lose a single drop of gravy, he filled two platters with chunks of dripping meat. As if exhausted by this task, he sat back in his chair, breathing heavily. "Gentlemen," he said, "to your good appetite."

Costain chewed his first mouthful with great deliberation and swallowed it. Then he looked at the empty tines of his fork with glazed eyes.

"Good God!" he breathed.

"It is good, hurr? Better than you imagined?"

Costain shook his head dazedly. "It is as impossible," he said slowly, "for the uninitiated to conceive the delights of lamb Amirstan as for mortal man to look into his own soul."

"Perhaps—" Sbirro thrust his head so close that Costain could feel the warm, fetid breath tickle his nostrils—"perhaps you have just had a glimpse into your soul, hurr?"

Costain tried to draw back slightly without giving offense. "Perhaps." He laughed. "And a gratifying picture it made: all fang and claw. But without intending any disrespect, I should hardly like to build my church on *lamb en casserole*."

Sbirro rose and laid a hand gently on his shoulder. "So perspicacious," he said. "Sometimes when you have nothing to do, nothing, perhaps, but sit for a very little while in a dark room and think of this world—what it is and what it is going to be—then you must turn your thoughts a little to the significance of the Lamb in religion. It will be so interesting. And now—" he bowed deeply to both men—"I have held you long enough from your dinner. I was most happy," he said, nodding to Costain, "and I am sure we will meet again." The teeth gleamed, the eyes glittered, and Sbirro was gone down the aisle of tables.

Costain twisted around to stare after the retreating figure. "Have I offended him in some way?" he asked.

Laffler looked up from his plate. "Offended him? He loves that kind of talk. Lamb Amirstan is a ritual with him; get him started and he'll be back at you a dozen times worse than a priest making a conversion."

Costain turned to his meal with the face still hovering before him. "Interesting man," he reflected. "Very."

It took him a month to discover the tantalizing familiarity of that face, and when he did, he laughed aloud in his bed. Why, of course! Sbirro might have sat as the model for the Cheshire cat in *Alice*!

He passed this thought on to Laffler the very next evening as they pushed their way down the street to the restaurant against a chill, blustering wind. Laffler only looked blank.

"You may be right," he said, "but I'm not a fit judge. It's a far cry back to the days when I read the book. A far cry, indeed."

As if taking up his words, a piercing howl came ringing down the street and stopped both men short in their tracks. "Someone's in trouble there," said Laffler. "Look!"

Not far from the entrance to Sbirro's two figures could be seen struggling in the near darkness. They swayed back and forth and suddenly tumbled into a writhing heap on the sidewalk. The piteous howl went up again, and Laffler, despite his girth, ran toward it at a fair speed with Costain tagging cautiously behind.

Stretched out full-length on the pavement was a slender figure with the dusky complexion and white hair of one of Sbirro's servitors. His fingers were futilely plucking at the huge hands which encircled his throat, and his knees pushed weakly up to the gigantic bulk of a man who brutally bore down with his full weight.

Laffler came up panting. "Stop this!" he shouted. "What's going on here?"

The pleading eyes almost bulging from their sockets turned toward Laffler. "Help, sair. This man—drunk—"

"Drunk am I, ya dirty—" Costain saw now that the man was a sailor in a badly soiled uniform. The air around him reeked with the stench of liquor. "Pick me pocket and then call me drunk, will ya!" He dug his fingers in harder, and his victim groaned.

Laffler seized the sailor's shoulder. "Let go of him, do you hear! Let go of him at once!" he cried, and the next instant was sent careening into Costain, who staggered back under the force of the blow.

The attack on his own person sent Laffler into immediate and berserk action. Without a sound he leaped at the sailor, striking and kicking furiously at the unprotected face and flanks. Stunned at first, the man came to his feet with a rush and turned on Laffler. For a moment they stood locked together, and then as Costain joined the attack, all three went sprawling to the ground. Slowly Laffler and Costain got to their feet and looked down at the body before them.

"He's either out cold from liquor," said Costain, "or he struck his head going down. In any case, it's a job for the police."

"No, no, sair!" The waiter crawled weakly to his feet, and stood swaying. "No police, sair. Mr. Sbirro do not want such. You understand, sair." He caught hold of Costain with a pleading hand, and Costain looked at Laffler.

"Of course not," said Laffler. "We won't have to bother with the police. They'll pick him up soon enough, the murderous sot. But what in the world started all this?"

"That man, sair. He make most erratic way while walking, and with no meaning I push against him. Then he attack me, accusing me to rob him."

"As I thought." Laffler pushed the waiter gently along. "Now go in and get yourself attended to."

The man seemed ready to burst into tears. "To you, sair, I owe my life. If there is anything I can do—"

Laffler turned into the areaway that led to Sbirro's door. "No, no, it was nothing. You go along, and if Sbirro has any questions send him to me. I'll straighten it out."

"My life, sair," were the last words they heard as the inner door closed behind them.

"There you are, Costain," said Laffler, as a few minutes later he drew his chair under the table, "civilized man in all his glory. Reeking with alcohol, strangling to death some miserable innocent who came too close."

Costain made an effort to gloss over the nerve-shattering memory of the episode. "It's the neurotic cat that takes to alcohol," he said. "Surely there's a reason for that sailor's condition."

"Reason? Of course there is. Plain atavistic savagery!" Laffler swept his arm in all-embracing gesture. "Why do we all sit here at our meat? Not only to appease physical demands, but because our atavistic selves cry for release. Think back, Costain. Do you remember that I once described Sbirro as the epitome of civilization? Can you now see why? A brilliant man, he fully understands the nature of human beings. But unlike lesser men he bends all his efforts to the satisfaction of our innate nature without resultant harm to some innocent bystander."

"When I think back on the wonders of lamb Amirstan," said Costain, "I quite understand what you're driving at. And, by the way, isn't it nearly due to appear on the bill of fare? It must have been over a month ago that it was last served."

The waiter, filling the tumblers, hesitated. "I am so sorry, sair. No special this evening."

"There's your answer," Laffler grunted, "and probably just my luck to miss out on it altogether the next time."

Costain stared at him. "Oh, come, that's impossible."

"No, blast it." Laffler drank off half his water at a gulp and the waiter immediately refilled the glass. "I'm off to South America for a surprise tour of inspection. One month, two months, Lord knows how long."

"Are things that bad down there?"

"They could be better." Laffler suddenly grinned. "Mustn't forget it takes very mundane dollars and cents to pay the tariff at Sbirro's."

"I haven't heard a word of this around the office."

"Wouldn't be a surprise tour if you had. Nobody knows about this except myself—and now you. I want to walk in on them completely unexpected. Find out what flimflammery they're up to down there. As far as the office is concerned, I'm off on a jaunt somewhere. Maybe recuperating in some sanatorium from my hard work. Anyhow, the business will be in good hands. Yours, among them."

"Mine?" said Costain, surprised.

"When you go in tomorrow you'll find yourself in receipt of a promotion, even if I'm not there to hand it to you personally. Mind you, it has nothing to do with our friendship either; you've done fine work, and I'm immensely grateful for it."

Costain reddened under the praise. "You don't expect to be in tomorrow. Then you're leaving tonight?"

Laffler nodded. "I've been trying to wangle some reservations. If they come through, well, this will be in the nature of a farewell celebration."

"You know," said Costain slowly. "I devoutly hope that your reservations don't come through. I believe our dinners here have come to mean more to me than I ever dared imagine."

The waiter's voice broke in. "Do you wish to be served now, sair?" and they both started.

"Of course, of course," said Laffler sharply, "I didn't' realize you were waiting."

"What bothers me," he told Costain as the waiter turned away, "is the thought of the lamb Amirstan I'm bound to miss. To tell you the truth, I've already put off my departure a week, hoping to hit a lucky night, and now I simply can't delay any more. I do hope that when you're sitting over your share of lamb Amirstan, you'll think of me with suitable regrets."

Costain laughed. "I will indeed," he said as he turned to his dinner.

Hardly had he cleared the plate when a waiter silently reached for it. It was not their usual waiter, he observed; it was none other than the victim of the assault.

"Well," Costain said, "how do you feel now? Still under the weather?"

The waiter paid no attention to him. Instead, with the air of a man under great strain, he turned to Laffler. "Sair," he whispered. "My life. I owe it to you. I can repay you!"

Laffler looked up in amazement, then shook his head firmly. "No," he said. "I want nothing from you, understand? You have repaid me sufficiently with your thanks. Now get on with your work and let's hear no more about it."

The waiter did not stir an inch, but his voice rose slightly. "By the body and blood of your God, sair, I will help you even if you do not want! *Do not go into the kitchen, sair.* I trade you my life for yours, sair, when I speak this. Tonight or any night of your life, do not go into the kitchen at Sbirro's!"

Laffler sat back, completely dumbfounded. "Not go into the kitchen? Why shouldn't I go into the kitchen if Mr. Sbirro ever took it into his head to invite me there? What's all this about?"

A hard hand was laid on Costain's back, and another gripped the waiter's arm. The waiter remained frozen to the spot, his lips compressed, his eyes downcast.

"What is all *what* about, gentlemen?" purred the voice. "So opportune an arrival. In time as ever, I see, to answer all the questions, hurr?"

Laffler breathed a sigh of relief. "Ah, Sbirro, thank heaven you're here. This man is saying something about my not going into your kitchen. Do you know what he means?"

The teeth showed in a broad grin. "But, of course. This good man was giving you advice in all amiability. It so happens that my too emotional chef heard some rumor that I might have a guest into his precious kitchen, and he flew into a fearful rage. Such a rage, gentlemen! He even threatened to give notice on the spot, and you can understand what that would mean to Sbirro's, hurr? Fortunately, I succeeded in showing him what a signal honor it is to have an esteemed patron and true connoisseur observe him at his work first-hand, and now he is quite amenable. Quite, hurr?"

He released the waiter's arm. "You are at the wrong table," he said softly. "See that it does not happen again."

The waiter slipped off without daring to raise his eyes and Sbirro drew a chair to the table. He seated himself and brushed his hand lightly over his hair. "Now I am afraid that the cat is out of the bag, hurr? This invitation to you, Mr. Laffler, was to be a surprise; but the surprise is gone, and all that is left is the invitation."

Laffler mopped beads of perspiration from his forehead. "Are you serious?" he said huskily. "Do you mean that we are really to witness the preparation of your food tonight?"

Sbirro drew a sharp fingernail along the tablecloth, leaving a thin, straight line printed in the linen. "Ah," he said, "I am faced with a dilemma of great proportions." He studied the line soberly. "You, Mr. Laffler, have been my guest for ten long years. But our friend here—"

Costain raised his hand in protest. "I understand perfectly. This invitation is solely to Mr. Laffler, and naturally my presence is embarrassing. As it happens, I have an early engagement for this evening and must be on my way anyhow. So you see there's no dilemma at all, really."

"No," said Laffler, "absolutely not. That wouldn't be fair at all. We've been sharing this until now, Costain, and I won't enjoy the experience half as much if you're not along. Surely Sbirro can make his conditions flexible, this one occasion."

They both looked at Sbirro who shrugged his shoulders regretfully.

Costain rose abruptly. "I'm not going to sit here, Laffler, and spoil your great adventure. And then, too," he bantered, "think of that ferocious chef waiting to get his cleaver on you. I prefer not to be at the scene. I'll just say goodbye," he went on, to cover Laffler's guilty silence, "and leave you to Sbirro. I'm sure he'll take pains to give you a good show." He held out his hand and Laffler squeezed it painfully hard.

"You're being very decent, Costain," he said. "I hope you'll continue to dine here until we meet again. It shouldn't be too long."

Sbirro made way for Costain to pass. "I will expect you," he said. "*Au 'voir.*"

Costain stopped briefly in the dim foyer to adjust his scarf and fix his Homburg at the proper angle. When he turned away from the mirror, satisfied at last, he saw with a final glance that Laffler and Sbirro were already at the kitchen door, Sbirro holding the door invitingly wide with one hand, while the other rested, almost tenderly, on Laffler's meaty shoulders.

SUSPICION

(1933)

Dorothy L. Sayers

In the following story a woman employed as a cook is supposed to have poisoned a family with arsenic. The cook disappears and the police are baffled. Has the cook reappeared elsewhere and is she up to her old tricks? Despite its grim theme, the story is lighthearted, with a nice touch of sardonic humor.

Dorothy L. Sayers (1893–1957) is one of the most important figures in the annals of mystery fiction. She created the character Lord Peter Wimsey, an aristocratic sleuth who stars in such novels as *Unnatural Death* (1927), *Strong Poison* (1930), and *The Five Red Herrings* (1933), and short story collections such as *Lord Peter Views the Body* (1928). Sayers also edited the twelve-hundred-page *Omnibus of Crime* in 1929, one of the first major mystery anthologies. Despite her enormous popularity as a British mystery writer, Sayers stopped writing in the field in 1940. She turned her attention to writing religious books, poetry, and plays.

"Suspicion" was first published in *Mystery League Magazine*.

As the atmosphere of the railway carriage thickened with tobacco smoke, Mr. Mummery became increasingly aware that his breakfast had not agreed with him.

There could have been nothing wrong with the breakfast itself. Brown bread, rich in vitamin content, as advised by the *Morning Star*'s health expert; bacon fried to a delicious crispness; eggs just nicely set; coffee made as only Mrs. Sutton knew how to make it. Mrs. Sutton had been a real find, and that was something to be thankful for. For Ethel, since her nervous breakdown in the summer, had really not been fit to wrestle with the untrained girls who had come and gone in tempestuous succession. It took very little to upset Ethel nowadays, poor child. Mr. Mummery, trying hard to ignore his growing internal discomfort, hoped he was not in for an illness. Apart from the trouble it would cause at the office, it would worry Ethel terribly, and Mr. Mummery would cheerfully have laid down his rather uninteresting little life to spare Ethel a moment's uneasiness.

He slipped a digestive tablet into his mouth—he had taken lately to carrying a few tablets about with him—and opened his paper. There did not seem to be very much news. A question had been asked in the House about Government typewriters. The Prince of Wales had smilingly opened an all-British exhibition of footwear. A further split had occurred in the Liberal party. The police were still looking for the woman who was supposed to have poisoned a family in Lincoln. Two girls had been trapped in a burning factory. A film star had obtained her fourth decree nisi.

At Paragon Station, Mr. Mummery descended and took a tram. The internal discomfort was taking form of a definite nausea. Happily he contrived to reach his office before the worst occurred. He was seated at his desk, pale but in control of himself, when his partner came breezing in.

"'Morning, Mummery," said Mr. Brookes in his loud tones, adding inevitably, "Cold enough for you?"

"Quite," replied Mr. Mummery. "Unpleasantly raw, in fact."

"Beastly, beastly," said Mr. Brookes. "Your bulbs all in?"

"Not quite all," confessed Mr. Mummery. "As a matter of fact I haven't been feeling—"

"Pity," interrupted his partner. "Great pity. Ought to get 'em in early. Mine were in last week. My little place will be a picture in the spring. For a town garden, that is. You're lucky, living in the country. Find it better than Hull, I expect, eh? Though we get plenty of fresh air up in the Avenues. How's the missus?"

"Thank you, she's very much better."

"Glad to hear that, very glad. Hope we shall have her about again this winter as usual. Can't do without her in the Drama Society, you know. By Jove I shan't forget her acting last year in 'Romance.' She and young Welbeck positively brought the house down, didn't they? The Welbecks were asking after her only yesterday."

"Thank you, yes. I hope she will soon be able to take up her social activities again. But the doctor says she mustn't overdo it. No worry, he says—that's the important thing. She is to go easy and not rush about or undertake too much."

"Quite right, quite right. Worry's the devil and all. I cut out worrying years ago and look at me! Fit as a fiddle, for all I shan't see fifty again. *You're* not looking altogether the thing, by the way."

"A touch of dyspepsia," said Mr. Mummery. "Nothing much. Chill on the liver, that's what I put it down to."

"That's what it is," said Mr. Brookes, seizing his opportunity. "Is life worth living? It depends upon the liver. Ha, ha! Well now, well now—we must do a spot of work, I suppose. Where's that lease of Ferraby's?"

Mr. Mummery, who did not feel at his conversational best that morning, rather welcomed this suggestion, and for half an hour was allowed to proceed in peace with the duties of an estate agent. Presently, however, Mr. Brookes burst into speech again.

"By the way," he said abruptly, "I suppose your wife doesn't know of a good cook, does she?"

"Well, no," replied Mr. Mummery. "They aren't so easy to find nowadays. In fact, we've only just got suited ourselves. But why? Surely your old Cookie isn't leaving you?"

"Good lord, no!" Mr. Brookes laughed heartily. "It would take an earthquake to shake off old Cookie. No. It's for the Philipsons. Their girl's getting married. That's the worst of girls. I said to Philipson, 'You mind what you're doing,' I said. 'Get somebody you know something about, or you may find yourself landed with this poisoning woman—what's her name—Andrews. Don't want to be sending wreaths to your funeral yet awhile,' I said. He laughed, but it's no laughing matter and so I told him. What we pay the police for I simply don't know. Nearly a month now, and they can't seem to lay hands on the woman. All they say is, they think she's hanging about the neighbourhood and 'may seek a situation as cook.' As cook! Now I ask you!"

"You don't think she committed suicide, then?" suggested Mr. Mummery.

"Suicide my foot!" retorted Mr. Brookes coarsely. "Don't you believe it, my boy. That coat found in the river was all eyewash. *They* don't commit suicide, that sort don't."

"What sort?"

"Those arsenic maniacs. They're too damned careful of their own skins. Cunning as weasels, that's what they are. It's only to be hoped they'll manage to catch her before she tries her hand on anybody else. As I told Philipson—"

"You think Mrs. Andrews did it, then?"

"Did it? Of course she did it. It's plain as the nose on your face. Looked after her old father, and he died suddenly—left her a bit of money, too. Then she keeps house for an elderly gentleman, and *he* dies suddenly. Now there's the husband and wife—man dies and woman taken very ill, of arsenic poisoning. Cook runs away, and you ask, did she do it? I don't mind betting that when they dig up the father and the other old bird they'll find *them* bung full of arsenic, too. Once that sort gets started, they don't stop. Grows on 'em, as you might say."

"I suppose it does," said Mr. Mummery. He picked up his paper again and studied the photograph of the missing woman. "She looks harmless enough," he remarked. "Rather a nice, motherly-looking kind of woman."

"She's got a bad mouth," pronounced Mr. Brookes. He had a theory that character showed in the mouth. "I wouldn't trust that woman an inch."

As the day went on, Mr. Mummery felt better. He was rather nervous about his lunch, choosing carefully a little boiled fish and custard pudding and being particular not to rush about immediately after the meal. To his great relief, the fish and custard remained where they were put, and he was not visited by that tiresome pain which had become almost habitual in the last fortnight. By the end of the day he became quite light-hearted. The bogey of illness and doctor's bills ceased to haunt him. He bought a bunch of bronze chrysanthemums to carry home to Ethel, and it was with a feeling of pleasant anticipation that he left the train and walked up the garden path of *Mon Abri*.

He was a little dashed by not finding his wife in the sitting room. Still clutching the bunch of chrysanthemums he pattered down the passage and pushed open the kitchen door.

Nobody was there but the cook. She was sitting at the table with her back to him, and started up almost guiltily as he approached.

"Lor', sir," she said, "you gave me quite a start. I didn't hear the front door go."

"Where is Mrs. Mummery? Not feeling bad again, is she?"

"Well, sir, she's got a bit of a headache, poor lamb. I made her lay down and took her up a nice cup o' tea at half past four. I think she's dozing nicely now."

"Dear, dear," said Mr. Mummery.

"It was turning out the dining room done it, if you ask me," said Mrs. Sutton. "'Now, don't you overdo yourself, ma'am,' I says to her, but you know how she is, sir. She gets that restless, she can't abear to be doing nothing."

"I know," said Mr. Mummery. "It's not your fault, Mrs. Sutton. I'm sure you look after us both admirably. I'll just run up and have a peep at her. I won't disturb her if she's asleep. By the way, what are we having for dinner?"

"Well, I *had* made a nice steak-and-kidney pie," said Mrs. Sutton, in accents suggesting that she would readily turn it into a pumpkin or a coach and four if it was not approved of.

"Oh!" said Mr. Mummery. "Pastry? Well, I—"

"You'll find it beautiful and light," protested the cook, whisking open the oven door for Mr. Mummery to see. "And it's made with butter, sir, you having said that you found lard indigestible."

"Thank you, thank you," said Mr. Mummery. "I'm sure it will be most excellent. I haven't been feeling altogether the thing just lately, and lard does not seem to suit me nowadays."

"Well, it don't suit some people, and that's a fact," agreed Mrs. Sutton. "I shouldn't wonder if you've got a bit of a chill on the liver. I'm sure this weather is enough to upset anybody."

She bustled to the table and cleared away the picture paper which she had been reading.

"Perhaps the mistress would like her dinner sent up to her?" she suggested.

Mr. Mummery said he would go and see, and tiptoed his way upstairs. Ethel was lying snuggled under the eiderdown and looked very small and fragile in the big double bed. She stirred as he came in and smiled up to him.

"Hullo, darling!" said Mr. Mummery.

"Hullo! You back? I must have been asleep. I got tired and headachy, and Mrs. Sutton packed me off upstairs."

"You've been doing too much, sweetheart," said her husband, taking her hand in his and sitting down on the edge of the bed.

"Yes—it was naughty of me. What lovely flowers, Harold. All for me?"

"All for you, Tiddleywinks," said Mr. Mummery tenderly. "Don't I deserve something for that?"

Mrs. Mummery smiled, and Mr. Mummery took his reward several times over.

"That's quite enough, you sentimental old thing," said Mrs. Mummery. "Run away, now, I'm going to get up."

"Much better go to bed, my precious, and let Mrs. Sutton send your dinner up," said her husband.

Ethel protested, but he was firm with her. If she didn't take care of herself, she wouldn't be allowed to go to the Drama Society meetings. And everybody was so anxious to have her back. The Welbecks had been asking after her and saying that they really couldn't get on without her.

"Did they?" said Ethel with some animation. "It's very sweet of them to want me. Well, perhaps I'll go to bed after all. And how has my old Hubby been all day?"

"Not too bad, not too bad."

"No more tummyaches?"

"Well, just a *little* tummyache. But it's quite gone now. Nothing for Tiddleywinks to worry about."

Mr. Mummery experienced no more distressing symptoms the next day or the next. Following the advice of the newspaper expert, he took to drinking orange juice, and was delighted with the results of the treatment. On Thursday, however, he was taken so ill in the night that Ethel was alarmed and insisted on sending for the doctor. The doctor felt his pulse and looked at his tongue and appeared to take the matter lightly. An inquiry into what he had been eating elicited the fact that dinner had consisted of pig's trotters, followed by a milk pudding, and that, before retiring, Mr. Mummery had consumed a large glass of orange juice, according to his new régime.

"There's your trouble," said Dr. Griffith cheerfully. "Orange juice is an excellent thing, and so are trotters, but not in combination. Pig and oranges together are extraordinarily bad for the liver. I don't know why they should be, but there's no doubt that they are. Now I'll send you round a little prescription and you stick to slops for a day or two and keep off pork. And don't you worry about him, Mrs. Mummery, he's as sound as a trout. *You're* the one we've got to look after. I don't want to see those black rings under the eyes, you know. Disturbed night, of course—yes. Taking your tonic regularly? That's right. Well, don't be alarmed about your hubby. We'll soon have him out and about again."

The prophecy was fulfilled, but not immediately. Mr. Mummery, though confining his diet to Benger's food, bread and milk and beef tea skilfully prepared by Mrs. Sutton and brought to his bedside by Ethel, remained very seedy all through Friday, and was only able to stagger rather shakily downstairs on Saturday afternoon. He had evidently suffered a "thorough upset." However, he was able to attend to a few papers which Brookes had sent down from the office for his signature, and to deal with the household books. Ethel was not a business woman, and Mr. Mummery always ran over the accounts with her. Having settled up with the butcher, the baker, the dairy and the coal merchant, Mr. Mummery looked up inquiringly.

"Anything more, darling?"

"Well, there's Mrs. Sutton. This is the end of her month, you know."

"So it is. Well, you're quite satisfied with her, aren't you, darling?"

"Yes, rather—aren't you? She's a good cook, and a sweet, motherly old thing, too. Don't you think it was a real brain wave of mine, engaging her like that, on the spot?"

"I do, indeed," said Mr. Mummery.

"It was a perfect providence, her turning up like that, just after that wretched Jane had gone off without even giving notice. I was in absolute *despair*. It was a little bit of a gamble, of course, taking her without any references, but naturally, if she'd been looking after a widowed mother, you couldn't expect her to give references."

"N-no," said Mr. Mummery. At the time he had felt uneasy about the matter, though he had not liked to say much because, of course, they simply had to have somebody. And the experiment had justified itself so triumphantly in practice that one couldn't say much about it now. He had once rather tentatively suggested writing to the clergyman of Mrs. Sutton's parish but, as Ethel had said, the clergyman wouldn't have been able to tell them anything about cooking, and cooking, after all, was the chief point.

Mr. Mummery counted out the month's money.

"And by the way, my dear," he said, "you might just mention to Mrs. Sutton that if she *must* read the morning paper before I come down, I should be obliged if she would fold it neatly afterwards."

"What an old fuss-box you are, darling," said his wife.

Mr. Mummery sighed. He could not explain that it was somehow important that the morning paper should come to him fresh and prim, like a virgin. Women did not feel these things.

On Sunday, Mr. Mummery felt very much better—quite his old self, in fact. He enjoyed the *News of the World* over breakfast in bed, reading the murders rather carefully. Mr. Mummery got quite a lot of pleasure out of murders—they gave him an agreeable thrill of vicarious adventure, for, naturally, they were matters quite remote from daily life in the outskirts of Hull.

He noticed that Brookes had been perfectly right. Mrs. Andrews's father and former employer had been "dug up" and had, indeed, proved to be "bung full" of arsenic.

He came downstairs for dinner—roast sirloin, with the potatoes done under the meat and Yorkshire pudding of delicious lightness, and an apple tart to follow. After three days of invalid diet, it was delightful to savour the crisp fat and underdone lean. He ate moderately, but with a sensuous enjoyment. Ethel, on the other hand, seemed a little lacking in appetite, but then, she had never been a great meat eater. She was fastidious and, besides, she was (quite unnecessarily) afraid of getting fat.

It was a fine afternoon, and at three o'clock, when he was quite certain that the roast beef was "settling" properly, it occurred to Mr. Mummery that it would be a good thing to put the rest of those bulbs in. He slipped on his old gardening coat and wandered out to the potting shed. Here he picked up a bag of tulips and a trowel, and then, remembering that he was wearing his good trousers, decided that it would be wise to take a mat to kneel on. When had he had the mat last? He could not recollect, but he rather fancied he had put it away in the corner under the potting shelf. Stooping down, he felt about in the dark among the flower pots. Yes, there it was, but there was a tin of something in the way. He lifted the tin carefully out. Of course, yes—the remains of the weed killer.

Mr. Mummery glanced at the pink label, printed in staring letters with the legend: "ARSENICAL WEED KILLER. *Poison*," and observed, with a mild feeling of excitement, that it was the same brand of stuff that had been associated with Mrs. Andrews's latest victim. He was rather pleased about it. It gave him a sensation of being remotely but definitely in touch with important events. Then he noticed, with surprise and a little annoyance, that the stopper had been put in quite loosely.

"However'd I come to leave it like that?" he grunted. "Shouldn't wonder if all the goodness has gone off." He removed the stopper and squinted into the can, which appeared to be half-full. Then he rammed the thing home again, giving it a sharp thump with the handle of the trowel for better security. After that he washed his hands carefully at the scullery tap, for he did not believe in taking risks.

He was a trifle disconcerted, when he came in after planting the tulips, to find visitors in the sitting room. He was always pleased to see Mrs. Welbeck and her son, but he would rather have had warning, so that he could have scrubbed the garden mould out of his nails more thoroughly. Not that Mrs. Welbeck appeared to notice. She was a talkative woman and paid little attention to anything but her own conversation. Much to Mr. Mummery's annoyance, she chose to prattle about the Lincoln Poisoning Case. A most unsuitable subject for the tea table, thought Mr. Mummery, at the best of times. His own "upset" was vivid enough in his memory to make him queasy over the discussion of medical symptoms, and besides, this kind of talk was not good for

Ethel. After all, the poisoner was still supposed to be in the neighbourhood. It was enough to make even a strong-nerved woman uneasy. A glance at Ethel showed him that she was looking quite white and tremulous. He must stop Mrs. Welbeck somehow, or there would be a repetition of one of the old, dreadful, hysterical scenes.

He broke into the conversation with violent abruptness.

"Those Forsyth cuttings, Mrs. Welbeck," he said. "Now is just about the time to take them. If you care to come down the garden I will get them for you."

He saw a relieved glance pass between Ethel and young Welbeck. Evidently the boy understood the situation and was chafing at his mother's tactlessness. Mrs. Welbeck, brought up all standing, gasped slightly and then veered off with obliging readiness on the new tack. She accompanied her host down the garden and chattered cheerfully about horticulture while he selected and trimmed the cuttings. She complimented Mr. Mummery on the immaculacy of his gravel paths. "I simply *cannot* keep the weeds down," she said.

Mr. Mummery mentioned the weed killer and praised its efficacy.

"That stuff!" Mrs. Welbeck stared at him. Then she shuddered. "I wouldn't have it in my place for a thousand pounds," she said, with emphasis.

Mr. Mummery smiled. "Oh, we keep it well away from the house," he said. "Even if I were a careless sort of person—"

He broke off. The recollection of the loosened stopper had come to him suddenly, and it was as though, deep down in his mind, some obscure assembling of ideas had taken place. He left it at that, and went into the kitchen to fetch a newspaper to wrap up the cuttings.

Their approach to the house had evidently been seen from the sitting room window, for when they entered, young Welbeck was already on his feet and holding Ethel's hand in the act of saying good-bye. He maneuvered his mother out of the house with tactful promptness and Mr. Mummery returned to the kitchen to clear up the newspapers he had fished out of the drawer. To clear them up and to examine them more closely. Something had struck him about them, which he wanted to verify. He turned them over very carefully, sheet by sheet. Yes—he had been right. Every portrait of Mrs. Andrews, every paragraph and line about the Lincoln Poisoning Case, had been carefully cut out.

Mr. Mummery sat down by the kitchen fire. He felt as though he needed warmth. There seemed to be a curious cold lump of something at the pit of his stomach—something that he was chary of investigating.

He tried to recall the appearance of Mrs. Andrews as shown in the newspaper photographs, but he had not a good visual memory. He remembered having remarked to Brookes that it was a "motherly" face. Then he tried counting up the time since the disappearance. Nearly a month, Brookes had said—and that was a week ago. Must be over a month now. A month. He had just paid Mrs. Sutton her month's money.

"Ethel!" was the thought that hammered at the door of his brain. At all costs, he must cope with this monstrous suspicion on his own. He must spare her any shock or anxiety. And he must be sure of his ground. To dismiss the only decent cook they had ever had out of sheer, unfounded panic, would be wanton cruelty to both women. If he did it at all, it would have to be done arbitrarily, preposterously—he could not suggest horrors to Ethel. However it was done, there would be trouble. Ethel would not understand and he dared not tell her.

But if by any chance there was anything in this ghastly doubt—how could he expose Ethel to the appalling danger of having the woman in the house a moment longer? He thought of the family at Lincoln—the husband dead, the wife escaped by a miracle with her life. Was not any shock, any risk, better than that?

Mr. Mummery felt suddenly very lonely and tired. His illness had taken it out of him.

Those illnesses—they had begun, when? Three weeks ago he had had the first attack. Yes, but then he had always been rather subject to gastric troubles. Bilious attacks. Not so violent, perhaps, as these last, but undoubted bilious attacks.

He pulled himself together and went, rather heavily, into the sitting room. Ethel was tucked up in a corner of the chesterfield.

"Tired, darling?"

"Yes, a little."

"That woman has worn you out with talking. She oughtn't to talk so much."

"No." Her head shifted wearily in the cushions. "All about that horrible case. I don't like hearing about such things."

"Of course not. Still, when a thing like that happens in the neighbourhood, people will gossip and talk. It would be a relief if they caught the woman. One doesn't like to think—"

"I don't want to think of anything so hateful. She must be a horrible creature."

"Horrible. Brookes was saying the other day—"

"I don't want to hear what he said. I don't want to hear about it at all. I want to be quiet. I want to be quiet!"

He recognised the note of rising hysteria.

"Tiddleywinks shall be quiet. Don't worry, darling. We won't talk about horrors."

No. It would not do to talk about them.

Ethel went to bed early. It was understood that on Sundays Mr. Mummery should sit up till Mrs. Sutton came in. Ethel was a little anxious about this, but he assured her that he felt quite strong enough. In body, indeed, he did; it was his mind that felt weak and confused. He had decided to make a casual remark about the mutilated newspapers—just to see what Mrs. Sutton would say.

He allowed himself the usual indulgence of a whiskey and soda as he sat waiting. At a quarter to ten he heard the familiar click of the garden gate. Footsteps passed up the gravel—squeak, squeak, to the back-door. Then the sound of the latch, the shutting of the door, the rattle of the bolts being shot home. Then a pause. Mrs. Sutton would be taking off her hat. The moment was coming.

The step sounded in the passage. The door opened. Mrs. Sutton in her neat black dress stood on the threshold. He was aware of a reluctance to face her. Then he looked up. A plump-faced woman, her eyes obscured by thick horn-rimmed spectacles. Was there, perhaps, something hard about the mouth? Or was it just that she had lost most of her front teeth?

"Would you be requiring anything tonight, sir, before I go up?"

"No thank you, Mrs. Sutton."

"I hope you are feeling better, sir." Her eager interest in his health seemed to him almost sinister, but the eyes, behind the thick glasses, were inscrutable.

"Quite better, thank you, Mrs. Sutton."

"Mrs. Mummery is not indisposed, is she, sir? Should I take her up a glass of hot milk or anything?"

"No, thank you, no." He spoke hurriedly, and fancied that she looked disappointed.

"Very well, sir. Good night, sir."

"Good night. Oh! by the way, Mrs. Sutton—"

"Yes, sir?"

"Oh, nothing," said Mr. Mummery, "nothing."

Next morning Mr. Mummery opened his paper eagerly. He would have been glad to learn that an arrest had been made over the weekend. But there was no news for him. The chairman of a trust company had blown out his brains, and the headlines were all occupied with tales about lost millions and ruined shareholders. Both in his own paper and in those he purchased on the way to the office, the Lincoln Poisoning Tragedy had been relegated to an obscure paragraph on a back page, which informed him that the police were still baffled.

The next few days were the most uncomfortable that Mr. Mummery had ever spent. He developed a habit of coming down early in the morning and prowling about the kitchen. This made Ethel nervous, but Mrs. Sutton offered no remark. She watched him tolerantly, even, he thought, with something like amusement. After all, it was ridiculous. What was the use of supervising the breakfast, when he had to be out of the house every day between half past nine and six?

At the office, Brookes rallied him on the frequency with which he rang up Ethel. Mr. Mummer paid no attention. It was reassuring to hear her voice and to know that she was safe and well.

Nothing happened, and by the following Thursday he began to think that he had been a fool. He came home late that night. Brookes had persuaded him to go with him to a little bachelor dinner for a friend who was about to get married. He left the others at eleven o'clock, however, refusing to make a night of it. The household was in bed when he got back but a note from Mrs. Sutton lay on the table, informing him that there was cocoa for him in the kitchen, ready for hotting up. He hotted it up accordingly in the little saucepan where it stood. There was just one good cupful.

He sipped it thoughtfully, standing by the kitchen stove. After the first sip, he put the cup down. Was it his fancy, or was there something queer about the taste? He sipped it again, rolling it upon his tongue. It seemed to him to have a faint tang, metallic and unpleasant. In a sudden dread he ran out to the scullery and spat the mouthful into the sink.

After this, he stood quite still for a moment or two. Then, with a curious deliberation, as though his movements had been dictated to him, he fetched an empty medicine bottle from the pantry shelf, rinsed it under the tap and tipped the contents of the cup carefully into it. He slipped the bottle into his coat pocket and moved on tiptoe to the back door. The bolts were difficult to draw without noise, but he managed it at last. Still on tiptoe, he stole across the garden to the potting shed. Stooping down, he struck a match. He knew exactly where he had left the tin of weed killer, under the shelf behind the pots at the back. Cautiously he lifted it out. The match flared up and burnt his fingers, but before he could light another his sense of touch had told him what he wanted to know. The stopper was loose again.

Panic seized Mr. Mummery, standing there in the earthy-smelling shed, in his dress suit and overcoat, holding the tin in one hand and the match box in the other. He wanted very badly to run and tell somebody what he had discovered.

Instead, he replaced the tin exactly where he had found it and went back to the house. As he crossed the garden again, he noticed a light in Mrs. Sutton's bedroom window. This terrified him more than anything which had gone before. Was she watching him? Ethel's window was dark. If she had drunk anything deadly there would be lights everywhere, movements, calls for the doctor, just as when he himself had been attacked. Attacked—that was the right word, he thought.

Still with the same odd presence of mind and precision, he went in, washed out the utensils and made a second brew of cocoa, which he left standing in the saucepan. He crept quietly to his bedroom. Ethel's voice greeted him on the threshold.

"How late you are, Harold. Naughty old boy! Have a good time?"

"Not bad. You all right, darling?"

"Quite all right. Did Mrs. Sutton leave something hot for you? She said she would."

"Yes, but I wasn't thirsty."

Ethel laughed. "Oh! it was *that* sort of party, was it?"

Mr. Mummery did not attempt any denials. He undressed and got into bed and clutched his wife to him as though defying death and hell to take her from him. Next morning he would act. He thanked God that he was not too late.

Mr. Dimthorpe, the chemist, was a great friend of Mr. Mummery's. They had often sat together in the untidy little shop on Spring Bank and exchanged views on green-fly and club-root. Mr. Mummery told his story frankly to Mr. Dimthorpe and handed over the bottle of cocoa. Mr. Dimthorpe congratulated him on his prudence and intelligence.

"I will have it ready for you by this evening," he said, "and if it's what you think it is, then we shall have a clear case on which to take action."

Mr. Mummery thanked him, and was extremely vague and inattentive at business all day. But that hardly mattered, for Mr. Brookes, who had seen the party through to a riotous end in the small hours, was in no very observant mood. At half past four, Mr. Mummery shut up his desk decisively and announced that he was off early, he had a call to make.

Mr. Dimthorpe was ready for him.

"No doubt about it," he said. "I used Marsh's test. It's a heavy dose—no wonder you tasted it. There must be four or five grains of pure arsenic in that bottle. Look, here's the mirror. You can see it for yourself."

Mr. Mummery gazed at the little glass tube with its ominous purple-black stain.

"Will you ring up the police from here?" asked the chemist.

"No," said Mr. Mummery. "No—I want to get home. God knows what's happening there. And I've only just time to catch my train."

"All right," said Mr. Dimthorpe. "Leave it to me. I'll ring them up for you."

The local train did not go fast enough for Mr. Mummery. Ethel—poisoned—dying—dead—Ethel—poisoned—dying—dead—the wheels drummed in his ears. He almost ran out of the station and along the road. A car was standing at his door. He saw it from the end of the street and broke into a gallop. It had happened already. The doctor was there. Fool, murderer that he was to have left things so late.

Then, while he was still a hundred and fifty yards off, he saw the front door open. A man came out followed by Ethel herself. The visitor got into his car and was driven away. Ethel went in again. She was safe—safe!

He could hardly control himself to hang up his hat and coat and go in looking reasonably calm. His wife had returned to the armchair by the fire and greeted him in some surprise. There were tea things on the table.

"Back early, aren't you?"

"Yes—business was slack. Somebody been to tea?"

"Yes, young Welbeck. About the arrangements for the Drama Society." She spoke briefly but with an undertone of excitement.

A qualm came over Mr. Mummery. Would a guest be any protection? His face must have shown his feelings, for Ethel stared at him in amazement.

"What's the matter, Harold, you look so queer."

"Darling," said Mr. Mummery, "there's something I want to tell you about." He sat down and took her hand in his. "Something a little unpleasant, I'm afraid—"

"Oh, ma'am!"

The cook was in the doorway.

"I beg your pardon, sir—I didn't know you was in. Will you be taking tea or can I clear away? And, oh, ma'am, there was a young man at the fish-monger's and he's just come from Grimsby and they've caught that dreadful woman—that Mrs. Andrews. Isn't it a good thing? It's worritted me dreadful to think she was going about like that, but they've caught her. Taken a job as housekeeper she had to two elderly ladies and they found the wicked poison on her. Girl as spotted her will get a reward. I been keeping my eyes open for her, but it's at Grimsby she was all the time."

Mr. Mummery clutched at the arm of his chair. It had all been a mad mistake then. He wanted to shout or cry. He wanted to apologise to this foolish, pleasant, excited woman. All a mistake.

But there had been the cocoa. Mr. Dimthorpe. Marsh's test. Five grains of arsenic. Who, then—?

He glanced around at his wife, and in her eyes he saw something that he had never seen before. . . .

THE ADVENTURE OF THE NEEDLE'S EYE

(1946)

Ellery Queen

The famous detective Ellery Queen is on a treasure hunt in this yarn (he's also credited as its author). None other than British privateer turned pirate William Kidd is supposed to have buried his booty on an island owned by Queen's client. Oddly enough, in 2007 Indiana University archeologists identified remnants of Captain Kidd's actual ship, the *Quedagh Merchant*, which had long eluded treasure hunters. Kidd had abandoned the ship in the Caribbean in 1699 when he went to New York City to try to clear his name.

The author is universally recognized as a master of mystery and detective stories, especially because *Ellery Queen's Mystery Magazine* is the most important outlet in the field today. In 1960 he was awarded the Grand Master Edgar. Yet the name Ellery Queen is in fact a pseudonym used by Frederic Dannay (1905–1982) and Manfred B. Lee (1905–1971). They collaborated on thirty-nine novels beginning with *The Roman Hat Mystery* (1929), as well as numerous short story collections. Among Queen's other novels are *Cat of Many Tales* (1949), *The Glass Village* (1954), and *The Hollywood Murders* (1957). His best short story collection is *Calendar of Crime* (1946), which includes the story below.

This being a tale of pirates and stolen treasure, it is a gratification to record that it all happened in that season of the year to which the moonstone and the poppy are traditionally dedicated. For the moonstone is a surprisingly moral object. To its lawful owner it brings nothing but good: Held in the mouth at the full of the moon, it reveals the future; it heats the lover and it cools the heated; it cures epilepsy; it fructifies trees; and so on. But rue and blight upon him who lays thievish hands on it, for then it invokes the black side of its nature and brings down upon the thief nothing but evil. Such exact justice is unarguably desirable in a story of piracy which, while boasting no moonstones—although there were buckets of other gems—did reach its apogee in Augustus Caesar's month, which is the moonstone's month. And the poppy springs from the blood of the slain, its scarlet blooms growing thickest on battlefields and in places of carnage. So it is a poetic duty to report that there is murder in this August tale, too.

The sea-robber involved was master of the galley *Adventure*, a Scotsman who was thoroughly hanged in London's Execution Dock two centuries and a half ago—alas, on a day in May—and whose name ever since has stood for piracy in general. Ellery had tangled with historical characters before, but never with one so exciting as this; and it must be confessed that he embarked on the case of Captain Kidd's treasure with a relish more suitable to a small boy in his first hot pursuit of Mr. Legrand's golden *scarabaeus* than to a weary workman in words and the case-hardened son of a modern New York policeman.

And then there was Eric Ericsson.

Ericsson was that most tragic of men, an explorer in an age when nothing of original note remained on earth to be explored. He had had to content himself with being, not the first in anything, but the farthest, or the highest, or the deepest. Where five channels in the Northwest Passage were known, Ericsson opened a sixth. He found a peak in Sikang Province of western China, in the Amne Machin Range, which was almost a thousand feet higher than Everest, but he lost his instruments and his companions and Mount Everest remained on the books the highest mountain on the planet. Ericsson went farther and wider in the great Juf depression of the Sahara than the Citroën expedition, but this did not salve the nettling fact that other men had blazed the trail. And so it had gone all his life. Now in middle age, broken in health, Ericsson rested on his bitter fame—honorary fellowships and medals from all the proper learned societies, membership and officership in clubs like the Explorers', Cosmos, Athenaeum—and brooded over his memories in his New York apartment or, occasionally, at the fireside of the old stone house on the island he owned off Montauk Point, Long Island.

Ellery had heard the story of William Kidd and Ericsson's Island as a result of his first meeting with Ericsson at the Explorers' Club. Not from Ericsson—their introduction had been by the way and their conversation brief; if any discoveries had been made it was by Ericsson, who explored Ellery with far swifter economy than that explorer in other spheres would have believed possible of anyone but himself. Then the large, burned, bowed man had shuffled off, leaving Ellery to quiz his host of the evening, a cartographer of eminence. When this amiable personae mentioned Ericsson's Island and the buccaneer of the *Adventure* in adjoining breaths, Ellery's bow plunged into the wind.

"You mean you've never heard that yarn?" asked the cartographer with the incredulity of the knowledgeable man. "I thought everyone had!" And he gripped his glass and set sail.

An Ericsson had taken possession of the little island in the fourth quarter of the seventeenth century, and he had managed to hold on to it through all the proprietary conflicts of that brawling era. Along the way the Northman acquired a royal patent which somehow weathered the long voyage of colonial and American history.

"Now did Kidd know Ericsson's Island?" asked the cartographer, settling himself as if for argument. "The circumstantial evidence is good. We know that in 1691, for instance, he was awarded £150 by the council of New York for his services during the disturbances in the colony 'after the rebellion of 1688.' And then, of course, there was the treasure found on Gardiner's Island off the tip of Long Island after Kidd's arrest in 1699 on a charge of murder and piracy. On a clear day you can see Ericsson's Island from Gardiner's Island with a glass. How could he have missed it?"

"It's your story," said Ellery judicially. "Go on."

William Kidd served respectably against the French in the West Indies, the cartographer continued, and in 1695 he was in London. Recommended as fit to command a vessel for the king, Captain Kidd received the royal commission to arrest all freebooters and *boucaniers*, and he sailed the galley *Adventure* from Plymouth in 1696 into a life, not of arresting pirates, but of outpirating them.

"The rest is history," said the cartographer, "although some of it is dubious history. We do know that in 1698 or thereabout he was in these parts in a small sloop. Well, the story has persisted for two hundred and fifty years that during this period—when Kidd deserted the *Adventure* in Madagascar and took to the sloop, eventually working his way to these waters—he paid a visit to Ericsson's Island."

"To Gardiner's Island," corrected Ellery.

"*And* Ericsson's," said his host stubbornly. "Why not? About £14,000 was recovered from Kidd's vessel and from Gardiner's Island afterward; there must have been a great deal more than that. Why, John Avery—'Long Ben'—once grabbed off 100,000 pieces of eight in a single haul, and a Mogul's daughter to boot!

"What happened to the rest of Kidd's booty? Is it likely he'd have cached it all in one place? He knew he was in for serious trouble—he tried to bribe Governor Bellomont, you'll recall. And with Ericsson's Island so handy . . ."

"What's the story?" murmured Ellery.

"Oh, that he put into the cove there with a small boat one night, by a ruse got into the Ericsson house—the original's still standing, by the way, beautifully preserved—gave Ericsson and his family fifteen minutes to get off the island, and used the place as his headquarters for a few days. When Kidd cleared out, to be seized and shipped to England shortly after, the Ericssons went back to their island—"

"And perforated it fore and aft and amidships for the treasure Kidd presumably buried there," said Ellery, trying to sound amused.

"Well, certainly," said the cartographer peevishly. "Wouldn't you have?"

"But they never found it."

"Neither they nor their heirs or assigns. But that doesn't mean it isn't there, Queen."

"Doesn't mean it is, either."

Nevertheless, Ellery went home that night feeling as if he had spent the evening in a hurricane off the Spanish Main, clinging to the wild rigging.

It was not quite two weeks later, in a mid-August spell of Dry Tortugan weather, that Eric Ericsson telephoned. The explorer sounded remote, as if deep—at least six fathoms deep—affairs were on his mind.

"Could you see me confidentially, Mr. Queen? I know you're a busy man, but if it's possible—"

"Are you calling from town, Mr. Ericsson?"

"Yes."

"You come right on over!"

Nikki could not understand Ellery's excitement. "Buried treasure," she sniffed. "A grown man."

"Women," pontificated Mr. Queen, "have no imagination."

"I suppose that's true," said his secretary coolly, "if you mean the kind that heats up at a bucket of nasty gore and a couple of rum-soaked yo-ho-hos. Who ever heard of a lady pirate?"

"Two of the bloodiest pirates in the business were Anne Bonny and Mary Read."

"Then they were no ladies!"

Twenty minutes later the doorbell rang and Nikki, still sniffishly, admitted the owner of the island whose clamshells had once been crunched by the tread of Captain Kidd and his cutthroat crew.

"Glad you didn't waste any time getting here, Mr. Ericsson," said Ellery enthusiastically. "The sooner we get going on it—"

"You know why I'm here?" The explorer frowned.

"It doesn't take a math shark to put a couple of twos together."

"What on earth are you talking about?"

"Oh, come, Mr. Ericsson," chortled Ellery. "If it's Nikki you're worried about, I assure you that not only is she the custodian of all my secrets, she also has no interest whatsoever in buried treasure."

"Buried treasure?" Ericsson waved a charred hand impatiently. "That's not what I wanted to see you about."

"It's . . . not?"

"I've never put any stock in that yarn, Mr. Queen. In fact, the whole picture of Kidd as a pirate in my opinion is a myth and historical libel. Kidd was the goat of a political intrigue, I'm convinced, not a pirate at all. Dalton's book presented some pretty conclusive evidence. If it's real pirates you're after, look up Bartholomew Roberts. Roberts took over four hundred ships during his career."

"Then the story of Kidd's seizure of Ericsson's Island—?"

"He may have visited the island around 1698, but if it was to bury anything I've never seen the slightest evidence of it. Mr. Queen, I'd like to tell you why I came."

"Yes," sighed Ellery, and Nikki felt almost sorry for him.

Ericsson's problem involved romance, it appeared, but not the kind that glittered under pirate moons. His only sister, a widow, had died shortly after Ericsson's retirement, leaving a daughter. The explorer's relationship with his sister had been distant, and he had last seen her child, Inga, as a leggy creature of twelve with a purple pimple on her nose. But at the sister's funeral he found himself embraced as "Uncle Eric" by a golden Norse goddess of nineteen. His niece was alone in the world and she had clung to him. Ericsson, a bachelor, found the girl filling a need he had never dreamed existed. Inga left college and came to live with him as his ward, the consolation of his empty retirement, and the sole heir of his modest fortune.

At first they were inseparable—in Ericsson's New York household, at the stone house on the island during long weekends. But Inga began to glow, and the moths came. They were young moths and they rather interfered. So Ericsson—selfishly, he admitted—had his yacht refurbished and sailed Inga away on a cruise of the Caribbean.

"Biggest mistake of my life," the explorer shrugged. "We stopped over in the Bahamas, and there Inga met a young Britisher, Anthony Hobbes-Watkins, who was living a gentlemanly beachcomber sort of existence out of Lyford Cay, at the other end of New Providence Island. It was Inga's first serious love affair. I should have taken her away immediately. When I woke up, it was too late."

"Elopement?" asked Nikki hopefully.

"No, no, Miss Porter, it was a cathedral wedding. I couldn't stand in Inga's way. And I really had nothing definite to go on."

Ellery said: "There's something fishy about Hobbes-Watkins?"

"I don't know, Mr. Queen." Ericsson's heavy, burned-out face remained expressionless, but not his eyes. "That's what I want you to find out."

"What do you know about him?"

"Only what he's told me and a few things I've picked up. Captaincy in the RAF during the war, and not much of anything since—I don't hold that against him, it's a rocky world. All the British upper class attainments—shoots well, plays an earnest game of polo, grouses about the fading star of empire; that sort of thing. Knew all the right people in Nassau; but he hadn't been there long.

"His father, a Colonel Hobbes-Watkins, came on from somewhere—England, he said—for the wedding," continued the explorer, and he shrugged again. "A stout, red, loud, horsy specimen, nearly a caricature of his type. They seem to have plenty of money, so it can't be that. But there *is* . . . something, a mystery, a vagueness about them that keeps disturbing me. They're like figures on a movie screen—you see them move, you hear them talk, but they never seem flesh and blood. Two-dimensional . . . I'm not saying this well," said Ericsson, flushing. "When a man's tramped mountains and deserts and jungles all his life, as I have, he develops in extra sense." He looked up. "I don't trust them."

"I suppose," said Nikki, "your niece does."

"Well, Inga's young and unsophisticated, and she's very much in love. That's what makes it so awkward. But she's become important to me, and for her sake I can't let this go on unless I'm satisfied she hasn't made some awful mistake."

"Have you noticed anything different since the wedding, Mr. Ericsson?" asked Ellery. "A change in their attitude?"

The explorer scraped the bark of his neck with a limp handkerchief. But he said defiantly, "They whisper together."

Ellery raised his brows.

But Ericsson went on doggedly. "Right after the wedding Colonel Hobbes-Watkins left for the States. On business, he said. I gave the yacht to Inga and Tony for a three-week honeymoon. On their way back they picked me up in Nassau and we sailed up to New York, meeting Tony's father here . . . On three different occasions I've come on the Hobbes-Watkinses having whispered conversations which break off like a shot. I don't like it, Mr. Queen. I don't like it to such an extent," said Ericsson quietly, "that I've deliberately kept us all in the city instead of doing the sensible thing in this heat and living down at the island. My island is pretty isolated, and it would make the ideal setting for a . . . Instead of which, Tony and Inga have my apartment, I'm stopping at one of my clubs, and the Colonel is sweating it out politely in a midtown hotel—business, unspecified, still keeping him in the States. But I can't stall any longer. Inga's been after me now for weeks to shove off for the Point, and she's beginning to look at me queerly. I've had to promise we'd all go down this weekend for the rest of the summer."

"It would make the ideal setting," said Ellery, "for a what?"

"You'll think I'm cracked."

"For a what, Mr. Ericsson?"

"All right!" The explorer gripped the arms of his chair. "For a murder," he muttered.

Nikki stared. "Oh, I'm sure—" she began.

But Ellery's foot shifted and somehow crushed Nikki's little toe. "Murder of whom, Mr. Ericsson?"

"Inga! Me! Both of us—I don't know!" He controlled himself with an effort. "Maybe I'm hallucinated. But I tell you those two are scoundrels and my island would be a perfect place for whatever they're up to. What I'd like you to do, Mr. Queen, is come down this weekend for an indefinite stay. Will you?"

Ellery glanced at his secretary; Nikki was often his umpire when he was playing the game of working. But she was regarding him with the grim smile of a spectator.

"Come down, too, Miss Porter," said the explorer, misinterpreting the glance. "Inga will love having you. Besides, your coming will make it appear purely social. I don't want Inga having the least suspicion that . . . Don't bother about a wardrobe; we lead the most primitive life on the island. And there's plenty of room; the house has tripled its original size. About the fee, Mr. Queen—"

"We'll discuss fees," murmured Ellery, "when there's something to charge a fee for. We'll be there, Mr. Ericsson. I can't leave, however, before Saturday morning. When are you planning to go down?"

"Friday." The explorer looked worried.

"I don't imagine they'd try anything the very first night," said Ellery soothingly. "And you're not exactly a helpless old gaffer."

"Good lord! You don't think it's myself I'm concerned about! It's Inga . . . married and . . ." Ericsson stopped abruptly. Then he smiled and rose. "Of course you're right. I'll have the launch waiting for you at Montauk Point. You don't know how this relieves me."

"But won't your niece suspect something by the mere fact of Ellery's being invited down?" asked Nikki. "Unless, Ellery, you cook up one of your stories."

"How's this?" beamed Ellery. "I met Mr. Ericsson at the Explorers' Club recently, heard the family tale about Captain Kidd's treasure, I couldn't resist it, and I'm coming down to try to solve a two-hundred-and-fifty-year-old mystery. Simple?"

"Simply perfect," exclaimed Ericsson. "Inga's had them half-believing this yarn ever since the Bahamas, and if I talk it up for the rest of the week you'll have them under your feet—they'll follow you around like tourists. See you both Saturday."

"It's simple, all right," said Nikki when the explorer had gone. "The simple truth! Shall I pack your extra cutlass, my bucko—and a couple of all-day suckers?"

Eric Ericsson and his niece met them at Montauk Point Saturday morning and hurtled them over blue water in a noisy launch. It was hard to think of wickedness. Inga was a big solid blonde girl with the uncomplicated loveliness of the North, friendly and charming and—Nikki thought—happy as a newlywed could be. The day was stainless, the sun brilliant, the horizon picketed with racing sails; a salt breeze blew the girls' hair about, and the world looked a jolly place. Even Ericsson was composed, as if he had slept unexpectedly well or the presence of serene, golden-legged Inga gave him the strength to dissemble his fears.

"I think it's so thrilling," Inga cried over the roar of the launch. "And Tony and the Colonel have talked of nothing else since Uncle Eric told us why you were coming down, Mr. Queen. Do you really feel there's hope?"

"I try to," Ellery shouted. "By the way, I'm disappointed. I thought your husband and father-in-law might be with you in the launch."

"Oh, that's Uncle Eric's fault," the girl said, and the explorer smiled. He kidnapped me before I could scream for help."

"Guilty." Ericsson's grip on the wheel gave the lie to his smile. "I don't see much of you now that you're Mrs. Hobbes-Watkins."

"Darling, I'm glad you kidnapped me. I really am."

"Even though Mr. Hobbes-Watkins is probably fit to be tied?"

Inga looked happy.

But Nikki, the sun notwithstanding, felt a chill. Ericsson had been afraid to leave Inga alone on the island with her husband and father-in-law.

Ellery kept chattering to Inga about the paragon she had married, while Ericsson stood quietly over the wheel. Nikki could have told the great man that he was wasting his celebrated breath: the girl was in the first heaven of wedded bliss, where the beloved hangs in space clothed in perfect light and there is no past.

From the horizon rose a seaweed-hung otter with a fish in its mouth, which changed rapidly into a long low-lying island thinly wooded and running down to a white beach and a pretty cove. As the launch drew near, they made out a shed, a boathouse, and a jetty. A lank, disjointed something stuck up from the jetty like a piece of driftwood. It turned surprisingly into a one-legged old man. His left leg was gone at the knee; the trouser of his bleached, fishy jeans was pinned back over the stump; and to the stump there was strapped a crude, massive pegleg. With a skin resembling the shed's corrugated roof, a nose that was a twist of bone, crafty and secretive eyes, and a greasy bandana tied behind his ears against the sun, the peglegged old man looked remarkably like a pirate; and Nikki said so.

"That's why we call him Long John," Inga said as her uncle maneuvered the launch toward the jetty. "At least Tony and I do. Uncle Eric calls him Fleugelheimer, or something as ridiculous, though I suppose it's his name. He's not very bright, and he has no manners at all. Hi, Long John!" she called. "Catch the line."

The old man hopped sidewise with great agility and caught the line, poorly tossed, in his powerful right hand. Immediately he wheeled on Ericsson, his bony jaws grinding.

"Bloodsucker!" he yelled.

"Now, John," said the explorer with a sigh.

"When ye givin' me more money?"

"John, we have guests . . ."

"Or d'ye want me to quit? Ye want me to quit!"

"Make the line fast," said Ericsson with a faint smile.

"I'm a poor man," whined the old pirate, obeying. Suddenly he squinted sidewise at Ellery. "This the great detective?"

"Yes, John."

"Henh!" said Long John, and he spat into the water, grinning evilly. He seemed to have forgotten all about his grievance.

"He's been on the island for years," Ericsson explained as they went up a rough path in the woods. "My caretaker. Surly old devil—not all there. He's a miser—hoards every penny I give him, and keeps dunning me for more with the regularity of a parrot. I ignore him and we get along fine."

And there was the stone house at the hump of the island's back. Clean wings stretched from a central building whose stones were grimy with weathered age. The old part of the house rose in a clapboard tower. The tower was square, with several small windows from which, Ellery thought, the whole island and a great spread of the sea must be visible. Undoubtedly the lookout tower of the original structure.

To one side of the house someone—Ericsson, or one of his more recent forebears—had built a rough but comfortable terrace. It was paved with oyster shells and there was a huge barbecue pit.

Two men—one portly and middleaged, the other slim and young—rose from deckchairs waving frosty glasses.

And the instant Ellery laid eyes on the Hobbes-Watkinses he knew Eric Ericsson had been right.

It was hard to say why. They were almost professionally British, especially Colonel Hobbes-Watkins, but that did not account for it; and for the rest of the day Ellery devoted himself to this riddle. He did not solve it.

On the surface the men were plausible. Inga's husband was handsome in a thin, underdone way; he slouched and lolled as if he were hopelessly tired; speech seemed forced out of him; and he drank a good deal. This was the very picture of the young postwar European, spoiled, sick, and disenchanted. Still . . . The elder Hobbes-Watkins was Colonel Blimp to the life, fussing and blustery and full of oldfashioned prejudices. A warmed-over mutton roast, as Nikki promptly dubbed him in a mumble. But there was something in the Colonel's bloated eye and occasionally in his blasting tone that had a lean and cynical energy in it, not at all in character.

During the afternoon Ellery, playing his role of historical detective, set off on a survey of the island. Inga, Tony, and the Colonel insisted on accompanying him.

Long John was fishing from a dory off the cove. When he spied them, he deliberately turned his back.

Ellery began to saunter along the beach, the others trotting eagerly behind.

"Needn't be bashful," he called, mindful of Inga between the two ogres at his back. "I'm merely casing the joint. Come up here, Inga."

"Casing the joint," wheezed Colonel Hobbes-Watkins. "Very good, haha! But I say, won't we trample the clues?"

"Not much danger of that, Colonel," said Ellery cheerfully, "after two and a half centuries. Inga, do join me."

"Glad I ambled along," said Tony Hobbes-Watkins in a languid voice. It sounded queerly dutiful for a groom. Ellery was conscious of the man's eyes; they kept a staring watch.

They went around the island in an hour. It was long and narrow and swelled to a ridge in the middle. The vegetation was scrubby and poor. There was no close anchorage except off the cove. None of the trees, which might have been landmarks, looked old; the island was exposed to the sea, and centuries of winter gales had kept it pruned.

"I don't suppose," Ellery asked Inga as they climbed the path back to the house in the dusk, "the story has ever had any documentation? Chart, map—anything like that?"

"Nothing that still exists. But it's said that there was once a letter or diary page or something left by the 1698 Ericsson—it's been lost, if it ever existed at all—telling about the clue in Captain Kidd's room, and of course that's been the big mystery ever since."

"Clue? Kidd's room?" exclaimed Ellery. "No one's mentioned that!"

"Didn't Eric tell you?" murmured the younger Englishman. "Fantastic fellow, Eric. No imagination."

"I wondered why you hadn't steamed up there immediately," panted the Colonel. "Fancy your uncle's not telling Mr. Queen the most exciting part of it, Inga! It's the chamber the pirate watched the sea from when he took the island over—didn't you say, my dear?"

"The tower room," said Inga, pointing through the dusk. "*That* was in the lost letter, and the reference to the clue Kidd left there."

"Clue left in the tower room?" Ellery squinted through the twilight hungrily. "And that's the original room up there, Inga?"

"Yes."

"What was the clue?"

But the terrace and Long John at the barbeque pit intervened; and since the one-legged caretaker was brandishing a veritable trident as he glowered at the latecomers, Ellery was not answered.

They had dinner. A great moon rose, and the air turned chilly. Ellery wandered to the edge of the terrace with his plate, and a moment later Eric Ericsson joined him.

"Well?" the explorer asked.

"Nothing tangible, Mr. Ericsson. But I agree—there's something in the wind."

"What about tonight? I've put you next to the Colonel's room, and I have an automatic, but Inga . . . alone with . . ."

"I've already fixed that. By a happy coincidence Nikki is going to be so nervous tonight in this primeval setting that she'll just have to sleep with somebody. Since she's had a strict upbringing, that means with Inga, the only other female here. A dirty trick to play on a new husband," said Ellery dryly, "but Tony can console himself with the prospect of a good night's sleep in the room next to mine." Ericsson pressed Ellery's arm rather pathetically. "For the rest of the evening, Mr. Ericsson," murmured Ellery, "please follow my lead. I'm going to be treasure-hunting like mad."

"Ha. Caught you whispering," said a voice at Ellery's elbow; it was young Hobbes-Watkins with a glass in his hand. "Pumping Eric about that clue, eh, Queen?"

"We were just getting round to it," said Ellery. "Girls couldn't take it, I see." Inga and Nikki were gone.

"Driven to cover by the mosquitoes and gnats," boomed the Colonel, slapping himself. "Lovely children, but females, what? Ah, there, you dog, don't shake your head at your old bachelor father! The moon's bloody, and it's the hour for high adventure, didn't some chap say? About that clue, Mr. Queen . . ."

"Yes, you never said a word to me about Captain Kidd's room, Mr. Ericsson," said Ellery reproachfully. "What's all this about a clue he's supposed to have left up there?"

"It's characteristically cryptic," said the explorer, pouring coffee. "The legend says that just before Kidd was to be hanged in London he sent a letter to my ancestor admitting that he'd buried a treasure on Ericsson's Island in '98, and saying that 'to find it you must look through the eye of the needle.'"

"Eye of the needle," said Ellery. "Eye of which needle?"

"Ah!" said Colonel Hobbes-Watkins ominously. "There's the rub, as the Bard says. No one knows—eh, Ericsson?"

"I'm afraid not, Colonel. And no one ever will, because it's all moonshine."

"Don't see why you say that, Eric, at all," said Tony, almost energetically. "Could have been a needle!"

"Even if there had been," Ericsson smiled in his moonshine, "two hundred and fifty years make a large haystack."

"One moment!" said Ellery. "Look through the eye of the needle *in the tower room*, Mr. Ericsson?"

"That's how it goes."

"What's in that room?"

"Nothing at all. Just four walls, a floor, and a ceiling. I assure you, Mr. Queen, everything's been tried—unsuccessfully—from hunting for a peculiar rock formation to conjuring up a tree fork viewed from a certain angle from the windows."

Ellery stared up at the tower. Suddenly he sprang to his feet. "How do I get up there?"

"There's the sleuth for you!" cried Colonel Hobbes-Watkins, hurling himself from his chair. "Been itching to have a go at that ruddy room myself!"

"But Eric's been so discouraging," murmured his son.

Nikki and Inga had their heads together before the fireplace, where Long John was laying a fire. Inga fell behind to say something to her young husband, who glanced quickly at Nikki and then shrugged.

The explorer led the way up a tiny narrow coiling staircase, holding a kerosene lamp high. "The tower's never been electrified," he called down, his deep voice reverberating. "Better use those flashlights or you'll break your necks on these stairs."

"Eeee," said Nikki convincingly; but it was only a dried-up wasps' nest. The stairs sagged perilously at every step.

The climb ended in a little landing and a heavy door of blackened oak and handforged iron. Ericsson set his big shoulder to the door. It gave angrily. The lamp bobbed off.

"A couple of you had better stay on the landing. This floor may not hold up under so much weight. Come in, Mr. Queen."

It was scarcely more than a large closet with miniature square windows. A floor of dirt-glazed random boards, undulant like the sea; a raftered ceiling only a few inches above the men's heads; and four papered walls. And that was all, except for dust and cobwebs. The windows, of imperfectly blown glass, were closed.

"Open them, Ellery," choked Nikki from the doorway. "You can't breathe up here."

"You can't open them," said Inga. "They've been stuck fast for six generations."

Ellery stood in the middle of the room looking about.

"Aren't you going to get down on all fours, Mr. Queen?" bellowed the Colonel from the landing. "Like the fellow from Baker Street?"

"I find these walls much more interesting."

But the only thing Nikki could see on the walls was the wallpaper. The paper showed an imitation colored marble design on a grainy background—ugly as sin, Nikki thought, and even uglier for being faded and mildewed in great patches.

Ellery was at one of the walls now, actually caressing it, holding the lamp close to the marbled paper. Finally he began at a corner and went over the paper inch by inch, from ceiling to floor. At one point he examined something for a long time. Then he resumed his deliberate inspection, and he neither spoke nor looked around until he had completed his tour of the room.

"This wallpaper," he said. "Do you know, Mr. Ericsson, what you have here?"

"Dash it all, sir," interrupted the Colonel explosively, "are you treasure-hunting, or what?"

"The wallpaper?" Ericsson frowned. "All I know about it is that it's very old."

"To be exact, late seventeenth century," said Ellery. "This is genuine flock paper, made by the famous Dunbar of Aldermanbury. It's probably quite valuable."

"There's a treasure for you," wailed Inga.

"If so," shrugged her uncle, "it's the first I've run across on the island."

"There may be a second," said Ellery. "If we look through the eye of the needle."

"Don't tell me, Queen," said Inga's husband with what might have been animation, "you've spotted something."

"Yes."

The Hobbes-Watkinses made admiring sounds and Inga embraced her spouse. The explorer seemed stunned.

"Do you mean to say," demanded Nikki in a loud voice, "that you walk into a strange room and in ten minutes solve a mystery that's baffled everybody for two hundred and fifty years? Come, come, Mr. Q!"

"It's still only theory," said Ellery apologetically. "Inga, may I borrow a broom?"

"A broom!"

Inga, Tony, and the Colonel shouted chaotically down the tower stairs for Long John to fetch the best broom on the premises. Then they ran into the little room and danced around Ellery, reckless of the aged floor.

"If the yarn is true at all," Ellery said, "Kidd couldn't have meant it literally when he instructed your ancestor, Mr. Ericsson, to 'look through the eye of the needle.' The early treasure-hunters saw that at once, or they wouldn't have looked for peculiar rock and tree formations. They just didn't look close enough to home. It was under their noses all the time."

"*What* was under their noses all the time?" asked Nikki.

"The marble design on this wallpaper. Marble's unique characteristic is its veining. Look at these veins in the pattern. Some are long and thin, tapering to a point—"

"*Like needles*," said the explorer slowly.

Everyone began scuttling along a wall.

"But where's one with an opening?" shrieked Inga. "Oh, I can't find a—a bloody eye!"

"An eye, an eye," mumbled the Colonel feverishly. "There must be one with an eye!"

"There is," said Ellery. "Just one, and here it is near this window."

And while they stared in awe at the place on the wall beyond the tip of Ellery's forefinger, Long John's boot and pegleg stumped into the tower room.

"Broom." He flung it.

Ellery seized it, placed the end of the broom handle on the open space in the needle-shaped vein, said with piety, "Let us pray," and pushed.

There was a ripping sound and the broom handle burst through the wall-paper and sank into the wall. Ellery kept pushing gently. The handle slid out of sight up to the sweep.

Ellery withdrew the broom and stepped back.

"Mr. Ericsson," he said, not without emotion, "the honor of the first look is yours."

"Well, don't just crouch there, Uncle Eric!" moaned Inga. "What do you see?"

"Can you see *anything?*"

"But he must—there's a bright moon!"

"Now, my dears, give the old chap a chance—"

"I see," said Eric Ericsson slowly, "a bit of the northeast shoreline. You know the place, Inga. It's that postage-stamp patch of beach with the slight overhang of flat rock. Where you've sunbathed."

"Let me see!"

"Let me!"

"It is!"

"It can't be. By George, not really—"

"What luck!"

There was a great deal of confusion.

Ellery said rapidly, "Mr. Ericsson, since you know just where the place is, take a hurricane lamp and a stake and get down there. We'll keep watch through the peephole. When we've got your lamp in the center of our sight, we'll signal with a flashlight three times from this window. Drive your stake into the sand at that point, and we'll join you there with shovels."

"I'll get 'em!" shrieked a voice; and they turned to see Long John's peg vanishing. Fifteen minutes later, with Inga sprinting ahead, they thrashed through the scrub toward the explorer's light.

They found Ericsson standing on an outcrop of silvery rock, smiling. "No hurry," he said. "And no treasure—not till low tide tomorrow morning, anyway."

Ericsson's stake was protruding from four and a half feet of ocean.

Nikki found herself able to play the part of a nervous city female with no difficulty at all. How could Inga *sleep?* she thought as she thrashed about in the twin bed. When in a few hours she was going to be the heiress of a pirate's treasure? . . . The . . . *piracy* of that pirate . . . to bury it so that for half the elapsed time the Atlantic rolled over it . . . He ought to be hanged . . .

Then Nikki remembered the he *had* been hanged; and that was her last thought until a hand clamped over her mouth and a light flashed briefly into her eyes and Ellery's voice said affectionately in her ear. "You certainly sleep soundly. Get into some clothes and join me outside. And don't wake anyone or I'll give you a taste of the cat."

Nikki slipped out of the house into a dead and lightless world. She could not even make out the terrace. But Ellery rose out of the void and led her down the path and into the woods, his grip forbidding noise. Not until they had gone several hundred yards did he turn on his flashlight, and even then he cupped its beam.

"Is it all right to talk now?" Nikki asked coldly. "What time is it? Where are we going? And why are you practically naked? And do you think this is cricket? After all, Ellery, it's not your treasure."

"It's not quite four, we're getting the jump on our friends, I expect it will be wet and mucky work, and pirate loot calls for pirate methods. Would you rather go back to your hot little bed?"

"No," said Nikki. "Though it all sounds pretty juvenile to me. How can you dig through sea water?"

"Low tide at 4:29 A.M.—I checked with a tide table at the house."

Nikki began to feel excited all over again.

And she almost burst into a yo-ho-ho when they came out on the flat rock and saw Ericsson's stake below them lapped by a mere inch or two of water.

The sun made its appearance with felicity. The first sliver of fried-egg radiance slipped over the edge of the sea's blue plate just as Ellery's spade rang a sort of breakfast bell. Nikki, who was flat on the wet sand with her head in the hole, and Ellery, whose salted hair bobbed a foot below Nikki's chin, responded to the sound with hungry cries.

"It's a metal box, Nikki!"

"Whee!"

"*Don't* come down here! Get that windlass ready."

"Where? What? What's a windlass?"

"That drum up there for hoisting!" Before turning in the previous night the men had lugged all the portable paraphernalia they could find in the shed down to the site of the treasure. "And unwind the line and pay it down to me—"

"Yaaaaa-hoo!" Nikki ran around in her little bare feet madly.

Twenty minutes later they knelt panting on the sand at the edge of the hole, staring at a brassbound iron chest with a fat convex lid. It was a black and green mass of corruption. Shreds of crumbled stuff told where leather had once been strapped. And the chest was heavy—

"Can you open it?" whispered Nikki.

Ellery set the heels of his hands on the edge of the lid and got his shoulders ready. The lid cracked off like a rotten nutshell.

Nikki gulped. The celestial egg was sunnyside up now, and beneath it a million little frying lights danced.

The chest was heaped with jewels.

"Diamonds," said Nikki dreamily. "Rubies. Emeralds. Pearls. Sapphires. So pretty. Look, Ellery. The booty of a real pirate. Wrenched from the throats and arms of dead Spanish women—"

"And the jewels in turn wrenched from their settings," muttered Ellery, "most of which were probably melted down. But here are some they overlooked. An empty gold setting. A silver one—"

"Here are more silver ones, Ellery . . ."

"Those aren't silver." Ellery picked one up. "This is platinum, Nikki . . ."

"And look at those old coins! What's this one?"

"What?"

"This coin!"

"Oh? *El peso duro.* A piece of eight."

"Gosh . . ." Nikki suddenly thrust both hands into the chest.

And at this precise moment, through the young air of the island's morning, there came a dull crack, like the faraway slam of a door, and quickly after—so quickly it sounded like an echo of the first—another.

Ellery vaulted across the hole and leaped onto the flat rock. "Nikki, those were gunshots—"

"Huh?" Nikki was still on a quarterdeck with her jewels. "But Ellery—the treasure! You can't leave—" But Ellery was gone.

They found Eric Ericsson in a robe and slippers lying in the doorway of Captain Kidd's roost, across the sill. He had tumbled head first into the empty room. In his right hand there was a .38 automatic pistol.

When they turned him over they saw a red hole in his forehead and red thickening fluid on the floor where the forehead had rested.

His body was still warm.

Ellery got up, and he said to the Hobbes-Watkinses and the marble-faced girl and the one-legged caretaker and Nikki, "We will go downstairs now and we will bar the tower door." So they went downstairs quietly, and Ellery excused himself for a moment and disappeared in his room, and when he appeared again he had a police revolver in his hand. "Nikki, you and Inga will take the launch and go over to the mainland and notify the Coast Guard and the Suffolk County police; there's no phone here. You won't come back until someone in authority can come with you. You gentlemen will wait here with me—with me, that is, and my shooting iron."

Late that day Ellery came downstairs from the tower room and conferred with the Coast Guard officer and the police captain from the mainland. Finally he said, "I appreciate that. It's something I owe poor Ericsson," and he waited until the people were brought in and seated before him.

The hearty bloat had gone out of Colonel Hobbes-Watkins; it was supplanted wholly by the muscular alertness Ellery had glimpsed the day before. Tony Hobbes-Watkins was very still, but he was no longer remotely languid. Inga was the palest projection of herself. Even Long John jiggled his peg nervously.

"Fifteen minutes or so after sunrise this morning," Ellery began, "just about the time I was down at the beach opening the treasure chest, Eric Ericsson was climbing the stairs in this house to the tower room. He was in his robe and slippers, and he carried his .38 automatic, with a full clip. His bedroom is below the tower shaft, which acts as an amplifier; evidently he was awakened by some noise from the tower room and decided to investigate. He took a gun with him because, even in his own house, he was afraid to be without it."

"I say—" began the Colonel furiously; but he did not say after all, he wiped the rolls on his neck.

"Someone was in the tower room. What was this person doing there—at dawn, in an empty room? There is only one thing of utility in that room—the peephole I punctured through the wall last night. The person Ericsson heard was watching me through the peephole. Watching me dig up the treasure."

They stared at him.

"Ericsson came to the landing and flung open the door. The man at the peephole whirled. Maybe they talked for a little while; maybe Ericsson was put off his guard. His gun came down, and the man across the room whipped out a revolver and fired a .22 caliber bullet into Ericsson's head, killing him instantly. But Ericsson's automatic had come up again instinctively as his murderer drew, and it went off, too—a split second after the murderer's. We know two shots were fired almost simultaneously because Miss Porter and I heard them, and because we found a .22 caliber bullet in Ericsson's head and a .38 shell on the floor near Ericsson's .38 automatic."

And Ellery said clearly, "The murderer ran down the tower stairs after the shots, heard the others coming—you'd all been awakened by the shots and dashed out of your rooms at once, you've said—realized he was trapped, and thereupon did the only thing he could: he pretended that he, too, had been awakened by the shots and he ran *back* up the stairs with the rest of you. The gun he managed to dispose of before I got back to the house from the beach.

"One of you," said Ellery, "was that murderer.

"Which one was it?"

There was no sound in the room at all.

"We found the empty shell of Ericsson's discharged cartridge, as I say, near his body. He had fired once at his murderer, his automatic had ejected the shell, and the bullet had sped on its way.

"But here is the interesting fact: *We haven't found Ericsson's bullet.*"

Ellery leaned their way. "The tower room has been gone over all day by these officers and me. The bullet isn't there. There is no sign of it or its passage anywhere in the room—floor, walls, ceiling. The windows remain intact. They weren't open at the time of Ericsson's shot; as you remarked yesterday, Inga, they've been stuck fast for generations; and when we tried to open them today without breaking something, we failed.

"Nor did Ericsson's shot go wild. He was killed instantly, falling into the room head first; this means that when he fired, he was facing into the room.

But just to be thorough, we went over the landing and the tower shaft, too. No bullet, no bullet mark, and no slightest opening through which the bullet might have passed."

"The peephole!" Nikki said involuntarily.

"No. There is considerable thickness to the walls. Ericsson in the doorway was at an extremely acute angle to the peephole. So while the bullet conceivably might have passed through the opening of the hole inside the tower room, it would have to have lodged inside the wall, or at least left some sign of its passage if it went clear through. We've torn down part of the wall to get a look inside. There is no bullet and no mark of a bullet.

"So the extraordinary fact is that while Ericsson's bullet must have struck something in that room, there is no sign of its having done so.

"Impossible? No.

"There is one logical explanation."

And Ellery said, "The bullet must have struck the only thing in that room which left it—the murderer. *One of you is concealing a bullet wound.*"

Ellery turned to the silent officers. "Let's have these three men stripped to the skin. And Nikki," he added, "go you somewhere with Inga—yes, I said Inga!—and do likewise."

And when the Colonel, raging, had been reduced to his fundamental pinkness, and his intent son stood similarly unclothed, and when what there was of Long John was grimly revealed also—and no wound was found on any of them, not so much as a scratch—Ellery merely blinked and faced the door through which Nikki had taken the murdered man's niece, the heir to his fortune and the treasure.

And the men redressed quickly, as if time were at their heels.

And when Nikki came back with Inga the police captain asked, "Where is Mrs. Hobbes-Watkins's wound, Miss Porter?"

"Mrs. Hobbes-Watkins," replied Nikki, "has no wound."

"No . . . ?"

"Maybe," said the Coast Guard officer awkwardly, "maybe you didn't look—uh—"

"And maybe I did," said Nikki with a sweet smile. "I work for the great Ellery Queen . . . you know?"

So now the two officers turned to look at the great Ellery Queen, but with no appreciation of his greatness at all.

And the Coast Guard officer said, "Well," and the police captain from the mainland did not say even that but turned on his heel.

He turned immediately back. For Ellery was growling, "If that's the case, it's obvious who killed Ericsson."

And Ellery produced a cigarette and a lighter and went to work on them, and then he said, "It all goes back to what I dug up this morning. And what did I dig up? An old chest, some old coins, a great number of unmounted gems, and some empty gem settings. Nikki, you saw the empty settings. Of which material were they made?"

"Gold, silver, platinum—"

"Platinum," said Ellery, and he waved his cigarette gently. "The metal platinum wasn't introduced into Europe until about 1750—*over fifty years after Kidd supposedly buried the chestful of jewels on this island.* It's even worse than that: *Platinum wasn't used for jewel settings until the year 1900,* at which time Kidd had been dead a hundred and ninety-nine years.

"A phony, gentleman. A plant. The whole thing.

"The 'treasure' I unearthed the morning was buried in that sand very recently, I'm afraid. It has no more connection with William Kidd or any other seventeenth century pirate than the loose change in my pocket. Oh, it was meant to be taken for a treasure Kidd buried—the chest is authentically old, and some old coins were strewn among the jewels. But the jewels, as proved by those platinum settings, are modern.

"Why should modern jewels be buried on an island in the guise of old pirate treasure? Well, suppose they were stolen property. As stolen property, they'd have to be disposed of through fences for a small proportion of their value. But as buried treasure they could be disposed of openly at market prices. Very clever.

"Eric Ericsson, gentlemen, suspected that Anthony Hobbes-Watkins and his 'father,' Colonel Hobbes-Watkins—who's probably not his father at all—were not what they seemed. He was tragically right—they're a pair of European jewel thieves and, from the size of their accumulations, they must hold some sort of record for prowess in their exacting profession.

"They were cooling off in the Bahamas, wondering how best to turn their loot into cash, when Eric Ericsson and his niece stopped over at New Providence Island for a visit. Hearing the purely mythical yarn about how Kidd had buried treasure on Ericsson's Island two hundred and fifty years ago—treasure that had never been found—these worthies got a remarkably ingenious idea. They would plant the jewels in a real old chest—the Bahamas were the headquarters of the buccaneers and are full of pirate relics; they would salt the stolen jewels with a few authentic old coins; and they would bury the chest on Ericsson's Island, to be 'discovered' by them at a later date. The plan revolved about Inga's infatuation for this fellow here; he pretended to reciprocate her love and he married her. As Ericsson's sole heir, Inga would inherit his entire estate, which included this island, when Ericsson died. And as Inga's husband, Tony Hobbes-Watkins would control it all, and when Inga died—an early and untimely death, eh, gentlemen?—our friends would be in the rosy clear . . . I'm sorry, Inga, but it seems to be a day for crushing blows."

Inga sat pallid and blank, her hand clutching Nikki's.

"If you're trying to pin Ericsson's murder on me—" began the younger man in a swift and nasal voice.

But the Colonel said harshly. "Be quiet."

"Oh, that?" said Ellery. "Let's see. We know that Ericsson's bullet struck his murderer. Yet none of his four possible murderers exhibits a wound. Obviously, the bullet buried itself in a part of the murderer which couldn't be wounded—" Ellery smiled—"*which couldn't be wounded because it's not flesh and blood.* Only one of you four fits that curious specification. The one who uses a wooden leg to compensate for his—*Stop him!*"

And when they had subdued the struggling caretaker and dug Eric Ericsson's bullet out of the pegleg, the police captain—who was glassy-eyed—said, "Then these two men, Mr. Queen . . . they weren't in on Ericsson's murder . . . ?"

"The whole plot, Captain, was geared to Ericsson's murder," said Ellery with a shrug, "though I'm afraid Long John rather jumped the gun.

"Don't you see that they were all in the plot together? How could our friend the Colonel, when he left the Bahamas after the wedding to smuggle the jewels into the States and get it to Ericsson's Island before the others sailed up to join him—how, I say, could the Colonel have planted the chest on the island unless the caretaker was taken into the gang? Also, the stage had to be set for the 'discovery' of the treasure: a hole bored through the tower room wall to sight on the chosen spot, the wallpaper doctored to implement the mythical clue of 'the needle's eye,' and so on—none of it possible unless Long John were declared in. He was, I suppose, to be paid off when Ericsson was disposed of and they got control, through Inga, of the estate and the island.

"What these gentry didn't figure on was the stupidity and avarice of Long John. They're far too clever operators to have planned to kill Ericsson the very night the treasure was located. Even if that had been their plan, they'd hardly have devised such a crude and obvious murder—especially with a trained investigator on the island. An 'accident' would have been more their style. At their leisure, under selected conditions . . . like a storm, say, and an overturned boat . . . perhaps even with Inga a victim of the same accident, in that way gaining their objective in one stroke and with no danger to themselves.

"But Long John is simple-minded and, as Ericsson told me, a miser. He just couldn't wait. He heard me leave in the dark, realized my purpose, saw the dawn coming up, and hurried to the tower room to spy on me. He watched me dig the jewels up, probably saw them sparkling in the sun. When Ericsson surprised him in the tower at that very moment, all he could see were those jewels and his share of them when Ericsson should be killed. So Long John killed him—then and there. Speeding up the great day . . .

"Haste makes waste, eh, Colonel? And Tony, I regret to inform you that I'm going to take your wife to the best lawyer in New York and see what can be done about an immediate annulment.

"And now, gentlemen, if you'll remove these pirates," said Ellery to the officers, but looking soberly at Inga, "Nikki and I have some holes to refill."

BECH NOIR

(1998)

John Updike

Henry Bech is a New York City writer created by John Updike and featured in novels such as *Bech Is Back* (1982). In this story a now-aged Bech decides it's time to settle some scores with old enemies, critics who gave his books negative reviews. Once he gets going, there's no stopping him. The story, told with wry humor, is a gem from one of America's greatest writers. Updike is the author of the bestselling *Rabbit* series, and he won a Pulitzer Prize for *Rabbit Is Rich* (1981). Other prominent books include *The Witches of Eastwick* (1984), *Rabbit at Rest* (1990), and *Due Considerations* (2007). He has also won the National Book Award and the American Book Award. Updike is a consummate short story stylist and literary critic. The following story is from *The New Yorker*.

Bech had a new sidekick. Her moniker was Robin. Rachel (Robin) Teagarten. Twenty-sex, post-Jewish, frizzy big hair, figure on the short and solid side. She interfaced for him with an IBM PS/1 his publisher had talked him into buying. She set up the defaults, rearranged the icons, programmed the style formats, accessed the ANSI character sets—Bech was a stickler for foreign accents. When he answered a letter, she typed it for him from dictation. When he took a creative leap, she deciphered his handwriting and turned it into digitized code. Neither happened very often. Bech was of the Ernest Hemingway save-your-juices school. To fill the time, he and Robin slept together. He was seventy-four, but they worked with that. Seventy-four plus twenty-six was one hundred; divided by two that was fifty, the prime of life. The energy of youth plus the wisdom of age. A team. A duo.

They were in his snug aerie on Crosby Street. He was reading the *Times* at breakfast. Caffeineless Folger's, D'Agostino orange juice, poppy-seed bagel lightly toasted. The crumbs and poppy seeds had scattered over the newspaper and into his lap but you don't get something for nothing, not on this hard planet. Bech announced to Robin, "Hey, Lucas Mishner is dead."

A creamy satisfaction—the finest quality, made extra easy to spread by the toasty warmth—thickly covered his heart.

"Who's Lucas Mishner?" Robin asked. She was deep in the D section—Business Day. She was a practical-minded broad with no experience of culture prior to 1975.

"Once-powerful critic," Bech told her, biting off his phrases. "Late *Partisan Review* school. Used to condescend to appear in the *Trib Book Review*, when the *Trib* was still alive on this side of the Atlantic. Despised my stuff. Called it 'superficially energetic but lacking in the true American fiber, the grit, the wrestle.' That's him talking, not me. The grit, the wrestle. Sanctimonious bastard. When *The Chosen* came out in '63, he wrote, 'Strive and squirm as he will, Bech will never, never be touched by the American sublime.' The simple, smug, know-it-all son of a bitch. You know what his idea of the real stuff was? James Jones. James Jones and James Gould Cozzens."

There Mishner's face was, in the *Times*, twenty years younger, with a fuzzy little rosebud smirk and a pathetic slicked-down comb-over, like limp venetian blinds throwing a shadow across the dome of his head. The thought of him dead filled Bech with creamy ease. He told Robin, "Lived way the hell up in Connecticut. Three wives, no flowers. Hadn't published in years. The rumor in the industry was he was gaga with alcoholic dementia."

"You seem happy."

"Very."

"Why? You say he had stopped being a critic anyway."

"Not in my head. He tried to hurt me. He did hurt me. Vengeance is mine."

"Who said that?"

"The Lord. In the Bible. Wake up, Robin."

"I thought it didn't sound like you," she admitted. "Stop hogging the Arts section."

He passed it over, with a pattering of poppy seeds on the teak breakfast table Robin had installed. For years he and his female guests had eaten at a low glass coffee table farther forward in the loft. The sun slanting in had been pretty, but eating all doubled up had been bad for their internal organs. He liked the cut of Robin's smooth broad jaw across the table. Her healthy big hair, her pushy plump lips, her little flattened nose. "One down," he told her, mysteriously.

A week later, he was in the subway. The Rockefeller Center station on Sixth Avenue, the old IND line. The downtown platform was jammed. All those McGraw-Hill, Exxon, and Time-Life execs were rushing back to their wives in the Heights. Or going down to West Fourth to have some herbal tea and put on drag for the evening. Monogamous transvestite executives were clogging the system. Bech was in a savage mood. He had been to MOMA, checking out the new art. It had all seemed pointless, poisonous, violent, inept. None of it had been Bech's bag. Art had passed him by. Literature was passing him by. Music he had never gotten exactly with, not since USO record hops. Those cuddly little WACs from Ohio in their starched uniforms. That war had been over too soon, before he got to kill enough Germans.

Down in the subway, three groups of electronic buskers—one country, one progressive jazz, and one doing Christian hip-hop—were competing. Overhead, a huge voice kept unintelligibly announcing cancellations and delays. In the cacophony, Bech spotted an English critic: Raymond Featherwaite, former Cambridge eminence lured to CUNY by American moola. From his perch in the CUNY crenellations, using his antique matchlock arquebus, he had been snottily potting American writers for twenty years, courtesy of the ravingly Anglophile *New York Review of Books*. "Prolix" and "*voulu*," Featherwaite had called Bech's best-selling comeback book, *Think Big*, in 1978. When, in 1985, Bech had ventured a harmless collection of sketches and stories, *Biding Time*, Featherwaite had written, "One's spirits, however initially well-disposed toward one of America's more carefully tended reputations, begin severely to sag under the repeated empathetic effort of watching Mr. Bech, page after page, strain to make something of very little."

The combined decibels of the buskers drowned out, for all but the most attuned city ears, the approach of the train whose delay had been so indistinctly bruited. Featherwaite, like all these Englishpersons who were breeding like wood lice in the rotting log piles of the New York literary industry, was no slouch at pushing ahead, through the malleable ex-colonials. Though there was hardly room to place one's shoes on the filthy speckled concrete, Featherwaite had shoved and wormed his way to the front of the crowd, right to the edge of the platform. His edgy profile, with its supercilious overbite and artfully projecting eyebrows, turned with arrogant expectancy toward the screamingly approaching D train, as though hailing a servile black London taxi or Victorian brougham. Featherwaite affected a wispy-banged Nero haircut. There were rougelike touches of color on his cheekbones. The tidy English head bit into Bech's vision like a branding iron.

Prolix, he thought. *Voulu.* He had had to look up "*voulu*" in his French dictionary. It put a sneering curse on Bech's entire oeuvre, for what, as Schopenhauer had asked, isn't willed?

Bech was three bodies back in the crush, tightly immersed in the odors, clothes, accents, breaths, and balked wills of others. Two broad-backed bodies, padded with junk food and fermented malt, intervened between himself and Featherwaite, while others importunately pushed at his own back. As if suddenly shoved from behind, he lowered his shoulder and rammed into the body ahead of his; like dominoes, it and the next tipped the third, the stiff-backed Englishman, off the platform. In the next moment the train with the force of a flash flood poured into the station, drowning all other noise under a shrieking gush of tortured metal. Featherwaite's hand in the last second of his life had shot up and his head jerked back as if in sudden recognition of an old acquaintance. Then he had vanished.

It was an instant's event, without time for the D-train driver to brake or a bystander to scream. Just one head pleasantly less in the compressed, malodorous mob. The man ahead of Bech, a ponderous African-American with bloodshot eyes, wearing a knit cap in the depths of summer, regained his balance and turned indignantly, but Bech, feigning a furious glance behind him, slipped sideways as the crowd arranged itself into funnels beside each door of the now halted train. A woman's raised voice—foreign, shrill—had begun to leak the horrible truth of what she had witnessed, and far away, beyond the turnstiles, a telepathic policeman's whistle was tweeting. But the crowd within the train was surging outward against the crowd trying to enter, and in the thick eddies of disgruntled and compressed humanity nimble, bookish, elderly Bech put more and more space between himself and his unwitting accomplices. He secreted himself a car's length away, hanging from a hand-burnished bar next to an ad publicizing free condoms and clean needles, with a dainty Oxford edition of Donne's poems pressed close to his face, as the whistles of distant authority drew nearer. The train refused to move and was finally emptied of passengers, while the official voice overhead, louder and less intelligible than ever, shouted word of cancellation, of disaster, of evacuation without panic.

Obediently Bech left the stalled train, blood on its wheels, and climbed the metallic stairs sparkling with pulverized glass. His insides shuddered in tune with the shoving, near-panicked mob about him. Gratefully he inhaled the outdoor air and Manhattan anonymity. Avenue of the Americas, a sign said, in stubborn upholding of an obsolete gesture of hemispheric good will. Bech walked south, then over to Seventh Avenue. Scrupulously he halted at each red light and deposited each handed-out leaflet (GIRLS! COLLEGE SEX KITTENS TOPLESS! BOTTOMLESS AFTER 6:30 P.M.!) in the nearest city trash receptacle. He descended into the Times Square station, where the old IRT's innumerable tunnels mingled their misery in a vast subterranean maze of passageways, stairs, signs, and candy stands. He caught an N train that took him to Broadway and Prince. Afternoon had sweetly turned to evening while he had been underground. The galleries were closing, the restaurants were opening. Robin was in the loft, keeping lasagna warm. "I thought MOMA closed at six," she said.

"There was a tieup in the Sixth Avenue subway. Nothing was running. I had to walk down to Times Square. I hated the stuff the museum had up. Violent, attention-getting."

"Maybe there comes a time," she said, "when new art isn't for you, it's for somebody else. I wonder what caused the tieup."

"Nobody knew. Power failure. A shootout uptown. Some maniac," he added, wondering at his own words. His insides felt agitated, purged, scrubbed, yet not yet creamy. Perhaps that needed to wait until the morning *Times*. He feared he could not sleep, out of nervous anticipation, yet he toppled into dreams while Robin still read beneath a burning light, as if he had done a long day's worth of physical labor.

"English Critic, Teacher Dead in West Side Subway Mishap," the headline read. The story was low on the front page and jumped to the obituaries. The obit photo, taken decades ago, glamorized Featherwaite—head facing one way, shoulders another—so he resembled a younger, less impish brother of George Sanders. High brow, thin lips, cocky glass chin. " . . . according to witnesses appeared to fling himself under the subway train as it approached the platform . . . colleagues at CUNY puzzled but agreed he had been under significant stress compiling permissions for his textbook of postmodern narrative strategies . . . former wife, reached in London, allowed the deceased had been subject to mood swings and fits of creative despair . . . the author of several youthful satirical novels and a single book of poems likened to those of Philip Larkin . . . born in Scunthorpe, Yorkshire, the third child and only son of a greengrocer and a part-time piano teacher . . ." and so on.

"Ray Featherwaite is dead," he announced to Robin, trying to keep a tremble of triumph out of his voice.

"Who was he?"

"A critic. More minor than Mishner. English. Came from Yorkshire, in fact—I had never known that. Went to Cambridge on a scholarship. I had figured him for inherited wealth; he wanted you to think so."

"That makes two critics this week," said Robin, preoccupied by the dense gray pages of stock prices.

"Every third person on this island is some kind of critic," Bech pointed out. He hoped the conversation would move on.

"How did he die?"

There was no way to hide it; she would be reading this section eventually. "Jumped under a subway train, oddly. Seems he'd been feeling low, trying to secure too many copyright permissions or something. These academics are under a lot of stress, competing for tenure."

"Oh?" Robin's eyes—bright, glossy, a living volatile brown, like a slick moist pelt—had left the stock prices. "What subway line?"

"Sixth Avenue, actually."

"Maybe that was the tieup you mentioned."

"Could be. Very likely, in fact."

"Why are your hands trembling? You can hardly hold your bagel." The poppy seeds were pattering on the obituary page.

"Who knows?" he asked her. "I may be coming down with something. I went out like a light last night."

"I'll say," said Robin, returning her eyes to the page.

"Sorry," he said, ease beginning to flow again within him. The past was sinking, every second, under fresher, obscuring layers of the recent past. "Did it make you feel neglected? A young woman needs her sex."

"No," she said, preoccupied by the market's faithful rise. "It made me feel tender. You seemed so innocent."

Robin, like Spider-man's wife, Mary Jane, worked in a computer emporium. She didn't so much sell them as share her insights with customers as they struggled in the crashing waves of innovation and the lightning-swift undertow of obsolescence. It thrilled Bech to view her in her outlet—Smart Circuits, on Third Avenue near Twenty-seventh Street, a few blocks from Bellevue—standing solid and calm in a gray suit whose lapels swerved to take in her bosom. Amid her array of putty-colored monitors and system-unit housings, she received the petitions of those in thrall to the computer revolution. They were mostly skinny young men with parched hair and sunless complexions. Sometimes Bech would enter the store, like some grizzled human glitch, and take Robin to lunch. Sometimes he would sneak away content with his glimpse of this princess decreeing in her realm. He marveled that at the end of the day she would find her path through the circuitry of the city and come to him. The tenacity of erotic connection anticipated the faithful transistor and the microchip.

Bech had not always been an object of criticism. His first stories and essays, appearing in defunct mass publications like *Liberty* and defunct avant-garde journals like *Displeasure*, roused little comment, and his dispatches, published in *The New Leader*, from Normandy in the wake of the 1944 invasion, and then from the Bulge and Berlin, went little noticed in a print world flooded with war coverage. But, ten years later, his first novel, *Travel Light*, made a small splash, and for the first time he saw, in print, spite directed at himself. Not just spite, but a willful mistaking of his intentions and a cheerfully ham-handed divulgence of all his plot's nicely calculated and hoarded twists. A New York Jew writing about Midwestern bikers infuriated some reviewers—some Jewish, some Midwestern—and the sly asceticism of his next, novella-length novel, *Brother Pig*, annoyed others: "The contemptuous medieval expression for the body which the author has used as a title serves only too well," one reviewer (female) wrote, "to prepare us for the sad orgy of Jewish self-hatred with which Mr. Bech will disappoint and repel his admirers—few, it is true, but in some rarefied circles curiously fervent."

As he aged, adverse phrases from the far past surfaced in his memory with an amazing vividness, word for word—"says utterly nothing with surprising aplomb," "too toothless or shrewd to tackle life's raw meat," "never doffs his velour exercise togs to break a sweat," "the sentimental coarseness of a pornographic valentine," "prose arabesques of phenomenal irrelevancy," "refusal or failure to ironize his reactionary positions," "starry-eyed sexism," "minor, minorer, minor-most"—and clamorously rattled around in his head, rendering him, some days, while his brain tried to be busy with something else, stupid with rage. It was as if these insults, these hurled mud balls, these stains on the robe of his vocation were, now that he was nearing the end, bleeding wounds. That a negative review might be a fallible verdict, delivered in haste, against a deadline, for a few dollars, by a writer with problems and limitations of his or her own, was a reasonable and weaseling supposition he could no longer, in the dignity of his years, entertain. Any adverse review, even a single timid phrase of qualification or reservation within a favorable and even adoring review, stood revealed as the piece of pure enmity it was—an assault, a virtual murder, a purely malicious attempt to unman and destroy him. The army of critics stood revealed as not fellow wordsmiths plying a dingy and dying trade but satanic legions, deserving only annihilation. A furious lava—an acidic indignation begging for the Maalox of creamy, murderous satisfaction—had gradually become Bech's essence, his angelic ichor.

The female reviewer, Deborah Frueh, who had in 1957 maligned *Brother Pig* as a flight of Jewish self-hatred was still alive, huddled in the haven of Seattle, amid New Age crystals and medicinal powders, between Boeing and Mount Rainier. Though she was grit too fine to be found in the coarse sieve of *Who's Who*, he discovered her address in the Poets & Writers' directory, which listed a few critical articles and her fewer books, all children's books with heart-tugging titles like *Jennifer's Lonely Birthday* and *The Day Dad Didn't Come Home* and *A Teddy Bear's Bequest*. These books, Bech saw, were her Achilles' heel.

He wrote her a fan letter, in a slow and childish hand, in black ballpoint, on blue-lined paper. "Dear Deborah Freuh," he wrote, deliberately misspelling, "You are my favrite writer. I have red your books over 'n' over. I would be greatful if you could find time to sign the two enclosed cards for me and my best friend Betsey and return them in the inclosed envelop. That would be really grate of you and many many thanx in advance." He signed it, "Your real fan, Mary Jane Mason."

He wrote it once and then rewrote it, holding the pen in what felt like a little girl's fist. Then he set the letter aside and worked carefully on the envelope. He had bought a cheap box of a hundred at an office-supply store on lower Broadway and destroyed a number before he got the alchemy right. With a paper towel he delicately moistened the dried gum on the envelope flap—not too much, or it curled. Then, gingerly using a glass martini-stirring rod, he placed three or four drops of colorless poison on the moist adhesive.

Prowling the cavernous basement of the renovated old sweatshop where he lived, Bech had found, in a cobwebbed janitor's closet, along with a quaint hand pump of tin and desiccated rubber, a thick brown-glass jar whose label, in the stiff and guileless typographic style of the nineteen-forties, proclaimed POISON and displayed along its border an array of dead vermin, roaches and rats and centipedes in dictionary-style engraving. In his thieving hand, the jar sloshed, half full. He took it upstairs to his loft and through a magnifying glass identified the effective ingredient as hydrocyanic acid. When the rusty lid was unscrewed, out rushed the penetrating whiff, cited in many a mystery novel, of bitter almonds. Lest the adhesive be betraying bitter when licked, and Deborah Frueh rush to ingest an antidote, he sweetened the doctored spots with some sugar water mixed in an orange-juice glass and applied with an eyedropper.

The edges of glue tended to curl as they dried, a difficulty he mitigated by rolling them the other way before applying the liquids. The afternoon waned; the roar of traffic up on Houston reached its crescendo unnoticed; the windows of the converted factory across Crosby Street entertained unseen the blazing amber of the lowering sun. Bech was wheezily panting in the intensity of his concentration. His nose was running; he kept wiping it with a trembling handkerchief. He had reverted to elementary school, where he and his peers had built tiny metropolises out of cereal boxes and scissored into being red valentines and black profiles of George Washington, even made paper Easter eggs and Christmas trees, under their young and starchy Irish and German instructresses, who without fear of objection swept their little Jewish-American pupils into the Christian calendar.

Bech thought hard about the return address on the envelope, which could become, once its fatal bait was taken, a dangerous clue. The poison, before hitting home, might give Deborah Frueh time to seal the thing, which in the confusion after her death might be mailed. That would be perfect—the clue consigned to a continental mailbag and arrived with the junk mail at an indifferent American household. In the Westchester directory he found a Mason in New Rochelle and fistily inscribed the address beneath the name of his phantom Frueh fan. Folding the envelope, he imagined he heard a faint crackling—microscopic sugar and cyanide crystals? His conscience, dried up by a century of atrocity and atheism, trying to come to life? He slipped the folded envelope with the letter and four (why not be generous?) three-by-five index cards into the envelope painstakingly addressed in the immature, girlish handwriting. He hurried downstairs, his worn heart pounding, to throw Mary Jane Mason's fan letter into the mailbox at Broadway and Prince.

Like the reflected light of a city set to burning, the lurid sunset hung low in the direction of New Jersey. The streets were crammed with the living and the guiltless, heading home in the day's horizontal rays, blinking from the subway's flicker and a long day spent at computer terminals. Bech hesitated a second before relinquishing his letter to the blue, graffiti-sprayed box, there in front of Victoria's Secret. A young black woman with an armful of metered nine-by-twelve envelopes impatiently arrived at his back, to make her more massive, less lethal drop. He stifled his qualm. The governmental box hollowly sounded with the slam of the lid upon the fathomless depths of sorting and delivery to which he consigned his missive. His life had been spent as a votary of the mails. This was but one more submission.

Morning after morning, the *Times* carried no word on the death of Deborah Frueh. Perhaps, just as she wasn't in *Who's Who*, she was too small a fish to be caught in the *Times*' obituary net. But no, they observed at respectful length the deaths of hundreds of people of whom Bech had never heard. Former aldermen, upstate prioresses, New Jersey judges, straight men on defunct TV comedies, founders of Manhattan dog-walking services—all got their space, their chiseled paragraphs, their farewell salute. Noticing the avidity with which he always turned to the back of the Metro section, Robin asked him, "What are you looking for?"

He couldn't tell her. "Familiar names," he said. "People I once knew."

"Henry, it seems morbid. Here, I'm done with Arts and Sports."

"I've read enough about arts and sports," he told this bossy tootsie, "to last me to the grave."

He went to the public library, the Hamilton Fish Park branch on East Houston, and in the children's section found one of Deborah Frueh's books,

Jennifer's Lonely Birthday, and checked it out. He read it and wrote her another letter, this time in blue ballpoint, on unlined stationery with a little Peter Maxish elf-figure up in one corner, the kind a very young girl might be given for her birthday by an aunt or uncle. "Dear Deborah Frueh," he wrote, "I love your exciting work. I love the way at the end of 'Jennifer's Lonely Birthday' Jennifer realizes that she has had a pretty good day after all and that in life you can't depend on anybody else to entertain you, you have to entertain your own mind. At the local library I have 'The Day Dad Didn't Come Home' on reserve. I hope it isn't too sad. 'Teddy Bear's Bequest' they never heard of at the library. I know you are a busy woman and must be working on more books but I hope you could send me a photograph of you for the wall of my room or if your too busy to do that please sign this zerox of the one on the cover of 'Jennifer's Lonely Birthday.' I like the way you do your hair, it's like my Aunt Daphne, up behind. Find enclosed a stamped envelope to send it in. Yours hopefully, Judith Green."

Miss Green in Bech's mind was a year or so older than Mary Jane Mason. She misspelled hardly at all, and had self-consciously converted her grammar-school handwriting to a stylish printing, which Bech slaved at for several hours before attaining the proper girlish plumpness in the *o*'s and *m*'s. He tried dotting the *i*'s with little circles and ultimately discarded the device as unpersuasive. He did venture, however, a little happy face, with smile and rudimentary pigtails. He intensified the dose of hydrocyanic acid on the envelope flap, and eased off on the sugar water. When Deborah Frueh took her lick—he pictured it as avid and thorough, not one but several swoops of her vicious, pointed tongue—the bitterness would register too late. The bitch would never know what hit her. A slowed heart, inhibited breathing, dilated pupils, convulsive movements, and complete loss of consciousness follow within seconds. He had done his research.

The postmark was a problem. Mary Jane up there in New Rochelle might well have had a father who, setting off in the morning with a full briefcase, would mail her letter for her in Manhattan, but two in a row and Frueh might smell a rat, especially if she had responded to the last request and was still feeling queasy. Bech took the Hoboken ferry from the World Financial Center, treating himself to a river view of his twinkling, aspiring home town. He looked up Greens in a telephone booth near the terminal. He picked one on Willow Street to be little Judy's family. He deposited his letter in a scabby dockside box and, leaving the missive to move on its own tides toward Seattle, took the ferry back to lower Manhattan. The writer's nerves hummed; his eyes narrowed against the river glare. What did Whitman write of such crossings? "Flood-tide below me! I see you face to face!" And, later on, speaking so urgently from the grave, "Just as you are refresh'd by the gladness of the river and the bright flow, I was refresh'd, Just as you stand and lean on the rail, yet hurry with the swift current, I stood yet was hurried." That "yet was hurried" was brilliant, with all of Whitman's brilliant homeliness.

A week went by. Ten days. The desired death was not reported in the *Times*. Bech wondered if a boy fan might win a better response, a more enthusiastic, heterosexual licking of the return envelope. "Dear Deborah Freuh," Bech typed, using the hideous Script face available on his IBM PS/1. "You are a great writer, the greatest as far as I am concerned in the world. Your book titled 'The Day Dad Didn't Come Home' broke me up, it was so sad and true. I don't want to waste any more of your time reading this so you can get back to writing another super book but it would be sensational if you would sign the enclosed first-day cover for Sarah Orne Jewett, the greatest female American writer until you came along. Even if you have a policy against signing I'd appreciate your returning it in the enclosed self-addressed stamped envelope since I am a collector and spent a week's allowance for it at the hobby shop here in Amityville, Long Island, NY. Sign it on the pencil line I have drawn. I will erase the line when you have signed. I look forward to hearing from you soon. Yours very sincerely, Jason Johnson, Jr."

It was a pleasant change, in the too-even tenor of Bech's days, to ride the Long Island Rail Road out to Amityville and mail Jason Johnson's letter. Just to visit Penn Station again offered a fresh perspective—all that Roman grandeur from his youth, that onetime temple to commuting Fortuna, reduced to these ignoble ceilings and Tartarean passageways. And then, after the elevated views of tar-roofed Queens, the touching suburban stations, like so many knobbed Victorian toys, with their carefully pointed stonework and gleaming rows of parked cars and stretches of suburban park. In Amityville he found a suitable Johnson—on Maple Drive—and mailed his letter and headed back to town, the stations accumulating ever shabbier, more commercial surroundings and the track bed becoming elevated and then, with a black roar, buried, underground, underriver, undercity, until the train stopped at Penn Station again and the passengers spilled out into a gaudy, perilous mess of consumeristic blandishments, deranged beggars, and furtive personal errands.

Four days later, there it was, in four inches of *Times* type, the death of Deborah Frueh. Respected educator was also a noted critic and author of children's books. Had earlier published scholarly articles on the English Metaphysicals and Swinburne and his circle. Taken suddenly ill while at her desk in her home in Hunts Point, near Seattle. Born in Conshohocken, near Philadelphia. Attended Barnard College and Duke University graduate school. Exact cause of death yet to be determined. Had been in troubled health lately—her weight a stubborn problem—colleagues at the University of Washington reported. Survived by a sister, Edith, of Ardmore, Pennsylvania, and a brother, Leonard, of Teaneck, New Jersey.

Another ho-hum exit notice, for every reader but Henry Bech. He knew what a deadly venom the deceased had harbored in her fangs.

"What's happened?" Robin asked from across the table.

"Nothing's happened," he said.

"Then why do you look like that?"

"Like what?"

"Like a man who's been told he's won a million dollars but isn't sure it's worth it, what with all the tax problems."

"What a strange, untrammeled imagination," he said.

"Let me see the page you're reading."

"No. I'm still reading it."

"Henry, are you going to make me stand up and walk around the table?"

He handed her the cream-cheese-stained obituary page. Robin, while the rounded points of her wide jaw thoughtfully clenched and unclenched on the last milky crumbs of her whole-bran flakes, flicked her quick brown eyes up and down the columns of print. Her eyes held points of red like the fur of a fox. Morning sun slanting through the big loft window made an outline of light, of incandescent fuzz, along her jaw. Her eyelashes glittered like a row of dewdrops on a spiderweb strand. "Who's Deborah Frueh?" she asked. "Did you know her?"

"A frightful literary scold," he said. "I never met the lady, I'm not sorry to say."

"Did she ever review you or anything?"

"I believe she did, once or twice."

"Favorably?"

"Not really."

"Really unfavorably?"

"It could be said. Her reservations about my work were unhedged, as I vaguely recall. You know I don't pay much attention to reviews."

"And that Englishman last month, who fell in front of the subway train—didn't you have some connection with him, too?"

"Darling, I've been publishing for over fifty years. I have slight connections with everybody in the print racket."

"You've not been quite yourself lately," Robin told him. "You've had some kind of secret. You don't talk to me the breezy way you used to. You're censoring."

"I'm not," he said, hating to lie, standing as he was knee-deep in the sweet clover of Deborah Frueh's extermination. He wondered what raced through that fat harpy's mind in the last second, as the terrible-tasting cyanide nipped down her esophagus and halted the oxidation process within her cells. Not of him, certainly. He was one of multitudes of writers she had put in their places. He was three thousand miles away, the anonymous progenitor of Jason Johnson Jr.

"Look at you!" Robin cried, on so high a note that her orange-juice glass emitted a surprised shiver. "You're triumphant! Henry, you killed her."

"How would I have done that?"

She was not balked. Her eyes narrowed. "At a distance, somehow," she guessed. "You sent her things. A couple of days, when I came home, there was a funny smell in the room, like something had been burning."

"This is fascinating," Bech said. "If I had your imagination, I'd be Balzac." He went on, to deflect her devastating insights, "Another assiduous critic of mine, Aldie Cannon—he used to be a mainstay of *The New Republic* but now he's on PBS and the Internet—says I can't imagine a thing. And hate women."

Robin was still musing, her smooth young mien puzzling at the crimes to which she was an as yet blind partner. She said, "I guess it depends on how you define 'hate.'"

But he loved her. He loved the luxurious silken whiteness of her slightly thickset young body, the soothing cool of her basically factual mind. He could not long maintain this wall between them, this ugly partition in the light-filled loft of their love match. The next day the *Times* ran a little follow-up squib on the same page as the daily book review—basically comic in its tone, for who would want to murder an elderly, overweight book critic and juvenile author—stating that the Seattle police had found suspicious chemical traces in Frueh's autopsied body. Bech confessed to Robin. The truth rose irrepressible in his throat like the acid burn of partial regurgitation. Pushing the large black man who pushed a body that pushed Featherwaite's. Writing Deborah Frueh three fan letters with doped return envelopes. Robin listened while reposing on his brown beanbag chair in a terry-cloth bathrobe. She had taken a shower, so her feet had babyish pink sides beneath the marblewhite insteps with their faint blue veins. It was Sunday morning. She said when he was done, "Henry, you can't just go around rubbing out people as if they existed only on paper."

"I can't? That's where they tried to rub me out, on paper. They preyed on my insecurities, to shut off my creative flow. They nearly succeeded. I haven't written nearly as much as I could have."

"Was that their fault?"

"Partly," he estimated. Perhaps he had made a fatal error, spilling his guts to this chesty broad. "Okay. Turn me in. Go to the bulls."

"The bulls?"

"The police—haven't you ever heard that expression? How about 'the fuzz'? Or 'the pigs'?"

"I've never heard them called that, either."

"My God, you're young. What have I ever done to deserve you, Robin? You're so pure, so straight. And now you loathe me."

"No, I don't, actually. I might have thought I would, but in fact I like you more than ever." She never said "love," she was too post-Jewish for that. "I think you've shown a lot of balls, frankly, translating your resentments into action instead of sublimating them into art."

He didn't much like it when young women said "balls" or called a man "an asshole," but today he was thrilled by the cool baldness of it. They were, he and his mistress, in a new realm, a computerized universe devoid of blame or guilt, as morally null as an Intel chip. There were only, in this purified universe, greater or lesser patches of electricity, and violence and sex were greater patches. She stood and opened her robe. She emitted a babyish scent, a whiff of sour milk; otherwise her body was unodiferous, so that Bech's own aromas, the product of seven and a half decades of marination in the ignominy of organic life, stood out like smears on a white vinyl wall. Penetrated, Robin felt like a fresh casing, and her spasms came rapidly, a tripping series of orgasms made almost pitiable by her habit of sucking one of his thumbs deep into her mouth as she came. When that was over, and their pulse rates had leveled off, she looked at him with her fox-fur irises shining expectantly, childishly.

"So who are you going to do next?" she asked. Her pupils, those inkwells as deep as the night sky's zenith, were dilated by excitement.

"Well, Aldie Cannon *is* very annoying," Bech reluctantly allowed. "He's a forty-something smart-aleck, from the West Coast somewhere. Palo Alto, maybe. He has one of these very rapid agile nerdy minds—whatever pops into it must be a thought. He began by being all over *The Nation* and *The New Republic* and then moved into the *Vanity Fair*/*GQ* orbit, writing about movies, books, TV, music, whatever, an authority on any sort of schlock, and then got more and more on radio and TV—they love that kind of guy, the thirty-second opinion, bing, bam—until now that's basically all he does, that and write some kind of junk on the Internet, his own Web site, I don't know—people send me printouts whenever he says anything about me, I wish they wouldn't."

"What sort of thing does he say?"

Bech shifted his weight off his elbow, which was hurting. Any joint in his body hurt, with a little use. His body wanted to retire but his raging spirit wouldn't let it. "He says I'm the embodiment of everything retrograde in pre-electronic American letters. He says my men are sex-obsessed narcissistic brutes and all my female characters are just anatomically correct dolls."

"Ooh," murmured Robin, as if softly struck by a bit of rough justice.

Bech went on, aggrieved, "He says things like, and I quote, 'Whenever Bech attempts to use his imagination, the fuse blows and sparks fall to the floor. But short circuits aren't the same as magic-realist fireworks.' End quote. On top of being a smart-aleck he's a closet prude. He hated the sex in *Think Big*; he wrote, as I dimly remember, 'These tawdry and impossible wet dreams tell us nothing about how men and women really interact.' Implying that he sure does, the creepy fag. He's never interacted with anything but a candy machine and the constant torrent of cultural crap."

"Henry, his striking you as a creepy fag isn't reason enough to kill him."

"It is for me."

"How would you go about it?"

"How would we go about it maybe is the formula. What do we know about this twerp? He's riddled with insecurities, has all this manicky energy, and is on the Internet."

"You have been mulling this over, haven't you?" Robin's eyes had widened; her lower lip hung slightly open, looking riper and wetter than usual, as she propped herself about him, bare-breasted, livid-nippled, her big hair tumbling in oiled coils. Her straight short nose didn't go with the rest of her face, giving her a slightly flattened expression, like a cat's. "My lover the killer," she breathed.

"My time on Earth is limited." Bech bit off his words. "I have noble work to do. I can't see Cannon licking return envelopes. He probably has an assistant for that. Or tosses them in the wastebasket, the arrogant little shit." He averted his eyes from Robin's bared breasts, their gleaming white weight like that of gourds still ripening, snapping their vines.

She said, "So? Where do I come in, big boy?"

"Computer expertise. You have it, or know those that do. My question of you, baby, is could we break into his computer?"

Robin's smooth face, its taut curves with their faint fuzz, hardened. "If he can get out," she said, "a cracker can get in. The Internet is one big happy family, like it or not."

The Aldie Cannon mini-industry was headquartered in his modest Upper East Side apartment. He lived, with his third wife and two maladjusted small children, not on one of the East Side's genteel, ginkgo-shaded side streets but in a raw new blue-green skyscraper, with balconies like stubby daisy petals, over by the river. His daily Internet feature, "Cannon Fodder," was produced in a child-resistant study on a Compaq PC equipped with Windows 95. His opinionated claptrap was twinkled by modem to a site in San Jose, where it was checked for obscenity and libel and misspellings before going out to the millions of green-skinned cyberspace goons paralyzed at their terminals. E-mail sent to fodder.com went to San Jose, where the less inane and more provocative communications were forwarded to Aldie, for possible use in one of his columns.

Robin, after consulting some goons of her acquaintance, explained to Bech that the ubiquitous program for E-mail, Sendmail, had been written in the Unix ferment of the late nineteen-seventies, when security had been of no concern; it was notoriously full of bugs. For instance, Sendmail performed security checks only on a user's first message; once the user passed, all his subsequent messages went straight through. Another weakness of the program was that a simple **|**, the "pipe" symbol, turned the part of the message following it into input, which could consist of a variety of Unix commands the computer was obliged to obey. These commands could give an intruder log-in status and, with some more manipulation, a "back door" access that would last until detected and deleted. Entry could be utilized to attach a "Trojan horse" that would flash messages onto the screen, with subliminal brevity if desired.

Bech's wicked idea was to undermine Cannon's confidence and sense of self—fragile, beneath all that polymathic, relentlessly with-it bluster—as the critic sat gazing at his monitor. Robin devised a virus: every time Aldie typed an upper-case "A" or a lower-case "x," a message would flash, too quickly for his conscious mind to register but distinctly enough to penetrate the neuronic complex of brain cells. The program took Robin some days to design; especially finicking were the specs of such brief interruptions, amid the seventy cathoderay refreshments of the screen each second, in letters large enough to make an impression. She labored while Bech slept; half-moon shadows smudged and dented the lovely smoothness of her face. Delicately she strung her binaries together. They could at any moment be destroyed by an automatic "sniffer" program or a human "sysadmin," a systems administrator. Federal laws were being violated; heavy penalties could be incurred. Nevertheless, out of love for Bech and the fascination of a technical challenge, Robin persevered and, by the third morning, succeeded.

Bech began, once the intricate, illicit commands had been lodged, with some hard-core Buddhism. BEING IS PAIN, the subliminal message read; NON-

BEING IS NIRVANA. Invisibly these truths rippled into the screens' pixels for a fifteenth of a second—that is, five refreshments of the screen, a single one being, Robin and a consulted neurophysiologist agreed, too brief to register even subliminally. After several days of these equations, Bech asked her to program the more advanced NO MISERY OF MIND IS THERE FOR HIM WHO HATH NO WANTS. It was critical that the idea of death be rendered not just palatable but inviting. NON-BEING IS AN ASPECT OF BEING, and BEING OF NON-BEING: this Bech had adapted from a Taoist poem by Seng Ts'an. From the same source he took TO BANISH REALITY IS TO SINK DEEPER INTO THE REAL. Out of his own inner resources he proposed ACTIVITY IS AVOIDANCE OF VICTORY OVER SELF.

Together he and Robin scanned Cannon's latest effusions, in print or on the computer screen, for signs of mental deterioration and spiritual surrender. Deborah Frueh had taken the bait in the dark, and Bech had been frustrated by his inability to see what was happening—whether she was licking an envelope or not, and what effect the diluted poison was having on her detestable innards. But in the case of Aldie Cannon, his daily outpouring of cleverness surely would betray symptoms. His review of a Sinead O'Conner concert felt apathetic, though he maintained it was her performance, now that she was no longer an anti-papal skinhead, that lacked drive and point. His roundup of recent books dwelling, with complacency or alarm, upon the erosion of the traditional literary canon—cannon fodder indeed, the ideal chance for him to do casual backflips of lightly borne erudition—drifted toward the passionless conclusion that "the presence or absence of a canon amounts to much the same thing; one is all, and none is equally all." This didn't sound like the Aldie Cannon who had opined of Bech's collection *When the Saints*, "Some of these cagey feuilletons sizzle but most fizzle; the author has moved from not having much to say to implying that anyone's having anything to say is a tiresome breach of good taste. Bech is a literary dandy, but one dressed in tatters—a kind of shreds and patches, as Hamlet said of another fraud."

It was good for Bech to remember these elaborate and gleeful dismissals, lest pity bring him to halt the program. Where the celebrant of pop culture would once wax rapturous over Julia Roberts's elastic mouth and avid eyes, Aldie now dwelt upon her ethereal emaciation in *My Best Friend's Wedding*, and the "triumphant emptiness" of her heroine's romantic defeat and the film's delivery of her into the arms of a homosexual. Of Saul Bellow's little novel, he noticed only the "thanatoptic beauty" of its culmination in a cemetery, where the hero's proposal had the chiseled gravity of an elegy or death sentence. The same review praised the book's brevity and confessed—this from Aldie Cannon, Pantagruelian consumer of cultural produce—that some days he just didn't want to read one more book, see one more movie, go to one more art show, look up one more reference, wrap up one more paragraph with one more fork-tongued apercu. And then, just as the Manhattan scene was kicking into another event-crammed fall season, "Cannon Fodder" now and then skipped a day on the Internet, or was replaced, with a terse explanatory note, by one of the writer's "classic" columns from a bygone year.

Bech had made a pilgrimage to the blue-green skyscraper near the river to make sure a suicide leap was feasible. Its towering mass receded above him like giant railroad tracks—an entire railroad yard of aluminum and glass. The jutting semicircular petals of its balconies formed a scalloped dark edge against the clouds as they hurtled in lock formation across the sere-blue late-summer sky. It always got to the pit of Bech's stomach, the way the tops of skyscrapers appeared to lunge across the sky when you looked up, like the prows of ships certain to crash. The building was fifty-five stories high and had curved sides. Its windows were sealed but the balconies were not caged. Within Bech a siren wailed, calling Aldie out, out of his cozy claustral nest of piped-in, faxed, E-mailed, messengered, videoed cultural fluff and straw—culture, that tawdry, cowardly anti-nature—into the open air, the stinging depths of space, cosmic nature pure and raw.

NON-BEING IS BLISS, Bech told Robin to make the Trojan horse spell, and SELFHOOD IS IMPURITY, and, at ever-faster intervals, the one word JUMP.

JUMP, the twittering little pixels cried, and JUMP YOU TWIT or JUMP YOU HOLLOW MAN or DO THE WORLD A FUCKING FAVOR AND JUMP.

"I can't believe this is you," Robin told him. "This killer."

"I have been grievously provoked," he said.

"Just by reviews? Henry, nobody takes them seriously."

"I thought I did not, but now I see that I have. I have suffered a lifetime's provocation. My mission has changed; I wanted to add to the world's beauty, but now I merely wish to rid it of ugliness."

"Poor Aldie Cannon. Don't you think he means well? Some of his columns I find quite entertaining."

"He may mean well but he commits atrocities. His facetious half-baked columns are crimes against art and against mankind. He has crass taste—no taste, in fact. He has a mouth to talk but no ears with which to listen." Liking in his own ear the rhythm of his tough talk, Bech got tougher. "Listen, sister," he called to Robin. "You want out? Out you can have any time. Walk down two flights. The subway's a block over, on Broadway. I'll give you the buck fifty. My treat."

She appeared to think it over. She said what women always say, to stall. "Henry, I love you."

"Why the hell would that be?"

"You're cute," Robin told him. "Especially these days. You seem more, you know, together. Before, you were some sort of a sponge, just sitting there, waiting for stuff to soak in. Now you've, like they say on the talk shows, taken charge of your life."

He pulled her into his arms with a roughness that darkened the fox-fur glints in her eyes. A quick murk of fear and desire clouded her features. His shaggy head cast a shadow on her silver face as he bowed his neck to kiss her. She made her lips as soft as she could, as soft as the primeval ooze. "And you like that, huh?" he grunted. "My becoming bad."

"It lets me be bad." Her voice had gotten small and hurried, as if she might faint. "I love you because I can be a bad girl with you and you love it. You eat it up. Yum, you say."

"Bad is relative," he told her, from the sage height of his antiquity. "For my purposes, you're a good girl. So it excites you, huh? Trying to bring this off."

Robin admitted, "It's kind of a rush." She added, with a touch of petulance as if to remind him how girlish she was, "It's my project. I want to stick with it."

"Now you're talking. Here, I woke up with an inspiration. Flash the twerp this." It was another scrap of Buddhist death-acceptance: LET THE ONE WITH ITS MYSTERY BLOT OUT ALL MEMORY OF COMPLICATIONS. JUMP.

"It seems pretty abstract."

"He'll buy it. I mean, his subconscious will buy it. He thinks of himself as an intellectual. He majored in philosophy at Berkeley, I read in that stuff you downloaded from the Internet."

She went to the terminal and pattered through the dance of computer control. "It went through, but I wonder," she said.

"Wonder what?"

"Wonder how much longer before they find us and wipe us out. There are more and more highly sophisticated security programs; crackers are costing industry billions."

"The seed is sown," Bech said, still somewhat in Buddhist mode. "Let's go to bed. I'll let you suck my thumb, if you beg nicely. You bad bitch," he added, to see if her eyes would darken again. They did.

But the sniffers were out there, racing at the speed of light through the transistors, scouring the binary code for alien configurations and rogue algorithms. It was Robin, now, who each morning rushed, in her terry-cloth bathrobe, on her pink-sided bare feet, down the two flights to the loft lobby and brought up the *Times* and scanned its obituary page. The very day after her Trojan horse, detected and killed, failed to respond, there it was: "Aldous Cannon, 43, Critic, Commentator." Jumped from the balcony of his apartment on the forty-eighth floor. No pedestrians hurt, but an automobile parked on York Avenue severely damaged. Wife, distraught, said the writer and radio personality, whose Web site on the Internet was one of the most visited for literary purposes by college students, had seemed preoccupied lately, and confessed to sensations of futility. Had always hoped to free up time to write a big novel. In a separate story in Section B, a wry collegial tribute from Christopher Lehmann-Haupt.

Bech and Robin should have felt jubilant. They had planted a flickering wedge of doubt beneath the threshold of consciousness and brought down a media-savvy smart-ass. But, it became clear after their initial, mutually congratulatory embrace, there above the breakfast-table confusion, the sweating carton of orange juice and the slowly toasting bagels, that they felt stunned, let down and ashamed. They avoided the sight and touch of each other for the rest of the day, though it was Saturday. They had planned to go up and cruise the Met and then try to get an outdoor table at the Stanhope, in the deliciously crisp September air. But the thought of art in any form sickened them: sweet icing on dung, thin ice over the abyss. Robin went shopping for black jeans at Barneys and then up in the train to visit her parents in Garrison, while Bech in a stupor like that of a snake digesting a poisonous toad sat watching two Midwestern college football teams batter at each other in a screaming, chanting stadium far west of the Hudson, where life was sunstruck and clean.

Robin spent the night with her parents. She returned so late on Sunday she must have hoped her lover would be asleep. But he was up, waiting for her, reading Donne. The day's lonely meal had generated a painful gas in his stomach. His mouth tasted chemically of nothingness. Robin's key timidly scratched at the lock and she entered; he met her near the threshold and they softly bumped heads in a show of contrition. They had together known sin. Like playmates who had mischievously destroyed a toy, they slowly repaired their relationship. As Aldie Cannon's wanton but not unusual (John Berryman, Jerzy Kosinski) self-erasure slipped deeper down into the stack of used newspapers, and the obligatory notes of memorial tribute tinnily, fadingly sounded in the PEN and Authors Guild newsletters, the duo on Crosby Street recovered their dynamism. Literary villains of Gotham, beware!

NEVER SHAKE A FAMILY TREE
(1961)
Donald E. Westlake

Recent years have seen a growing interest in genealogy, as people search back over time to learn about their ancestral roots. Wouldn't it be great to find out that one is related to some distinguished historical personage like Mozart or Lincoln? But, of course, the opposite might also hold, if one discovered a lowdown scoundrel in the family tree. Donald E. Westlake writes a delightful spoof of genealogy in this story.

Perhaps the greatest living mystery writer, Westlake began his career with hard-boiled crime novels but later expanded his repertoire to include comical parodies and send-ups. Westlake has won an Edgar Award, as well as the Grand Master Edgar Award for lifetime achievement in 1993. Many of his books have been made into movies: *The Hunter* (1963) was filmed as *Point Blank* in 1967 with Lee Marvin and Angie Dickinson, and remade as *Payback* in 1998 with Mel Gibson. *The Hot Rock* (1970) was filmed in 1972 with Robert Redford. Westlake has written approximately thirty novels under his own name, as well as about twenty others under the pseudonym Richard Stark and another five under the name of Tucker Coe. About Westlake's recent Richard Stark book *Lemons Never Lie* (2006), a reviewer said that it "reads like Raymond Chandler with a dark literary whisper—as faint as the vermouth in a martini—of Cormac McCarthy."

"Never Shake a Family Tree" was originally published in *Alfred Hitchcock's Mystery Magazine.*

Actually, I was never so surprised in my life, and I seventy-three my last birthday and eleven times a grandmother and twice a great-grandmother. But never in my life did I see the like, and that's the truth.

It all began with my interest in genealogy, which I got from Mrs. Ernestine Simpson, a widow I met at Bay Arbor, in Florida, when I went there three summers ago. I certainly didn't like Florida—far too expensive, if you ask me, and far too bright, and with just too many mosquitoes and other insects to be believed—but I wouldn't say the trip was a total loss, since it did interest me in genealogical research, which is certainly a wonderful hobby, as well as being very valuable, what with one thing and another.

Actually, my genealogical researches have been valuable in more ways than one, since they have also been instrumental in my meeting some very pleasant ladies and gentlemen, although some of them only by postal, and of course it was through this hobby that I met Mr. Gerald Fowlkes in the first place.

But I'm getting far ahead of my story, and ought to begin at the beginning, except that I'm blessed if I know where the beginning actually is. In one way of looking at things, the beginning is my introduction to genealogy through Mrs. Ernestine Simpson, who has since passed on, but in another way the beginning is really almost two hundred years ago, and in still another way the story doesn't really begin until the first time I came across the name of Euphemia Barber.

Well. Actually, I suppose, I ought to begin by explaining just what genealogical research is. It is the study of one's family tree. One checks marriage and birth and death records, searches old family Bibles and talks to various members of one's family, and one gradually builds up a family tree, showing who fathered whom and what year, and when so-and-so got married, and when so-and-so died, and so on. It's really fascinating work, and there are any number of amateur genealogical societies throughout the country, and when one has one's family tree built up for as far as one wants—seven generations, or nine generations, or however long one wants—then it is possible to write this all up in a folder and bequeath it to the local library, and then there is a *record* of one's family for all time to come, and I for one think that's important and valuable to have even if my youngest boy, Tom, does laugh at it and say it's just a silly hobby. Well, it *isn't* a silly hobby. After all, I found evidence of murder that way, didn't I?

So, actually, I suppose the whole thing really begins when I first come across the name of Euphemia Barber. Euphemia Barber was John Anderson's second wife. John Anderson was born in Goochland County, Virginia, in 1754. He married Ethel Rita Mary Rayborn in 1777, just around the time of the Revolution, and they had seven children, which wasn't at all strange for that time, though large families have, I notice, gone out of style today, and I for one think it's a shame.

At any rate, it was John and Ethel Anderson's third child, a girl named Prudence, who is in my direct line on my mother's father's side, so of course I had them in my family tree. But then, in going through Appomattox County records—Goochland County being now a part of Appomattox, and no longer a separate county of its own—I came across the name of Euphemia Barber. It seems that Ethel Anderson died in 1793, in giving birth to her eighth child—who also died—and three years later, 1796, John Anderson remarried, this time marrying a widow named Euphemia Barber. At that time he was forty-two years of age, and her age was given as thirty-nine.

Of course, Euphemia Barber was not at all in my direct line, being John Anderson's second wife, but I was interested to some extent in her pedigree as well, wanting to add her parents' names and her place of birth to my family chart, and also because there were some Barbers fairly distantly related on my father's mother's side, and I was wondering if this Euphemia might be kin to them. But the records were very incomplete, and all I could learn was that

Euphemia Barber was not a native of Virginia, and had apparently only been in the area for a year or two when she married John Anderson. Shortly after John's death in 1798, two years after their marriage, she sold the Anderson farm, which was apparently a somewhat prosperous location, and moved away again. So that I had neither birth nor death records on her, nor any record of her first husband, whose last name had apparently been Barber, but only the one lone record of her marriage to my great-great-great-great-great-grandfather on my mother's father's side.

Actually, there was no reason for me to pursue the question further, since Euphemia Barber wasn't in my direct line anyway, but I had worked diligently and, I think, well, on my family tree, and had it almost complete back nine generations, and there was really very little left to do with it, so I was glad to do some tracking down.

Which is why I included Euphemia Barber in my next entry in the *Genealogical Exchange*. Now, I suppose I ought to explain what the *Genealogical Exchange* is. There are any number of people throughout the country who are amateur genealogists, concerned primarily with their own family trees, but of course family trees do interlock, and any one of these people is liable to know about just the one record which has been eluding some other searcher for months. And so there are magazines devoted to the exchanging of such information, for nominal fees. In the last few years I had picked up all sorts of valuable leads in this way. And so my entry in the summer issue of the *Genealogical Exchange* read:

> BUCKLEY, Mrs. Henrietta Rhodes, 119A Newbury St., Boston, Mass. Xch data on *Rhodes, Anderson, Richards, Pryor, Marshall, Lord*. Want any info Euphemia *Barber*, m. John Anderson, Va. 1796.

Well. The *Genealogical Exchange* had been helpful to me in the past, but I never received anywhere near the response caused by Euphemia Barber. And the first response of all came from Mr. Gerald Fowlkes.

It was a scant two days after I received my own copy of the summer issue of the *Exchange*. I was still poring over it myself, looking for people who might be linked to various branches of my family tree, when the telephone rang. Actually, I suppose I was somewhat irked at being taken from my studies, and perhaps I sounded a bit impatient when I answered the phone.

If so, the gentleman at the other end gave no sign of it. His voice was most pleasant, quite deep and masculine, and he said, "May I speak, please, with Mrs. Henrietta Buckley?"

"This is Mrs. Buckley," I told him.

"Ah," he said. "Forgive my telephoning, please, Mrs. Buckley. We have never met. But I noticed your entry in the current issue of the *Genealogical Exchange*—"

"Oh?" I was immediately excited, all thought of impatience gone. This was surely the fastest reply I'd ever had to date!

"Yes," he said. "I noticed the reference to Euphemia Barber. I do believe that may be the Euphemia Stover who married Jason Barber in Savannah, Georgia, in 1791. Jason Barber is in my direct line, on my mother's side. Jason and Euphemia had only the one child, Abner, and I am descended from him."

"Well," I said. "You certainly do seem to have complete information."

"Oh, yes," he said. "My own family chart is almost complete. For twelve generations, that is. I'm not sure whether I'll try to go back farther than that or not. The English records before 1600 are so incomplete, you know."

"Yes, of course," I said. I was, I admit, taken aback. Twelve generations! Surely that was the most ambitious family tree I had ever heard of, though I had read sometimes of people who had carried particular branches back as many as fifteen generations. But to actually be speaking to a person who had traced his entire family back twelve generations!

"Perhaps," he said, "it would be possible for us to meet, and I could give you the information I have on Euphemia Barber. There are also some Marshalls in one branch of my family; perhaps I can be of help to you there, as well." He laughed, a deep and pleasant sound, which reminded me of my late husband, Edward, when he was most particularly pleased. "And, of course," he said, "there is always the chance that you have some information on the Marshalls which can help me."

"I think that would be very nice," I said, and so I invited him to come to the apartment the very next afternoon.

At one point the next day, perhaps half an hour before Gerald Fowlkes was to arrive, I stopped my fluttering around to take stock of myself and to realize that if ever there were an indication of second childhood taking over, my thoughts and actions preparatory to Mr. Fowlkes' arrival were certainly it. I had been rushing hither and thither, dusting, rearranging, polishing, pausing incessantly to look in the mirror and touch my hair with fluttering fingers, all as though I were a flighty teenager before her very first date. "Henrietta," I told myself sharply, "you are seventy-three years old, and all that nonsense is well behind you now. Eleven times a grandmother, and just look at how you carry on!"

But poor Edward had been dead and gone these past nine years, my brothers and sisters were all in their graves, and as for my children, all but Tom, the youngest, were thousands of miles away, living their own lives—as of course they should—and only occasionally remembering to write a duty letter to Mother. And I am much too aware of the dangers of the clinging mother to force my presence too often upon Tom and his family. So I am very much alone, except of course for my friends in the various church activities and for those I have met, albeit only by postal, through my genealogical research.

So it *was* pleasant to be visited by a charming gentleman caller, and particularly so when that gentleman shared my own particular interests.

And Mr. Gerald Fowlkes, on his arrival, was surely no disappointment. He looked to be no more than fifty-five years of age, though he swore to sixty-two, and had a fine shock of gray hair above a strong and kindly face. He dressed very well, with that combination of expense and breeding so little found these days, when the well-bred seem invariably to be poor and the well-to-do seem invariably to be horribly plebeian. His manner was refined and gentlemanly, what we used to call courtly, and he had some very nice things to say about the appearance of my living room.

Actually, I make no unusual claims as a housekeeper. Living alone, and with quite a comfortable income having been left me by Edward, it is no problem at all to choose tasteful furnishings and keep them neat. (Besides, I had scrubbed the apartment from top to bottom in preparation for Mr. Fowlkes' visit.)

He had brought his pedigree along, and what a really beautiful job he had done. Pedigree charts, photostats of all sorts of records, a running history typed very neatly on bond paper and inserted in a loose-leaf notebook—all in all, the kind of careful, planned, well-thought-out perfection so unsuccessfully striven for by all amateur genealogists.

From Mr. Fowlkes, I got the missing information on Euphemia Barber. She was born in 1765, in Salem, Massachusetts, the fourth child of seven born to John and Alicia Stover. She married Jason Barber in Savannah in 1791. Jason, a well-to-do merchant, passed on in 1794, shortly after the birth of their first child, Abner. Abner was brought up by his paternal grandparents, and Euphemia moved away from Savannah. As I already knew, she had gone to Virginia, where she had married John Anderson. After that, Mr. Fowlkes had no record of her, until her death in Cincinnati, Ohio, in 1852. She was buried as Euphemia Stover Barber, apparently not having used the Anderson name after John Anderson's death.

This done, we went on to compare family histories and discover an Alan Marshall of Liverpool, England, around 1680, common to both trees. I was able to give Mr. Fowlkes Alan Marshall's birth date. And then the specific purpose of our meeting was finished. I offered tea and cakes, it then being four-thirty in the afternoon, and Mr. Fowlkes graciously accepted.

Before leaving, Mr. Fowlkes asked me to accompany him to a concert on Friday evening, and I very readily agreed. And so began the strangest three months of my entire life.

It didn't take me long to realize that I was being courted. Actually, I couldn't believe it at first. After all, at *my* age! But I myself did know some very nice couples who had married late in life—a widow and a widower, both lonely, sharing interests, and deciding to lighten their remaining years together—and looked at in that light it wasn't at all as ridiculous as it might appear at first.

Actually, I had expected my son Tom to laugh at the idea, and to dislike Mr. Fowlkes instantly upon meeting him. I suppose various fictional works that I have read had given me this expectation. So I was most pleasantly surprised when Tom and Mr. Fowlkes got along famously together from their very first meeting, and even more surprised when Tom came to me and told me Mr. Fowlkes had asked him if he would have any objection to his, Mr. Fowlkes', asking for my hand in matrimony. Tom said he had no objection at all, but actually thought it a wonderful idea, for he knew that both Mr. Fowlkes and myself were rather lonely, with nothing but our genealogical hobbies to occupy our minds.

As to Mr. Fowlkes' background, he very early gave me his entire history. He came from a fairly well-to-do family in upstate New York, and was himself now retired from his business, which had been a stock brokerage in Albany. He was a widower these last six years, and his first marriage had not been blessed with any children, so that he was completely alone in the world.

The next three months were certainly active ones. Mr. Fowlkes—Gerald—squired me everywhere, to concerts and to museums and even, after we had come to know one another well enough, to the theater. He was at all times most polite and thoughtful, and there was scarcely a day went by but what we were together.

During this entire time, of course, my own genealogical researches came to an absolute standstill. I was much too busy, and my mind was much to full of Gerald, for me to concern myself with family members who were long since gone to their rewards. Promising leads from the *Genealogical Exchange* were not followed up, for I didn't write a single letter. And though I did receive many in the *Exchange*, they all went unopened into a cubbyhole in my desk. And so the matter stayed, while the courtship progressed.

After three months Gerald at last proposed. "I am not a young man, Henrietta," he said. "Nor a particularly handsome man"—though he most certainly was very handsome, indeed—"nor even a very rich man, although I do have sufficient for my declining years. And I have little to offer you, Henrietta, save my own self, whatever poor companionship I can give you, and the assurance that I will be ever at your side."

What a beautiful proposal! After being nine years a widow, and never expecting even in fanciful daydreams to be once more a wife, what a beautiful proposal and from what a charming gentleman!

I agreed at once, of course, and telephoned Tom, the good news that very minute. Tom and his wife, Estelle, had a dinner party for us, and then we made our plans. We would be married three weeks hence. A short time? Yes, of course, it was, but there was really no reason to wait. And we would honeymoon in Washington, D.C., where my oldest boy, Roger, had quite a responsible position with the State Department. After which, we would return to Boston and take up our residence in a lovely old home on Beacon Hill, which was then for sale and which we would jointly purchase.

Ah, the plans! The preparations! How newly filled were my so recently empty days!

I spent most of the last week closing my apartment on Newbury Street. The furnishings would be moved to our new house by Tom, while Gerald and I were in Washington. But, of course, there was ever so much packing to be done, and I got at it with a will.

And so at last I came to my desk, and my genealogical researches lying as I had left them. I sat down at the desk, somewhat weary, for it was late afternoon and I had been hard at work since sunup, and I decided to spend a short while getting my papers into order before packing them away. And so I opened the mail which had accumulated over the last three months.

There were twenty-three letters. Twelve asked for information on various family names mentioned in my entry in the *Exchange*, five offered to give me information, and six concerned Euphemia Barber. It was, after all, Euphemia Barber who had brought Gerald and me together in the first place, and so I took time out to read these letters.

And so came the shock. I read the six letters, and then I simply sat limp at the desk, staring into space, and watched the monstrous pattern as it grew in my mind. For there was no question of the truth, no question at all.

Consider: Before starting the letters, this is what I knew of Euphemia Barber: She had been born Euphemia Stover in Salem, Massachusetts, in 1765. In 1791 she married Jason Barber, a widower of Savannah, Georgia. Jason died two years later, in 1793, of a stomach upset. Three years later Euphemia appeared in Virginia and married John Anderson, also a widower. John Anderson died two years thereafter, in 1798, of stomach upset. In both cases Euphemia sold her late husband's property and moved on.

And here is what the letters added to that, in chronological order:

From Mrs. Winnie Mae Cuthbert, Dallas, Texas: Euphemia Barber, in 1800, two years after John Anderson's death, appeared in Harrisburg, Pennsylvania, and married one Andrew Cuthbert, a widower and a prosperous feed merchant. Andrew died in 1801, of a stomach upset. The widow sold his store, and moved on.

From Miss Ethel Sutton, Louisville, Kentucky: Euphemia Barber, in 1804, married Samuel Nicholson of Louisville, a widower and a well-to-do tobacco farmer. Samuel Nicholson passed on in 1807, of a stomach upset. The widow sold his farm and moved on.

From Mrs. Isabelle Padgett, Concord, California: In 1808 Euphemia Barber married Thomas Norton, then Mayor of Dover, New Jersey, and a widower. In 1809 Thomas Norton died of a stomach upset.

From Mrs. Luella Miller, Bicknell, Utah: Euphemia Barber married Jonas Miller, a wealthy shipowner of Portsmouth, New Hampshire, a widower, in 1811. The same year Jonas Miller died of a stomach upset. The widow sold his property, and moved on.

From Mrs. Lola Hopkins, Vancouver, Washington: In 1813, in southern Indiana, Euphemia Barber married Edward Hopkins, a widower and a farmer. Edward Hopkins died in 1816 of a stomach upset. The widow sold the farm, and moved on.

From Mr. Roy Cumbie, Kansas City, Missouri: In 1819 Euphemia Barber married Stanley Thatcher of Kansas City, Missouri, a river barge owner and a widower. Stanley Thatcher died, of a stomach upset, in 1821. The widow sold his property, and moved on.

The evidence was clear, and complete. The intervals of time without dates could mean that there had been other widowers who had succumbed to Euphemia Barber's fatal charms, and whose descendants did not number among themselves an amateur genealogist. Who could tell just how many husbands Euphemia had murdered? For murder it quite clearly was, brutal murder, for profit. I had evidence of eight murders, and who knew but what there were eight more, or eighteen more? Who could tell, at this late date, just how many times Euphemia Barber had murdered for profit, and had never been caught?

Such a woman is unconceivable. Her husbands were always widowers, sure to be lonely, sure to be susceptible to a wily woman. She preyed on widowers, and left them all, a widow.

Gerald.

The thought came to me, and I pushed it firmly away. It couldn't possibly be true; it couldn't possibly have a single grain of truth.

But what did I know of Gerald Fowlkes, other than what he had told me? And wasn't I a widow, lonely and susceptible? And wasn't I financially well off?

Like father, like son, they say. Could it be also, like great-great-great-great-great-grandmother, like great-great-great-great-great-grandson?

What a thought! It came to me that there must be any number of widows in the country, like myself, who were interested in tracing their family trees. Women who had a bit of money and leisure, whose children were grown and gone out into the world to live their own lives, and who filled some of the empty hours with the hobby of genealogy. An unscrupulous man, preying on well-to-do widows, could find no better introduction than a common interest in genealogy.

What a terrible thought to have about Gerald! And yet I couldn't push it from my mind, and at last I decided that the only thing I could possibly do was try to substantiate the autobiography he had given me, for if he had told the truth about himself, then he could surely not be a beast of the type I was imagining.

A stockbroker, he had claimed to have been, in Albany, New York. I at once telephoned an old friend of my first husband's, who was himself a Boston stockbroker, and asked him if it would be possible for him to find out if there had been, at any time in the last fifteen or twenty years, an Albany stockbroker named Gerald Fowlkes. He said he could do so with ease, using some sort of directory he had, and would call me back. He did so, with the shattering news that no such individual was listed!

Still I refused to believe. Donning my coat and hat, I left the apartment at once and went directly to the telephone company, where, after an incredible number of white lies concerning genealogical research, I at last persuaded someone to search for an old Albany, New York, telephone book. I knew that the main office of the company kept books for other major cities, as a convenience for the public, but I wasn't sure they would have any from past years. Nor was the clerk I talked to, but at last she did go and search, and came back finally with the 1946 telephone book from Albany, dusty and somewhat ripped, but still intact, with both the normal listings and the yellow pages.

No Gerald Fowlkes was listed in the white pages, or in the yellow pages under Stocks & Bonds.

So. It was true. And I could see exactly what Gerald's method was. Whenever he was ready to find another victim, he searched one or another of the genealogical magazines until he found someone who shared one of his own past relations. He then proceeded to effect a meeting with that person, found out quickly enough whether or not the intended victim was a widow, of the proper age range, and with the properly large bank account, and then the courtship began.

I imagined that this was the first time he had made the mistake of using Euphemia Barber as the go-between. And I doubted that he even realized he was following in Euphemia's footsteps. Certainly, none of the six people who had written to me about Euphemia could possibly guess, knowing only of the one marriage and death, what Euphemia's role in life had actually been.

And what was I to do now? In the taxi, on the way back to my apartment, I sat huddled in a corner, and tried to think.

For this *was* a severe shock, and a terrible disappointment. And how could I face Tom, or my other children, or any of my friends, to whom I had already written the glad news of my impending marriage? And how could I return to the drabness of my days before Gerald had come to bring me gaiety and companionship and courtly grace?

Could I even call the police? I was sufficiently convinced myself, but could I possibly convince anyone else?

All at once, I made my decision. And, having made it, I immediately felt ten years younger, ten pounds lighter, and quite a bit less foolish. For, I might as well admit, in addition to everything else, this had been a terrible blow to my pride.

But the decision was made, and I returned to my apartment cheerful and happy.

And so we were married.

Married? Of course. Why not?

Because he will try to murder me? Well, of course, he *will* try to murder me. As a matter of fact, he has already tried, half a dozen times.

But Gerald is working at a terrible disadvantage. For he cannot murder me in any way that looks like murder. It must appear to be a natural death, or, at the very worst, an accident. Which means that he must be devious, and he must plot and plan, and never come at me openly to do me in.

And there is the source of his disadvantage. For I am forewarned, and forewarned is forearmed.

But what, really, do I have to lose? At seventy-three, how many days on this earth do I have left? And how *rich* life is these days! How rich compared to my life before Gerald came into it! Spiced with the thrill of danger, the excitement of cat and mouse, the intricate moves and countermoves of the most fascinating game of all.

And, of course, a pleasant and charming husband. Gerald *has* to be pleasant and charming. He can never disagree with me, at least not very forcefully, for he can't afford the danger of my leaving him. Nor can he afford to believe that I suspect him. I have never spoken of the matter to him, and so far as he is concerned I know nothing. We go to concerts and museums and the theater together. Gerald is attentive and gentlemanly, quite the best sort of companion at all times.

Of course, I can't allow him to feed me breakfast in bed, as he would so love to do. No, I told him, I was an old-fashioned woman, and believed that cooking was a woman's job, and so I won't let him near the kitchen. Poor Gerald!

And we don't take trips, no matter how much he suggests them.

And we've closed off the second story of our home, since I pointed out that the first floor was certainly spacious enough for just the two of us, and I felt I was getting a little old for climbing stairs. He could do nothing, of course, but agree.

And, in the meantime, I have found another hobby, though of course Gerald knows nothing of it. Through discreet inquiries, and careful perusal of past issues of the various genealogical magazines, and the use of the family names in Gerald's family tree, I am gradually compiling another sort of tree. Not a family tree, no. One might facetiously call it a hanging tree. It is a list of Gerald's wives. It is in with my genealogical files, which I have willed to the

Boston library. Should Gerald manage to catch me after all, what a surprise is in store for the librarian who sorts out those files of mine! Not as big a surprise as the one in store for Gerald, of course.

Ah, here comes Gerald now, in the automobile he bought last week. He's going to ask me again to go for a ride with him.

But I shan't go.

DARK JOURNEY

(1934)

Francis Iles

Norm Cayley's girlfriend Rose Fenton wants to get married. Cayley doesn't, and so he decides to kill her. This wildly irrational decision leads nonetheless to a careful plan of execution, which presents a terrifying portrait of a murderer.

As noted earlier, the name Francis Iles is one of the pseudonyms of Anthony Berkeley Cox (1893–1971). Like Cox's other nom de plume Anthony Berkeley, Iles is an acclaimed British mystery writer. His masterpiece is one of the greatest psychological mystery novels of all time, *Before the Fact* (1932). That book was made into the movie *Suspense* (1941), directed by Alfred Hitchcock and starring Cary Grant and Joan Fontaine, who won the Academy Award for Best Actress.

Cayley was going to commit murder.

He had worked it all out very carefully. For weeks now his plan had been maturing. He had pondered over it, examined it, tested it in the light of every possibility; and he was satisfied that it was impregnable. Now he was going to put it into practice.

Cayley did not really want to kill Rose Fenton.

Indeed, the idea made him shudder, even when he had been drinking. But what else could he do? He was desperate. Rose would not leave him alone. She thought, too, now that she had a claim on him; and she was plainly determined to exercise it. And Cayley very much did not want to marry Rose Fenton.

He never had thought of marrying her. A solicitor's clerk, with a position to make in the world—a solicitor's clerk with every chance of an ultimate partnership in his firm—cannot afford to marry a girl like Rose Fenton. Respectability is the bread of a solicitor's life. Besides, now there was Miriam. Miriam Seale, the only daughter of old Seale himself, the senior partner in Cayley's own firm. . . .

Cayley knew now that he had been risking his whole future by taking up with Rose at all. It had not seemed like that at first. Other men have adventures, why not he? But adventures in any case are not safe for solicitors, and now Rose had decided not to be an adventure at all, but a job. As Cayley knew only too well, Rose was a determined girl. Rose knew nothing of Miriam.

It seemed curious to Cayley now to remember that once he had been quite fond of Rose. Now, of course, he detested her. He would sit for hours in his cottage over a bottle of whisky, thinking how much he hated Rose. Before Rose became impossible, Cayley had never drunk whisky alone. Now he was depending on it more and more, and one cannot go on like that. One must make an end somehow.

Rose had brought it on herself. She would not leave him alone. She would not see when an affair was—finished. Cayley did not at all want to kill Rose, but he gloated over the idea of Rose dead. And he would never be his own man again till Rose was dead. He knew that. No; Cayley did not at all want to kill Rose, but what else could he do?

And now he was waiting for Rose to come; waiting on the side of the road, in the dark, with his stomach full of whisky and a revolver in his pocket.

As he waited, Cayley felt as if he were made of lead. The night was warm, but he felt neither warm nor cold, afraid nor brave, despairing nor exultant. He felt nothing at all. Both body and mind seemed to have gone inert, so that he just waited and hardly noticed whether the time went fast or slowly.

The noise of the bus roused him from his torpor. He followed its progress along the main road: loud when the line between it and himself was clear, with curious mufflings and dim silences when hedges or a fold in the ground intervened. Rose was in the bus, but Cayley did not feel any excitement at the thought. Everything had become in some strange way inevitable.

Cayley was waiting a couple of hundred yards down a side turning. It was a convenient little lane which Cayley had marked weeks and weeks ago, when he first thought of killing Rose. He and Rose had picnicked there one Sunday, on Rose's afternoon off. They had sat on the wide grassy margin which bordered one side, and Cayley had thought then how he would be able to wheel his motor-bicycle on to it and put out the lights while he waited for Rose. In such a deserted spot, in the dark, with his headlights out, it would be impossible that their meeting could be seen.

Rose had not been able to understand at first why Cayley should want to meet her in such an out-of-the-way place and so far from both the cottage and from Merchester; but Cayley had been able to make her see reason.

Both the plan in his heart and the plan on his lips depended on his meeting with Rose remaining secret, and that had been very convenient for the former. That explained why Rose was coming to meet him in the last bus from Stanford to Merchester and not in that from Merchester to

Stanford, although it was in Merchester that Rose was in service and Cayley worked.

Stanford and Merchester, both towns of some size, were eighteen miles apart, and while it was unlikely that Rose, not indigenous to the district, should be recognized leaving Merchester, it was almost impossible that she could be recognized leaving Stanford. Cayley had been taking no chances at all.

The bus had grumbled to a halt just beyond the turning and roared on again. Cayley heard footsteps coming towards him, scraping in the dark on the gritty surface of the lane. He waited where he stood until they were almost abreast of him, disregarding the calls of his name, rather louder than he liked, which Rose sent out before her in waves of sound through the still night like a swimmer urging the water in front of her.

"Rose," he said quietly.

Rose uttered a little scream. "Coo! You didn't half make me jump. Why didn't you answer when I called?"

"Have you put your trunk and things in the cloakroom?" It was essential to Cayley's plan that Rose should have left her luggage that afternoon at Liverpool Street Station, in London.

"Course I have. . . . Well," added Rose archly, "aren't you going to give us a kiss?"

"What else do you think I've been waiting for?" Cayley's heart was beating a little faster as he kissed Rose for the last time. He thought of Judas. It made him feel uncomfortable, and he cut the kiss as short as he decently could.

Rose sniffed at him. "Been drinking, haven't you?"

"Nothing, really," Cayley returned easily, feeling for his bicycle in the darkness. "Just a drop."

"It's been too many drops with you lately, my lad. I'm going to put a stop to it. Not going to have a drunkard for a husband, I'm not."

Cayley writhed. Rose's voice was full of possession; full of complacent assurance that in future he would have no life but what she chose to allow him. Had any qualms remained in him, that tone of Rose's would have dispelled them.

"Come on," he said sharply. "Let's get off."

"All right, all right. In a great hurry, aren't you? Where's the bike? Coo, I never saw it. It's that dark."

Cayley had wheeled the bicycle into the lane and switched on the headlight. He helped Rose into the sidecar, and jumped into his saddle.

"All serene. So off we go, on our honeymoon," giggled Rose. "Fancy you and me on our honeymoon, Norm."

"Yes," said Cayley. It was odd that, though this was the last time they would ever be together, Rose's hideous shortening of his Christian name grated on him as much as ever.

He drove slowly down the lane. "See anyone you know in Stanford?" he asked as casually as possible.

"So likely, isn't it? I fat lot of people I know."

"But did you?"

"No, Mr. Inquisitive, I did not. Any more questions?"

They turned into the main road, and Cayley increased his speed.

The whisky he had drunk did not affect his driving. His hands held the machine quite steady, though he was now pushing it along as fast as it would go, anxious to arrive and get the business finished. He did not glance at Rose in the sidecar beside him. Although it was the last time that Rose would ever ride in that sidecar alive, yet her presence exasperated him as much as ever, and the way she would cock her feet up under her so that her knees stuck up in the air. In a dim way Cayley recognized the fact, and was surprised by it. He had expected to feel tolerant now towards Rose's irritating ways. It was a relief to find that, in fact, he had not softened.

Nor had his resolution weakened.

Now that it had come to the point, Cayley was quite calm.

He knew that, normally, he was not always calm, and he had feared lest he might lose his head and somehow bungle things: be queer in his manner, tremble, let Rose see that something dreadful was afoot. But there was no longer any danger of that. Rose could not guess what was going to happen to her; and as for Cayley himself, he felt almost indifferent, as if the matter had all been taken somehow out of his hands. The whole affair was pre-ordained; events were moving forward of their own volition; nothing that he, or Rose, or anyone else, might do now could alter them.

Cayley drove on in a fatalistic trance. He realized vaguely that Rose was protesting against the speed, but disregarded her. It was no use Rose protesting against anything now.

Cayley's lonely little cottage was not on the main road. It, too, was down a side turning, and a good half-mile from the village. The village itself, with its couple of dozen cottages and two little shops, was tiny enough, but Cayley had always been glad that he was half a mile from it. He liked solitude. Since he had determined to kill Rose, he had realized how his liking for solitude had played into his hands. Even so small a thing as that was going to help to destroy Rose.

As he turned off the main road his love of solitude rose up in him in a passionate wave. Had Rose really imagined that he was going to let her into that little corner of the world that he had made for himself—Rose, with her inevitable vulgarity of speech and mind?

A tremor of hatred shook him as he saw her sturdy form trampling about the house which, a fire-blackened ruin when he bought it out of his small savings, he had rebuilt with his own hands; Rose, marching like a grenadier through the garden he had created; Rose, so assured in her ownership of it all that he would be made to feel an interloper in his own tiny domain. Miriam would never be like that. Besides, Miriam was . . .

Cayley thought fiercely how peaceful everything would be again once Rose was dead: how peaceful, and how hopeful.

A hundred yards away from the cottage he shut off his engine. Late though the time was, it was just possible that old Mrs. Wace, who "did" for him, might not yet have gone. She liked to potter and potter in the evenings, and Cayley had not been so foolish as to try to hustle her off the premises early. And slightly deaf though she was, Cayley had already been careful to find out that she could hear his motorcycle drive up to the little shed at the bottom of the garden where he kept it.

Rose, of course, expostulated when his engine stopped, but Cayley was ready for that.

"Run out of juice," he explained glibly. "Lucky we got nearly home. Give me a hand to push her, Rose."

"Well, that's a nice thing to ask a girl, I must say," objected Rose for form's sake.

Between them they pushed the bicycle past the cottage.

Before they reached the shed, Rose evidently considered it due to herself to protest further.

"Here, this is a bit too much like hard work for me. You didn't ought to ask me to do a thing like that, Norm, and that's a fact."

"All right," Cayley said mildly. "I can manage alone now." There were indeed only a few more yards to cover.

"Well, it's your own fault, isn't it?"

Cayley did not answer. The bicycle was heavy, and he needed all his breath. Rose walked behind him.

"Here, half a mo'. I'll get my suitcase out before you put the bike away, if you *don't* mind."

"It doesn't matter," Cayley threw back over his shoulder. "I'll get it out in a minute."

He brought the bicycle to a standstill outside the shed and opened the door.

Rose, a dim figure in the velvety August night, was peering up at the stars.

"Coo, it's black enough for you to-night, I should think. Never known it so dark, I haven't."

"The moon doesn't rise till after midnight," Cayley answered absently, busy turning the bicycle round in the lane. It was better to turn it now, then it would be ready.

"Proper night to elope, and no mistake," Rose's voice came rallyingly. "Is that why you chose it, eh? Getting quite sloppy in your old age, Norm, aren't you? Well, that'll be a nice change, I must say."

Cayley straightened up from the bicycle and wiped the sweat from his forehead, "Why?"

"Oh, nothing. I just thought you'd been a bit standoffish lately."

There was a sentimental, almost a yearning note in Rose's voice.

"Nonsense, darling. Of course, I haven't."

"In fact, I don't mind telling you, I thought at one time you didn't mean to treat me right."

"I'm going to treat you right, Rose," said Cayley.

"Still love us, Norm?"

"Of course I do."

"Where are you, then?"

Cayley's fingers closed round the small revolver in his pocket. "Here."

"Well, can't you come a bit closer?" Rose giggled.

Cayley took her arm. "Come inside the shed for a minute, Rose."

"What ever for?"

"I want you to."

Rose giggled again. "Coo, Norm, you are a one, aren't you?"

Cayley's mouth and throat were dry as he drew Rose across the threshold and closed the door. But he was not really afraid. The dream-like state was on him again. Things were not real. All this had happened somewhere before. Rose was dead already. The two of them were only enacting, like ghosts, a deed that had been performed ages and ages ago, in some other existence; every movement and word had been already laid down, and there could be neither deviation nor will to deviate.

Once more Rose uttered her silly, throaty giggle.

"What do you want to shut the door for? I should have thought it was dark enough already."

Cayley had already proved, by repeated experiment, that with the door of the shed closed Mrs. Wace, even if she were in the cottage, could not hear a revolver-shot; but of course, he could not tell Rose that.

He drew the revolver from his pocket. He was still quite calm.

Hot hands were clutching for him in the darkness and he held the revolver out of their reach.

"Honest, I'm ever so fond of you, Norm," whispered Rose.

"So am I of you, Rose. Where are you?"

"Well, that's a nice question. Where do you think I am? Can't you feel me?"

"Yes." Cayley found her shoulder and gripped it gently while he edged behind her. Methodically he felt for the back of her neck and placed the muzzle of the revolver against it.

"Here, mind my hat, *if* you please. Here . . . what's the game, Norm?"

Cayley fired.

The shot sounded so deafeningly loud in the little shed that it seemed to Cayley as if anyone not only at the cottage but in the village, too, must have heard it. A spasm of terror shook him. How could anyone in the whole of England not have heard it? He stood rigid, listening for the alarm that must inevitably follow.

Everything was quiet.

Cayley pulled himself together. Of course, the shot had been no louder than his experiments in the daytime. There was no time now to give way to fantastic panic of that sort. He realized that he was still holding Rose's body in his arms. He had been so close to her when he fired that she had slumped down against him, and he had caught her mechanically. He laid her now on the floor of the shed. Then he lighted a stub of candle which he had brought here days ago for just that purpose. There was no window in the shed, and the door was still closed.

Cayley could not believe that Rose was dead.

It had been too easy, too quick. She could not have died in that tiny instant. Not Rose. She was too vigorous, too vital, to have the life blown out of her like that in a tiny fraction of a second.

He looked at her lying there, in her best frock of saxe-blue silk, her black straw hat, brown shoes, and pink silk stockings. People bled, didn't they, when they were shot? But there was no blood. Rose was not bleeding at all.

Cayley's forehead broke out in a cold sweat. Rose was not really dead, after all! He had missed her, somehow, in the darkness. The gun had not been touching her head at all, it had been touching something else. Rose was only stunned. Perhaps not even stunned: just pretending to be stunned: shamming.

Cayley dropped on his knees beside her and felt frantically for her heart. He knew Rose was dead, but he could not believe it. Her heart gave no movement.

"Rose!" he said, in a shaky voice. "Rose—can't you speak to me? Rose!" He could not believe Rose was dead.

Rose lay on her back staring up at the roof of the little shed, her eyelids just drooping over her eyes. Cayley did not know why he had spoken to her aloud. Of course Rose could not answer. She was dead.

The tears came into Cayley's own eyes. He understood now that it was too late, that there had never been any need to kill Rose at all. He could have managed everything by being firm. Just by being firm. Rose would have understood. Rose had always been sensible. And now, for the want of a little firmness, Rose was dead and he was a murderer.

"Oh, God," he moaned, "I wish I hadn't done it. Oh, God, I wish I hadn't done it."

But he had done it, and Rose was dead. Cayley got up slowly from his knees.

It was dreadful to see Rose lying there, with her head on the floor. There was an old pillion cushion on the shelf. Cayley took it down and put it under Rose's head. Somehow that made her look better.

Besides—Rose might not be dead. If she came to it would be nicer for her to have a cushion under her head.

Cayley stiffened. Had that been a noise outside? He stood stock-still, hardly daring to breathe. Was someone prowling about? He listened desperately. It was not easy to listen very well, because the blood was pounding so in his ears. It made a kind of muffled drumming, like waves on a distant shingle beach. Beyond the drumming he could detect no sound.

Very slowly he lifted the latch of the door. It was stiff, and for all his caution rose with a final jerk. Cayley started violently. The latch had made only a tiny click, but in his ears it sounded like the crack of doom.

He edged the door open, got outside, and closed it behind him. Then he stood still, listening again. There was no sound. He began to walk softly towards the cottage, fifty yards away.

He walked more and more slowly. A horrible feeling had suddenly taken possession of him: that someone was following, just as softly, in his tracks. The back of his head tingled and pricked as the hair lifted itself on his scalp; for something was telling him that the door of the shed had opened and Rose had come noiselessly out. Now she was following him.

He could feel her presence, just behind him. Cold beads chased each other down his back. He tried to turn his head to make sure that Rose was not really there, but could not. It was physically impossible for him to look back towards the door of the shed. All he could do was to stand still and listen, between the pounding of the waves in his ears. The flesh of his back quivered and crept. Every second he expected Rose to come up and touch him on it. He could almost feel her touch already. It was all he could do to stop himself from shrieking.

At last, with a little sob, he forced himself to turn round.

There was nothing but inky darkness behind him.

But somewhere in that inky darkness, between himself and the shed, Cayley could not get rid of the feeling that someone, or something stood. He dragged the revolver out of his pocket again and leveled it at the shed. At any moment a shape might loom towards him out of the blackness, and he must be ready. He stood rigid, waiting, his tongue parched and his throat dry. Then, with a sudden effort, he walked rapidly back to the shed.

The door was still closed.

Cayley put the revolver back into his pocket and walked quickly over to the cottage.

Outside it he halted for a few moments, working his jaws to obtain some saliva in order to moisten his tongue and throat. The kitchen was at the back of the cottage. As he peered round the angle, Cayley could see the light streaming out of the window. Mrs. Wace had not gone.

Cayley's knees shook together. Mrs. Wace had not gone, and she must have heard the shot. It was impossible that she could not have heard it, deaf as she was. He had miscalculated in his experiments. They had been made in the daytime, and sound travels further in the silence of the night. He had not allowed for that. Mrs. Wace had heard the shot, and now she was waiting to find out what it meant. Cayley stood for a minute in the grip of a panic so violent that his limbs shook and his teeth chattered, and he could not control them. It was all he could do at last to drag himself round the corner of the house and, unseen, stare through the uncurtained kitchen window.

Mrs. Wace was doing something by the larder door. She had her hat and coat on. Cayley watched her take up three onions, look at them, drop one into a string bag and put the other two back into the larder. He searched her face. There seemed to be nothing on it but preoccupation with what she was doing. Was it possible that she had not heard the shot after all?

He walked quickly round to the front of the house and went into his living room.

From a cupboard on the wall he took a whisky bottle and a glass. Then, putting back the glass, he pulled the cork out of the bottle and put the mouth of it to his lips, gulping down the neat spirit in thirsty haste. Not until half its remaining contents had gone did he put the bottle back on the shelf.

Almost immediately the stuff did him good. He waited a moment while the heartening glow steadied his limbs. Then he walked firmly into the kitchen.

Mrs. Wace was just going out through the back door. She stopped when she saw him, and it seemed to Cayley that she looked at him queerly.

Cayley's fingers tightened round the revolver in his pocket as he searched her face.

"Ah, back are you?" said Mrs. Wace comfortably.

Cayley breathed with relief. His fingers relaxed on the revolver. The next instant they tightened again.

"Back? I haven't been away. I've been sitting in the garden, smoking."

"Well, there's no accounting for tastes," observed Mrs. Wace indifferently. "Good night, Mr. Cayley."

"Good night, Mrs. Wace."

Cayley went back to his living room, his knees weak with relief. If Mrs. Wace had heard anything, or voiced any suspicion, he would have shot her dead. He knew he would. It would have been madness, but he would have done it. He took the whisky bottle and tumbler from the shelf and poured himself out a stiff dose. He realized now that he was trembling.

Instantly the same feeling came to him as in the shed. Rose was not dead at all. She had only been stunned. She would come to if he gave her some whisky. He caught up the bottle and hurried with it down the garden through the dark.

Outside the door of the shed he stopped. He could not go in: he just could not go inside. Suppose after all that . . .

"Rose!" he called shakily. "Rose!"

It took a full minute, and another swig at the bottle, before he could get a grip on himself again.

Rose was lying just as he had left her. She was quite dead.

Cayley took another, smaller mouthful of whisky and set the bottle down on the shelf with a hand that no longer shook. What a fool he had been! Everything had gone splendidly. All he had to do now was to proceed with his plan.

It was a good plan.

To her mistress in Merchester and to her only living relative, an elderly aunt, living in Streatham, Rose had written, on Cayley's instructions, that she was going out to Canada to be married. Canada somehow sounded more convincing than America. Rose really had believed that Cayley was going out to Canada, to open a branch there for his firm.

Over her luggage Cayley had been equally clever. Rose was to have left Merchester that afternoon for London, and deposited her trunk at Liverpool Street Station. In a busy place like Liverpool Street Rose would never be noticed or remembered. Equally unnoticed, Cayley would be able to claim the trunk later with the check that would be in Rose's handbag, and dispose of it at his leisure. There would be nothing at all to connect him with Rose's disappearance.

Rose had made objections, of course. When, in Merchester, she was only half-a-dozen miles from Cayley's cottage, why travel all the way up to London and come back to Stanford? But Cayley had been able to convince her. He was not leaving for Canada till the next day.

It was essential that Rose should not be seen coming to the cottage. If she were, her good name would be lost, even though they were getting married in London the next morning before sailing. The argument had gone home, for Rose was always very careful about "what people would say."

So though she had demurred at the expense, for she had a parsimonious mind, Rose had in the end consented. If she had not consented, Cayley would never have dared to kill her. Rose had agreed to her own death when she agreed to take her trunk up to Liverpool Street Station.

Cayley stood now, looking down at her.

He was no longer afraid of Rose's dead body. The whisky he had drunk was making him sentimental. Two tears oozed out of his eyes and ran absurdly down his cheeks. Poor old Rose. She had not been such a bad sort, really. It was a shame that he had had to kill her. A rotten shame. Cayley wished very much that he had not had to kill Rose.

In a flash, sentiment fled before a sudden jab of terror.

Suppose Rose had not brought the check for the trunk with her after all! Suppose she had left it somewhere, or given it to someone else to claim for her! Cayley saw now that he had left this weak spot in the armour of his plan.

He had taken no steps to ensure that Rose should have the check with her: he had simply taken it for granted that she would. And if she had not, and he were unable to claim the trunk, everything would miscarry. In that case the trunk would sooner or later be opened, and then it would be known that Rose had disappeared, and then . . .

Cayley shivered with fear.

In vain he tried to point out to himself that even if it did become known that Rose had disappeared, there would still be nothing to connect her disappearance with himself. In Merchester he had always kept very quiet about his relations with Rose. But his mind, numb with panic, refused to accept the reasoning. Everything hung for him on the vital question: had Rose brought the check with her?

Rose's handbag lay on the floor, half underneath her. Cayley pushed her body roughly aside to snatch it up. His fingers shook so much that he could hardly open it.

The next moment he uttered a sob of relief. The check was there. "One trunk . . ." The words danced before his eyes. He was safe.

He took another pull at the whisky bottle.

He was safe: and now he must proceed, quite calmly, with the rest of his plan.

Cayley would never have believed that Rose was so heavy.

It had seemed simple, in advance, to put her into the sidecar, prop her there to look natural, and drive with her to the disused quarry, where her grave was already prepared, and the spade waiting to fill it in. But now that it had come to the point, it was dreadful to have to pick her up and stagger with her through the darkness, like a sack of potatoes in his arms. Cayley was gasping for breath by the time he reached the sidecar.

But the physical effort had helped him. He was no longer nervous. He was exultant. It takes courage and brains to commit a successful murder. Cayley, doubtful at times before, knew now that he had both. And there were people who thought him—Cayley knew they did!—a weakling, a little rat. Now he could smile at them. Rats can bite.

Before he set out for the quarry, Cayley went back to the shed. The candle had to be put out, and he wanted to have a good look round to make sure that no traces were left. The risk was infinitesimal, but Cayley was not taking even infinitesimal risks; and there are always tramps.

There were no traces. Only a few spots of blood on the leather of the cushion, which Cayley wiped off with a wisp of cotton waste, burning the waste at once in the flame of the candle. No one could possibly tell that a newly-dead body had been lying in that shed.

Before he blew out the candle Cayley pulled the precious check for the trunk out of his trouser pocket, where he had stuffed it, in order to stow it away more carefully in his wallet. It was funny how he had nearly lost his head just now over a little thing like that. He glanced through it gloatingly before tucking it away. The wording, which before had shimmered in a blurred way before his panic-stricken eyes, was now soberly legible.

The next instant his heart seemed to stop beating. Then it began to race faster than the engine of his own motorcycle. For the check was not on Liverpool Street at all, not even on Stanford. It was on the station quite close to Cayley's cottage. Rose had not been up to London. She had kept the money Cayley had given her, and traveled only to the local station. Cayley had committed the fatal mistake of underrating Rose's parsimony. And by her parsimony Rose had ensured that her last appearance alive should be inevitably connected with her lover.

With a sick horror Cayley sat down in the doorway of the shed and nursed his head in his hands. Then he moaned aloud. What was he to do now? What, in Heaven's name, could he do now?

Cayley never knew how long he had sat like that, in a lethargy of self-pity and despair, nor how long it was before coherent thought returned to him. The first shock, which galvanized his mind into activity once more, was the realization that all this time Rose was waiting for him—waiting, in the sidecar. Cayley choked down the hysterical laugh which leapt in his throat. Rose never had liked waiting.

He jumped up.

Instantly, as if it had only needed the reflex action of his muscles to stimulate his brain, he saw that the position was not, after all, so desperate. The trunk would remain in the cloakroom for days, perhaps for weeks, before anything was done about it. By that time Cayley could, if the worst came to the worst, be in South America.

But perhaps the best thing to do would be to claim it boldly, in a day or two's time. It was quite unlikely that the porter-cum-clerk would remember who had left it. Rose was not known there. It was not as if suspicion would ever be roused. Suspicion is only roused when a person is reported missing. Rose never would be so reported. No, the position was not desperate at all. Cayley's spirits began to rise. The position was not even bad. Except for a small adjustment or two, his plan still held perfectly good.

He began to whistle as he wrapped a rug carefully over Rose, and drove her off. It was only a couple of miles to the quarry. In a quarter of an hour the whole business would be done.

Yes, the boldest course usually paid. He would claim the trunk himself. And he could arrange some slight disguise, just in case of accidents. A disguise, yes. Why . . .

Cayley's thoughts broke off with a jerk. He cursed. His engine had stopped.

He came to a standstill by the side of the road. The trouble was simple: he had run out of petrol. Cayley felt terribly frightened. He had filled the tank before first setting out to meet Rose; how could it have emptied so soon? It almost looked as though Providence . . .

It was not Providence, but a leaking feed-pipe. Feverishly Cayley screwed up the loose nut and delved into the sidecar for the spare tin of petrol, pushing Rose to one side without a thought. He blessed his foresight in having put the tin there. Really, every possibility had been foreseen.

As he got back into the saddle once more, a sound struck his whole body into frozen immobility. Someone was approaching along the lonely country road. Someone with large, heavy feet. Someone who flashed a lamp. It was the millionth chance, and it had come off.

Cayley kicked in agony at his starter, but the carburetor had emptied. He kicked and kicked, but not even a splutter came from the engine. Then, as the footsteps drew abreast of him, he stopped kicking and waited, petrified.

"Hullo," said the constable. "Breakdown?"

Cayley's dry tongue rustled over his drier lips. "No," he managed to mutter. "Just—just filling up . . . petrol."

"Oh, it's you, Mr. Cayley. Ah! Fine night."

"Yes. Well, I must be getting on." Cayley prayed that his voice did not sound such a croak as he feared. The light of the constable's lamp flickered over him, and he winced. Before he could stop himself, the words had jumped out. "Switch that light of yours off, man."

"Sorry, Mr. Cayley, I'm sure." The constable sounded hurt.

"It was blinding me," Cayley muttered.

"Ah, new battery. Well good night, Mr. Cayley. Nothing I can do?"

"Nothing, thanks." Cayley kicked at his starter. Nothing happened.

The constable lingered. "Quite a treat to see someone, on a lonely beat like this."

"Yes, it must be." Cayley was still kicking. He wanted to scream at the man to go. He would scream in a minute. No, he must not scream. He must hold the edges of his nerves together like flesh over a wound, to keep the panic within from welling out. "Good night," he said clearly.

"Well, good night, Mr. Cayley. Got a load, I see?"

"Yes," Cayley's head was bent. He spoke through almost closed teeth. "Some potatoes I . . ."

"Potatoes?"

"Yes, a sack. Look here, man. I said switch that light out."

"Now, now, Mr. Cayley, I don't take orders from you. I know my duty, and it's my belief—"

"Leave that rug alone!" screamed Cayley.

The constable paused, startled. Then he spoke weightily, the corner of the rug in his great hand.

"Mr. Cayley, I must ask you to show me what you've got in this here sidecar. It don't look like potatoes to me, and that's a fact. Besides—"

"All right then, damn you!" Cayley's voice was pitched hysterically. "All right!"

The sound of the shot mingled with the sudden roar of the engine. As he twisted to fire Cayley's foot had trodden on the starter. This time it worked. The bicycle leapt forward.

Cayley drove on, as fast as his machine would carry him. His face was stiff with terror. He knew he had not killed the policeman, for he had seen him jump aside as the bicycle plunged forward.

What had possessed him to fire like that? And what, ten times more fatal, had possessed him to fire and not to kill? Now he was done for. Cayley knew that his only chance was to go back and find the policeman: to hunt him down and kill him where he stood. That was his only chance now—and he could not do it. No, he could not. Too late Cayley realized that he was not the man for murder.

What was he going to do?

Already the constable would be giving the alarm. Policemen everywhere would be on the look-out for him soon. He must not stop. His only hope was to get as far away as possible, in the quickest time.

He sped on madly, not knowing where he was going, turning now right, now left, as the road forked, intent only on putting as long and as confused a trail as possible between himself and the constable.

He drove till his eyes were almost blind and his arms were numb with pain, and Rose drove with him.

Rose!

He could not dispossess himself of her, he dared not leave her anywhere. He dared not even stop. If he stopped, they might pounce on him. And then they would find her. And if he did not stop—just stop to bury her somewhere—then they would find her just the same in the end. But he dared not stop. His one hope was to keep flying along. So long as he was moving he was safe.

He drove on: insanely, anywhere, everywhere, so long as he was still driving. His eyes never shifted from the road ahead of him; but after a time his lips began to move. He was talking to Rose, in the sidecar.

"I got it for you, Rose. You would have it, instead of riding pillion. Well, now you've got it. This is our last drive together, Rose, so I hope you're enjoying it."

What was to happen when his petrol gave out he dared not think. He could not think. His brain was numb. All he knew was that he must keep on driving: away, away, from that policeman and the alarm he had given. Where he might be he had no idea; nor any idea of the names of the villages and little towns through which he tore.

It did not matter so long as he kept on. One word only fixed itself in his sliding mind: Scotland. For some reason he had the idea that if he could but reach Scotland he would have a chance.

At breakneck speed he thrust on, with Rose, to Scotland.

But Cayley was not to reach Scotland that night. Whether it is that, in panic, the human animal really does move in circles, whether it was that in his numbed brain there still glowed an unconscious spark of his great plan, the fact is left that, while Cayley still thought himself headed for Scotland, he instinctively took a rough track which presented itself on the right of the road when he came to it, and that track led to the top of the same quarry in which he had meant to bury Rose.

But Cayley never knew that, any more than he recognized the wooden rails bordering the edge when they seemed to leap towards him in the beam of his headlight. Then it was too late to recognize anything, in this world.

There were other things, too, which Cayley never knew. He never knew that the constable, a motorcyclist himself, had seen his inadvertent treading on the self-starter. He did not know that the constable, highly amused, had thought that Cayley's motorcycle had run away with him. Above all, he did not know that the constable never had the remotest idea that a shot was ever fired at him.

THE FALL OF A COIN

(1975)

Ruth Rendell

Burdened with an unhappy marriage, a couple engage in psychological warfare. The reader becomes engrossed in the tattered fabric of their relationship as they grope their way toward a tragic conclusion.

If Agatha Christie and Dorothy L. Sayers were the grand dames of English mystery writing in the "Golden Age," Ruth Rendell is one of their modern successors. She is the winner of three Edgar Awards, the Grand Master Edgar Award (1997), and three Gold Dagger Awards, Britain's equivalent of the Edgar. In 1996 Rendell, like Christie, was awarded the CBE (Commander of the Order of the British Empire), the country's highest honor. She is a mainstream novelist as well as a mystery/crime writer, and her short stories are second to none. About a dozen of her novels feature Chief Inspector Reginald Wexford, including the recent *Harm Done* (2000) and *End in Tears* (2006). Other well-known books are *A Sleeping Life* (1976), *Make Death Love Me* (1979), and *An Unkindness of Ravens* (1983). Under the pseudonym Barbara Vine, Rendell has written several books such as *A Dark-Adapted Eye* (1986), which won an Edgar Award. The popularity of Rendell's stories has led to numerous television adaptations. Many of them are collected in *The Ruth Rendell Mysteries*, released on DVD in 2007.

This story initially appeared in *Ellery Queen's Mystery Magazine*.

The manageress of the hotel took them up two flights of stairs to their room. There was no lift. There was no central heating either and, though April, it was very cold.

"A bit small, isn't it?" said Nina Armadale.

"It's a double room and I'm afraid it's all we had left."

"I suppose I'll have to be thankful it hasn't got a double bed," said Nina.

Her husband winced at that, which pleased her. She went over to the window and looked down into a narrow alley bounded by brick walls. The cathedral clock struck five. Nina imagined what that would be like chiming every hour throughout the night, and maybe every quarter as well, and was glad she had brought her sleeping pills.

The manageress was still making excuses for the lack of accommodation. "You see, there's this big wedding in the cathedral tomorrow. Sir William Tarrant's daughter. There'll be five hundred guests and most of them are putting up in the town."

"We're going to it," said James Armadale. "That's why we're here."

"Then you'll appreciate the problem. Now the bathroom's just down the passage, turn right and it's the third door on the left. Dinner at seven-thirty and breakfast from eight till nine. Oh, and I'd better show Mrs. Armadale how to work the gas fire."

"Don't bother," said Nina, enraged. "I can work a gas fire." She was struggling with the wardrobe door, which at first wouldn't open, and when opened refused to close.

The manageress watched her, apparently decided it was hopeless to assist, and said to James, "I really meant about working the gas *meter*. There's a coin-in-the-slot meter—it takes fivepence pieces—and we really find it the best way for guests to manage."

James squatted on the floor beside her and studied the grey metal box. It was an old-fashioned gas meter with brass fittings of the kind he hadn't seen since he had been a student living in a furnished room. A gauge with a red arrow marker indicated the amount of gas paid for, and at present it showed empty. So if you turned the dial on the gas fire to "on" no gas would come from the meter unless you had previously fed it with one or more fivepence pieces. But what was the purpose of that brass handle? There were differences between this contraption and the one he'd had in his college days. Maybe, while his had been for the old toxic coal gas, this had been converted for the supply of natural gas. He looked enquiringly at the manageress, and asked her.

"No, we're still waiting for natural in this part of the country and when it comes the old meters will have to go."

"What's the handle for?"

"You turn it to the left like this, insert your coin in the slot, and then turn it to the right. Have you got fivepence on you?"

James hadn't. Nina had stopped listening, he was glad to see. Perhaps when the inevitable quarrel started, as it would as soon as the woman had gone, it would turn upon the awfulness of going to this wedding, for which he could hardly be blamed, instead of the squalid arrangements in the hotel, for which he could.

"Never mind," the manageress was saying. "You can't go wrong, it's very simple. When you've put your fivepence in, you just turn the handle to the right as far at it will go and you hear the coin fall. Then you can switch on the fire and light the gas. Is that clear?"

James said it was quite clear, thanks very much, and immediately the manageress had left the room. Nina, who wasted no time, said. "Can you tell me one good reason why we couldn't have come here tomorrow?"

"I could tell you several," said James, getting up from the floor, turning his back on that antediluvian thing and the gas fire which looked as if it hadn't given out a therm of heat for about thirty years. "The principal one is that I didn't fancy driving a hundred and fifty miles in a morning coat and top hat."

"Didn't fancy driving with your usual Saturday morning hangover, you mean."

"Let's not start a row, Nina. Let's have a bit of peace for just one evening. Sir William is my company chairman. I have to take it as an honour that we were asked to this wedding, and if we have an uncomfortable evening and night because of it, that can't be helped. It's part of the job."

"Just how pompous can you get?" said Nina with what in a less attractive woman would have been called a snarl. "I wonder what Sir William-Bloody-Tarrant would say if he could see his sales director after he's got a bottle of whisky inside him."

"He doesn't see me," said James, lighting a cigarette, and adding because she hadn't yet broken his spirit, "That's your privilege."

"*Privilege!*" Nina, who had been furiously unpacking her case and throwing clothes onto one of the beds, now stopped doing this because it sapped some of the energy she needed for quarrelling. She sat down on the bed and snapped, "Give me a cigarette. You've no manners, have you? Do you know how uncouth you are? This place'll suit you fine, it's just up to your mark, gas meters and a loo about five hundred yards away. That won't bother you as long as there's a bar. I'll be able to have the *privilege* of sharing my bedroom with a disgusting soak." She drew breath like a swimmer and plunged on. "Do you realise we haven't slept in the same room for two years? Didn't think of that, did you, when you left booking up till the last minute? Or maybe—yes, that was it, my God!—maybe you did think of it. Oh, I know you so well, James Armadale. You thought being in here with me, undressing with me, would work the miracle. I'd come round. I'd—what's the expression?—*resume marital relations*. You got them to give us this—this cell on purpose. You bloody fixed it!"

"No," said James. He said it quietly and rather feebly because he had experienced such a strong inner recoil that he could hardly speak at all.

"You liar! D'you think I've forgotten the fuss you made when I got you to sleep in the spare room? D'you think I've forgotten about that woman, that Frances? I'll never forget and I'll never forgive you. So don't think I'm going to let bygones by bygones when you try pawing me about when the bar closes."

"I shan't do that," said James, reflecting that in a quarter of an hour the bar would be opening. "I shall never again try what you so charmingly describe as pawing you about."

"No, because you know you wouldn't get anywhere. You know you'd get a slap round the face you wouldn't forget in a hurry."

"Nina," he said, "let's stop this. It's hypothetical, it won't happen. If we are going to go on living together—and I suppose we are, though God knows why—can't we try to live in peace?"

She flushed and said in a thick sullen voice, "You should have thought of that before you were unfaithful to me with that woman."

"That," he said, "was three years ago, *three years*. I don't want to provoke you and we've been into this enough times, but you know very well why I was unfaithful to you. I'm only thirty-five, I'm still young. I couldn't stand being permitted *marital relations*—pawing you about, if you like that better—about six times a year. Do I have to go over it all again?"

"Not on my account. It won't make any difference to me what excuses you make." The smoke in the tiny room made her cough and, opening the window, she inhaled the damp, cold air. "You asked me," she said, turning round, "why we have to go on living together. I'll tell you why. Because you married me. I've got a right to you and I'll never divorce you. You've got me till death parts us. Till death, James. Right?"

He didn't answer. An icy blast had come into the room when she had opened the window, and he felt in his pocket. "If you're going to stay in here till dinner," he said, "you'll want the gas fire on. Have you got any fivepence pieces? I haven't, unless I can get some change."

"Oh, you'll get some all right. In the bar. And just for your information. I haven't brought any money with me. That's *your* privilege."

When he had left her alone, she sat in the cold room for some minutes, staring at the brick wall. Till death parts us, she had told him, and she meant it. She would never leave him and he must never be allowed to leave her, but she hoped he would die. It wasn't her fault she was frigid. She had always supposed he understood. She had supposed her good looks and her capacity as housewife and hostess compensated for a revulsion she couldn't help. And it wasn't just against him, but against all men, any man. He had seemed to accept it and to be happy with her. In her sexless way, she had loved him. And then, when he had seemed happier and more at ease than at any time in their marriage, when he had ceased to make those painful demands and had become so sweet to her, so generous with presents, he had suddenly and without shame confessed it. She wouldn't mind, he had told her, he knew that. She wouldn't resent his finding elsewhere what she so evidently disliked giving him. While he provided for her and spent nearly all his leisure with her and respected her as his wife, she should be relieved, disliking sex as she did, that he had found someone else.

He had said it was the pent-up energy caused by her repressions that made her fly at him, beat at him with her hands, scream at him words he didn't know she knew. To her dying day she would remember his astonishment. He had genuinely thought she wouldn't mind. And it had taken weeks of nagging and screaming and threats to make him agree to give Frances up. She had driven him out of her bedroom and settled into the bitter, unremitting vendetta she would keep up till death parted them. Even now, he didn't understand how agonizingly he had hurt her. But there were no more women and he had begun to drink. He was drinking now, she thought, and by nine o'clock he would be stretched out, dead drunk on that bed separated by only eighteen inches from her own.

The room was too cold to sit in any longer. She tried the gas fire, turning on the switch to "full," but the match she held to it refused to ignite it, and presently she made her way downstairs and into a little lounge where there was a coal fire and people were watching television.

They met again at the dinner table.

James Armadale had drunk getting on for half a pint of whisky, and now, to go with the brown Windsor soup and hotted-up roast lamb, he ordered a bottle of burgundy.

"Just as a matter of idle curiosity," said Nina, "why do you drink so much?"

"To drown my sorrows," said James. "The classic reason. Happens to be true in my case. Would you like some wine?"

"I'd better have a glass, hadn't I, otherwise you'll drink the whole bottle."

The dining room was full and most of the other diners were middle-aged or elderly. Many of them, he supposed, would be wedding guests like themselves. He could see that their arrival had been noted and that at the surrounding tables their appearance was being favourably commented upon. It afforded him a thin, wry amusement to think that they would be judged a handsome, well-suited and perhaps happy couple.

"Nina," he said, "we can't go on like this. It's not fair on either of us. We're destroying ourselves and each other. We have to talk about what we're going to do."

"Pick your moments, don't you? I'm not going to talk about it in a public place."

She had spoken in a low, subdued voice, quite different from her hectoring tone in their bedroom, and she shot quick, nervous glances at the neighbouring tables.

"It's because this is a public place that I think we stand a better chance of talking about it reasonably. When we're alone you get hysterical and then neither of us can be rational. If we talk about it now, I think I know you well enough to say you won't scream at me."

"I could walk out though, couldn't I? Besides, you're drunk."

"I am not drunk. Frankly, I probably shall be in an hour's time and that's another reason why we ought to talk here and now. Look, Nina, you don't love me, you've said so often enough, and whatever crazy ideas you have about my having designs on you, I don't love you either. We've been into the reasons for that so many times that I don't need to go into them now, but can't we come to some sort of amicable arrangement to split up?"

"So that you can have all the women you want? So that you can bring that bitch into my house?"

"No," he said, "you can have the house. The court would probably award you a third of my income, but I'll give you more if you want. I'd give you half." He had nearly added, "to be rid of you," but he bit off the words as being too provocative. His speech was already thickening and slurring.

It was disconcerting—though this was what he had wanted—to hear how inhibition made her voice soft and kept her face controlled. The words she used were the same, though. He had heard them a thousand times before. "If you leave me, I'll follow you. I'll go to your office and tell them all about it. I'll sit on your doorstep. I won't be abandoned. I'd rather die. I won't be a divorced woman just because you've got tired of me."

"If you to on like this," he said thickly, "you'll find yourself a widow. Will you like that?"

Had they been alone, she would have screamed the affirmative at him. Because they weren't, she gave him a thin, sharp, and concentrated smile, a smile which an observer might have taken for amusement at some married couple's private joke. "Yes," she said, "I'd like to be a widow, *your* widow. Drink yourself to death, why don't you? That's what you have to do if you want to be rid of me."

The waitress came to their table. James ordered a double brandy and "coffee for my wife." He knew he would never be rid of her. He wasn't the sort of man who can stand public disruption of his life, scenes at work, molestation, the involvement of friends and employers. It must be, he knew, an amicable split or none at all. And since she would never see reason, never understand or forgive, he must soldier on. With the help of this, he thought, as the brandy spread its dim, cloudy euphoria through his brain. He drained his glass quickly, muttered an "excuse me" to her for the benefit of listeners, and left the dining room.

Nina returned to the television lounge. There was a play on whose theme was a marital situation that almost paralleled her own. The old ladies with their knitting and the old men with their after-dinner cigars watched it apathetically. She thought she might take the car and go somewhere for a drive. It didn't much matter where, anywhere would do that was far enough from this hotel and James and that cathedral clock whose chimes split the hours into fifteen-minute segments with long brazen peals. There must be somewhere in this town where one could get a decent cup of coffee, some cinema maybe where they weren't showing a film about marriage or what people, she thought shudderingly, called sexual relationships. She went upstairs to get the car keys and some money.

James was fast asleep. He had taken off his tie and his shoes, but otherwise he was fully dressed, lying on his back and snoring. Stupid of him not to get under the covers. He'd freeze. Maybe he'd die of exposure. Well, she wasn't going to cover him up, but she'd close the window for when she came in. The car keys were in his jacket pocket, mixed up with a lot of loose change. The feel of his warm body through the material made her shiver. His breath smelt of spirits and he was sweating in spite of the cold. Among the change were two fivepence pieces. She'd take one of those and keep it till the morning to feed that gas meter. It would be horrible dressing for that wedding in here at zero temperature. Why not feed it now so that it would be ready for the morning, ready to turn the gas fire on and give her some heat when she came in at midnight, come to that?

The room was faintly illuminated by the yellow light from the street lamp in the alley. She crouched down in front of the gas fire, and noticed she hadn't turned the dial to "off" after her match had failed to ignite the jets. It wouldn't do to feed that meter now with the dial turned to "full" and have fivepence worth of old-fashioned toxic gas flood the room. Not with the window tight shut and not a crack round that heavy old door. Slowly she put her hand out to turn off the dial.

Her fingers touched it. Her hand remained still, poised. She heard her heart begin to thud softly in the silence as the idea in all its brilliant awfulness took hold of her. Wouldn't do . . . ? Was she mad? It wouldn't do to feed that meter now with the gas-fire dial turned to "full"? What would do as well, as efficiently, as finally? She withdrew her hand and clasped it in the other to steady it.

Rising to her feet, she contemplated her sleeping husband. The sweat was standing on his pale forehead now. He snored as rhythmically, as stertorously, as her own heart beat. A widow, she thought, alone and free in her own unshared house. Not divorced, despised, disowned, laughed at by judges and solicitors for her crippling frigidity, not mocked by that Frances and her successors, but a widow whom all the world would pity and respect. Comfortably-off too, if not rich, with an income from James's life assurance and very likely a pension from Sir William Tarrant.

James wouldn't wake up till midnight. No, that was wrong. He wouldn't *have* wakened up till midnight. What she meant was he wouldn't wake up at all.

The dial on the gas fire was still on, full on. She took the fivepence coin and tiptoed over to the meter. Nothing would wake him but still she tiptoed. The window was tight shut, with nothing beyond it but that alley, that glistening lamp, and the towering wall of the cathedral.

She studied the meter, kneeling down. It was the first time in her sheltered, cosseted, snug life that she had ever actually seen a coin-in-the-slot gas meter. But if morons like hotel servants and the sort of people who would stay in a place like this could work it, she could. There was the slot where the coin went in, there the gauge whose red arrow showed empty. All you had to do, presumably, was slip in the coin, fiddle about with that handle, and then, if the gas-fire dial was on, toxic coal gas—the kind of gas that had killed thousands in the past, careless old people, suicides, accident-prone fools—would rapidly begin to seep out of the unlighted jets in the fire. James wouldn't smell it. Drink paralysed him into an unconsciousness as deep as that which her own sleeping tablets brought to her.

Nina was certain it wouldn't matter that she hadn't attended closely to the manageress's instructions. What had she said? Turn the handle to the left, insert the coin, turn it to the right. She hesitated for a moment, just long enough for brief fractured memories to cross her mind—James when they were first married, James patient and self-denying on their honeymoon, James promising that her coldness didn't matter, that with time and love . . . James confessing with a defiant smirk, throwing Frances's name at her, James going on a three-day bender because she couldn't pretend the wound he'd given her was just a surface scratch, James drunk night after night after night. . . .

She didn't hesitate for long.

She got her coat, put the car keys in her handbag. Then she knelt down again between the gas fire and the meter. First she checked that the dial, which was small and almost at ground level, was set at "full." She took hold of the brass handle on the meter and turned it to the left. The coin slot was now fully exposed and open. She pressed in the fivepence piece and flicked the handle to the right. There was no need to wait for the warning smell, oniony, acrid, of the escaping gas. Without looking back, she walked swiftly from the room, closing the door behind her.

The cathedral clock chimed the last quarter before nine.

When the bar closed at eleven-thirty, the crowd of people coming upstairs and chattering in loud voices would have awakened even the deepest sleeper. They woke James. He didn't move for some time but lay there with his eyes open till he heard the clock chime midnight. When the last stroke died away he reached out and turned on the bedside lamp. The light was like knives going into his head, and he groaned. But he felt like this most nights at midnight and there was no use making a fuss. Who would hear or care if he did? Nina was evidently still downstairs in that lounge. It was too much to hope she might stay there all night out of fear of being alone with him. No, she'd be up now the television had closed down and she'd start berating him for his drunkenness and his infidelity—not that there had been any since Frances—and they would lie there bickering and smarting until grey light mingled with that yellow light, and the cathedral clock told them it was dawn.

And yet she had been so sweet once, so pathetic and desperate in her sad failure. It had never occurred to him to blame her, though his body suffered. And his own solution, honestly confessed, might have worked so well for all three of them if she had been rational. He wondered vaguely, for the thousandth time, why he had been such a fool as to confess, when, with a little deception, he might be happier now than at any time in his marriage. But he was in no fit state to think. Where had that woman said the bathroom was? Turn right down the passage and the third door on the left. He lay there till the clock struck the quarter before he felt he couldn't last out any longer and he'd have to find it.

The cold air in the passage—God, it was more like January than April—steadied him a little and made his head bang and throb. He must be crazy to go on like this. What the hell was he doing, turning himself into an alcoholic at thirty-five? Because there were no two ways about it, he was an alcoholic all right, a drunk. And if he stayed with Nina he'd be a dead alcoholic by forty. But how can you leave a woman who won't leave you? Give up his job, run away, go to the ends of the earth. . . . It wasn't unusual for him to have wild thoughts like this at midnight, but when the morning came he knew he would just soldier on.

He stayed in the bathroom for about ten minutes. Coming back along the passage, he heard footsteps on the stairs, and knowing he must look horrible and smell horribly of liquor, he retreated behind the open door of what proved to be a broom cupboard. But it was only his wife. She approached their room door slowly as if she were bracing herself to face something—himself, probably, he thought. Had she really that much loathing of him that she had to draw in her breath and clench her hands before confronting him? She was very pale. She looked ill and frightened, and when she had opened the door and gone inside he heard her give a kind of shrill gasp that was almost a shriek.

He followed her into the room, and when she turned and saw him he thought she was going to faint. She had been pale before, but now she turned paper white. Once, when he had still loved her and had hoped he might teach her to love him, he would have been concerned. But now he didn't care, and all he said was, "Been watching something nasty on the T.V.?"

She didn't answer him. She sat down on her bed and put her head into her hands. James undressed and got into bed. Presently Nina got up and began taking her clothes off slowly and mechanically. His head and body had begun to twitch as they did when he was recovering from the effects of a drinking bout. It left him wide awake. He wouldn't sleep again for hours. He watched her curiously but dispassionately, for he had long ago ceased to derive the slightest pleasure or excitement from seeing her undress. What intrigued him now was that, though she was evidently in some sort of state of shock, her hands shaking, she still couldn't discard those modest subterfuges of hers, her way of turning her back when she stepped out of her dress, of pulling her nightgown over her head before she took off her underclothes.

She put on her dressing gown and went to the bathroom. When she came back her face was greasy where she had cleaned off the make-up and she was shivering.

"You'd better take a sleeping tablet," he said.

"I've already taken one in the bathroom. I wanted a bath but there wasn't any hot water." Getting into bed, she exclaimed in her normal fierce way, "Nothing works in this damned place! Nothing goes right!"

"Put out the light and go to sleep. Anyone would think you'd got to spend the rest of your life here instead of just one night."

She made no reply. They never said good night to each other. When she had put her light out the room wasn't really dark because a street lamp was still lit in the alley outside. He had seldom felt less like sleep, and now he was aware of a sensation he hadn't expected because he hadn't thought about it. He didn't want to share a bedroom with her.

That cold modesty, which had once been enticing, now repelled him. He raised himself on one elbow and peered at her. She lay in the defensive attitude of a woman who fears assault, flat on her stomach, her arms folded under her head. Although the sleeping pill had taken effect and she was deeply asleep, her body seemed stiff, prepared to galvanise into violence at a touch. She smelt cold. A sour saltiness emanated from her as if there were sea water in her veins instead of blood. He thought of real women with warm blood, women who woke from sleep when their husbands' faces neared theirs, who never recoiled but smiled and put out their arms. Forever she would keep him from them until the drink or time made him as frozen as she.

Suddenly he knew he couldn't stay in that room. He might do something dreadful, beat her up perhaps or even kill her. And much as he wanted to be rid of her, spend no more time with her, no more money on her, the notion of killing her was as absurd as it was grotesque. It was unthinkable. But he couldn't stay here.

He got up and put on his dressing gown. He'd go to that lounge where she'd watched television, take a blanket, and spend the rest of the night there. She wouldn't wake till nine and by then he'd be back, ready to dress for that wedding. Funny, really, their going to a wedding, to watch someone else getting into the same boat. But it wouldn't be the same boat, for if office gossip was to be relied on, Sir William's daughter had already opened her warm arms to many men. . . .

The cathedral clock struck one. By nine the room would be icy and they'd need that gas fire. Why not put a fivepence piece in the meter now so that the fire would work when he wanted it?

The fire itself lay in shadow but the meter was clearly illuminated by the street lamp. James knelt down, trying to remember the instructions of the manageress. Better try it out first before he put his coin in, his only fivepence coin. Strange, that. He could have sworn he'd had two when he first went to bed.

What had that woman said? Turn the handle to the left, insert the coin, turn the handle to the right. . . . No, turn it to the right as far as it will go until *you hear the coin fall.* Keeping hold of his coin—he didn't want to waste it if what Nina said was true and nothing worked in this place—he turned the handle to the left, then hard to the right as far as it would go.

Inside the meter a coin fell with a small dull clang. The red arrow marker on the gauge, which had stood at empty, moved along to register payment. Good. He was glad he hadn't wasted his money. The previous guest must have put a coin in and failed to turn the handle until it fell. So Nina had been wrong about things not working. Still, it wasn't unusual for her to get the wrong idea, not unusual at all. . . .

Gas would come through now once the dial was switched on. James checked that the window was shut to keep out the cold, gave a last look at the sleeping, heavily sedated woman, and went out of the room, closing the door behind him.

THE TWO BOTTLES OF RELISH

(1922)

Lord Dunsany

This story may perplex the reader, because the narrator is subtle about the answer to the mystery: how did the victim disappear? Author Lord Dunsany (1878–1957) was an Irish poet, dramatist, and novelist who wrote occasional short stories. His full name was Edward John Moreton Drax Plunkett and he was the eighteenth Baron Dunsany. Fellow poet W. B. Yeats called Dunsany "a man of genius" and compared him to Baudelaire. The adventuresome Dunsany joined the Coldstream Guards in 1899 and sailed off to South Africa to fight in the Boer War. He served in World War I and participated in the 1916 Easter Rebellion of Irish nationalists, in which he was wounded. Although Dunsany's writings, often featuring fantasy and mythology, were enormously popular in the first two decades of the twentieth century, he is not widely read today. "The Two Bottles of Relish" is therefore exceptional for having remained one of the best mystery stories ever written. *Bon appetit!*

Smithers is my name. I'm what you might call a small man and in a small way of business. I travel for Num-numo, a relish for meats and savouries—the world-famous relish I ought to say. It's really quite good, no deleterious acids in it, and does not affect the heart; so it is quite easy to push. I wouldn't have got the job if it weren't. But I hope some day to get something that's harder to push, as of course the harder they are to push, the better the pay. At present I can just make my way, with nothing at all over; but then I live in a very expensive flat. It happened like this, and that brings me to my story. And it isn't the story you'd expect from a small man like me, yet there's nobody else to tell it. Those that know anything of it besides me are all for hushing it up. Well, I was looking for a room to live in in London when first I got my job. It had to be in London, to be central; and I went to a block of buildings, very gloomy they looked, and saw the man that ran them and asked him for what I wanted. Flats they called them; just a bedroom and a sort of cupboard. Well, he was showing a man round at the time who was a gent, in fact more than that, so he didn't take much notice of me—the man that ran all those flats didn't, I mean. So I just ran behind for a bit, seeing all sorts of rooms and waiting till I could be shown my class of thing. We came to a very nice flat, a sitting room, bedroom and bathroom, and a sort of little place that they called a hall. And that's how I came to know Linley. He was the bloke that was being shown round.

"Bit expensive," he said.

And the man that ran the flats turned away to the window and picked his teeth. It's funny how much you can show by a simple thing like. What he meant to say was that he'd hundreds of flats like that, and thousands of people looking for them, and he didn't care who had them or whether they all went on looking. There was no mistaking him, somehow. And yet he never said a word, only looked away out of the window and picked his teeth. And I ventured to speak to Mr. Linley then; and I said, "How about it, sir, if I paid half, and shared it? I wouldn't be in the way, and I'm out all day, and whatever you said would go, and really I wouldn't be no more in your way than a cat."

You may be surprised at my doing it; and you'll be much more surprised at him accepting it—at least, you would if you knew me, just a small man in a small way of business. And yet I could see at once that he was taking to me more than he was taking to the man at the window.

"But there's only one bedroom," he said.

"I could make up my bed easy in that little room there," I said.

"The Hall," said the man, looking round from the window, without taking his toothpick out.

"And I'd have the bed out of the way and hid in the cupboard by any hour you like," I said.

He looked thoughtful, and the other man looked out over London; and in the end, do you know, he accepted.

"Friend of yours?" said the flat man.

"Yes," answered Mr. Linley.

It was really very nice of him.

I'll tell you why I did it. Able to afford it? Of course not. But I heard him tell the flat man that he had just come down from Oxford and wanted to live for a few months in London. It turned out he wanted just to be comfortable and do nothing for a bit while he looked things over and chose a job, or probably just as long as he could afford it. Well, I said to myself, what's the Oxford manner worth in business, especially a business like mine? Why, simply everything you've got. If I picked up only a quarter of it from this Mr. Linley I'd be able to double my sales, and that would soon mean I'd be given something a lot harder to push, with perhaps treble the pay. Worth it every time. And you can make a quarter of an education go twice as far again, if you're careful with it. I mean you don't have to quote the whole of the *Inferno* to show that you've read Milton; half a line may do it.

Well, about that story I have to tell. And you mightn't think that a little man like me could make you shudder. Well, I soon forgot about the Oxford manner when we settled down in our flat. I forgot it in the sheer wonder of the man himself. He had a mind like an acrobat's body, like a bird's body. It didn't want education. You didn't notice whether he was educated or not. Ideas were always leaping up in him, things you'd never have thought of. And not only that, but if any ideas were about, he'd sort of catch them. Time and again I've found him knowing just what I was going to say. Not thought reading, but what they call intuition. I used to try to learn a bit about chess, just to take my thoughts off Num-numo in the evening, when I'd done with it. But problems I never could do. Yet he'd come along and glance at my problem and say, "You probably move that piece first," and I'd say, "But where?" and he'd say, "Oh, one of those three squares." And I'd say, "But it will be taken on all of them." And the piece a queen all the time, mind you. And he'd say, "Yes, it's doing no good there; you're probably meant to lose it."

And, do you know, he'd be right.

You see, he'd been following out what the other man had been thinking. That's what he'd been doing.

Well, one day there was that ghastly murder at Unge. I don't know if you remember it. But Steeger had gone down to live with a girl in a bungalow on the North Downs, and that was the first we had heard of him.

The girl had £200, and he got every penny of it, and she utterly disappeared. And Scotland Yard couldn't find her.

Well, I'd happened to read that Steeger had bought two bottles of Num-numo; for the Otherthorpe police had found out everything about him, except what he did with the girl; and that of course attracted my attention, or I should have never thought again about the case or said a word of it to Linley. Num-numo was always on my mind, as I always spent every day pushing it, and that kept me from forgetting the other thing. And so one day I said to Linley, "I wonder with all that knack you have for seeing through a chess problem, and thinking of one thing and another, that you don't have a go at that Otherthorpe mystery. It's a problem as much as chess," I said.

"There's not the mystery in ten murders that there is in one game of chess," he answered.

"It's beaten Scotland Yard," I said.

"Has it?" he asked.

"Knocked them endwise," I said.

"It shouldn't have done that," he said. And almost immediately after he said, "What are the facts?"

We were both sitting at supper, and I told him the facts, as I had them straight from the papers. She was a pretty blonde, she was small, she was called Nancy Elth, she had £200, they lived at the bungalow for five days. After that he stayed there for another fortnight, but nobody ever saw her alive again. Steeger said she had gone to South America, but later said he had never said South America, but South Africa. None of her money remained in the bank where she had kept it, and Steeger was shown to have come by at least £150 just at that time. Then Steeger turned out to be a vegetarian, getting all his food from the greengrocer, and that made the constable in the village of Unge suspicious of him, for a vegetarian was something new to the constable. He watched Steeger after that, and it's well he did, for there was nothing that Scotland Yard asked him that he couldn't tell them about him, except of course the one thing. And he told the police at Otherthorpe five or six miles away, and they came and took a hand at it too. They were able to say for one thing that he never went outside the bungalow and its tidy garden ever since she disappeared. You see, the more they watched him the more suspicious they got, as you naturally do if you're watching a man; so that very soon they were watching every move he made, but if it hadn't been for his being a vegetarian they'd never have started to suspect him, and there wouldn't have been enough evidence even for Linley. Not that they found out anything much against him, except that £150 dropping in from nowhere, and it was Scotland Yard that found that, not the police of Otherthorpe. No, what the constable of

Unge found out was about the larch trees, and that beat Scotland Yard utterly, and beat Linley up to the very last, and of course it beat me. There were ten larch trees in the bit of a garden, and he'd made some sort of an arrangement with the landlord, Steeger had, before he took the bungalow, by which he would do what he liked with the larch trees. And then from about the time that little Nancy Elth must have died he cut every one of them down. Three times a day he went at it for nearly a week, and when they were all down he cut them all up into logs no more than two foot long and laid them all in neat heaps. You never saw such work. And what for? To give an excuse for the axe was one theory. But the excuse was bigger than the axe; it took him a fortnight, hard work every day. And he could have killed a little thing like Nancy Elth without an axe, and cut her up too. Another theory was that he wanted firewood, to make away with the body. But he never used it. He left it all standing there in those neat stacks. It fairly beat everybody.

Well, those are the facts I told Linley. Oh yes, and he bought a big butcher's knife. Funny thing, they all do. And yet it isn't so funny after all; if you've got to cut a woman up, you've got to cut her up; and you can't do that without a knife. Then, there were some negative facts. He hadn't burned her. Only had a fire in the small stove now and then, and only used it for cooking. They got on to that pretty smartly, the Unge constable did, and the men that were lending him a hand from Otherthorpe. There were some little woody places lying round, shaws they call them in that part of the country, the country people do, and they could climb a tree handy and unobserved and get a sniff at the smoke in almost any direction it might be blowing. They did that now and then, and there was no smell of flesh burning, just ordinary cooking. Pretty smart of the Otherthorpe police that was, though of course it didn't help to hang Steeger. Then later on the Scotland Yard men went down and got another fact—negative, but narrowing things down all the while. And that was that the chalk under the bungalow and under the little garden had none of it been disturbed. And he'd never been outside it since Nancy disappeared. Oh yes, and he had a big file besides the knife. But there was no sign of any ground bones found on the file, or, any blood on the knife. He'd washed them of course. I told all that to Linley.

Now I ought to warn you before I go any further. I am a small man myself and you probably don't expect anything horrible from me. But I ought to warn you this man was a murderer, or at any rate somebody was; the woman had been made away with, a nice pretty little girl too, and the man that had done that wasn't necessarily going to stop at things you might think he'd stop at. With the mind to do a thing like that, and with the long thin shadow of the rope to drive him further, you can't say what he'll stop at. Murder tales seem nice things sometimes for a lady to sit and read all by herself by the fire. But murder isn't a nice thing, and when a murderer's desperate and trying to hide his tracks he isn't even as nice as he was before. I'll ask you to bear that in mind. Well, I've warned you.

So I says to Linley, "And what do you make of it?"

"Drains?" said Linley.

"No," I says, "you're wrong there. Scotland Yard has been into that. And the Otherthorpe people before them. They've had a look in the drains, such as they are, a little thing running into a cesspool beyond the garden; and nothing has gone down it—nothing that oughtn't to have, I mean."

He made one or two other suggestions, but Scotland Yard had been before him in every case. That's really the crab of my story, if you'll excuse the expression. You want a man who sets out to be a detective to take his magnifying glass and go down to the spot; to go to the spot before everything; and then to measure the footmarks and pick up the clues and find the knife that the police have overlooked. But Linley never even went near the place, and he hadn't got a magnifying glass, not as I ever saw, and Scotland Yard were before him every time.

In fact they had more clues than anybody could make head or tail of. Every kind of clue to show that he'd murdered the poor little girl; every kind of clue to show that he hadn't disposed of the body; and yet the body wasn't there. It wasn't in South America either, and not much more likely in

South Africa. And all the time, mind you, that enormous bunch of chopped larchwood, a clue that was staring everyone in the face and leading nowhere. No, we didn't seem to want any more clues, and Linley never went near the place. The trouble was to deal with the clues we'd got. I was completely mystified; so was Scotland Yard; and Linley seemed to be getting no forwarder; and all the while the mystery was hanging on me. I mean if it were not for the trifle I'd chanced to remember, and if it were not for one chance word I said to Linley, that mystery would have gone the way of all the other mysteries that men have made nothing of, a darkness, a little patch of night in history.

Well, the fact was Linley didn't take much interest in it at first, but I was so absolutely sure that he could do it that I kept him to the idea. "You can do chess problems," I said.

"That's ten times harder," he said, sticking to his point.

"Then why don't you do this?" I said.

"Then go and take a look at the board for me," said Linley.

That was his way of talking. We'd been a fortnight together, and I knew it by now. He meant to go down to the bungalow at Unge. I know you'll say why didn't he go himself; but the plain truth of it is that if he'd been tearing about the countryside he'd never have been thinking, whereas sitting there in his chair by the fire in our flat there was no limit to the ground he could cover, if you follow my meaning. So down I went by train next day, and got out at Unge station. And there were the North Downs rising up before me, somehow like music.

"It's up there, isn't it?" I said to the porter.

"That's right," he said. "Up there by the lane; and mind to turn to your right when you get to the old yew tree, a very big tree, you can't mistake it, and then . . ." and he told me the way so that I couldn't go wrong. I found them all like that, very nice and helpful. You see, it was Unge's day at last. Everyone had heard of Unge now; you could have got a letter there any time just then without putting the country or post town; and this was what Unge had to show. I dare say if you tried to find Unge now . . . well, anyway, they were making hay while the sun shone.

Well, there the hill was, going up into sunlight, going up like a song. You don't want to hear about the spring, and all the may rioting, and the colour that came down over everything later on in the day, and all those birds; but I thought, "What a nice place to bring a girl to." And then when I thought that he'd killed her there, well I'm only a small man, as I said, but when I thought of her on that hill with all the birds singing, I said to myself, "Wouldn't it be odd if it turned out to be me after all that got that man killed, if he did murder her." So I soon found my way up to the bungalow and began prying about, looking over the hedge into the garden. And I didn't find much, and I found nothing at all that the police hadn't found already, but there were those heaps of larch logs staring me in the face and looking very queer.

I did a lot of thinking, leaning against the hedge, breathing the smell of the may, and looking over the top of it at the larch logs, and the neat little bungalow the other side of the garden. Lots of theories I thought of, till I came to the best thought of all; and that was that if I left the thinking to Linley, with his Oxford-and-Cambridge education, and only brought him the facts, as he had told me, I should be doing more good in my way than if I tried to do any big thinking. I forgot to tell you that I had gone to Scotland Yard in the morning. Well, there wasn't really much to tell. What they asked me was what I wanted. And, not having an answer exactly ready, I didn't find out very much from them. But it was quite different at Unge; everyone was most obliging; it was their day there, as I said. The constable let me go indoors, so long as I didn't touch anything, and he gave me a look at the garden from the inside. And I saw the stumps of the ten larch trees, and I noticed one thing that Linley said was very observant of me, not that it turned out to be any use, but anyway I was doing my best: I noticed that the stumps had been all chopped anyhow. And from that I thought that the man that did it didn't know much about chopping. The constable said that was a deduction. So then I said that the axe was blunt when he used it; and that certainly made the constable think, though he didn't actually say I was right this time. Did I tell you that Steeger never went outdoors, except to the little garden to chop wood, ever since Nancy disappeared? I think I did. Well, it was perfectly true. They'd watched him night and day, one or another of them, and the Unge constable told me that himself. That limited things a good deal. The only thing I didn't like about it was that I felt Linley ought to have found all that out instead of ordinary policemen, and I felt that he could have too. There'd have been romance in a story like that. And they'd never have done it if the news hadn't gone round that the man was a vegetarian and only dealt at the greengrocer's. Likely as not even that was only started out of pique by the butcher. It's queer what little things may trip a man up. Best to keep straight is my motto. But perhaps I'm straying a bit away from my story. I should like to do that for ever—forget that it ever was; but I can't.

Well, I picked up all sorts of information; clues I suppose I should call it in a story like this, though they none of them seemed to lead anywhere. For instance, I found out everything he ever bought at the village, I could even tell you the kind of salt he bought, quite plain with no phosphates in it, that they sometimes put in to make it tidy. And then he got ice from the fishmonger's, and plenty of vegetables, as I said, from the greengrocer, Mergin & Sons. And I had a bit of a talk over it all with the constable. Slugger he said his name was. I wondered why he hadn't come in and searched the place as soon as the girl was missing. "Well, you can't do that," he said. "And besides, we didn't suspect at once, not about the girl, that is. We only suspected there was something wrong about him on account of him being a vegetarian. He stayed a good fortnight after the last that was seen of her. And then we slipped in like a knife. But, you see, no one had been enquiring about her, there was no warrant out."

"And what did you find?" I asked Slugger, "when you went in?"

"Just a big file," he said, "and the knife and the axe that he must have got to chop her up with."

"But he got the axe to chop trees with," I said.

"Well, yes," he said, but rather grudgingly.

"And what did he chop them for?" I asked.

"Well, of course, my superiors has theories about that," he said, "that they mightn't tell to everybody."

You see, it was those logs that were beating them.

"But did he cut her up at all?" I asked.

"Well, he said that she was going to South America," he answered. Which was really very fair-minded of him.

I don't remember now much else that he told me. Steeger left the plates and dishes all washed up and very neat, he said.

Well, I brought all this back to Linley, going up by the train that started just about sunset. I'd like to tell you about the late spring evening, so calm over that grim bungalow, closing in with a glory all round it as though it were blessing it; but you'll want to hear of the murder. Well, I told Linley everything, though much of it didn't seem to me to be worth the telling. The trouble was that the moment I began to leave anything out, he'd know it, and make me drag it in. "You can't tell what may be vital," he'd say. "A tin tack swept away by a housemaid might hang a man."

All very well, but be consistent, even if you are educated at Eton and Harrow, and whenever I mentioned Num-numo, which after all was the beginning of the whole story, because he wouldn't have heard of it if it hadn't been for me, and my noticing that Steeger had bought two bottles of it, why then he said that things like that were trivial and we should keep to the main issues. I naturally talked a bit about Num-numo, because only that day I had pushed close on fifty bottles of it in Unge. A murder certainly stimulates people's minds, and Steeger's two bottles gave me an opportunity that only a fool could have failed to make something of. But of course all that was nothing at all to Linley.

You can't see a man's thoughts, and you can't look into his mind, so that all the most exciting things in the world can never be told of. But what I think happened all that evening with Linley, while I talked to him before supper, and all through supper, and sitting smoking afterwards in front of our fire, was that his thoughts were stuck at a barrier there was no getting over. And the barrier wasn't the difficulty of finding ways and means by which Steeger might have made away with the body, but the impossibility of finding why he chopped those masses of wood every day for a fortnight, and paid, as I'd just found out, £25 to his landlord to be allowed to do it. That's what was beating Linley. As for the ways by which Steeger might have hidden the body, it seemed to me that every way was blocked by the police. If you said he buried it, they said the chalk was undisturbed; if you said he carried it away, they said he never left the place; if you said he burned it, they said no smell of burning was ever noticed when the smoke blew low, and when it didn't they climbed trees after it. I'd taken to Linley wonderfully, and I didn't have to be educated to see there was something big in a mind like his, and I thought that he could have done it. When I saw the police getting in before him like that, and no way that I could see of getting past them, I felt really sorry.

Did anyone come to the house, he asked me once or twice. Did anyone take anything away from it? But we couldn't account for it that way. Then perhaps I made some suggestion that was no good, or perhaps I started talking of Num-numo again, and he interrupted me rather sharply.

"But what would you do, Smithers?" he said. "What would you do yourself?"

"If I'd murdered poor Nancy Elth?" I asked.

"Yes," he said.

"I can't ever imagine doing such a thing," I told him.

He sighed at that, as though it were something against me.

"I suppose I should never be a detective," I said. And he just shook his head.

Then he looked broodingly into the fire for what seemed an hour. And then he shook his head again. We both went to bed after that.

I shall remember the next day all my life. I was till evening, as usual, pushing Num-numo. And we sat down to supper about nine. You couldn't get things cooked at those flats, so of course we had it cold. And Linley began with a salad. I can see it now, every bit of it. Well, I was still a bit full of what I'd done in Unge, pushing Num-numo. Only a fool, I know, would have been unable to push it there; but still, I *had* pushed it; and about fifty bottles, forty-eight to be exact, are something in a small village, whatever the circumstances. So I was talking about it a bit; and then all of a sudden I realized that Num-numo was nothing to Linley, and I pulled myself up with a jerk. It was really very kind of him; do you know what he did? He must have known at once why I stopped talking, and he just stretched out a hand and said, "Would you give me a little of your Num-numo for my salad?"

I was so touched I nearly gave it him. But of course you don't take Num-numo with salad. Only for meats and savouries. That's on the bottle.

So I just said to him, "Only for meats and savouries." Though I don't know what savouries are. Never had any.

I never saw a man's face go like that before.

He seemed still for a whole minute. And nothing speaking about him but that expression. Like a man that's seen a ghost, one is tempted to write. But it wasn't really at all. I'll tell you what he looked like. Like a man that's seen something that no one has ever looked at before, something he thought couldn't be.

And then he said in a voice that was all quite changed, more low and gentle and quiet it seemed, "No good for vegetables, eh?"

"Not a bit," I said.

And at that he gave a kind of sob in his throat. I hadn't thought he could feel things like that. Of course I didn't know what it was all about; but, whatever it was, I thought all that sort of thing would have been knocked out of him at Eton and Harrow, an educated man like that. There were no tears in his eyes, but he was feeling something horribly.

And then he began to speak with big spaces between his words, saying, "A man might make a mistake perhaps, and use Num-numo with vegetables."

"Not twice," I said. What else could I say?

And he repeated that after me as though I had told of the end of the world, and adding an awful emphasis to my words, till they seemed all clammy with some frightful significance, and shaking his head as he said it.

Then he was quite silent.

"What is it?" I asked.

"Smithers," he said.

"Yes," I said.

"Smithers," said he.

And I said, "Well?"

"Look here, Smithers," he said, "you must phone down to the grocer at Unge and find out from him this."

"Yes?" I said.

"Whether Steeger bought those two bottles, as I expect he did, on the same day, and not a few days apart. He couldn't have done that."

I waited to see if any more was coming, and then I ran out and did what I was told. It took me some time, being after nine o'clock, and only then with the help of the police. About six days apart they said; and so I came back and told Linley. He looked up at me so hopefully when I came in, but I saw that it was the wrong answer by his eyes.

You can't take things to heart like that without being ill, and when he didn't speak I said, "What you want is a good brandy, and go to bed early."

And he said, "No. I must see someone from Scotland Yard. Phone round to them. Say here at once."

But I said, "I can't get an inspector from Scotland Yard to call on us at this hour."

His eyes were all lit up. He was all there all right.

"Then tell them," he said, "they'll never find Nancy Elth. Tell one of them to come here, and I'll tell him why." And he added, I think only for me, "They must watch Steeger, till one day they get him over something else."

And, do you know, he came. Inspector Ulton; he came himself.

While we were waiting I tried to talk to Linley. Partly curiosity, I admit. But I didn't want to leave him to those thoughts of his, brooding away by the fire. I tried to ask him what it was all about. But he wouldn't tell me. "Murder is horrible," is all he would say. "And as a man covers his tracks up it only gets worse."

He wouldn't tell me. "There are tales," he said, "that one never wants to hear."

That's true enough. I wish I'd never heard this one. I never did actually. But I guessed it from Linley's last words to Inspector Ulton, the only ones that I overheard. And perhaps this is the point at which to stop reading my story, so that you don't guess it too; even if you think you want murder stories. For don't you rather want a murder story with a bit of a romantic twist, and not a story about real foul murder? Well, just as you like.

In came Inspector Ulton, and Linley shook hands in silence, and pointed the way to his bedroom; and they went in there and talked in low voices, and I never heard a word.

A fairly hearty-looking man was the inspector when they went into that room.

They walked through our sitting room in silence when they came out, and together they went into the hall, and there I heard the only words they said to each other. It was the inspector that first broke that silence.

"But why," he said, "did he cut down the trees?"

"Solely," said Linley, "in order to get an appetite."

THE ELEVENTH JUROR

(1927)

Vincent Starrett

The narrator of this classic mystery story is the sole member of a jury who holds out for the acquittal of an alleged murderer. Will he convince the other jury members to declare the accused not guilty? Author Vincent Starrett (1886–1974) was one of the great mystery writers, as evidenced when he won the Grand Master Edgar Award in 1957. He was only the second recipient of this honor; Agatha Christie won the first in 1954. Starrett was considered by many to be the most learned authority on Holmesiana, as revealed in books such as *The Unique Hamlet* (1920), *221-B: Studies in Sherlock Holmes* (1940), and *The Adventures of Sherlock Holmes* (1950). He also authored *Real Detective Tales and Mystery Stories* (1927), which contains "The Eleventh Juror."

There are few practicing citizens of the republic, I guess, who some time or other have not been called for jury service. The system is impartial, and, like lightning, you never know where it is going to strike.

It's unlike lightning, though—or the way lightning is supposed to operate—in one respect. It does, often, strike more than once in the same place. I have a friend, for instance, who has served on a dozen juries in as many years, in cases ranging anywhere from leasehold troubles to first degree murder. He doesn't particularly like to serve, but he's one of those citizens who think they owe a duty to the state, and all that sort of thing. And I have another friend who has been called a dozen times and hasn't served yet. He's an accomplished liar, and always manages to get the judge to excuse him.

Of course, it's easier to get excused in a big case than in a little one. The lawyers are more particular in a big case. If you want to dodge, just wait for the right question, and then give the wrong answer. If the prosecutor wants to hang a man for murder, tell him you are opposed to the death penalty, and before you know it you'll be collecting your coat and hat and heading back for the office. Or just suggest that you have followed the case pretty closely in the newspapers, and have formed a strong opinion about it. Something like that. It will always work; nearly always.

They don't really need you on a jury. There are always enough men who *want* to serve because they like it. It's a vacation from home and work, and it gives them a feeling of consequence to be sitting around in court, as important as the judge. Fountains of wisdom, and all that. They claim to be unprejudiced, and really they are a lot more prejudiced than the fellows who beg off. God help the prisoner who gets a jury of wiseacres that really want to sit in judgment on him! Who claim they haven't formed an opinion!

However, this isn't an essay. What I started out to tell was the story of my own first jury service. We were out for ten days without getting a verdict, and all the time—from first to last—the count stood eleven for hanging and one for acquittal. I was the juror who held out. On the eleventh day, we returned a verdict of not guilty, and the prisoner was acquitted. He became one of my best friends, for of course the newspapers found out that I had swung the jury, and he came around to thank me. About a year after the end of the trial, without any urging on my part, he told me something I had suspected form the beginning of the case. In fact, it had been part of my argument to the other jurors during ten days of talking, though I didn't dwell on it a lot. He said he didn't know—actually didn't know—whether he had committed the crime or not!

Of course, that didn't come out at the trial, although the idiot wanted to tell it. He was too honest to live. Fortunately, his lawyer was less scrupulous.

Horace Thistlethwaite was his lawyer—a tongue twister of a name that made the courtroom laugh every time the prosecutor mispronounced it, which he did every chance he got. Ricketts was the prosecutor's name, so he didn't have much call to laugh at Thistlethwaite; but it never occurred to Ricketts that there could be *anything* funny about himself. I suppose the case is pretty well forgotten by this time, but it was a good one while it lasted. Good enough, anyway. Chicago may have two or three bigger and better ones, every year, but this one caused some talk in its day.

I had been interested in the case from the beginning, and had read everything I could about it, in all the newspapers; but the last thing I thought of was that I would get a chance to serve on the jury that tried Murray. I was never more surprised in my life than I was the day the summons came. But I knew at once that I was going to serve on that jury unless I was thrown off by one side or the other. I couldn't think of any reason why I would not make a perfectly fair juror, and that was the attitude I intended to carry into court. But it struck me as remarkable that after the years the jury call had missed me, I should be called for service in a case that fascinated me the way this one did.

Of course, I couldn't be positive till I was sitting in the antechamber of the courtroom that it *was* the Murray case I was in for; but I was sure enough, for I had been following the papers, as I say, and I knew they were having a hard time getting a jury. They had already exhausted a couple of panels of veniremen, because it seemed that everybody had read about the case and had an opinion. The defense lawyers were afraid of men who had read about the case, and I didn't blame them. It certainly looked bad for Murray. But who *hadn't* read about it?

However, they got a jury. It was touch and go, as far as I was concerned, for they already had ten men accepted when I came in; ten whopping liars, sitting there as big as life, itching for the case to commence. I lied too, for I wanted the job as much as they did, and after the usual line of questions I got it. I said I had read very little about the case, had no opinions about it whatever, and was not averse to the death penalty; and I never told three bigger lies in a row in my life. After awhile, they caught another plausible liar, and there we were, twelve of us, all innocent as—I was going to say innocent as the twelve apostles.

The case began to unfold next day. As I looked around at my fellow jurors, it occurred to me that I had never seen eleven more ridiculous fatheads. However, that was what the prosecution wanted, and probably what Thistlethwaite wanted, too. It's a great system, the jury system in this country! If you look as if you might have an ounce of intelligence, neither side wants you; but give a lawyer twelve complete fools, without an idea between them, and he's happy. He knows if he loses his case it's his own fault.

Well, the wheels began to go round, and before long I was listening to everything I had already read and knew all about. The principal witness for the state was Patrolman Witte of the Waterside Station, a good-natured fat old hippopotamus, who must have been on the force to prove that the Irish don't have a monopoly on all the appointments. He told a straight story, though, and stuck to it like a good copper. . . . On the night of umpty-ump, or about two o'clock the next morning, to be exact, he had heard three shots fired in close order, and had hurried toward the sound. At Lambeth Avenue and Belvedere Road, he had found the prisoner, James Murray, standing still, looking at a revolver in his hand. Not far away was the body of a man, and the man had been shot to death. Questioned by Witte, the prisoner had denied all knowledge of the shooting, but was unable to tell why he carried a recently discharged revolver. He seemed dazed, Witte said, and had evidently been drinking heavily. He made no attempt to escape, but went along quietly when Witte told him he was under arrest.

In a little while the whole story had been outlined. The dead man had been identified as Howard Blessing, a widower, and death had resulted from a bullet wound in the neck and another in the heart. Murray had been taken to the station, and the body of Howard Blessing had been taken to a neighboring undertaking establishment. Nobody called it a parlor, I remember, and I decided that only undertakers called their places parlors. Murray had been locked up and had slept like a log all night and part of the morning; then he had wakened and continued his denials. Later, after a coroner's committee had held him to the grand jury, he had been formally charged with the murder and indicted. Witte didn't tell all this, but it came out early in the case and was corroborated by everybody concerned.

Naturally, the mystery was considerable. Murray denied flatly that he ever knew Howard Blessing, the inference being that in those circumstances he would hardly have killed him, even as a matter of drunken target practice—which didn't necessarily follow. He also denied that he ever carried or ever had owned a revolver, and in this he was supported by a lot of his friends, all very good citizens. Murray was a good citizen, himself; that was one of the things against him, really. He was smug, and prosperous, and he wore good clothes; and, even worse, he had a reputation as a sort of small-time reformer. That sort of fellow, when he's caught in something disreputable, like bootlegging or murder, doesn't make much of a hit with a jury of average citizens.

He was one of the last witnesses in his own behalf, and he made only a fair impression; and when he told his story of what had happened that night at

Lambeth Avenue and Belvedere Road, he didn't make any impression at all. It was a pretty thin tale, and even his lawyer knew it. Murray admitted that he'd been drinking pretty heavily with some of the "boys," and the "boys" had already supported him in that. In fact, they all swore that he couldn't have held a revolver steady, even if he'd had one, which they knew he didn't. A fine tale to have to tell about a fellow associated with reform!

Murray also admitted that he wasn't walking toward home when the shots were fired on the corner, but he blamed that on the drink. He said, with an air of great candor, that he had been completely malted on the night in question, and hadn't any idea why he was at that intersection, holding a revolver in his hand. Somebody must have given it to him. Anyway, he knew he hadn't shot Blessing. He was clear enough to know that, he said. Personally, I doubted it. He was a rather good-looking fellow, with a young wife who seemed to be all legs and eyes. She was probably pretty, but she looked like a corpse, herself, sitting there beside Thistlethwaite at the table.

Ricketts, a thin small man, with a sharp nose and eyes like a cornered rat, rode Murray pretty hard, but the prisoner stood up to it and stuck to his story. They didn't shake him an ounce, not even after the Pearson woman had weakened under Ricketts's battering.

This Pearson woman was one of the star witnesses for the defense, or was supposed to be; but she wasn't strong enough for Ricketts's bullying, and after a while nobody could tell whose witness she was. She was a plump little, peering sort of old lady, the sort that *would* see everything that was going on around her, and tell about it, too. Her story, on direct examination, was clear enough, although she had to be coached a little. She had been sitting at her window, in Lambeth Avenue, waiting for her husband to come home—He *wasn't* one of the "boys," she snapped, when Ricketts interrupted—and she had seen two men pass her window, a short time before the shooting. She had heard them quarreling—violently. One of them was waving his arms. She had taken particular notice of them, and she was sure that neither of the men was James Murray; they were both much bigger men. She was also pretty sure that one of them *was* Howard Blessing. It was pretty dark, she admitted on cross-examination, but she saw them quite clearly, because there was light not very far from her house. She had heard their voices, too, and neither one of them sounded like the voice of James Murray.

Then Ricketts exploded a couple of bombs. He was particularly sarcastic on the subject of Murray's voice, but there was no need for his being so brutal with her. Even the boobs on the jury had noticed all *he* had. The woman was hard of hearing. She was all right when Thistlethwaite had her, for he kept his voice up—it's pretty high, anyway—and she knew what he was going to ask; but Ricketts turned her inside out. What she had to tell wasn't so much, but it was less when Ricketts had finished with her. He kept his voice down on purpose, and all the time she was saying "What?" and "How?" and putting her hands up to her ears. First of all, he made her admit that she hadn't heard the shots. Thistlethwaite had carefully kept away from that question. And in the end, Ricketts forced her to confess that she wasn't very sure of anything. She *might* have made a mistake. She couldn't *swear* that one of the voices she had heard was *not* Murray's. The man she had taken for Howard Blessing *might* have been someone else.

The things Ricketts said can be imagined. She hadn't even heard the shots, a quarter of a block away; she couldn't even hear his questions right there in the courtroom; and yet she could testify about the voices of two men passing her window! And, of course, he looked over at us, triumphantly, every time he made a point. The woman was nearly crying. Thistlethwaite got her again, as quickly as he could, and tried to soothe her. He managed to bring out that the immediate reason for her poor hearing was a cold in her head, whereas on the night of the voices her head had been clearer; but even the judge grinned at that.

The other defense ace was a janitor who had seen a man running. That was all. The man who was running had been seen by the janitor, on Lambeth Avenue, some blocks from the scene of the shooting, not long after it had occurred. The suggestion there, of course, was that this running man had shot

Howard Blessing and then taken to his heels. Which was all right as far as it went; but it didn't explain James Murray, standing there on the spot with a revolver in his hand, and three of the chambers empty.

However, the defense had a trump card that even Ricketts couldn't beat. Blessing, a widower, always carried around with him a miniature portrait of his wife. All his friends knew this, and some of them testified about it; one of them swore he had seen it in Blessing's possession the very night of Blessing's death. Blessing had shown it to him, in the friend's home, just before he—Blessing, that is—started for his own home on the trip that he never finished. And the miniature was missing. It hadn't been found on Murray, and it hadn't been found in the neighborhood of the murder; and it hadn't been found on Blessing's body.

It was a lovely point, and it hinted at all sorts of things. It furnished just about the only hint of romance the case had, and the newspapers had played it strong, from the beginning. Pictures of the girl—Blessing's wife—were in every edition. Every man on the jury knew what she looked like, although she had been dead for some years. Thistlethwaite, of course, made the most of that missing miniature. Ricketts just shrugged it out of existence, as if it didn't matter, anyway.

I suppose nearly everybody believed Murray to be guilty, and probably everybody thought something discreditable was being hidden, or wasn't known; something that would connect Murray with Blessing's dead wife, or something that would connect Blessing with Murray's wife. I heard some pretty rough guesses made in the jury room, myself, the first night out.

From the beginning, Thistlethwaite stuck to one story. It wasn't much of a story to impress a jury, but it was all he had, and he did what he could with it, which was a lot. Everything he brought out contributed to it, and finally got into his plea to the jury. He knew that his only chance to clear Murray was a great speech, and when the time came he made it. The fellow certainly could talk. He was tall and thin, and would have been good-looking if his face hadn't been pock-marked. His hair had a curl and a wave that was the envy of every woman in the courtroom—and they were there in regiments. He looked like an actor, and he should have been one. He won most of his cases. That's why he was in this one. Without Thistlethwaite, Murray wouldn't have had a chance.

Well, it was my first jury service and I listened for all I was worth. I was interested in the case, anyway, as I said, and had my own opinions about it. It was as good as a vaudeville show, sometimes, to watch Ricketts and Thistlethwaite in action, particularly when they got after each other. Ricketts was a snarly, sarcastic little devil, and sharp as a whip. I remember once when Thistlethwaite was going after Witte pretty strong, early in the trial, about the exact minute he had heard the shots, and just where Murray was standing with reference to the body, and what the position of the moon was, and so on, Ricketts smiled out of the corner of his face, with one eye on the jury, and said: "Apparently it is Mr. Whistlewhite's idea that we have erred in failing to call the moon as an essential witness in this case."

Everybody snickered at the name, as usual, then everybody roared; and the bailiff pounded and howled for order, although he was grinning like a black comedian himself. Thistlethwaite's only reply was: "I should have been very glad, Mr. Prosecutor, had it been possible, to call the moon as a witness for the defense. I have no doubt that its long experience as an eyewitness would have enabled it to interpret what it saw more correctly than the human eyes of Officer Witte." Which wasn't so good, I imagine, for nobody laughed.

Later, though, Thistlethwaite got a chance to compare the combination of Ricketts's voice and Ricketts's argument with a jew's harp, and all the defense followers cheered up and chuckled. And, of course, whenever anything of that sort was sprung, we in the jury box got a smile and a glance from the orator who was doing the talking. That sort of thing is always for the benefit of the jury. We didn't any of us like Ricketts, but he had Murray dead to the rights, and he knew it, and we knew it. Not that Thistlethwaite was popular in the jury room; he wasn't. He was a bit too oily, and half the time he was over the heads of—well, say eleven of us. But on the whole, I think we liked him better than we did Ricketts—maybe because he had a losing case and was putting up a good fight.

Sometimes the two of them wrangled together over nothing in particular until the judge, who always looked half asleep when he wasn't drawing heads or something on his blotter, would get tired of it and ask them to get along with the case. Sometimes the judge called a recess when the razzing was getting pretty furious, and when he came back from his chambers he would always have a fresh chew of tobacco in his cheek. He had a chopped moustache, and reminded me of a veterinary surgeon I used to know.

After the evidence was all in, the main talking began, as I said. Rickets, sneery as ever, talked as if it was all over but the shouting. The newspapers called him a "hanging prosecutor," and it was a hanging he wanted in this case. He drew a lot of inferences that weren't justified by the evidence, it seemed to me, to give Murray a motive for the crime; but there wasn't much that it was necessary for him to say. His case was complete when Witte finished giving his testimony. Murray had been caught red-handed, whatever his motives may have been, and that was that. He had taken a human life, and the law demanded his own in return. A silly idea, but there are a lot of silly ideas in the world, parading as wisdom.

Thistlethwaite, of course, took another tone. He was bitter when he referred to Ricketts's conduct of the case; but for the most part he delivered an address that might have come out of a Sunday serial. He pictured Murray as a victim of circumstances, a man of fine reputation who was to be blamed only because he was fool enough to get drunk and stagger into a mess. Considering the little he had to build on, his story was a good one. You could see the whole scene the way he described it: Murray, so fuddled he didn't know what was going on, meandering home the wrong way, probably making speeches to the moon, blundering onto the body of Howard Blessing a minute or two after the shooting, seeing the revolver on the ground beside the body, picking it up like an idiot, and finally standing there dazed as Witte came up and arrested him. Meanwhile, Thistlethwaite said, the real murderer was fleeing for his life, making a clean getaway, seen only by an owl janitor who hadn't even caught a glimpse of the runner's face.

In support of Thistlethwaite's reconstruction, we had, of course, the janitor's slender testimony, and the evidence of the Pearson woman, as much of it as hadn't been laughed out of court. I always believed, myself, that she *did* hear the voices she said she did. The men were quarreling, and their voices probably were pretty high.

Finally, Thistlethwaite continued, there was the matter of the missing miniature. It completely exonerated Murray, he contended. It had to be either on Blessing or Murray, if Murray was the murderer; there hadn't been time for Murray to throw it away or hide it. So he ran on, and it was a first-class speech. He pointed to Murray's blameless life, and his distinguished friends, and wanted to know why under the canopy a man who had never handled a revolver in his life should on this occasion beg, borrow, or steal one and murder a man he had never seen or heard of before.

Oh, it was a masterpiece of a talk, but as Ricketts pointed out in his final address, it was all pure guesswork. In spite of everything anybody could say, one *fact* remained unshaken—James Murray, standing over his victim on the corner, with the discharged revolver in his hand.

As for Murray's drunkenness, Ricketts said, it was no excuse. He was willing to admit that in cold sobriety Murray might not have lost his temper and Blessing might have gone on living. It was absurd to assert, however, that there had been no quarrel between them. Whatever their differences may have been, they were obviously enemies. If we, the jury, believed that drunkenness excused cold-blooded murder, he added sarcastically, then we would, or course, acquit Murray and thereby encourage others to get drunk and go man-hunting; but if we believed that human life should be protected against the insanity of drunken beasts, whatever their reputations when sober, it was our duty to make an example of this particularly obnoxious specimen. And so on. It wasn't as picturesque a speech as Thistlethwaite's, but it carried a lot more conviction.

As a matter of fact, as far as the other eleven jurors were concerned, Murray's goose was cooked long before the final addresses. I knew that. Even the eyes and legs of Mrs. Murray hadn't helped much.

Then the judge adjusted his nose glasses and shoved his stomach up against the corner of the bench, and read his instructions, which were a fair enough summing up of what we had heard from both sides. On the whole, the instructions were a bit favorable to the prosecution, which was to be expected; but we were told that if we entertained—that was the word—a reasonable doubt of Murray's guilt, it was up to us to acquit him of the charge. After that we paraded to the jury room, and the real trial of the case began.

A smug animal named Dean, a printing superintendent somewhere, was our foreman, and he was as important about it as if he had been appointed minister to Dublin. Dean had served on juries before, although he'd never been a foreman until now, and he knew the ropes. We began by taking a trial ballot, just to see where we stood, and the vote was eleven for conviction and one for acquittal.

I knew who the *one* was, and I didn't see any reason for leaving the others in doubt.

"I'm the fellow, boys," I said. "Try to convince me."

They did. Dean in particular seemed to take it as a personal quarrel with him that I had. He seemed to think it inconsiderate of me to hold an opinion opposed to the views of eleven others. He had an idea that if we had all been agreed, somehow it would have been a feather in his cap to report right back to the judge, like a bunch of boy scouts, who had finished an assignment. The others thought it was funny, at first, and were chiefly interested to know my reasons for believing Murray innocent. They hadn't seen a chance for him at any time, they said. They were kind of sorry for him, but not much. As for his being innocent—!

"It's an open-and-shut case, Russell," one of them said. "Thistlethwaite made a good talk, all right, but he didn't have a single fact. It was all moonshine. I wouldn't hustle anybody off to the gallows, or even to the pen, if I had any doubts; but I haven't—not a doubt. This guy's going to get what is coming to him. He's as guilty as Judas Iscariot."

"He's being framed," I said. "He was drunk, and he happened along at the right time, and the murderer used him. That's the way I figure it. Thistlethwaite thinks Murray came along and saw the gun, and like a damn fool picked it up, just in time to get caught with it. I think the murderer stuck the gun into Murray's hand, just before he ran off himself. No wonder Murray was dazed!"

"Bunk!" said one of the others. "He was dazed because he was soused. He planned it all in cold blood, then licked up a lot of liquor to give him nerve to see it through."

"You think Murray knew Blessing?" I asked. And they all answered at once: "Sure thing!"

"There wasn't any testimony to show it," I said. "Ricketts just said that. There wasn't any proof."

"There didn't have to be," Dean said. "It stuck out all through the case. Why would he want to shoot him if he didn't know him?"

"That's what Thistlethwaite wanted to know," I told him. "He wouldn't—and he didn't. That's the answer. And how about the miniature?"

"He didn't have it on him," said Dean, meaning Blessing didn't have it on him. "Ricketts had the dope on that. He couldn't have had it on him. The fellow who said he did was probably lying."

"Lying, your grandmother," I said. "He saw it half an hour before Blessing was shot. If that miniature could be located, we'd know a lot more about this case than we do now, and Murray wouldn't be in danger of swinging."

"If your grandmother had four wheels she'd be a box car," said Dean.

"You fellows are just sore at Murray because he's a reformer who got drunk," I said. "I don't blame you for that, but it's no reason for supposing he committed murder."

"That's a lie," said Dean. "Anyway, it's a good reason, in my opinion."

So it went, off and on, for ten days. We picked that case to pieces. We went over every bit of testimony. And it ended just the way it began. Everybody but me wanted to convict Murray, and most of them wanted him hung. The longer we were out, the sorer they all got at Murray—and, of course, at me. They hated me like poison. They probably thought I'd been fixed, and was holding out on orders.

One of them—Dean—started to say something about it, one day, but I said some things that quieted him for a couple of hours. In one way, I had the whip hand. I didn't have any family waiting for me at home, and all the others had. They were all married men, and they were pretty sick about being kept away from home, after they'd been out a few days. At first, they had all thought it was a great lark.

I didn't care how long we were out. I knew it was my job to save Murray's neck. Not that I cared a hoot about Murray, but I was positive he was an innocent of the murder as Dean himself. Every once in a while the judge would send his bailiff in to see how we stood and whether there was any chance of our reaching a verdict. I thought a number of times he would call it a mistrial and discharge the jury, but he didn't. Eleven to one sounded pretty good to him, I guess. He figured that sooner or later I would cave, and there would be a verdict for the state.

The bailiff used to take a hand in the argument, sometimes. He thought I was a stubborn ass, and didn't hesitate to say so. He said he had heard all the evidence, too, and he was sure Murray was guilty.

"What do you care whether he swings or not?" he asked. "It ain't your funeral. Come on, boys, let's get a verdict, and we'll all go home." At other times he would say: "What do you think you are, Russell? Chief Justice or something? What right have you to say this man isn't guilty when these eleven men say he is? Do you think your brains are better than other people's?"

So it went. They didn't budge me an inch. I argued right back, and went over the whole ground with them like a teacher, time and again. And I didn't budge them an inch, either.

After a while they began to get even with me. The bailiff was at the bottom of that, I think. The other eleven used to have cigars, all of a sudden, when I didn't; and a couple of times I thought my food wasn't quite up to scratch, though it all came from the same hotel kitchen. Then one night somebody upset a pitcher of water in my bed, just before I had to use it; and my clothes used to disappear mysteriously, a few minutes before I needed them. I was taken over the jumps, all right. It was a regular initiation. It narrowed down, at last, to a survival contest. Nobody spoke to me, and I didn't speak to anybody. Any one of them would have been glad to take a punch at me, and a few times I thought some of them were going to do it. And every once in a while Dean would call for another ballot, just to see whether I had changed my mind.

Well, the eleventh morning rolled around, and the ratio was still eleven to one. The judge's bailiff came in and dropped a hint. He said if we didn't reach a verdict that day we were going to be discharged. He may have been lying; I don't know; but that's what he said. Everybody cheered up but me. It was going to be over soon, one way or another, they figured. They weren't so angry at me that morning.

When I still held out, they just laughed a little, and Dean said: "Well, you certainly stuck it out, Russell. I've got to hand it to you."

"Thanks!" I said.

But I wasn't pleased at all. A discharge of the jury meant another trial for Murray, probably, and I knew that next time he wouldn't have someone like me on the jury to save his neck. I thought it all over, and there was only one thing to do; so after dinner I did it.

"Boys," I said, "or gentlemen, if you like, the time has come to end all this funny business. We haven't been able to agree, and it looks as if the judge is going to let us disagree. That doesn't suit me, for I believe Murray is innocent. I don't want another jury to convict him. I want this jury to free him. Last night, I went over this case pretty carefully, and I can tell you just what happened that night on that street corner, as clearly as if I was there. Maybe I dreamed it; maybe I just figured it out; but this is the way it goes. . . .

"About ten years ago, let's imagine there was a man named Smith—call him George Smith. Suppose he fell in love with a girl, and that it was an honest-to-God thing. Maybe he was an electrician or something like that, in a small town in Ohio, where the girl lived. Anyway, I imagine he didn't have money enough to get married, so he and the girl just drifted along, liking each other a lot, and hoping that some day it would be all right. He would have taken a chance, and so would the girl; but suppose her father was dead against it. Then suppose Smith got a chance to make some money—good money—in another city, and went away. The girl, of course, was going to wait for him, and maybe she would have waited, if it hadn't been for another fellow. Suppose this other fellow was a hardware salesman, a fellow who made that town every once in a while, a flashy, good-looking young fellow, with enough money to make it look like it was more than it was. Then suppose he took a fancy to this girl, too, and that his name was Howard Blessing."

That gave them all a shock. At first they hadn't known what I was talking about. Now they began to prick up their ears and look at each other.

"Well," I said, "suppose all that, and the rest ought to be easy to guess. It's the sort of thing that happens in life, a lot oftener than you think. What happens? As soon as Smith is out of the way, Blessing begins to work on the girl. He fills her up with a lot of stories about Smith, some of them pretty tough; and, with the girl's father to help him, it isn't long before Smith isn't getting any answer to his letters. Then, one day, he gets a letter from the girl that knocks him over. Maybe it's a year after he's gone away; about the time he's thinking about going back to marry her. And she says she's going to marry Blessing.

"There's the situation, and you can't blame the girl altogether, because Blessing is a good plausible liar, and Smith isn't there to defend himself. There isn't anything Smith can do, is there? He can't figure it out, of course, because he doesn't know all the dirty stories Blessing has been telling about him. Maybe it doesn't break his heart exactly, because men's hearts don't break easily; but it makes him pretty mad. He already hates Blessing, who is a pup. Smith has always known that, the way men know about each other. All right!

Smith stays on where he is, and after a time he gets the wedding announcement, and that's that. The chapter's over. That's what Smith thinks; and probably that's what Blessing thinks."

Well, I had them, all right. The story got them, as I thought maybe it would. They began to smell a rat. But Dean wasn't letting me get away with too much. "That's very pretty," he said. "You ought to write a story about it, Russell. You've sure got an imagination. But what's it got to do with Murray?"

"Let me finish," I said. "Maybe I'm only supposing a case, but you'll find it fits the facts. What happens afterwards? You don't need three guesses to know that. The years begin to run, and after enough of them have gone by, one day Smith gets a letter from the girl's mother. She's always liked Smith, and she writes to tell him that her daughter—that is, Mrs. Blessing—is dead. She doesn't beat around the bush for words, either, and what she has to say about Blessing is plenty. He's everything that Smith already knows, and then some. The old woman is broken-hearted, and she's mad—both of them. She writes to Smith because she's got to write to somebody. And, of course, it's the old story again—as old as what happened to Smith. Blessing hadn't panned out very well, and when he'd got to running around with other women, it was the finish for the girl. But instead of getting a divorce, the girl commits suicide, being that kind of girl. She must have had a terrible time, to do that. Maybe you can imagine her. She probably looked like the pictures you've seen of Mrs. Blessing.

"Well," I said, "now you've got the beginning of the story. Smith, of course, writes a letter to the old woman, trying to buck her up; and privately he tells himself what he's going to do to Blessing if he ever meets him. Because Blessing has killed the girl just as surely as if he had knifed her. They don't call it murder, maybe, but that's what it is. Isn't it?"

About half of them nodded their heads; and I was pretty glad they were all married men. Probably some of them had daughters; I don't know.

"The girl's mother, you see, has spilled the beans," I went on, "and Smith knows now how Blessing happened to cut him out. And the end of the story, of course, is what happened the night Smith met Blessing at Lambeth Avenue and Belvedere Road; the night Mrs. Pearson was looking out of her window, and didn't have a cold in her head. It was a long time after the girl had died, of course, and Smith and Blessing had met once before that, but Blessing had got away. He ran. That's how Smith knew Blessing was in the same city as himself, this city in which we're sitting now. If Blessing had known it in time, he'd probably have shipped for Africa. That's the sort of a coward he was."

By this time the whole eleven of them were listening with both ears, for they had tumbled to the fact that I knew Smith and knew his story; they knew I *must*. Well, I did. Even so, one of them sneered a bit, and said: "You seem to know a lot about it!"

"I do!" I said, and went on with the story:

"The second time Smith met Blessing was that night, and Blessing was ready. He'd got a gun, apparently, and carried it every night after that first meeting. He wasn't taking any chances. Smith didn't have a gun. He didn't intend to kill Blessing. He just intended to thrash him within an inch of his life. They met, accidentally, and Blessing began to argue—to justify himself. That's what the Pearson woman heard as the two of them passed her window. But Smith was cold. He knew what he was going to do; but he let Blessing talk, to see what he'd say. Finally, Blessing produced his miniature, and began to sob about it; and that was the last straw. Smith knocked it out of his hands and swung on him. And Blessing ducked and got out his gun. He didn't get a chance to use it, for Smith grabbed him and took that away from him, too. The gun went off in the air, just as Smith got it. That was the first shot. Then there were two more.

"I'm not trying to justify Smith, exactly. Something happened to him, just then, and maybe he wasn't responsible. Maybe you think he *was*. He let Blessing have it, just as Blessing jumped for him. It was all over in a minute, and Smith was a murderer. That sort of thing happens in life, too. It wasn't intended, there isn't any plan; it just happens because you're mad, and somebody has it coming to him. Something pops inside of you, and there you are. It might be you; it might be me. This time it was Smith."

Dean got the floor, then, for a minute. He had listened hard, and now he had a question to ask. "Who is Smith?" he wanted to know. "Is he—Murray?"

"No," I said, "he's the fellow the janitor saw running. I told you Murray was framed, and so he was. He came up just in time to be useful. He came up staggering, drunk; and he stopped and looked around to see what was going on. And Smith, who was pretty horrified by what he'd done, and had to get away quick, shoved the gun into Murray's hand, grabbed the miniature off the sidewalk, and ran. When Witte came up, a few minutes later—it took him longer than he thought—there was Murray standing over the body of Blessing, holding the gun, too drunk to know what was going on; wondering what it was all about. He said he was innocent, when he got his wits back, but he hadn't a leg to stand on.

"Now," I said, "that's what happened, that night, and there's only one thing for us to do, and that's acquit Murray."

They didn't say a word for a while. They couldn't. They just sat—or stood—and looked at me. Finally, Dean had an idea—another one. He stood up and aimed his finger at me.

"Russell," he said, "it's a good story, and if it's true, of course it goes without saying that you know this fellow Smith. Well, that's all right; though how you got onto the jury, I don't know. But it needs a lot more than your word to prove it. We'll free Murray—sure!—as soon as we know *you* know what you're talking about. If you're just making up a fairy tale, to get Murray off . . ."

Well, that was that. I knew again what I had to do. "All right, Dean," I said. "What would you consider was proof?"

He thought a minute. "If you could produce this fellow Smith," he said at last, "it would be something, eh, boys? But even then, Smith would have to produce the miniature, I guess, to prove that *he* was telling the truth. Yes, I guess the miniature is the only real proof. Eh, boys?"

They all agreed with him. They always agreed with everybody and with each other—with everybody except me.

"All right then," I said again, "but the question is: what about Smith? Does he have to take Murray's place? You know the truth about him. Do you want him to go to the gallows for killing Blessing? If you tell the court about Smith, he has to take *his* chance in the dock, and maybe get a jury that wouldn't understand him the way this one does. Assume that all I've told you is true, and that you're sitting in judgment on Smith. Would you free him or convict him?"

"Free him," said about four of them at once. The others hadn't thought about it; but I could see the answer in their faces. They wouldn't have hanged Smith. He had done the sort of thing every one of them knew he might have done himself. I chanced it.

"There's the miniature, boys," I said, pulling it out of my coat. "Take a look at it. I've had it in my pocket ever since that night. Then take a look at me. I'm Smith."

They had to believe it. It was true. There was the miniature, and they knew the face. It had been in all papers. They looked at it for a while, then at me, and then out of the window. For a minute I felt the rope around my neck. But I had read their minds. They were a bit stunned, but they believed me. They were ashamed of the things they had hinted about Mrs. Blessing, that first day out. It was all right. All they wanted was for someone to say the right thing, and finally a little wrinkled fellow, who had been one of the craziest to hang Murray, said it.

"Don't be scared," he said, good-naturedly. "Nobody's going to tell on you. Come on, you fellows. This is the last ballot. Not guilty—and that goes for Russell, too!"

I can tell about it now. It was a long time ago; and I'm a long way off.

THE INQUISITIVE BUTCHER OF NICE

(1963)

James Holding

Although murder is a solemn affair, this story has a nice touch of humor, as a French butcher finds himself involved in a different kind of meat business. James Holding is a renowned mystery writer. His books include *Mr. Moonlight and Omar* (1963), *Sherlock on the Trail* (1964), and *The Robber of Featherbed Lane* (1970). This story first appeared in *Ellery Queen's Mystery Magazine*.

Until the morning he discovered the dead man in his refrigerated display case, nothing very exciting had ever happened to Jacques Beauregard.

Beauregard was a butcher. Not a "purveyor of meats," mind you. Not yet a "provisioner" dealing in quality viands. M. Beauregard was much too unpretentious to allow himself and his vocation to be described in these agreeable modern terms. He was a plain man who believed in calling a butcher a butcher. He had a small, cool, spotless meat market in a side street off the Avenue de la Victoire in Nice. There, he sold cuts of top-grade meat to any who sought them. He was well-liked and well-patronized. He, in turn, liked his customers. And he liked his work.

He lived above his shop, alone, having never, alas, acquired a wife—a fact he laughingly explained by saying that since no woman in her right mind would ever consent to marry a butcher, he had never bothered to ask one to. He did, however, have an apprentice, a lad of seventeen named Martin Roget. Martin was learning the butcher's art by working for Jacques Beauregard at starvation wages, but with board and keep thrown in. And since the "keep" provided him with as much excellent beef, pork, mutton, and fowl as he could possibly desire, he felt himself to be quite a fortunate fellow and had nothing but the greatest respect and affection for his mentor.

This *garçon boucher*, Martin, was a bright, cheerful boy, and shared with M. Beauregard a lively interest in *boule*, the cinema, and detective stories. He, too, lived above the shop, in a small garret room directly across the hall from M. Beauregard's own somewhat more lavishly furnished quarters.

It was actually Martin who discovered the cadaver.

One of his duties as Beauregard's apprentice was to rise at seven o'clock each morning, descend to the butcher shop below, and prepare the store for the day's business. This meant scattering fresh sawdust on the floor, raising the steel shutter that protected the store front at night, unlocking the commodious refrigeration room at the rear of the store where the supplies of meat were hygienically stored, and refilling the white enameled trays of cold meats in the refrigerated display case.

When these chores were attended to, Martin normally climbed slowly upstairs again, still half asleep, and awakened M. Beauregard by knocking on the butcher's door. M. Beauregard would then rise, prepare himself a leisurely breakfast, consume it, and by opening time at 8:30, be down in his butcher shop, swathed in a fresh white apron, ready to serve whatever customers the day might produce.

On the 28th of July, however, this routine was rudely interrupted.

At 7:10 Martin came clattering up the stairs from the butcher shop three at a time. His knock on M. Beauregard's door had none of its usual apologetic politeness. He thundered on the panel with both hands. At the same time, he called in a loud voice through the door. "M. Beauregard! Awake! Instantly! Come quickly to the shop! There is a dead man in our display case, lying on the cold cuts!"

Thus violently shaken from slumber, Jacques Beauregard lost no time in descending to his shop, still clad in his pajamas which Martin, even though half hysterical, was charmed to see were of a gaudy purple color. "You are dreaming, Martin!" cried Beauregard as he ran down the stairs. "A dead man on the cold cuts! It is impossible. What wine did you drink last night with your onion sandwich at bedtime? You are *fou*, crazy!" He burst into the shop. "Where is this dead man, imbecile?"

"Right there, Monsieur," said Martin, pointing at the long refrigerated display case that divided the shop. "When I went to fill the trays of cold cuts . . ." He ceased talking because his *patron* was no longer listening.

Beauregard was looking aghast at the figure reclining full length in his display case. With a little gasp, half sick, half indignant, he noted that Martin had been accurate in his description. The man was, in truth, dead. His wide-open staring eyes testified to that. His hands were crossed on his chest. And he was, indeed, lying on the unsold cold cuts from yesterday, looking for all the world like a man laid out in a transparent coffin.

M. Beauregard stooped to look through the triple-glazed front of the display case. In his shock and horror he used his strongest oath. "Sacred name of a stuck swan!" he breathed, "*Sacré nom d'un cygne percé!*" Martin made a mental note to remember this manly expletive for his own later use. "Martin! Look who it is! It is M. Maurice!"

"Yes," said Martin, studiously avoiding the dead face with his eyes. He felt a bit squeamish. After all, it was still before breakfast. "It is truly M. Maurice. One customer who always paid cash, alas!"

"Force yourself to be less mercenary," Beauregard snapped. "We have here a dead man, a customer, on our cold cuts. Whether he paid cash or we extended him credit does not signify at a time like this. Call the police, Martin. At once."

"Certainly, *mon patron*. Immediately." Martin moved toward the wall telephone.

"Wait!" said M. Beauregard before his apprentice had taken two steps. "I must think."

Obligingly, Martin paused and rested a hip on the chopping block. Beauregard held his chin in one muscular hand. His bare feet shuffled contemplatively on the sawdusted floor. "It occurs to me," he said finally, "that M. Maurice may have been murdered. There is blood on that tray under his back."

"But of course," said Martin, snickering feebly. "It is the blood sausage tray."

"No jokes, idiot!" said his employer. "Let us make sure." He went around behind the display case.

"The police will be angry if we touch anything," suggested Martin. "They will no doubt look for fingerprints, clues, signs of a struggle. Thus it is always done in Ellery Queen's Mystère Magazine which I read each month."

Beauregard squinted at the unsmudged shiny surface of the sliding panels that formed the back of the display case. "There are no fingerprints," he said assuredly. He looked around his neat, undisturbed butcher shop. "There are no signs of a struggle. Any fool can clearly see that. And there are no clues except a corpse in our meat case. Help me here, Martin."

Together they slid back the panels and shifted the body of M. Maurice enough to see the slash in his bloodstained clothing and, through that, the lips of a deep and ugly knife wound in the corpse's back.

"Enough!" said M. Beauregard. "I must think again."

"M. Maurice was murdered, was he not? Only so could such a wound . . ."

"Quiet, boy. I think."

"I, also," said Martin valiantly. "I shall help you think, *mon patron*. Two heads . . ."

"*Alors*, think! But for the love of God, keep the mouth closed meanwhile, eh?"

Silence descended on the butcher shop, broken only by the solemn ticking of the round clock with a rusted hand that hung on the wall. The hour was now 7:45. They must open the shop at 8:30.

At length Beauregard hitched up his pajama pants. He said, "I have decided. We will not summon the police, Martin. Not yet."

Martin was amazed. "Not call the police? But surely, if ever the police were required . . ."

"Listen, my young ignoramus. If we call the police, what are we doing?"

"Behaving like good citizens of France, *mon patron*." Martin said this stoutly.

"Perhaps. But we shall also be doing just what the murderer expects us to do, shall we not?"

"Admittedly."

"So we shall not do it. We will confuse this killer."

"Why?"

"Out of confusion emerges truth," Beauregard said sententiously. "I have read that somewhere."

"In M. Queen's Mystère Magazine, without doubt," said Martin respectfully.

"I do not remember. But it is only the least of our reasons for not summoning the *flics*. There are others, more powerful. First, publicity. You are too young to appreciate the effects on our business of such a contretemps as this. To have all of Nice know that a dead corpse, formerly a good customer of ours, has been found lying on our cold cuts in our thrice-accursed display case! It is unthinkable, Martin. What customer of ours could stand the thought? No one would want to buy meat in a butcher shop where such things occur, *hein?*"

"That I can comprehend very clearly, young as I am."

"So. And still a third reason forbids me to call the police."

"What is it?"

M. Beauregard ran his hands over his tousled hair in a gesture of near-despair. "They might think *I* killed M. Maurice," he said in a stricken voice. "Or you, Martin."

Martin blinked and sat up with a jerk on the chopping block. "Why should they think that?" he asked. "We didn't."

"Of course we didn't. But consider. The corpse is found in our shop. In our display case. Among our cold cuts. He is a customer of ours. The cause of death seems to be a knife wound in the back. What better source of a long, sharp knife than M. Jacques Beauregard's butcher shop, where the murdered man is found?"

"Ah," said Martin, awe-struck by this dazzling deduction. "You are right, my dear *patron*. Let us not call the police. It would be suicidal. But if not . . ." his voice cracked a little and trailed off weakly, "what do we do?"

"We prepare to open for business as usual," said Beauregard briskly. "Take his legs."

They worked the cadaver out of the display case. "But we are destroying evidence," protested Martin, pulling and hauling until his face was red.

"Not so, thou great worrier," said Jacques. "I intend to keep M. Maurice well refrigerated still." They carried the body to the door of the refrigeration room at the rear of the shop. They carried it inside, their breath showing white in the cold room. "Back here, Martin."

In the most distant corner of the cold room they leaned M. Maurice against the wall behind several sides of beef that hung from sturdy hooks. The cow carcasses partially concealed the cadaver. "There," said Beauregard with a sigh of relief, "no one will suspect he is here. Now, that blood stained tray."

Martin quickly replaced that with another in the display case. Beauregard cast a professional eye around the shop. "Good. Now, Martin, dress yourself. Have your breakfast. I shall do likewise. And if you ever hope to become a master butcher, permit no word of this to escape your lips. Do you promise?"

"But certainly."

"*Bien.*"

As they climbed the stairs to their respective rooms, Beauregard said without immodesty, "I have already reduced this problem to its basic elements, Martin—as one reduces the body of a pig to its basic cuts of pork. And although my conclusions have little to do with an apprentice's training, I shall relate them to you. You are young, and a mystery story reader. Therefore listen, and tell me if I have reasoned well."

"Three questions immediately present themselves in this bizarre affair. One, who killed M. Maurice? Two, why was he killed? And three—our major concern—why was the corpse left in our shop, deliberately placed on top of our cold cuts? Do you agree?"

Flattered that M. Beauregard should consult him in such a delicate matter, Martin nodded eagerly. "You have reason," he said. "If we knew the answers to those three problems, we should know where we stand."

Mr. Beauregard said with satisfaction, "Exactly."

"But how shall we learn these so-important answers?" asked Martin reasonably enough.

"Silence, boy," said the butcher brusquely. "I must think."

They separated on the landing before their doors. At 8:30 on the dot they opened the butcher shop for business. And as the day wore on, their customers detected nothing unusual about the butcher and his apprentice except a tendency on both their parts to become a little absent-minded in their tasks, and a certain thoughtful expression on M. Beauregard's ordinarily candid and open countenance.

Between trimming an *entrecote* for Madame Sevigny and grinding up half a *kilogramme* of round steak for Madame Cothelle, M. Beauregard suddenly snapped his fingers with the air of remembering something important.

"What is it, *mon patron?*" Martin asked as soon as Madame Cothelle had left. "You have thought of something?"

"I have, Martin. Cast your mind back to yesterday," said Beauregard as though yesterday were a hundred years ago. "Do you remember M. Maurice coming in for two loin lamb chops and four lamb kidneys?"

"Of course. I stood right here beside you when you served him."

"Well. As M. Maurice turned to leave the shop with his meat, who came in the door?"

"M. Bonfils, the *avocat*," said Martin promptly. "The one who owes us a meat bill of nine hundred and fifty francs."

"You are an observant boy," his patron complimented him. "And did you by any chance observe that which followed this encounter of M. Maurice and M. Bonfils?"

"No, Monsieur. I did not."

"Ah. M. Maurice stopped as though surprised when he saw M. Bonfils. Then he laughed in a peculiar way—a rather unpleasant way, I thought—and said to the *avocat*, 'How do you do, M. Bonfils? I didn't know you were affluent enough to patronize a quality butcher shop like this? I am delighted to know it.' And M. Bonfils nodded coldly to him and said nothing. Then M. Maurice, laughing again, said, 'And how is Madame Bonfils today, *mon ami?*' I remember it because I did not know M. Bonfils was married. He always buys the meat as though for himself alone, and never enough, surely, for two grown people. Yet 'Madame Bonfils' is what M. Maurice said."

"And how did M. Bonfils reply to that?"

"In a voice very low, scarcely to be heard, he said, 'She is well, thank you,' and M. Maurice went out of the store and M. Bonfils came on to the counter to ask for further credit, as it turned out. But—and this is the marrow of the bone, Martin—for just one moment M. Bonfils' eyes blazed with such a savage hatred as to be almost incredible in a quiet, well-mannered man of the law like M. Bonfils."

"And . . . ?" said Martin, deeply interested.

"That was the entire incident," said Beauregard somewhat weakly. "It does not seem significant to you?"

"No," said Martin bluntly. "Two customers meet in the shop and exchange civilities. What could be significant about that?"

"M. Bonfils' glare of hatred. I only remembered how savage it was just now as I ground up Madame Cothelle's beef."

When lunchtime came, Martin shut the door of the shop as usual and went to the rear door that opened on a dirty alley behind the block of buildings. Beauregard followed him. "It is through this back door," the butcher said slowly, "that the murderer of M. Maurice must have brought the body to deposit among our *viandes*." He stooped to look at the primitive lock on the door. "Bah," he added in disgust, "a child with a toothpick could open this lock." He turned to Martin. "I am going out to lunch, Martin. Tend things here till I return, understood? I cannot forget that look on M. Bonfils' face."

"He is a lawyer," warned Martin. "Do nothing rash, Monsieur, or he will have us both in the *bastille* for lawbreakers."

"Be easy," M. Beauregard said. "I was not weaned yesterday." He clapped on his hat and left the shop.

It was an hour before he returned. And not until a mid-afternoon lull occurred in the butcher shop could Martin ask eagerly. "You have found a clue, *mon patron?*"

Beauregard gave a short barking laugh. "A clue!" he said, obviously pleased with himself. "I have personally discovered, Martin, in less than a single hour of investigation, the solution to two-thirds of our problem! I have answered the 'who' and the 'why' of M. Maurice's murder."

Martin's eyes rounded. He regarded his mentor with the air of a boy who has ordered brisket of beef and been served with tenderloin at the same price. "*Prodigeux!*" he said, startled. "Who is the who and why is the why?"

"Allow me," Beauregard said, "to state a hypothetical case, my young colleague. That is what the famous detectives do without fail, *n'est-ce pas?*" He took a deep breath and fixed his eyes on Martin's. "Suppose you were a struggling young *avocat* in Paris. Married to a woman who was not only quite wealthy, but beautiful also."

"It is a pleasure even to imagine," said Martin with enthusiasm.

"Wait. The wife is wealthy and beautiful, yes. But she is also, alas, a hellcat. For in spite of her background and money, her appetites are carnal and uncontrolled. Can you imagine having such a wife?"

"It is still a pleasure," Martin said. The butcher cast a quizzical glance at the young man but continued.

"It is no pleasure for her husband, whom you are supposing yourself to be. Your wife becomes the talk of Paris, you its laughing stock. You want a divorce, to cleanse your dishonored name. She will not agree, both because the church forbids it and because, being your wife, she enjoys the protection of your ancient name in her indiscretions. In addition, she has a fantastic fortune, *tu sais*—enough money to buy off or intimidate any witnesses you might bring against her. *Eh, bien.*" Beauregard spread his hands and shrugged in a peculiarly Gallic fashion. "You are in despair. Your life is ruined. Your legal practice evaporates. And after some time . . . you disappear."

"Disappear?"

"You vanish, you drop out of existence, as far as anyone can find out. Your wife hires detectives to find you, but without success. You are seen no more in Paris. You have chosen flight rather than further humiliation."

"Where have I flown to?" asked Martin.

Beauregard flashed him a smile. "To Nice. To our lovely city, big enough to hide in, small enough to take the taste of Paris out of your mouth."

Martin snickered. "And now I am a butcher's apprentice in Nice, working for M. Jacques Beauregard while I try to forget my sexy wife and heal my broken heart."

"Very humorous," said the butcher disapprovingly. "I urge you to remember what we have in the corner of our cold room at this moment, Martin. To continue: you establish yourself in Nice. As an *avocat*, naturally—it is all you know. You have changed your name. You build up a new practice. You are beginning to find a new, supportable life. Then—and this is the heart of the matter, Martin—you suddenly fall in love! Hopelessly and gloriously in love with a simple girl in the flower market, down by the Old Town. She is everything your wife is not—sweet, pure, understanding, generous. You resist temptation as long as possible, naturally. But finally you say to yourself, *Diable!* I must have her!" And you marry her."

"One moment," said Martin shrewdly. "I already have a wife in Paris."

"To be sure. But you have changed your name. Nobody in Nice knows who you really are. What harm can come of it? You marry the flower girl. You have a baby, a little girl named Zou-Zou—"

"I refuse," Martin protested. "The child would be illegitimate."

"You anticipate me," said Beauregard with dignity. "Pray permit me to finish this hypothetical case, my good imbecile. All goes well with you and your family for a while. Then—pouf!—the whole affair blows up in your face. Someone who has known you in Paris suddenly recognizes you in Nice. And discovers you have another wife here. And a baby. What happens to you then?"

"It depends on the one who recognizes me," said Martin. "If he is a man of sympathetic humanity, nothing happens. If he is, on the other hand, a scoundrel, a *mauvais sujet*—"

"He *is* a scoundrel."

"Then—blackmail!" breathed Martin dramatically, entering into the spirit of the hypothesis. "I am the perfect blackmail victim, am I not? I am a bigamist. I have a child who will be branded, if my secret comes out, an *enfant naturel.* I have a wife whom I adore in Nice and a wife whom I detest in Paris. To return to my true wife is unthinkable. I shall pay whatever the blackmailer asks to guard my secret and protect my second family!" Martin's eyes flashed.

"Bravo!" applauded Beauregard. "Now. You pay blackmail to this scoundrel until you are bled white. You cannot even settle your butcher's bill. You cannot feed your wife and child in adequate fashion. Then, to cap it all, you meet this blackmailer in a butcher shop one day and he twits you, publicly, about your poverty that he himself has induced. He makes two-edged inquiries about your wife before witnesses. He fills you with renewed dread of exposure. You are roused to the very peak of hate and desperation. What do you do then?"

Martin hesitated not a single second. "I kill the pig," he cried.

"Exactly," M. Beauregard honed his largest knife against the whetstone on his chopping block. "I believe that is what happened."

"M. Bonfils is the *avocat?*" asked Martin, somewhat deflated at having to substitute a real person, and a customer at that, for his own imaginary role in the drama.

The butcher nodded solemnly. "Not the smallest doubt of it."

"And M. Maurice is—was—the blackmailer?"

"It must be so."

"How have you learned so many things, *mon patron,*" asked Martin in humble hero worship, "in the course of a single lunchtime?"

M. Beauregard preened himself. "It was simple," he replied. "I called at M. Bonfils home. He was not there, naturally, since the telephone book clearly demonstrates that he has an office on the Gambetta. I ask the concierge for *Madame* Bonfils, to discuss with her my unpaid bill. She, I am informed by the concierge—who is our good customer, Madame Constance, by the way—has taken little Zou-Zou and gone to visit her mother for the day, who resides near the Casino Municipal. I therefore chat with Madame Constance about these admirable but debt-ridden people, the family Bonfils. Skillfully I extract from her all the gossip she knows—their love affair, their marriage, the birth of Zou-Zou, their evident poverty, although M. Bonfils does a good business, she believes. She, too, it appears, must wait for her rent money."

"Madame Constance would rather gossip than eat," Martin remarked.

"Yes. She would be still talking if I had permitted. But I say I shall wait for a few moments, on the chance that Monsieur or Madame Bonfils may return. Madame Constance, because she is aware of my honesty, permits me to wait in the Bonfils' room abovestairs. I wait. Neither Monsieur nor Madame returns. Not even Zou-Zou. I grow restless. I prowl the room. I inspect the potted plants on the window sill. I look at the books on a shelf. And on the flyleaf of one of these books I find a name that is *not* Bonfils, as it should be. 'This book,' says the flyleaf, 'belongs to Pierre St. Clair.' It is written in round, back-slanting, stylish handwriting. And below it is written 'Paris, 1959.'"

"It could have been another's book," protested Martin. "Surely M. Bonfils could have borrowed it from a friend named St. Clair?"

"Not so," said Beauregard with a superior smile. "The name 'Bonfils' written in the mailbox slot on the Bonfils' front door is written in identically the same back-slanting stylish handwriting. You see the significance of that?"

"Yes, of course."

"Very well. I have a name, a city, a date. I ask Madame Constance not to mention my abortive visit. I go to the public library. There, in the gossip columns of *Le Soir*, among the files of Paris newspapers, I find all I need to know about the Paris *avocat*, Pierre St. Clair, who disappeared when his wife disgraced him."

Martin, impressed, said, "You are truly a genius." He nodded. "You could instruct Auguste Dupin!"

"I deny it. If I could, I could also solve the third question we asked ourselves this morning: why was M. Maurice's body left in our display case? This is the crux of the affair, my boy. Why *here?*"

Martin shrugged eloquently. "Who knows? Perhaps he wants us to be suspected of the murder, as you suggested this morning."

"I think not, now that I know who he is. I have extended him generous credit. I have always been polite. I have sold him quality meat. He has no reason to wish me in trouble. Or you, either."

"Perhaps," said Martin, "we should examine the clothing and effects of M. Maurice in our cold room?"

"A capital idea," said Beauregard warmly. "It never occurred to me."

They could not, however, carry out this ghoulish search until the shop was closed for the day. Then, with the front and rear doors locked against interruption, they repaired somewhat hesitantly to the cold room.

"Hold him," said the butcher to his apprentice, "while I search him."

Martin propped up the icy body of M. Maurice. His employer went through the corpse's pockets. "Nothing," he announced at length. "Nothing—not even a sou. No document, no tailor's label."

"You missed the watch pocket in the trousers," said Martin. Holding the dead body erect gave him a decidedly queer feeling in the pit of his stomach.

Beauregard's fingers dipped into the small watch pocket of the corpse. They withdrew slowly a piece of paper, folded very small. "Lean him back in the corner," directed the butcher. "We will read this outside."

Under the drop light over the display case they pored over the unfolded paper. Martin exhaled sharply.

The paper showed a picture of a bald-headed man, with circles of dissipation ringing his eyes. Under the picture, in bold type, was the caption: WANTED—DEAD OR ALIVE! 5000 FRANCS REWARD! Under this caption a small block of type read: "Grigoire (The Pullet) Bussier. Authorities will pay the above reward for information about this man, dead or alive. He is wanted for murder, robbery, embezzlement, and other crimes. Height: about 1¾ meters. Age: approximately 37. Eyes: blue. Bald. Clean-shaven. If you know anything of this man, call the Police at once."

Beauregard and Martin raised their heads and stared at each other.

"Bald!" said Beauregard. "But M. Maurice had thick black hair."

Martin said, "Blue eyes. But M. Maurice's were brown."

"Clean-shaven," said Beauregard. M. Maurice wore a black mustache." He looked once more at the picture on the handbill. "Yet M. Maurice is perhaps one and three-quarters meters tall and could have been thirty-seven."

"And the eyes with the big circles. They *could* be M. Maurice's—if they were only blue."

M. Beauregard selected a short sharp knife from his rack. "Come," he said, "we shall experiment."

Once more in the cold room, before M. Maurice's body, Beauregard gently inserted the point of his knife under the skin at M. Maurice's hairline. He pried tenderly with the knife.

"*Mon Dieu!*" said Martin, staring. "You would scalp a corpse, Monsieur?"

"Not scalp, idiot. This is a toupee." Beauregard ripped the mat of black hair from M. Maurice's head. Disclosing an almost bald cranium. "Now, the eyes." His knife point delicately detached brown contact lenses from dead eyes that still showed blue pigment. "And the mustache." He used the razor-sharp knife to shave the corpse's upper lip. "*Regardez!*" he said, stepping back proudly, like a magician calling attention to a rabbit drawn from his hat. "M. Grigoire—The Pullet—Bussier!"

Martin went right to the heart of the matter. "Five thousand francs reward!" he said. "Dead or alive!" His voice cracked with excitement.

Beauregard pondered aloud. "So M. Maurice, too, was a fake. A hardened criminal in disguise, living an easy life on M. Bonfils' blackmail money. How, Martin, could he have known M. Bonfils, a respectable *avocat*, in Paris? So that he would recognize him in Nice?"

Martin said, "It springs to mind that M. Bonfils, or rather, M. St. Clair, as *avocat* acting for the state, may once have prosecuted this man and sent him to prison, perhaps? If so, Grigoire Bussier would remember and hate him forever?"

"Clearly," Beauregard said kindly, "you have been reading detective fiction when you should have been studying your butcher charts, little idiot. Nevertheless, I am prepared to wager that you are right." He took his strong chin in his hand. "Let me see. M. Bonfils must have expected we would call the police the instant we discovered the body this morning. So the reward notice was plainly meant for the police to find. Why?"

"In order that the police might properly identify M. Maurice, just as we did. And therefore, so that you would get the reward, having delivered this criminal to them."

Beauregard laughed aloud with simple delight. "Exactly my own analysis."

The apprentice frowned. "One wonders why M. Bonfils did not himself collect the reward on M. Maurice, since he knew who he was."

"No, no," the butcher said. "Impossible. Possessing a false name, a bigamous marriage, and an illegitimate Zou-Zou, would *you* care to become involved with the police on *any* matter?"

"Well, then," said Martin, returning with commendable directness to the immediate problem, "how can we get this reward to which we are now unquestionably entitled, and still prevent the police from thinking *we* killed M. Maurice?"

"Allow me to think once more," replied Beauregard.

Martin flapped his thin arms to warm himself in the chilly air of the refrigeration room while M. Beauregard thought furiously. "Ah!" the butcher said at last. "Help me carry him out." They carted the body, now bald, blue-eyed, and clean-shaven, from the cold room. "We shall allow him to defrost," said Beauregard. "Until three o'clock in the morning. Then I shall call the police. Place him by the back door."

So when two officers of the law arrived in answer to Beauregard's telephone call at three in the morning, they found a butcher in purple pajamas and a butcher's boy in his undershirt and drawers, standing above a recumbent body outside the rear door of the butcher shop.

"Messieurs," explained the butcher, stammering with excitement, "my bedroom window is directly above this door. I was awakened just now by sounds of a scuffle at this door, and by angry voices. I woke my apprentice here and we descended to investigate, suspecting burglars. And this is what we found."

He pointed dramatically to the dead body of M. Maurice, warm and limber now, with some fresh steer's blood artistically splashed on his clothing and about the flesh of the knife wound in his back. "Do you suppose they could have quarreled, as they jointly attempted to break into my shop—this man and a companion, perhaps? And the companion, in a fit of temper, killed him on this spot? The fellow died just before you arrived."

The ranking policeman took a close look at M. Maurice in the light of the flash his comrade held. "*Attendez!*" he cried then, in amazement. "This man, my friends, is *Le Poulet!* For seven years we seek him. I am glad to see him dead, M. Beauregard. No matter how he came by his end, it was too good for him. His killer has done society a favor. You have no idea what a blackguard he was, this one. *Le Poulet!* There is a reward for him!"

"A reward?" asked Beauregard innocently. Martin coughed into his shirt tail.

"Most certainly a reward!" The policeman paused, as though struck by a sudden thought. "And I shall see that you get it, M. Beauregard. For turning over this filth to us." He kicked the body of M. Maurice idly. Then he said, "The reward is three thousand francs, if I am not mistaken. Is that not correct, Raoul? You have seen the handbill at the station."

"That is right, *mon chef*," said the second policeman, smiling. "Three thousand francs exactly."

When the police had departed, moving the peripatetic body of M. Maurice for the last time, it is to be hoped, Beauregard sighed. "They will give us three thousand francs of the reward," he said to Martin. "The remaining two thousand will indubitably go to their favorite charity—themselves."

Martin said nothing, sobered by this first aching knowledge of man's corruption.

Three days later M. Bonfils walked into the butcher shop. He was cheerful. He greeted M. Beauregard almost gaily. "I read in the newspapers of your recent brush with crime," he said. "You are a famous man, now, *hein?*"

"Too famous for my taste," Beauregard said pleasantly. He regarded the *avocat* with narrowed gaze. Surely this small inoffensive man with two wives and a baby could not have crept on that hardened criminal in some dark alley, stabbed him in the back, stolen a car perhaps to cart the body to M. Beauregard's shop, and then laid the corpse on the cold cuts?

The butcher was all at once assailed by doubt. He said tentatively, "We received a reward, Monsieur. A handsome one. And in view of this unexpected windfall, I am serving meat on the house, as it were. A kilo free for every customer. Whatever you choose. For today only, of course, and only to my good customers. What is your pleasure? I can recommend the cold cuts very highly."

M. Bonfils fluttered his eyes toward the display case. And surely, as the *avocat's* glance rested where M. Maurice's body had so recently lain, the small man seemed to change color slightly and the suggestion of a shiver seemed to shake his narrow shoulders? Yes. M. Beauregard was certain of it. It was enough.

"No cold cuts, thank you," said Bonfils, perhaps a shade too quickly. "Perhaps a kilo of veal chops? But as it happens, I have come in to pay you a small token on my account. A delinquent client has at last settled with me today."

"Ah," said M. Beauregard, nodding and cutting veal chops. "About your bill. I am glad you reminded me. We have discovered a regrettable error in your account. You owe us absolutely nothing, Monsieur. Nothing." He turned to Martin, who was listening avidly to every word. "Martin! Kindly look up Monsieur's account in the book. Does he owe us anything?"

Martin rose to the occasion nobly. He found the account book and riffled through it. "No, *mon patron*," he said in a carefully bored voice. "He owes us nothing—not a sou."

The little *avocat's* smile was like the sun coming out. He accepted the kilo of veal chops, thanked the butcher profusely, and left the shop with a spring in his walk.

Beauregard turned to his apprentice. "Just consider, Martin, what brilliance, what sentiment, what a delicate feeling for true economy of action M. Bonfils has displayed in this affair! To rid oneself of a blackmailer and pay one's meat bill, both at a single stroke! It is no less than magnificent!"

THE SILVER MASK

(1933)

Hugh Walpole

No murder takes place in this story. Instead, there is an amputation of the means of life and a killing of the spirit. The crime of living death is terrifying, and the prolonged suffering it causes is far worse than the brief agony of actually being murdered. This story was dramatized in the play *Kind Lady*, which became a big hit on Broadway.

Sir Hugh Seymour Walpole (1884–1941) was a distinguished English novelist. Among his books are *The Dark Forest* (1916), *Jeremy* (1919), *The Inquisitor* (1935), and *The Old Ladies* (1940).

Miss Sonia Herries, coming home from a dinner party at the Westons', heard a voice at her elbow.

"If you please—only a moment——"

She had walked from the Westons' flat because it was only three streets away, and now she was only a few steps from her door, but it was late, there was no one about and the King's Road rattle was muffled and dim.

"I am afraid I can't—" she began. It was cold, and the wind nipped her cheeks.

"If you would only—" he went on.

She turned and saw one of the handsomest young men possible. He was the handsome young man of all romantic stories, tall, dark, pale, slim, distinguished—oh! everything!—and he was wearing a shabby blue suit and shivering with the cold just as he should have been.

"I'm afraid I can't—" she repeated, beginning to move on.

"Oh, I know," he interrupted quickly. "Everyone says the same, and quite naturally. I should if our positions were reversed. But I *must* go on with it. I *can't* go back to my wife and baby with simply nothing. We have no fire, no food, nothing except the ceiling we are under. It is my fault, all of it. I don't want your pity, but I *have* to attack your comfort."

He trembled. He shivered as though he were going to fall. Involuntarily she put out her hand to steady him. She touched his arm and felt it quiver under the thin sleeve.

"It's all right . . ." he murmured. "I'm hungry . . . I can't help it."

She had had an excellent dinner. She had drunk perhaps just enough to lead to recklessness—in any case, before she realised it, she was ushering him in, through her dark-blue painted door. A crazy thing to do! Nor was it as though she were too young to know any better, for she was fifty if she was a day and, although sturdy of body and as strong as a horse (except for a little unsteadiness of the heart), intelligent enough to be thin, neurotic and abnormal; but she was none of these.

Although intelligent she suffered dreadfully from impulsive kindness. All her life she had done so. The mistakes that she had made—and there had been quite a few—had all arisen from the triumph of her heart over her brain. She knew it—how well she knew it!—and all her friends were forever dinning it into her. When she reached her fiftieth birthday she said to herself, "Well, now at last I'm too old to be foolish any more." And here she was, helping an entirely unknown young man into her house at dead of night, and he in all probability the worst sort of criminal.

Very soon he was sitting on her rose-coloured sofa, eating sandwiches and drinking a whisky and soda. He seemed to be entirely overcome by the beauty of her possessions. "If he's acting he's doing it very well," she thought to herself. But he had taste and he had knowledge. He knew that the Utrillo was an early one, the only period of importance in that master's work, he knew that the two old men talking under a window belonged to Sickert's "Middle Italian," he recognised the Dobson head and the wonderful green bronze Elk of Carl Milles.

"You are an artist," she said. "You paint?"

"No, I am a pimp, a thief, a what you like—anything bad," he answered fiercely. "And now I must go," he added, springing up from the sofa.

He seemed most certainly invigorated. She could scarcely believe that he was the same young man who only half an hour before had had to lean on her arm for support. And he was a gentleman. Of that there could be no sort of question. And he was astoundingly beautiful in the spirit of a hundred years ago, a young Byron, a young Shelley, not a young Ramon Navarro or a young Ronald Colman.

Well, it was better that he should go, and she did hope (for his own sake rather than hers) that he would not demand money and threaten a scene. After all, with her snow-white hair, firm broad chin, firm broad body, she did not look like someone who could be threatened. He had not apparently the slightest intention of threatening her. He moved towards the door.

"Oh!" he murmured with a little gasp of wonder. He had stopped before one of the loveliest things that she had—a mask in silver of a clown's face, the clown smiling, gay, joyful, not hinting at perpetual sadness as all clowns are traditionally supposed to do. It was one of the most successful efforts of the famous Sorat, greatest living master of masks.

"Yes. Isn't that lovely?" she said. "It was one of Sorat's earliest things, and still, I think, one of his best."

"Silver is the right material for that clown," he said.

"Yes, I think so too," she agreed. She realised that she had asked him nothing about his troubles, about his poor wife and baby, about his past history. It was better perhaps like this.

"You have saved my life," he said to her in the hall. She had in her hand a pound note.

"Well," she answered cheerfully, "I was a fool to risk a strange man in my house at this time of night—or so my friends would tell me. But such an old woman like me—where's the risk?"

"I could have cut your throat," he said quite seriously.

"So you could," she admitted. "But with horrid consequences to yourself."

"Oh no," he said. "Not in these days. The police are never able to catch anybody."

"Well, good night. Do take this. It can get you some warmth at least."

He took the pound. "Thanks," he said carelessly. Then at the door he remarked: "That mask. The loveliest thing I ever saw."

When the door had closed and she went back into the sitting room she sighed:—

"What a good-looking young man!" Then she saw that her most beautiful white jade cigarette case was gone. It had been lying on the little table by the sofa. She had seen it just before she went into the pantry to cut the sandwiches. He had stolen it. She looked everywhere. No, undoubtedly he had stolen it.

"What a good-looking young man!" she thought as she went up to bed.

Sonia Herries was a woman of her time in that outwardly she was cynical and destructive while inwardly she was a creature longing for affection and appreciation. For though she had white hair and she was fifty she was outwardly active, young, could do with little sleep and less food, could dance and drink cocktails and play bridge to the end of all time. Inwardly she cared for neither cocktails nor bridge. She was above all things maternal and she had a weak heart, not only a spiritual weak heart but also a physical one. When she suffered, must take her drops, lie down and rest, she allowed no one to see her. Like all the other women of her period and manner of life she had a courage worthy of a better cause.

She was a heroine for no reason at all.

But, beyond everything else, she was maternal. Twice at least she would have married had she loved enough, but the man she had really loved had not loved her (that was twenty-five years ago), so she had pretended to despise matrimony. Had she had a child her nature would have been fulfilled; as she had not had that good fortune she had been maternal (with outward cynical indifference) to numbers of people who had made use of her, sometimes laughed at her, never deeply cared for her. She was named "a jolly good sort," and was always "just outside" the real life of her friends. Her Herries relations, Rockages and Cards and Newmarks, used her to take odd places at table, to fill up spare rooms at house parties, to make purchases for them in London, to talk to when things went wrong with them or people abused them. She was a very lonely woman.

She saw her young thief for the second time a fortnight later. She saw him because he came to her house one evening when she was dressing for dinner.

"A young man at the door," said her maid Rose.

"A young man? Who?" But she knew.

"I don't know, Miss Sonia. He won't give his name."

She came down and found him in the hall, the cigarette case in his hand. He was wearing a decent suit of clothes, but he still looked hungry, haggard, desperate and incredibly handsome. She took him into the room where they had been before. He gave her the cigarette case. "I pawned it," he said, his eyes on the silver mask.

"What a disgraceful thing to do!" she said. "And what are you going to steal next?"

"My wife made some money last week," he said. "That will see us through for a while."

"Do you never do any work?" she asked him.

"I paint," he answered. "But no one will touch my pictures. They are not modern enough."

"You must show me some of your pictures," she said, and realised how weak she was. It was not his good looks that gave him his power over her, but something both helpless and defiant, like a wicked child who hates his mother but is always coming to her for help.

"I have some here," he said, went into the hall, and returned with several canvases. He displayed them. They were very bad—sugary landscapes and sentimental figures.

"They are very bad," she said.

"I know they are. You must understand that my aesthetic taste is very fine. I appreciate only the best things in art, like your cigarette case, that mask there, the Utrillo. But I can paint nothing but these. It is very exasperating." He smiled at her.

"Won't you buy one?" he asked her.

"Oh, but I don't want one," she answered. "I should have to hide it." She was aware that in ten minutes her guests would be here.

"Oh, do buy one."

"No, but of course not——"

"Yes, please." He came nearer and looked up into her broad kindly face like a beseeching child.

"Well . . . how much are they?"

"This is twenty pounds. This twenty-five——"

"But how absurd! They are not worth anything at all."

"They may be one day. You never know with modern pictures."

"I am quite sure about these."

"Please buy one. That one with the cows is not so bad."

She sat down and wrote a cheque.

"I'm a perfect fool. Take this, and understand I never want to see you again. Never! You will never be admitted. It is no use speaking to me in the street. If you bother me I shall tell the police."

He took the cheque with quiet satisfaction, held out his hand and pressed hers a little.

"Hang that in the right light and it will not be so bad——"

"You want new boots," she said. "Those are terrible."

"I shall be able to get some now," he said and went away.

All that evening while she listened to the hard and crackling ironies of her friends she thought of the young man. She did not know his name. The only thing that she knew about him was that by his own confession he was a scoundrel and had at his mercy a poor young wife and a starving child. The picture that she formed of these three haunted her. It had been, in a way, honest of him to return the cigarette case. Ah, but he knew, of course, that did he not return it he could never have seen her again. He had discovered at once that she was a splendid source of supply, and now that she had bought one of his wretched pictures——Nevertheless he could not be altogether bad. No one who cared so passionately for beautiful things could be quite worthless. The way that he had gone straight to the silver mask as soon as he entered the room and gazed at it as though with his very soul! And, sitting at her dinner table, uttering the most cynical sentiments, she was all softness as she gazed across to the wall upon whose pale surface the silver mask was hanging. There was, she thought, a certain look of the young man in that jolly shining surface. But where? The clown's cheek was fat, his mouth broad, his lips thick—and yet, and yet——

For the next few days as she went about London she looked in spite of herself at the passers-by to see whether he might not be there. One thing she soon discovered, that he was very much more handsome than anyone else whom she saw. But it was not for his handsomeness that he haunted her. It was because he wanted her to be kind to him, and because she wanted—oh, so terribly—to be kind to someone!

The silver mask, she had the fancy, was gradually changing, the rotundity thinning, some new light coming into the empty eyes. It was most certainly a beautiful thing.

Then, as unexpectedly as on the other occasions, he appeared again. One night as she, back from a theatre smoking one last cigarette, was preparing to climb the stairs to bed, there was a knock on the door. Everyone of course rang the bell—no one attempted the old-fashioned knocker shaped like an owl that she had bought, one idle day, in an old curiosity shop. The knock made her sure that it was he. Rose had gone to bed, so she went herself to the door. There he was—and with him a young girl and a baby. They all came into the sitting room and stood awkwardly by the fire. It was at that moment when she saw them in a group by the fire that she felt her first sharp pang of fear. She knew suddenly how weak she was—she seemed to be turned to water at sight of them, she, Sonia Herries, fifty years of age, independent and strong, save for that little flutter of the heart—yes, turned to water! She was afraid as though someone had whispered a warning in her ear.

The girl was striking, with red hair and a white face, a thin graceful little thing. The baby, wrapped in a shawl, was soaked in sleep. She gave them drinks and the remainder of the sandwiches that had been put there for herself. The young man looked at her with his charming smile.

"We haven't come to cadge anything this time," he said. "But I wanted you to see my wife and I wanted her to see some of your lovely things."

"Well," she said sharply, "you can only stay a minute or two. It's late. I'm off to bed. Besides, I told you not to come here again."

"Ada made me," he said, nodding at the girl. "She was so anxious to see you."

The girl never said a word but only stared sulkily in front of her.

"All right. But you must go soon. By the way, you've never told me your name."

"Henry Abbott, and that's Ada, and the baby's called Henry too."

"All right. How have you been getting on since I saw you?"

"Oh, fine! Living on the fat of the land." But he soon fell into silence and the girl never said a word. After an intolerable pause Sonia Herries suggested that they should go. They didn't move. Half an hour later she insisted. They got up. But, standing by the door, Henry Abbott jerked his head towards the writing desk.

"Who writes your letters for you?"

"Nobody. I write them myself."

"You ought to have somebody. Save a lot of trouble. I'll do them for you."

"Oh no, thank you. That would never do. Well, good night, good night——"

"Of course I'll do them for you. And you needn't pay me anything either. Fill up my time."

"Nonsense . . . good night, good night." She closed the door on them. She could not sleep. She lay there thinking of him. She was moved, partly by a maternal tenderness for them that warmed her body (the girl and the baby had looked so helpless sitting there), partly by a shiver of apprehension that chilled her veins. Well, she hoped that she would never see them again. Or did she? Would she not to-morrow, as she walked down Sloane Street, stare at everyone to see whether by chance that was he?

Three mornings later he arrived. It was a wet morning and she had decided to devote it to the settling of accounts. She was sitting there at her table when Rose showed him in.

"I've come to do your letters," he said.

"I should think not," she said sharply. "Now, Henry Abbott, out you go. I've had enough——"

"Oh no, you haven't," he said, and sat down at her desk.

She would be ashamed for ever, but half an hour later she was seated in the corner of the sofa telling him what to write. She hated to confess it to herself, but she liked to see him sitting there. He was company for her, and to whatever depths he might by now have sunk, he was most certainly a gentleman. He behaved very well that morning; he wrote an excellent hand. He seemed to know just what to say.

A week later she said, laughing, to Amy Weston: "My dear, would you believe it? I've had to take on a secretary. A very good-looking young man—but you needn't look down your nose. You know that good-looking young men are nothing to *me*—and he does save me endless bother."

For three weeks he behaved very well, arriving punctually, offering her no insults, doing as she suggested about everything. In the fourth week, about a quarter to one on a day, his wife arrived. On this occasion she looked astonishingly young, sixteen perhaps. She wore a simple grey cotton dress. Her red bobbed hair was strikingly vibrant about her pale face.

The young man already knew that Miss Herries was lunching alone. He had seen the table laid for one with its simple appurtenances. It seemed to be very difficult not to ask them to remain. She did, although she did not wish to. The meal was not a success. The two of them together were tiresome, for the man said little when his wife was there, and the woman said nothing at all. Also the pair of them were in a way sinister.

She sent them away after luncheon. They departed without protest. But as she walked, engaged on her shopping that afternoon, she decided that she must rid herself of them, once and for all. It was true that it had been rather agreeable having him there; his smile, his wicked humorous remarks, the suggestion that he was a kind of malevolent gamin who preyed on the world in general but spared her because he liked her—all this had attracted her—but what really alarmed her was that during all these weeks he had made no request for money, made indeed no request for anything. He must be piling up a fine account, must have some plan in his head with which one morning he would balefully startle her! For a moment there in the bright sunlight, with the purr of the traffic, the rustle of the trees about her, she saw herself in surprising colour. She was behaving with a weakness that was astonishing. Her stout, thick-set, resolute body, her cheery rosy face, her strong white hair—all these disappeared, and in their place, there almost clinging for support to the park railings, was a timorous little old woman with frightened eyes and trembling knees. What was there to be afraid of? She had done nothing wrong. There were the police at hand. She had never been a coward before. She went home, however, with an odd impulse to leave her comfortable little house in Walpole Street and hide herself somewhere, somewhere that no one could discover.

That evening they appeared again, husband, wife and baby. She had settled herself down for a cosy evening with a book and an "early to bed." There came the knock on the door.

On this occasion she was most certainly firm with them. When they were gathered in a little group she got up and addressed them.

"Here is five pounds," she said, "and this is the end. If one of you shows his or her face inside this door again I call the police. Now go."

The girl gave a little gasp and fell in a dead faint at her feet. It was a perfectly genuine faint. Rose was summoned. Everything possible was done.

"She has simply not had enough to eat," said Henry Abbott. In the end (so determined and resolved was the faint) Ada Abbott was put to bed in the spare room and a doctor was summoned. After examining her he said that she needed rest and nourishment. This was perhaps the critical moment of the whole affair. Had Sonia Herries been at this crisis properly resolute and bundled the Abbott family, faint and all, into the cold unsympathising street, she might at this moment be a hale and hearty old woman enjoying bridge with her friends. It was, however, just here that her maternal temperament was too strong for her. The poor young thing lay exhausted, her eyes closed, her cheeks almost the colour of her pillow. The baby (surely the quietest baby ever known) lay in a cot beside the bed. Henry Abbott wrote letters to dictation downstairs. Once Sonia Herries, glancing up at the silver mask, was struck by the grin on the clown's face. It seemed to her now a thin sharp grin—almost derisive.

Three days after Ada Abbott's collapse there arrived her aunt and her uncle, Mr. and Mrs. Edwards. Mr. Edwards was a large red-faced man with a hearty manner and a bright waistcoat. He looked like a publican. Mrs. Edwards was a thin sharp-nosed woman with a bass voice. She was very, very thin, and wore a large old-fashioned brooch on her flat but emotional chest. They sat side by side on the sofa and explained that they had come to enquire after Ada, their favourite niece. Mrs. Edwards cried, Mr. Edwards was friendly and familiar. Unfortunately Mrs. Weston and a friend came and called just then. They did not stay very long. They were frankly amazed at the Edwards couple and deeply startled by Henry Abbott's familiarity. Sonia Herries could see that they drew the very worst conclusions.

A week later Ada Abbott was still in bed in the upstairs room. It seemed to be impossible to move her. The Edwardses were constant visitors. On one occasion they brought Mr. and Mrs. Harper and their girl Agnes. They were profusely apologetic, but Miss Herries would understand that "with the interest they took in Ada it was impossible to stay passive." They all crowded into the spare bedroom and gazed at the pale figure with the closed eyes sympathetically.

Then two things happened together. Rose gave notice and Mrs. Weston came and had a frank talk with her friend. She began with that most sinister opening: "I think you ought to know, dear, what everyone is saying—" What everyone was saying was that Sonia Herries was living with a young ruffian from the streets, young enough to be her son.

"You must get rid of them all and at once," said Mrs. Weston, "or you won't have a friend left in London, darling."

Left to herself, Sonia Herries did what she had not done for years, she burst into tears. What had happened to her? Not only had her will and determination gone but she felt most unwell. Her heart was bad again; she could not sleep; the house, too, was tumbling to pieces. There was dust over everything. How was she ever to replace Rose? She was living in some horrible nightmare. This dreadful handsome young man seemed to have some authority over her. Yet he did not threaten her. All he did was to smile. Nor was she in the very least in love with him. This must come to an end or she would be lost.

Two days later, at tea time, her opportunity arrived. Mr. and Mrs. Edwards had called to see how Ada was; Ada was downstairs at last, very weak and pale. Henry Abbott was there, also the baby. Sonia Herries, although she was feeling dreadfully unwell, addressed them all with vigour. She especially addressed the sharp-nosed Mrs. Edwards.

"You must understand," she said. "I don't want to be unkind, but I have my own life to consider. I am a very busy woman, and this has all been forced on me. I don't want to seem brutal. I'm glad to have been of some assistance to you, but I think Mrs. Abbott is well enough to go home now—and I wish you all good night."

"I am sure," said Mrs. Edwards, looking up at her from the sofa, "that you've been kindness itself, Miss Herries. Ada recognizes it, I'm sure. But to move her now would be to kill her, that's all. Any movement and she'll drop at your feet."

"We have nowhere to go," said Henry Abbott.

"But, Mrs. Edwards—" began Miss Herries, her anger rising.

"We have only two rooms," said Mrs. Edwards quietly. "I'm sorry, but just now, what with my husband coughing all night——"

"Oh, but this is monstrous!" Miss Herries cried. "I have had enough of this. I have been generous to a degree——"

"What about my pay," said Henry, "for all these weeks?"

"Pay! Why, of course—" Miss Herries began. Then she stopped. She realised several things. She realised that she was alone in the house, the cook having departed that afternoon. She realised that none of them had moved. She realised that her "things"—the Sickert, the Utrillo, the sofa—were alive with apprehension. She was fearfully frightened of their silence, their immobility. She moved towards her desk, and her heart turned, squeezed itself dry, shot through her body the most dreadful agony.

"Please," she gasped. "In the drawer—the little green bottle—oh, quick! Please, please!"

The last thing of which she was aware was the quiet handsome features of Henry Abbott bending over her.

When, a week later, Mrs. Weston called, the girl, Ada Abbott, opened the door to her.

"I came to enquire for Miss Herries," she said. "I haven't seen her about. I have telephoned several times and received no answer."

"Miss Herries is very ill."

"Oh, I'm so sorry. Can I not see her?"

Ada Abbott's quiet gentle tones were reassuring her. "The doctor does not wish her to see anyone at present. May I have your address? I will let you know as soon as she is well enough."

Mrs. Weston went away. She recounted the event. "Poor Sonia, she's pretty bad. They seem to be looking after her. As soon as she's better we'll go and see her."

The London life moves swiftly. Sonia Herries had never been of very great importance to anyone. Herries relations enquired. They received a very polite note assuring them that as soon as she was better—

Sonia Herries was in bed, but not in her own room. She was in the little attic bedroom but lately occupied by Rose the maid. She lay at first in a strange apathy. She was ill. She slept and woke and slept again. Ada Abbott, sometimes Mrs. Edwards, sometimes a woman she did not know, attended to her. They were all very kind. Did she need a doctor? No, of course she did not need a doctor, they assured her. They would see that she had everything that she wanted.

Then life began to flow back into her. Why was she in this room? Where were her friends? What was this horrible food that they were bringing her? What were they doing here, these women?

She had a terrible scene with Ada Abbott. She tried to get out of bed. The girl restrained her—and easily, for all the strength seemed to have gone from her bones. She protested, she was as furious as her weakness allowed her, then she cried. She cried most bitterly. Next day she was alone and she crawled out of bed; the door was locked; she beat on it. There was no sound but her beating. Her heart was beginning again that terrible strangled throb. She crept back into bed. She lay there, weakly, feebly crying. When Ada arrived with some bread, some soup, some water, she demanded that the door should be unlocked, that she should get up, have her bath, come downstairs to her own room.

"You are not well enough," Ada said gently.

"Of course I am well enough. When I get out I will have you put in prison for this——"

"Please don't get excited. It is so bad for you heart."

Mrs. Edwards and Ada washed her. She had not enough to eat. She was always hungry.

Summer had come. Mrs. Weston went to Etretat. Everyone was out of town.

"What's happened to Sonia Herries?" Mabel Newmark wrote to Agatha Benson. "I haven't seen her for ages. . . ."

But no one had time to enquire. There were so many things to do. Sonia was a good sort, but she had been nobody's business. . . .

Once Henry Abbott paid her a visit. "I am so sorry that you are not better," he said smiling. "We are doing everything we can for you. It is lucky we were around when you were so ill. You had better sign these papers. Someone must look after your affairs until you are better. You will be downstairs in a week or two."

Looking at him with wide-open terrified eyes, Sonia Herries signed the papers.

The first rains of autumn lashed the streets. In the sitting room the gramophone was turned on. Ada and young Mr. Jackson, Maggie Trent and stout

Henry Bennett were dancing. All the furniture was flung against the walls. Mr. Edwards drank his beer; Mrs. Edwards was toasting her toes before the fire.

Henry Abbott came in. He had just sold the Utrillo. His arrival was greeted with cheers.

He took the silver mask from the wall and went upstairs. He climbed to the top of the house, entered, switched on the naked light.

"Oh! Who—what—" A voice of terror came from the bed.

"It's all right," he said soothingly. "Ada will be bringing your tea in a minute."

He had a hammer and nail and hung the silver mask on the speckled, mottled wall paper where Miss Herries could see it.

"I know you're fond of it," he said. "I thought you'd like it to look at."

She made no reply. She only stared.

"You'll want something to look at," he went on. "You're too ill, I'm afraid, ever to leave this room again. So it'll be nice for you. Something to look at."

He went out, gently closing the door behind him.

KELLER ON THE SPOT

(1997)

Lawrence Block

Mike Keller, hit man deluxe, is generously rewarded for his services. He is "on the spot" because he may not want to kill his contracted victim. Lawrence Block has written over fifty books, creating not only Keller but such other memorable characters as Matthew Scudder, Chip Harrison, Bernie Rhodenbarr, and Evan Tanner. He is renowned for his humor and suspense, and has received several Shamus and Edgar awards, including the Grand Master Edgar in 1994. Among his books are *The Burglar in the Closet* (1978), *Eight Million Ways to Die* (1982), *The Burglar in the Rye* (1999), *Hope to Die* (2001), and *All the Flowers Are Dying* (2005). He wrote this Edgar-winning story for *Playboy*.

Keller, drink in hand, agreed with the woman in the pink dress that it was indeed a lovely evening. He threaded his way through a crowd of young marrieds on what he supposed you would call the patio. A waitress passed carrying a tray of drinks in stemmed glasses and he traded in his own for a fresh one. He sipped as he walked along, wondering what he was drinking. Some sort of vodka sour, he decided, and decided as well that he didn't need to narrow it down any further than that. He figured he'd have this one and one more, but he could have ten more if he wanted, because he wasn't working tonight. He could relax and cut loose and have a good time.

Well, almost. He couldn't relax completely, couldn't cut loose altogether. Because, while this might not be work, neither was it entirely recreational. The garden party this evening was a heaven-sent opportunity for reconnaissance, and he would use it to get a close look at his quarry. He had been handed a picture back in White Plains, and he had brought that picture with him to Dallas, but even the best photo wasn't the same as a glimpse of the fellow in the flesh, and in his native habitat.

And a lush habitat it was. Keller hadn't been inside the house yet, but it was clearly immense, a sprawling multilevel affair of innumerable large rooms. The grounds sprawled as well, covering an acre or two, with enough plants and shrubbery to stock an arboretum. Keller didn't know anything about flowers, but five minutes in a garden like this one had him thinking he ought to know more about the subject. Maybe they had evening classes at Hunter or NYU; maybe they'd take you on field trips to the Brooklyn Botanical Gardens.

He walked along a brick path, smiling at this stranger, nodding at that one, and wound up standing alongside the swimming pool. Some 12 or 15 people sat at poolside tables, talking and drinking, the volume of their conversations rising as they drank. In the enormous pool, a young boy swam back and forth, back and forth.

Keller felt a curious kinship with the kid. He was standing instead of swimming, but he felt as distant as the kid from everybody else around. There were two parties going on, he decided. There was the hearty social whirl, and there was the solitude he felt in the midst of it all, akin to the solitude of the swimming boy.

Huge pool. The boy was swimming its width, but that dimension was still greater than the length of your typical backyard pool. Keller wasn't sure if this was an Olympic-size pool, but he figured you could just call it enormous and let it go at that.

Ages ago he'd heard about some college-boy stunt, filling a swimming pool with Jell-O, and he'd wondered how many little boxes of the gelatin dessert it would have required, and how the college boys could have afforded it. It would cost a fortune, he decided, to fill this pool with Jell-O, but if you could afford the pool in the first place, he supposed the Jell-O would be the least of your worries.

There were cut flowers on all the tables, and the blooms looked like ones Keller had seen in the garden. It stood to reason. If you grew all these flowers, you wouldn't have to order from the florist. You could cut your own.

What good would it do, he wondered, to know the names of all the shrubs and flowers? Wouldn't it just leave you wanting to dig in the soil and grow your own? And he didn't want to get into all that, for God's sake.

So maybe he'd just forget about evening classes at Hunter, and field trips to Brooklyn. If he wanted to get close to nature he could walk in Central Park, and if he didn't know the names of the flowers he would just hold off on introducing himself to them. And if—

Where was the kid?

The boy, the swimmer. Keller's companion in solitude. Where the hell did he go? The pool was empty, its surface still. Keller saw a ripple toward the far end, saw bubbles break the surface.

He didn't react without thinking. That was how he'd always heard that sort of thing described, but that wasn't what happened, because the thoughts were there, loud and clear. *He's down there. He's in trouble. He's drowning.* And, echoing in his head in a voice sour with exasperation: *Keller, for Christ's sake, do something!*

He set his glass on a table, shucked his coat, kicked off his shoes, dropped his pants and stepped out of them. Ages ago he'd earned a Red Cross lifesaving certificate, and the first thing they taught you was to strip before you hit the water. The six or seven seconds you spent peeling off your clothes would be repaid many times over in quickness and mobility.

But the strip show did not go unnoticed. Everybody at poolside had a comment, one more hilarious than the next. He barely heard them. In no time at all he was down to his underwear. Then he was out of range of their cleverness, hitting the water in a flat racing dive, churning the water till he reached the spot where he'd seen the bubbles, then diving, eyes wide, barely noticing the burn of the chlorine.

Searching for the boy. Groping, searching, then finding him, reaching to grab hold of him. And pushing off against the bottom, lungs bursting, racing to the surface.

People were saying things to Keller, thanking him, congratulating him, but it wasn't really registering. A man clapped him on the back, a woman handed him a glass of brandy. He heard the word hero and realized people were saying it all over the place, and applying it to him.

Hell of a note.

Keller sipped the brandy. It gave him heartburn, which assured him of its quality; good cognac always gave him heartburn. He turned to look at the boy. He was a little fellow, 12 or 13 years old, his hair lightened and his skin bronzed by the summer sun. He was sitting up now, Keller saw, and looking none the worse for his near-death experience.

"Timothy," a woman said, "this is the man who saved your life. Do you have something to say to him?"

"Thanks," Timothy said, predictably.

"Is that all you have to say, young man?" the woman asked.

"It's enough," Keller said, and smiled. To the boy he said, "There's something I've always wondered. Did your life actually flash before your eyes?"

Timothy shook his head. "I got this cramp," he said, "and it was like my whole body turned into one big knot, and there wasn't anything I could do to untie it. And I didn't even think about drowning. I was just fighting the cramp, 'cause it hurt, and about the next thing I knew I was up here, coughing and puking up water." He made a face. "I must have swallowed half the pool. All I have to do is think about it and I can taste vomit and chlorine."

"Timothy," the woman said, rolling her eyes.

"Something to be said for plain speech," an older man said. He had a mane of white hair and prominent white eyebrows, and his eyes were a vivid blue. He was holding a glass of brandy in one hand and a bottle in the other, and he reached with the bottle to fill Keller's glass to the brim. "'Claret for boys and port for men,'" he said. "'But he who aspires to be a hero must drink brandy.' That's Samuel Johnson, though I may have gotten a word wrong."

The woman patted his hand. "If you did, Daddy, I'm sure you just improved Mr. Johnson's wording."

"Dr. Johnson," he said, "and one could hardly do that. Improve the man's wording, that is. 'Being in a ship is like being in a jail, with the chance of being drowned.' He said that as well, and I defy anyone to comment more trenchantly on the experience, or to say it better." He beamed at Keller. "I owe you more than a glass of brandy and a well-turned Johnsonian phrase. This little rascal whose life you've saved is my grandson, and the apple—nay, sir, the very nectarine—of my eye. And we'd have all stood around drinking and laughing while he drowned. You observed, and you acted, and God bless you for it."

What did you say to that, Keller wondered. *It was nothing? Well, shucks?* There had to be some sort of apt phrase, and maybe Samuel Johnson could have found it, but Keller couldn't. So he said nothing, and tried not to look po-faced.

"I don't even know your name," the white-haired man went on. "That's not remarkable in and of itself. I don't know half the people here, and I'm content to remain in my ignorance. But I ought to know your name, wouldn't you agree?"

Keller might have picked a name out of the air, but the one that leaped to mind was Boswell, and he couldn't say that to a man who quoted Samuel Johnson. So he supplied the name he'd traveled under, the one he'd signed when he checked into the hotel, the one on the driver's license and credit cards in his wallet.

"It's Michael Soderholm," he said, "and I can't even tell you the name of the fellow who brought me here. We met over drinks in the hotel bar, and he said he was going to a party and it would be perfectly all right if I came along. I felt a little funny about it, but—"

"Please," the man said. "You can't possibly propose to apologize for your presence here. It has kept my grandson from a watery if chlorinated grave. And I've just told you I don't know half my guests, but that doesn't make them any the less welcome." He took a deep drink of his brandy and topped up both glasses. "Michael Soderholm," he said. "Swedish?"

"A mixture of everything," Keller said, improvising. "My great-grandfather Soderholm came over from Sweden, but my other ancestors came from all over Europe, plus I'm something like a sixteenth American Indian."

"Oh? Which tribe?"

"Cherokee," Keller said, thinking of the jazz tune.

"I'm an eighth Comanche," the man said. "So, I'm afraid we're not tribal blood brothers. The rest's British Isles, a mix of Scots and Irish and English. Old Texas stock. But you're not Texan yourself."

"No."

"Well, it can't be helped, as the saying goes. Unless you decide to move here, and who's to say you won't? It's a fine place for a man to live."

"Daddy thinks that everybody should love Texas the same way he does," the woman said.

"Everybody should," her father said. "The only thing wrong with Texans is we're a long-winded lot. Look at the time it's taking me to introduce myself! Mr. Soderholm, Mr. Michael Soderholm, my name's Garrity, Wallace Penrose Garrity, and I'm your grateful host this evening."

No kidding, thought Keller.

The party, lifesaving and all, took place on Saturday night. The next day Keller sat in his hotel room and watched the Cowboys beat the Vikings with a field goal in the last three minutes of double overtime. The game seesawed back and forth, with interceptions and runbacks, and the announcers kept telling each other what a great game it was.

Keller supposed they were right. It had all the ingredients, and it wasn't the players' fault that he was entirely unmoved by their performance. He could watch sports, and often did, but he almost never got caught up in it. He had occasionally wondered if his work might have something to do with it. On one level, when your job involved dealing regularly with life and death, how could you care if some overpaid steroid abuser had a touchdown run called back? And, on another level, you saw unorthodox solutions to a team's problems on the field. When Emmitt Smith kept crashing through the Minnesota line, Keller wondered why they didn't deputize someone to shoot the son of a bitch in the back of the neck, right below his star-covered helmet.

Still, it was better than watching golf, say, which had to be better than playing golf. And he couldn't get out and work, because there was nothing for him to do. Last night's reconnaissance mission had been both better and worse than he could have hoped, and what was he supposed to do now? Park his rented Ford across the street from the Garrity mansion and clock the comings and goings?

No need for that. He could bide his time, just so he got there in time for Sunday dinner.

"More potatoes, Mr. Soderholm?"

"They are delicious," Keller said. "But I'm full. Really."

"And we can't keep calling you 'Mr. Soderholm,'" Garrity said. "I've only held off this long for not knowing whether you prefer Mike or Michael."

"Mike's fine," Keller said.

"Then Mike it is. And I'm Wally, Mike, or W.P., though there are those who call me the Walrus."

Timmy laughed and clapped both hands over his mouth.

"Though never to his face," said the woman who had offered Keller more potatoes. She was Ellen Garrity, Timmy's aunt and Garrity's daughter-in-law, and Keller was now instructed to call her Ellie. Her husband, a big-shouldered fellow who seemed to be smiling bravely through the heartbreak of male-pattern baldness, was Garrity's son, Hank.

Keller remembered Timothy's mother from the night before, but hadn't caught her name, or her relationship to Garrity. She was Rhonda Sue Butler, as it turned out, and everybody called her Rhonda Sue, except for her husband, who called her Ronnie. His name was Doak Butler, and he looked like a college jock who'd been too light for pro ball, though he now seemed to be closing the gap.

Hank and Ellie, Doak and Rhonda Sue. And, at the far end of the table, Vanessa, who was married to Wally but who was clearly not the mother of Hank or Rhonda Sue, or anyone else. Keller supposed you could describe her as Wally's trophy wife, a sign of his success. She was no older than Wally's kids, and she looked to be well bred and elegant, and she even had the good grace to hide the boredom Keller was sure she felt.

And that was the lot of them. Wally and Vanessa. Hank and Ellen, Doak and Rhonda Sue. And Timothy, who had been swimming that very afternoon, the aquatic equivalent of getting right back on the horse. He'd had no cramps this time, but he'd had an attentive eye kept on him throughout.

Seven of them, then. And Keller . . . also known as Mike.

"So you're here on business," Wally said. "And stuck here over the weekend, which is the worst part of a business trip, as far as I'm concerned. More trouble than it's worth to fly back to Chicago?"

The two of them were in Wally's den, a fine room paneled in knotty pecan and trimmed in red leather, with Western doodads on the walls—here a branding iron, there a longhorn skull. Keller had accepted a brandy and declined a cigar, but the aroma of Wally's Havana was giving him second thoughts. Keller didn't smoke, but from the smell of it the cigar wasn't smoking. It was more along the lines of a religious experience.

"Seemed that way," Keller said. He had supplied Chicago as Michael Soderholm's home base, even though Soderholm's license placed him in southern California. "By the time I fly there and back—"

"You've spent your weekend on airplanes. Well, it's our good fortune you decided to stay. Now what I'd like to do is find a way to make it your good fortune as well."

"You've already done that," Keller told him. "I crashed a great party last night and actually got to feel like a hero for a few minutes. And tonight I get a fine dinner with nice people and get to top it off with a glass of outstanding brandy."

The heartburn told him how outstanding it was.

"What I had in mind," Wally said smoothly, "was to get you to work for me."

Who did he want him to kill? Keller almost blurted out the question until he remembered that Garrity didn't know what he did for a living.

"You won't say who you work for?" Garrity went on.

"I can't."

"Because the job's hush-hush for now. Well, I can respect that, and from the hints you've dropped I gather you're here scouting out something in the way of mergers and acquisitions."

"That's close."

"And I'm sure it's well paid, and you must like the work or I don't think you'd stay with it. So what do I have to do to get you to switch horses and come work for me? I'll tell you one thing—Chicago's a nice place, but nobody who ever moved from there to Big D went around with a sour face about it.

I don't know you well yet, but I can tell you're our kind of people and Dallas will be your kind of town. I don't know what they're paying you, but I suspect I can top it and offer you a stake in a growing company with all sorts of attractive possibilities."

Keller listened, nodded judiciously, sipped a little brandy. It was amazing, he thought, the way things came along when you weren't looking for them. It was straight out of Horatio Alger, for God's sake—Ragged Dick stops the runaway horse and saves the daughter of the captain of industry, and the next thing you know he's president of IBM with rising expectations.

"Maybe I'll have that cigar after all," Keller said.

"Now come on, Keller," Dot said. "You know the rules. I can't give you that information."

"It's sort of important," he said.

"One of the things the client buys," she said, "is confidentiality. That's what he wants and it's what we provide. Even if the agent in place—"

"The agent in place?"

"That's you," she said. "You're the agent, and Dallas is the place. Even if you get caught red-handed, the confidentiality of the client remains uncompromised. And do you know why?"

"Because the agent in place knows how to keep mum."

"Mum's the word," she agreed, "and there's no question you're the strong, silent type. But even if your lip loosens, you can't sink a ship if you don't know when it's sailing."

Keller thought that over. "You lost me," he said.

"Yeah, it came out a little abstruse, didn't it? Point is, you can't tell what you don't know, Keller, which is why the agent doesn't get to know the client's name."

"Dot," he said, trying to sound injured, "how long have you known me?"

"Ages, Keller. Many lifetimes."

"Many lifetimes?"

"We were in Atlantis together. Look, I know nobody's going to catch you red-handed, and I know you wouldn't blab if they did. But *I* can't tell what *I* don't know."

"Oh."

"Right. I think the spies call it a double cutout. The client made arrangements with somebody we know, and that person called us. But he didn't give us the client's name, and why should he? Come to think of it, Keller, why do you have to know, anyway?"

He had his answer ready. "It might not be a single," he said.

"Oh?"

"The target's always got people around him," he said, "and the best way to do it might be a sort of group plan, if you follow me."

"Two for the price of one."

"Or three or four," he said. "But if one of those innocent bystanders turned out to be the client, it might make things a little awkward."

"Well, I can see where we might have trouble collecting the final payment."

"If we knew for a fact that the client was fishing for trout in Montana," he said, "it would be no problem. But if he's here in Dallas . . ."

"It would help to know his name." Dot sighed. "Give me an hour or two, huh? Then call me back."

If Keller knew who the client was, the client could have an accident.

It would have to be an artful accident, too. It would have to look good not only to the police but also to whoever was aware of the client's intentions. The local go-between, the helpful fellow who had hooked up the client to the old man in White Plains—and, thus, to Keller—could be expected to cast a cold eye on any suspicious death. So it would have to be a damn good accident, but Keller had managed a few of those in his day. It took a little planning, but it wasn't brain surgery. You just figured out a method and took your best shot.

If, as he rather hoped, the client was some business rival in Houston or Denver or San Diego, he'd have to slip off to that city without anyone noting his absence. Then, having induced a quick attack of accidental death, he'd fly back to Dallas and hang around until someone called him off the case. He'd need a different ID for Houston or Denver or San Diego—it wouldn't do to overexpose Michael Soderholm—and he'd need to mask his actions from all concerned: Garrity, his homicidal rival and, perhaps most important, Dot and the old man.

All told, it was a great deal more complicated (if easier to stomach) than the alternative.

Which was to carry out the assignment professionally and kill Wallace Penrose Garrity the first good chance he got.

And he really didn't want to do that. He'd eaten at the man's table, he'd drunk the man's brandy, he'd smoked the man's cigars. He'd been offered not merely a job but a well-paid executive position with a future, and, later that night, light-headed from alcohol and nicotine, he'd had fantasies of taking Wally up on it.

Hell, why not? He could live out his days as Michael Soderholm, doing whatever unspecified tasks Garrity was hiring him to perform. He probably lacked the requisite experience, but how hard could it be to pick up the skills he needed as he went along? Whatever he had to do, it would be easier than flying from town to town killing people. He could learn on the job. He could pull it off.

The fantasy had about as much substance as a dream, and, like a dream, it was gone when he awoke the next morning. No one would put him on the payroll without some sort of background check, and the most cursory scan would knock him out of the box. Michael Soderholm had no more substance than the fake ID in Keller's wallet.

Even if he somehow finessed a background check, even if the old man in White Plains let him walk out of one life and into another, he knew he couldn't really make it work. He already had a life. Misshapen though it was, it fit him like a glove.

He went out for a sandwich and a cup of coffee. He got back in his car and drove around for a while. Then he found a pay phone and called White Plains.

"Do a single," Dot said.

"How's that?"

"No added extras, no free dividends. Just do what they signed on for."

"Because the client's here in town," he said. "Well, I could work around that if I knew his name. I could make sure he was out of it."

"Forget it," Dot said. "The client wants a long and happy life for everybody but the designated vic. Maybe the DV's close associates are near and dear to the client. That's just a guess, but all that really matters is that nobody else gets hurt. *Capisce?*"

"*Capisce?*"

"It's Italian, it means—"

"I know what it means. It just sounded odd from your lips, that's all. But yes, I understand." He took a breath. "Whole thing may take a little time," he said.

"Then here comes the good news," she said. "Time's not of the essence. They don't care how long it takes, just so you get it right."

"I understand W.P. offered you a job," Vanessa said. "I know he hopes you'll take him up on it."

"I think he was just being generous," Keller told her. "I was in the right place at the right time, and he'd like to do me a favor. But I don't think he really expects me to come to work for him."

"He'd like it if you did," she said, "or he never would have made the offer. He'd have just given you money, or a car, or something like that. And as far as what he expects, well, W.P. generally expects to get whatever he wants. Because that's the way things usually work out."

And had she been saving up her pennies to get things to work out a little differently? You had to wonder. Was she truly under Garrity's spell, in awe of his power, as she seemed to be? Or was she in it only for the money, and was there a sharp edge of irony under her worshipful remarks?

Hard to say. Hard to tell about any of them. Was Hank the loyal son he appeared to be, content to live in the old man's shadow and take what got tossed his way? Or was he secretly resentful and ambitious?

What about the son-in-law, Doak? On the surface, he looked to be delighted with the aftermath of his college football career—his work for his father-in-law consisted largely of playing golf with business associates and drinking with them afterward. But did he seethe inside, sure he was fit for greater things?

How about Hank's wife, Ellie? She struck Keller as an unlikely Lady Macbeth. Keller could fabricate scenarios in which she or Rhonda Sue had a reason for wanting Wally dead, but they were the sort of thing you dreamed up watching reruns of *Dallas* and trying to guess who shot J.R. Maybe one of their marriages was in trouble. Maybe Garrity had put the moves on his daughter-in-law, or maybe a little too much brandy had led him into his daughter's bedroom now and then. Maybe Doak or Hank was playing footsie with Vanessa. Maybe. . . .

Pointless to speculate, he decided. You could go around and around like that, but it didn't get you anywhere. Even if he managed to dope out which of them was the client, then what? Having saved young Timothy, and thus feeling obligated to spare his doting grandfather, what was he going to do? Kill the boy's father? Or mother or aunt or uncle?

Of course he could just go home. He could explain the situation to the old man. Nobody loved it when you took yourself off a contract for personal reasons, but it wasn't something they could talk you out of, either. If you made a habit of that sort of thing, well, that was different, but that wasn't the case with Keller. He was a solid pro. Quirky perhaps, even whimsical, but a pro all the way. Tell him what to do and he does it.

So, if he had a personal reason to bow out, you honored it. You let him come home and sit on the porch and drink iced tea with Dot.

And you picked up the phone and sent somebody else to Dallas.

Because, either way, the job was going to be done. If a hit man had a change of heart, it would be followed in short order by a change of hit man. If Keller didn't pull the trigger, somebody else would.

His mistake, Keller thought savagely, was that he had jumped into the goddamn pool in the first place. All he'd have had to do was look the other way and let the little bastard drown. A few days later he could have taken Garrity out, possibly making it look like suicide, a natural consequence of despondency over the boy's tragic accident.

But no, he thought, glaring at himself in the mirror. No, you had to go and get involved. You had to be a hero, for God's sake. Had to strip down to your skivvies and prove you deserved that lifesaving certificate the Red Cross had given you all those years ago.

He wondered what had happened to that certificate.

It was gone, of course, like everything he'd owned in his childhood and youth. Gone like his high school diploma, like his Boy Scout merit badge sash, like his sack of marbles and his stack of baseball cards. He didn't mind that these things were gone, didn't waste time wishing he had them any more than he wanted those years back.

The certificate, when all was said and done, was only a piece of paper. What was important was the skill itself, and what was truly remarkable was that he'd retained it. Because of it, Timothy Butler was alive. Which was all well and good for the boy, but a great big headache for Keller.

Later, sitting with a cup of coffee, Keller thought some more about Wallace Penrose Garrity, a man who seemed to have not an enemy in the world.

Suppose Keller had let the kid drown. Suppose he just plain hadn't noticed the boy's disappearance beneath the water just as everyone else had failed to notice it. Garrity would have been despondent. It was his party, his pool, his failure to provide supervision. He'd probably have blamed himself for the boy's death.

When Keller took him out, it would have been the kindest thing he could have done for him.

He caught the waiter's eye and signaled for more coffee.

"Mike," Garrity said, with a hand outstretched. "Sorry to keep you waiting. Had a call from a fellow with a hankering to buy a little five-acre lot of mine on the south edge of town. Thing is, I don't want to sell it to him."

"I see."

"There's ten acres on the other side of town I'd be perfectly happy to sell to him, but he'll only want it if he thinks of it himself. So that left me on the phone longer than I would have liked. Now then, what would you say to a glass of brandy?"

"Maybe a small one."

Garrity led the way to the den, poured drinks for both of them. "You should have come earlier," he said. "In time for dinner. I hope you know you don't need an invitation. There'll always be a place for you at our table."

"Well," Keller said.

"I know you can't talk about it," Garrity said, "but I hope your project here in town is shaping up nicely."

"Slow but sure," Keller said.

"Some things can't be hurried," Garrity allowed, and sipped brandy and winced. If Keller hadn't been looking for it, he might have missed the shadow that crossed his host's face.

Gently he asked, "Is the pain bad, Wally?"

"How's that, Mike?"

Keller put his glass on the table. "I spoke to Dr. Jacklin," he said. "I know what you're going through."

"That son of a bitch," Garrity said, "was supposed to keep his mouth shut."

"Well, he thought it was all right to talk to me," Keller said. "He thought I was Dr. Edward Fishman from the Mayo Clinic."

"Calling for a consultation."

"Something like that."

"I did go to Mayo," Garrity said, "but they didn't need to call Harold Jacklin to double-check their results. They just confirmed his diagnosis and told me not to buy any long-playing records." He looked to one side. "They said they couldn't say for sure how much time I had left, but that the pain would be manageable for a while. And then it wouldn't."

"I see."

"And I'd have all my faculties for a while," he said. "And then I wouldn't."

Keller didn't say anything.

"Well, hell," Garrity said. "A man wants to take the bull by the horns, doesn't he? I decided I'd go out for a walk with a shotgun and have a little hunting accident. Or I'd be cleaning a handgun here at my desk and have it go off. But it turned out I just couldn't tolerate the idea of killing myself. Don't know why, can't explain it, but that seems to be the way I'm made."

He picked up his glass and looked at the brandy. "Funny how we hang on to life," he said. "Something else I think Sam Johnson said, that there wasn't a week of his life he would voluntarily live through again. I've had more good times than bad, Mike, and even the bad times haven't been that god-awful. But I think I know what he was getting at. I wouldn't want to repeat any of it, but that doesn't mean there's a minute of it I'd have been willing to miss. I don't want to miss whatever's coming next, and I don't guess Dr. Johnson did either. That's what keeps us going, isn't it? Wanting to find out what's around the next bend in the river?"

"I guess so."

"I thought that would make the end easier to face," he said, "not knowing when it was coming, or how or where. And I recalled that years ago a fellow told me to let him know if I ever needed to have somebody killed. 'You just let me know,' he had said, and I laughed, and that was the last said on the subject. A month or so ago I looked up his number and called him, and he gave me another number to call."

"And you put out a contract."

"Is that the expression? Then that's what I did."

"Suicide by proxy," Keller said.

"And I guess you're holding my proxy," Garrity said, and drank some brandy. "You know, the thought flashed across my mind that first night, talking with you after you pulled my grandson out of the pool. I got this little glimmer, but I told myself I was being ridiculous. A hired killer doesn't turn up and save somebody's life."

"It's out of character," Keller agreed.

"Besides, what would you be doing at the party in the first place? Wouldn't you stay out of sight and wait until you could get me alone?"

"If I'd been thinking straight," Keller said. "I told myself it wouldn't hurt to have a look around. And this joker from the hotel bar assured me I had nothing to worry about. 'Half the town will be at Wally's tonight,' he said."

"Half the town was. You wouldn't have tried anything that night, would you?"

"God, no."

"I remember thinking, I hope he's not here. I hope it's not tonight. Because I was enjoying the party and I didn't want to miss anything. But you *were* there, and a good thing, wasn't it?"

"Yes."

"Saved the boy from drowning. According to the Chinese, you save somebody's life, you're responsible for him for the rest of your life. Because you've interfered with the natural order of things. That make sense to you?"

"Not really."

"Or me either. You can't beat them for whipping up a meal or laundering a shirt, but they've got some queer ideas on other subjects. Of course, they'd probably say the same for some of my notions."

"Probably."

Garrity looked at his glass. "You called my doctor," he said. "Must have been to confirm a suspicion you had. What tipped you off? Is it starting to show in my face, or how I move around?"

Keller shook his head. "I couldn't find anybody else with a motive," he said, "or a grudge against you. You were the only one left. And then I saw you wince once or twice and try to hide it. I barely noticed at the time, but then I started to think about it."

"I thought it would be easier than doing it myself," Garrity said. "I thought I'd just let a professional take me by surprise. I'd be like an old bull elk on a hillside, never expecting the bullet that takes him out in his prime."

"It makes sense."

"No, it doesn't. Because the elk didn't arrange for the hunter to be there. Far as the elk knows, he's all alone. He's not wondering every damn day if today's the day. He's not bracing himself, trying to sense the crosshairs centering on his shoulder."

"I never thought of that."

"Neither did I," said Garrity. "Or I never would have called that fellow in the first place. Mike, what the hell are you doing here tonight? Don't tell me you came over to kill me."

"I came over to tell you I can't."

"Because we've come to know each other."

Keller nodded.

"I grew up on a farm," Garrity said. "One of those vanishing family farms you hear about, and of course it's vanished, and I say good riddance. But we raised our own beef and pork, and we kept a milk cow and a flock of laying hens. And we never named the animals we were going to wind up eating. The cow had a name, but not the bull calf she dropped. The breeder sow's name was Elsie, but we never named her piglets."

"Makes sense," Keller said.

"I guess it doesn't take a Chinaman to see how you can't kill me once you've hauled Timmy out of the drink. Let alone after you've sat at my table and smoked my cigars. Reminds me, care for a cigar?"

"No, thank you."

"Well, where do we go from here, Mike? I have to say I'm relieved. I feel like I've been bracing myself for a bullet for weeks now. All of a sudden I've got a new lease on life. I'd say this calls for a drink, except we're already having one and you've scarcely touched yours."

"There is one thing," Keller said.

He left the den while Garrity made his phone call. Timothy was in the living room, puzzling over a chessboard. Keller played a game with him and lost badly. "Can't win 'em all," he said, and tipped over his king.

"I was going to checkmate you," the boy said, "in a few more moves."

"I could see it coming," Keller told him.

He went back to the den. Garrity was selecting a cigar from his humidor. "Sit down," he said. "I'm fixing to smoke one of these things. If you won't kill me, maybe it will."

"You never know."

"I made the call, Mike, and it's all taken care of. Be a while before the word filters through the chain of command, but sooner or later they'll call you and tell you the client changed his mind. He paid in full and called off the job."

They talked some, then sat awhile in silence. At length Keller said he ought to get going. "I should be at my hotel," he said, "in case they call."

"Be a couple of days, won't it?"

"Probably," he said, "but you never know. If everyone involved makes a phone call right away, the word could get to me in a couple of hours."

"Calling you off, telling you to come home. Be glad to get home, I bet."

"It's nice here," he said, "but yes, I'll be glad to get home."

"Wherever it is, they say there's no place like it." Garrity leaned back, then allowed himself to wince at the pain that came over him. "If it never hurts worse than this," he said, "then I can stand it. But of course it will get worse. And I'll decide I can stand *that*, and then it'll get worse again."

There was nothing to say to that.

"I guess I'll know when it's time to do something," Garrity said. "And who knows? Maybe my heart will cut out on me out of the blue. Or I'll get hit by a bus, or I don't know what. Struck by lightning?"

"It could happen."

"Anything can happen," Garrity agreed. He got to his feet. "Mike," he said, "I guess we won't be seeing any more of each other, and I have to say I'm a little bit sorry about that. I've truly enjoyed our time together."

"So have I, Wally."

"I wondered, you know, what he'd be like. The man they'd send to do this kind of work. I don't know what I expected, but you're not it."

He stuck out his hand, and Keller gripped it. "Take care," Garrity said. "Be well, Mike."

Back at his hotel, Keller took a hot bath and got a good night's sleep. In the morning he went out for breakfast, and when he got back there was a message at the desk for him: *Mr. Soderholm—Please call your office.*

He called from a pay phone, even though it didn't matter, and was careful not to overreact when Dot told him to come home, the mission was aborted.

"You told me I had all the time in the world," he said. "If I'd known the guy was in such a rush—"

"Keller," she said, "it's a good thing you waited. What he did, he changed his mind."

"He changed his mind?"

"It used to be a woman's prerogative," Dot said, "but now we've got equality between the sexes, so that means anyone can do it. It works out fine because we're getting paid in full. So kick the dust of Texas off your feet and come on home."

"I'll do that," he said, "but I may hang out here for a few more days."

"Oh?"

"Or even a week," he said. "It's a pretty nice town."

"Don't tell me you're itching to move there, Keller. We've been through this before."

"Nothing like that," he said. "But there's this girl I met."

"Oh, Keller."

"Well, she's nice," he said. "And if I'm off the job there's no reason not to have a date or two with her, is there?"

"Not as long as you don't decide to move in."

"She's not that nice," he said, and Dot laughed and told him not to change.

He hung up and drove around and found a movie he'd been meaning to see. The next morning he packed and checked out of his hotel.

He drove across town and to a room on the motel strip, paying cash in advance for four nights and registering as J. D. Smith from Los Angeles.

There was no girl he'd met, no girl he wanted to meet. But it wasn't time to go home yet.

He had unfinished business, and four days should give him time to do it. Time for Wallace Garrity to get used to the idea of not feeling those imaginary crosshairs on his shoulder blade.

But not so much time that the pain would be too much to bear.

And, sometime in those four days, Keller would deliver a gift. If he could, he'd make it look natural—a heart attack, say, or an accident. In any event it would be swift and without warning, and as close as he could make it to painless.

And it would be unexpected. Garrity would never see it coming.

Keller frowned, trying to figure out how he would manage it. It would be a lot trickier than the task that had drawn him to town originally, but he'd brought it on himself. Getting involved, fishing the boy out of the pool. He'd interfered in the natural order of things. He was under an obligation.

It was the least he could do.

THE INVISIBLE WITNESS

(1973)

Anthony Gilbert

The setting of this story is a picturesque London park. It is ostensibly a cheerful place, but murder is lurking in the greenery. Anthony Gilbert's (1899–1973) work is always freshly original and shows a grasp of a certain type of character, like the elderly lady in this story. Among Gilbert's many books are *A Case for Mr. Crook* (1952), *Fingerprint* (1965), and *The Looking Glass Murder* (1967). "The Invisible Witness" was first published in *Ellery Queen's Mystery Magazine*.

I suppose I originally noticed the old woman because she always occupied the same seat in the park. It had a copper plate on the back which read:

In Memory of
Mrs. CHARLOTTE RACE
Who loved this place

A good many of the benches in Phillimore Park have similar inscriptions to commemorate the army of old people who came here for a few hours in the sun during their declining years. The seats were full of them—the old people, I mean. This one looked much like the rest; she wore a black and white tweed coat and a felt basin of a hat over her white hair and a long dark red scarf—the scarf the gift of a dead-and-gone nephew, she told me.

She carried a solid black leather bag that probably contained most of her worldly treasures, and she differed from the rest in that she never had a newspaper or a bit of knitting to occupy her time. She sat with her hands in her lap; nothing moved but her eyes.

One afternoon when she was the sole occupant of the bench I took a place at the farther end, shaking out my morning paper. On fine days I often walked through the park to my subway station; being a freelance journalist I could choose my own hours. That afternoon, I remember, a wave of pigeons had settled on the asphalt, strutting, and preening their shining breasts. One of them, even plumper than the rest, reminded me of my Aunt Selina who used to attend church in a purple marabout and shawl. The Old Indestructible, they called her.

I hadn't been seated more than a minute or two when the old woman leaned toward me.

"Can you tell me the time, sir?"

I told her it was 3:30.

She leaned back, smiling.

"Then I can stay a little longer," she said.

I supposed her appointment, whatever it might be, was for four o'clock. I wondered whom she was expecting to meet, other than, of course, Death in due course.

After a moment she spoke again. "They're such greedy birds, aren't they?" and she pointed to the pigeons. "Bring a little bit of bread for the sparrows or the ducks and it's always the pigeons that get it."

"Not the gulls?" I murmured. I don't know why I let my self be drawn into a conversation. But it was a pleasant afternoon and I had a few minutes to spare. I liked to watch the gulls flying—like a ballet they were, swooping, diving, soaring again with their prey.

"Only if you throw it up into the air," said the old woman seriously. "And I never do that. Mind you," she added. "it's not much I bring. I'm against wasting food, but a bit of crust sometimes—it doesn't run to more than that when you're living on a small pension."

"I don't know how anyone does. Unless they have friends or something." I meant children; she had a wedding ring worn deep into her finger. It didn't occur to me she might be going to beg. She didn't look the type.

"The Old Age Pension helps," she told me. "Of course, I never taste meat. It's out of the question, the price the way it is. If only people would take a stand and refuse to buy, prices would come down."

I suppose she thought I looked restive, for she rapidly changed the subject, saying how fortunate Londoners were to have these lovely parks.

"I go up to the pond sometimes," she said. "Last year's cygnets are as big as their parents now, such beautiful birds. And did you know the Chinese geese had a family last year? If it wasn't for the parks we should have to go to China to see a thing like that."

A few minutes later she said she must be getting home. "I make myself a cup of tea at four o'clock," she confided. "I find if you don't keep regular hours, that's when you start going downhill. When you've only yourself to keep house for, you get all hugger-mugger if you're not careful."

As she picked up her gloves I saw that her fingernails were beautifully tended and painted a deep coral pink, and her hair under her indifferent hat was carefully arranged.

You'll never let yourself go to pieces, I thought. And then I put her out of my mind. She was just one of a host of elderly women sitting in the sun in the evening of her days. I didn't even know her name.

I saw her again a few days later, still alone on her bench. She smiled and said she'd been watching a baby poodle trying to play with a swan.

"It didn't understand," she said. "Well, they don't at that age. A swan could drown a little dog like that. And the owner was not even noticing. I screamed and the swan went away and then the man came up. I think he thought I was mad, I think they all did."

I murmured something about it being the breeding season, so you had to be careful.

"It's cruel how they have to learn, isn't it?" she agreed. "It just wanted to play." A man went past and she chuckled slyly.

"See that one?" she said. "I call him Mr. Drake. The way he puts his feet down—see?"

I wouldn't have noticed it myself, but she was quite right. He walked exactly in a duck's splay-footed fashion.

"You're very noticing," I congratulated her.

"You might say it's my hobby. He comes here three or four times a week. It's their little habits that turn people into individuals, you see. Some of them would be surprised to realize how much I know about them."

I saw her quite often after that. Sometimes she shared the seat with some other old biddy and then she'd just glance up and smile. At other times she was alone, but she never gave the impression of being solitary. She felt herself part of the pattern, I suppose. I wondered what stories she made up about the other passersby.

I got into the habit of stopping for a few minutes if she was alone, though I didn't learn much more about her—just that she had a single room in a big apartment house near the park, had her own gas-ring but shared domestic facilities. It was the history of hundreds of thousands of elderly folk with no home ties. She never complained. Once she said it would be nice to have a meal out now and again, but of course the small pension would never permit that.

As I got to know her better a few more facts emerged. She was a widow, had married a man who had a little neighborhood store business, but he'd gone bankrupt and died soon after. She'd gone back to work in a shop, selling behind a counter. She'd enjoyed that—all the different people, see? Now at 70 she enjoyed her leisure, and there was always someone nice to talk to. She never spoke of a child; usually if there have been any, some whisper creeps in.

Once I offered her a newspaper but though she took it, she laid it on the seat. The passersby were her newspaper—"and then I have my little radio. That keeps me in touch." Now and again she went to the public library, but it was a bit of a walk—"and anyway," she added, "it's people I mind about. I mean, there's nothing you can do about strikes and rising prices, but people are always real. You get to recognize them after a time, though my sight's not quite what it was. But I've good hearing still. Some of the bits of conversation you pick up—it makes you wonder. And some of them have a child or a dog. There's one woman limps on a big stick with a dog's head for the handle. I think to myself sometimes, you've probably never noticed me, but say you were in trouble with the police—couldn't show where you were at such and such a time—out walking you might say, on your own; well, I might be able to give you an alibi. But no one would think of asking me—the invisible witness."

She laughed. She had a pretty tinkling laugh.

Another visitor and one frequently occupying a seat near my old girl was an old tramp in a tattered black coat and a black hat that no self-respecting bird would have accepted for a nest. He was always laden with a huge haversack packed with parcels, food, debris—that he'd unpack and lay out along the seat—presumably to prevent anyone else from sharing it. My old friend spoke of him once.

"I don't want you to think I'm a vain old woman," she said, "but I'm sometimes terrified he'll come and settle along of me. He gives me such funny looks—it wouldn't do, no, it wouldn't at all."

"He wouldn't do any harm," I assured her. "There are people all about."

"If he was to ask me for money, what could I say? I don't have any, and that's the truth, but if you keep yourself looking respectable no one believes you. And you do read such awful things. There was that old woman not so far from Harrods, attacked in broad daylight just for the few pounds in her purse. She'd come up to buy blankets, been saving months. And they never got the man who did it."

I insisted she was working herself up over nothing, though I didn't much care for the look of the old tramp myself.

"If you're really nervous you could sit on a seat that was already occupied," I suggested. But she looked startled.

"Oh, I couldn't do that. I like to think of this as my place. Sometimes I wonder if I ever saw her—Charlotte Race, I mean. I could even have spoken to her. There wouldn't have been a plaque on the seat in those days, of course. And you never exchange names. Well, you like to keep yourself to yourself, you know. But I think she'd be a widow like me—a married woman wouldn't have the time to sit around. I daresay she liked the trees and the birds, the same as I do, and a bit of company. I can almost feel her here sometimes. It gives you a sense of belonging."

If her seat was occupied I might find her up by the pond, where the children sailed their boats and the elderly gentlemen flew their kites. That made her laugh.

"So serious," she said. "You'd think it was the Grand Prix. There's one has a kite shaped like a falcon, ever so realistic. I like to watch out for that. Might have been a gamekeeper's, I think."

The days I didn't go to the park I didn't think about her at all; that was where she belonged and, so far as I was concerned, outside the park she had no existence. I liked her courage, and sometimes wished I could help her; but I had my own troubles—as haven't we all—and they took up a lot of my time.

It was a blustery summer; she still wore the black and white tweed coat and tied the red scarf round her throat.

"Odd," she said, "to think that Humphrey who gave me this has been gone these many years, and I linger on."

It was during that wet July it happened, an event that set the whole neighborhood ablaze, though it didn't rate much above a paragraph in the national press. After all, the news was full of wars and rumors of wars, strikes and violence everywhere, death falling out of the skies—so the death of one little trollop was pretty small beer. Only not in the place where it happened. As my old lady said, there's always the personal element. It might have been me, she said, and that was the general feeling.

The young woman's body was found in a little private garden designed a century earlier for a royal princess, within the precincts of the park. In spring and summer, when the weather was fine, this was a favorite spot, especially for visitors, from both home and overseas. There was a stretch of water, covered with rose-colored lilies whose like I have seen nowhere else, and each season a white duck brought forth her brood and exercised them among the lilies' broad umbrella leaves.

The whole garden was roofed by thick vinery and surrounded by a paved walk within a box hedge; and there were seats at intervals round three sides of the garden. It was on one of the seats, the farthest one from the entrance, that the body was found. The previous afternoon had been cloudy with storm, breaking into thundery rain, and at such times there was something sinister about the little garden—it became a place of shadows and pattering raindrops.

One such afternoon I had dived into the shelter of the vinery during a sudden storm and found my old friend on one of the seats there.

She was wrapped in a huge gray raincoat with sleeves like the flukes of a whale.

"You're very brave to be out in such weather," I told her. "Brave and rash."

"It was better when I started out," she said. "I haven't seen you this last day or so."

"I'm not the regular you are," I reminded her. "I go by bus or subway if the weather's unpromising."

"You get tired of your own company," she explained. "And, of course, you can't have even a bird where I live. I like to think Charlotte Race wouldn't let a little bit of bad weather defeat her."

That had been one week ago. And now, not a hundred yards from where we'd been sitting, a woman had been murdered, strangled by her own scarf pulled tight round her throat—garroting, they called it. The body was found huddled in a corner of the seat in the early morning by one of the park keepers. He'd given his usual cry—"All out, all out!"—the previous night, and no one, so far as he could recall, had left the garden. The whole park, in fact, was nearly empty thanks to the thunder and the sudden onslaught of rain, and he hadn't gone round the little garden; he had other duties. And, of course, murder isn't what you come to look for in a Royal Park.

The papers nosed out quite a lot of information about the murdered woman: Thelma Hughes, married, but believed to be living apart from her husband, aged 29, living in a flat in Marylebone. She had a job in a Bayswater Hotel. The previous day she'd been off duty since three o'clock. She'd been leaving the hotel a bit later, presumably to keep an appointment. The weather of the early afternoon had been fresh and a little cloudy, but the ensuing storm had taken everyone by surprise. Great black clouds had scudded across the sky, the wind had risen, thunder had pealed; later had come the rain, but the girl's clothes weren't wet. She must have met her fate, as they used to say, before the storm broke.

On such an afternoon it would be a sort of twilight in the little garden, and she'd been found lying back against the seat, as though resting or asleep.

No one would have tried to speak to her or disturb her. Whatever had been the motive of the crime, it wasn't theft, for her bag containing ten pounds in notes hadn't been touched, and there were rings on her fingers and a brooch and necklace at her throat. Nor, we were assured, had there been any attempt at assault. She would have chosen this place thinking it was secret and safe. But if you're shut off from the world, the world is equally shut off from you.

The hotel where she was employed couldn't supply much information; she'd been working for them for a little more than a year, having come from a reputable hotel on the west coast. They knew of no particular men friends, and she had confided in no one. It wasn't even certain that her husband was still alive, or, if alive, was still a resident in England. She'd never spoken of him to anyone. The police advertised for him, of course, but no one came forward. Taken by and large, she was a woman of mystery, and, until now, of no particular interest to anyone.

A day or so after the news broke I was hurrying through the park in the late afternoon; the sky looked ominous and I wanted to escape a wetting. My old lady wasn't on her usual seat, but to my surprise I found her up by the pond. The shelter cut off a lot of the wind, she explained. When she saw me, for the first time she jumped up and came toward me.

"I hoped I'd see you," she said. "You weren't here yesterday."

"I wasn't in this part of London," I explained. "We've had a bit of a rush on. You know, you'll catch your death of cold."

"I wanted to see you," she said. "I want some advice and there's no one else to ask."

She spoke more loudly than usual, and I looked round, but people had packed up with the threatened break in the weather and we had this part of the park to ourselves. The few ducks that were about were blown clownishly by the wind, and all the kite flyers had gone.

"I couldn't ask them," she repeated.

I knew she meant her fellow boarders.

"Ask them what?" I said.

"What I ought to do. About that poor girl."

"What poor girl?" For a moment I hadn't got the drift of her meaning.

"The one they found in the garden, of course. You must have heard—it was on the radio—being a royal garden, I mean."

"That one," I said a bit blankly. "But I don't understand where you come in. If you're afraid you might be next you've only got to keep away from the spot and—"

She was almost shaking me in her agitation. "You don't understand. I saw him!"

That staggered me. "You saw . . . ? Think what you're saying. Whom did you see?"

"I don't know. But he must have been the one." She calmed a little, and became more coherent. "You remember how the weather broke that afternoon. I'd been up here by the pond, all the cygnets were out and the parent birds, a lovely show, and then suddenly it got dark and I thought the storm might break before I got back, so I made for the garden as being the nearest shelter."

"Yes," I encouraged her.

"And I saw them."

"Get this straight," I said. "You saw—what? Two people in the garden. There were probably others."

"No. Only those two. I was walking round looking at the flowers and as I turned the corner there they were, sitting in the farthest seat. I thought at first they were a pair of lovers having a tiff, the way young people do, goodness knows, it's natural enough, and I was going to move away because no one wants eavesdroppers at a time like that when I heard her. . . ."

She paused, drawing a deep breath.

"You mean you heard her speak?" I said.

"Yes, I couldn't help it. Anyone near me would have heard her, too. She said, 'It's no use, Gerald. I've got you like *that*.' I thought at first it might be—" She hesitated.

"You thought—?"

"I did think she might be telling him she was going to have a baby and he'd have to marry her. You read about that kind of thing."

"But there was nothing in the paper about her being pregnant," I said.

"Yes. I noticed that. But—oh, sir"—she had never called me sir and she had never held onto my sleeve as she was holding onto it now—"there was no love there. I know the voice of love, even when you're quarreling, but this was something different. She was dangerous to him."

"Since he presumably murdered her—" I began and then I stopped. "Did you see him?" I asked.

She shook her head. "I told you, I went back."

"Then how can you be sure it was the same couple? I daresay there were plenty of people in the garden that afternoon?"

"There was a flash of lightening. I saw that little gold cap she was wearing—the papers made a point of that, they thought someone might remember seeing it. Oh, she was the one, I'm sure. What I wanted to ask you was what should I do now? I mean, should I tell the police? My husband always said, 'Keep away from the police, Alice.' They don't do any good, being mixed up with them, I mean."

"If you have any idea who he is—" I said doubtfully.

"I do have a feeling I've seen him somewhere, but of course I see so many, and they all look so very much alike. If they've a dog or a child, that's different, or if they're like that old tramp—didn't someone say once it was depressing how alike old women become? But I do know they say that when anything sensational happens, there are always people coming forward to get the limelight."

"You don't want the limelight," I said.

"I want to do what's right. It must be someone who knows the neighborhood or he'd never have suggested the garden."

"Unless she suggested it."

"I hadn't thought of that," she admitted. "I hoped I'd see you yesterday—if I was to ask any of them at the house, even mention the police, I'd find my room was wanted. Oh, I daresay it's against the law turning people out for no real reason, but there's ways of getting round the law. They can say you're not fit to look after yourself or something."

I imagined her at the police station, and some ambitious young constable listening to her and perhaps writing her off as one of those old sensation-mongers, just as she'd said. There'd be the newspapers, too.

"Do you think you really saw enough of him?" I wondered. "You didn't hear him speak."

"I've been trying to remember. But I didn't stop," she went on quickly, "the thunder had started and the lightning and I wanted to get home. I thought, it's nothing to do with me, people are always quarreling, and they don't thank you to interfere. I mean, I couldn't have done anything, could I? I couldn't guess how it would end, but I do think now if they'd known I was there, it might not have come to this."

"You can't torture yourself like that," I said roughly. We had moved away from the pond, toward her gate. The thunder that had been growling softly burst into a sudden roar. I felt her shudder.

"I've always hated thunder," she said. "My mother used to tell me it was the angels quarreling. And I shouldn't have troubled you. I ought to be able to make up my own mind. That's what William would have said—William was my husband. I won't do anything tonight, I want to get back before the rain breaks, but I'll sleep on it. My mother always said things are clearer in the dawn, before your ideas have had a chance to get muddled. I'll think about it"—I felt oddly sure she meant she would also pray about it—"and in the morning I'll know what to do."

In the distance I heard the anonymous voice calling, "All out, all out!" I looked round. We virtually had the park to ourselves.

"We don't want to get locked in," said Alice. "I'll take the short cut through the trees."

"Mind how you go," I said.

I saw her feet slipping on the wet grass.

"I'll be all right," she called. "You don't have to worry about me."

She was like some strange spirit dodging among the tree trunks.

I reached the gate in the north wall just before it was locked. The rain was coming down hard by then, and there was no hope of a taxi and the buses were crammed. I remembered my old lady's voice.

Things are clearer in the dawn.

Next morning I woke to what might have been a different world. The sun shone, the whole world sparkled. I took my short cut through the park, but there was no Alice—what was her other name? We never exchanged names, she had said. You like to keep yourself to yourself. Charlotte Race's seat was occupied, though, by the villainous old tramp, who was busy spreading his flotsam and jetsam. He was grinning evilly to himself.

I strode past without meeting his eye. She wasn't up by the pond, either, though the children were coming along with their mothers or *au pair* girls, and the first kite flyers were gathering. Someone went past whistling. I recognized the tune. It had been old when I was a child. How did it go? Something like—*Alice, where are you?* I remembered I still didn't know her second name.

I learned it, though, that night. It had been one of those busy days and the evening rush was accumulating round the subway station where people were stopping to buy copies of the evening editions. There was no paper seller there—there never was; people just threw down their money and helped themselves. I never saw anyone take a paper without paying for it or saw anyone help himself to the loose change lying around. It's one of the odd quirks of honesty in a society that isn't particularly thin-skinned.

The man in front of me threw down his money and picked up a paper. For a moment the staring black headlines almost hit me in the face.

Second Park Murder
Another Woman
Found Strangled

it ran, and I put my money down and grabbed a paper.

"An elderly woman who has been identified as Mrs. Alice Calcraft, a pensioner living in an apartment house in W. 8., was found in the early hours of this morning among the trees near the North Gate of Phillimore Park. She had been strangled by a scarf she was wearing. This is the second case of a woman being found garroted in the park during the past 48 hours. The police are examining a theory that a maniacal killer has escaped from some mental home or hospital and is roaming at large."

There was even a warning that unaccompanied women shouldn't roam in the park after dusk.

I stood there like a man riven in stone. People went past and the pile of papers rapidly reduced.

Alice Calcraft, I thought. So that was her full name. A harmless innocent old woman—but that wasn't true any more. Not harmless, not innocent. She'd heard a blackmailing little trollop threaten a man's life—that was what it amounted to, years of dependence winding up in ruin—oh, there are some chances a man can't take. And just because of those few words she'd had to forfeit her life.

A hand fell on my arm. I almost jumped out of my skin.

"What's up, Gerald?" said a voice. I looked up and it was a chap I knew in Fleet Street.

"You're as white as a sheet. Burning the candle . . . ?"

"She called him Gerald," insisted a ghostly voice.

It's no use, Gerald. I've got you like *that.*

"You look as though you could do with a strengthener at The Bull before you join the rush-hour crowd," the chap went on. "Join me."

I looked round. There was no one else with us.

So I folded my paper under my arm and followed him to The Bull.

UNDER SUSPICION

(2000)

Clark Howard

The procedural school of mystery writing is nicely demonstrated in this story. Detectives go about their business of investigating homicides in a systematic and methodical manner, gathering information that they hope will lead them to the murderer.

Clark Howard grew up in Chicago, where this story takes place. He served in combat in the Korean War as a member of the Marine Corps. Author of eighteen books and over a hundred short stories, Howard is a five-time winner of the Ellery Queen Magazine Readers Award, and has won an Edgar for short story writing. His books include *Six Against the Rock* (1977), *Quick Silver* (1988), *City Blood* (1994), and *Crème de la Crime* (2000). "Under Suspicion" was originally published in *Ellery Queen's Mystery Magazine*.

Frank Dell walked into the Three Corners Club shortly after five, as he usually did every day, and took a seat at the end of the bar. The bartender, seeing him, put together, without being told, a double Tanqueray over two ice cubes with two large olives, and set it in front of him on a cork coaster. Down at the middle of the bar, Dell saw two minor stickup men he remembered from somewhere and began staring at them without touching his drink. Frank Dell's stare was glacial and unblinking. After three disconcerting minutes of it, the two stickup men paid for their drinks and left. Only then did Dell lift his own glass.

Tim Callan, the club owner, came over and sat opposite Dell. "Well, I see you just cost me a couple more customers, Frankie," he said wryly.

"Hoodlums," Dell replied. "I'm just helping you keep the place respectable, Timmy."

"Bring some of your policemen buddies in to drink," Callan suggested. "That'll keep me respectable *and* profitable."

"You're not hurting for profits," Dell said. "Not with that after-hours poker game you run in the apartment upstairs."

Callan laughed. "Ah, Frankie, Frankie. Been quick with the answers all your life. You should've been a lawyer. Even my old dad, rest his soul, used to say that."

"I'm not crooked enough to be a lawyer," Dell said, sipping his drink.

"Not crooked *enough*! Hell, you're not crooked at all, Frankie. You're probably the straightest cop in Chicago." Callan leaned forward on one elbow. "How long we known each other, Frank?"

"What's on your mind, Tim?" Dell asked knowingly. Reminiscing, he had learned, frequently led to other things.

"We go back thirty years, do you realize that, Frank?" Callan replied, ignoring Dell's suspicion. "First grade at St. Mel's school out on the West Side."

"What's on your mind, Tim?" Dell's expression hardened just a hint. He hated asking the same question twice.

"Remember my baby sister, Francie?" Callan asked, lowering his voice.

"Sure. Cute little kid. Carrot-red hair. Freckles. Eight or ten years younger than us."

"Nine. She's twenty-seven now. She married this Guinea a few years ago, name of Nicky Santore. They moved up to Milwaukee where the guy's uncle got him a job in a brewery. Well, they started having problems. You know the greaseballs, they're all Don Juans, chasing broads all the time—"

"Get to the point, Tim," said Dell. He hated embellishment.

"OK. Francie left him and came back to live with my brother, Dennis—you know him, the fireman. Anyhow, after she got back, she found out she's expecting. Then Nicky finds out, and he comes back too. Guy begs Francie to take him back, and she does. Now, the only job he can get down here is pumping gas at a Texaco station, which only pays minimum wage. He's worried about doctor bills and everything with the baby coming, so he agrees, for a cut, to let a cousin of his use the station storeroom to stash hot goods. It works OK for a while, but then the cousin gets busted and leads the cops to the station. They find a load of laptop computers. Nick gets charged with receiving stolen property. He comes up for a preliminary hearing in three weeks."

"Tough break," Dell allowed, sipping again. "But he should get probation if he's got no priors."

"He's got a prior," Callan said, looking down at the bar.

"What is it?"

"Burglary. Him and that same cousin robbed some hotel rooms down at the Hilton when they was working as bellmen. Years ago. Both of them got probation on that."

"Then he's looking at one-to-four on this fall," Dell said.

Callan swallowed. "Can you help me out on this, Frankie?"

Dell gave him the stare. "You don't mean help you, Tim. You mean help Nicky Santore. What do you think I can do?"

"Give your personal voucher for him."

"Are you serious? You want me to go to an assistant state's attorney handling an RSP case and personally vouch for some Guinea with a prior that I don't even know?"

"Frank, it's for Francie—"

"No, it isn't. If Francie was charged, I'd get her off in a heartbeat. But it's not Francie; it's some two-bit loser she married."

"Frank, please, listen—"

"No. Forget it."

There was a soft buzzing signal from the pager clipped to Dell's belt. Reaching under his coat, he got it out and looked at it. It was a 911 page from the Lakeside station house out on the South Side, where he was assigned.

"I have to answer this," he told Callan. Taking a cellular phone from his coat pocket, he opened it and dialed one of the station house's unlisted numbers. When someone answered, he said, "This is Dell. I got a nine-one-one page."

"Yeah, it's Captain Larne. Hold on."

A moment later, an older, huskier voice spoke. "Dell? Mike Larne. Where's Dan?" He was asking about Dan Malone, Dell's partner, a widower in his fifties.

"Probably at home," Dell told the captain. "I dropped him off there less than an hour ago. What's up, Cap?"

"Edie Malone was found dead in her apartment a little while ago. It looks like she's been strangled."

Dell said nothing. He froze, absolutely still, the little phone at his ear. Edie was Dan's only child.

"Dell? Did you hear me?"

"Yessir, I heard you. Captain, I can't tell him—"

"You won't have to. The department chaplain and Dan's parish priest get that dirty job. What I want you to do is help me keep Dan from going off the deep end over this. You know how he is. We can't have *him* going wild thinking he'll solve this himself."

"What do you want me to do?"

"I'm going to assign you temporary duty to the homicide team working the case. If Dan knows you're on it, he might stay calm. Understand where I'm coming from?"

"Yessir." Dell was still frozen, motionless.

"Take down this address," Larne said. Dell animated, taking a small spiral notebook and ballpoint from his shirt pocket. He wrote down the address Larne gave him. "The homicide boys have only been there a little while. Kenmare and Garvan. Know them?"

"Yeah, Kenmare, slightly. They know I'm coming?"

"Absolutely. This has all been cleared with headquarters." Larne paused a beat, then said, "You knew the girl, did you?"

"Yessir."

"Well," Larne sighed heavily. "I hate to do this to you, Frank—"

"It's all right, Cap. I understand."

"Call me at home later."

"Right."

Dell closed the phone and slipped it back into his pocket. He walked away from the bar and out of the club without another word to Tim Callan.

Edie Malone's address was one of the trendy new apartment buildings remodeled from old commercial high-rises on the near North Side. The sixth floor had been cordoned off to permit only residents of that floor to exit the elevator, and they were required to go directly to their apartments. Edie Malone's apartment was posted as a crime scene. In addition to homicide detectives Kenmare and Garvan, there were half a dozen uniformed officers guarding the hallways and stairwells, personnel from the city crime lab in the apartment itself, and a deputy coroner and Cook County morgue attendants waiting to transport the victim to the county hospital complex for autopsy.

When Frank Dell arrived, Kenmare and Garvan took him into the bedroom to view the body. Edie Malone was wearing a white cotton sweatshirt with MONICA FOR PRESIDENT lettered on it, and a pair of cutoff denim shorts.

Barefoot, she was lying on her back, elbows bent, hands a few inches from her ears, feet apart as if she were resting, with her long, dark red hair splayed out on the white shag carpet like spilled paint. Her eyes were wide open in a bloated face, the neck below it ringed with ugly purplish bruises. Looking at her, Dell had to blink back tears.

"I guess you knew her, your partner's daughter and all," said Kenmare. Dell nodded.

"Who found her?"

"Building super," said Garvan. "She didn't show up for work today and didn't answer the phone when her boss called. Then a coworker got nervous about it and told the boss that the victim had just broken up with a guy who she was afraid was going to rough her up over it. They finally came over and convinced the super to take a look in the apartment. The boss and the coworker were down in his office when we got here. We questioned them briefly, then sent them home. They've been instructed not to talk about it until after we see them tomorrow."

The three detectives went into the kitchen and sat at Edie's table, where the two from homicide continued to share their notes with Dell.

"Coroner guy says she looks like she's been dead sixteen, eighteen hours, which would mean sometime late last night, early this morning," said Garvan.

"She worked for Able, Bennett, and Crain Advertising Agency in the Loop," said Kenmare, then paused, adding, "Maybe you know some of this stuff already, from your partner."

Dell shook his head. "Dan and his daughter hadn't been close for a while. He didn't approve of Edie's lifestyle. He and his wife had saved for years to send her to the University of Chicago so she could become a teacher, but then Dan's wife died, and a little while after that Edie quit school and moved out to be on her own. Dan didn't talk much about her after that."

"But Captain Larne still thinks Dan might jump ranks and try to work the case himself?"

"Sure." Dell shrugged. "She was still his daughter, his only kid."

"OK," Kenmare said, "we'll give you everything, then. Her boss was a Ronald Deever, one of the ad agency execs. The coworker who tipped him about the ex-boyfriend is a copywriter named Sally Simms."

"Did she know the guy's name?" Dell asked.

"Yeah." Kenmare flipped a page in his notebook. "Bob Pilcher. He's some kind of redneck. Works as a bouncer at one of those line-dancing clubs over in Hee-Haw town. The Simms woman met him a couple times on double dates with the victim." He closed his notebook. "That's it so far."

"Where do we go from here?" Dell asked.

Kenmare and Garvan exchanged glances. "We haven't figured that out yet," said the former. "You've been assigned by a district captain, with headquarters approval and a nod from our own commander, and the victim is the daughter of a veteran cop who's your senior partner. We'll be honest, Dell: We're not sure what your agenda is here."

Dell shook his head. "No agenda," he said. "I'm here to make it look good to Dan Malone so he'll get through this thing as calmly as possible. But it's your case. You two tell me what I can do to help and I'll do it. Or I'll just stand around and watch, if that's how you want it. Your call."

Kenmare and Garvan looked at each other for a moment, then both nodded. "OK," said Kenmare, "we can live with that. We'll work together on it." The two homicide detectives shook hands with Dell, the first time they had done so. Then Kenmare, who was the senior officer, said, "Let's line it up. First thing is to toss the bedroom as soon as the body is out and the crime lab guys are done. Maybe we'll get lucky, find a diary, love letters, stuff like that. You do the bedroom, Frank. You knew her; you might tumble to something that we might not think was important. While you're doing that, we'll work this floor, the one above, and the one below, canvassing the neighbors. We'll have uniforms working the other floors. Then we'll regroup."

With that agreed to, the detectives split up.

It was after ten when they got back together.

"Bedroom?" asked Kenmare. Dell handed him a small red address book.

"Just this. Looks like it might be old. Lot of neighborhood names where Dan still lives. None of the new telephone exchanges in it."

"That's it?"

"Everything else looks normal to me." Dell nodded. "Clothes, makeup, couple of paperback novels, Valium and birth-control pills in the medicine cabinet, that kind of stuff. But I'd feel better if one of you guys would do a follow-up toss."

"Good idea." Kenmare motioned to Garvan, who went into the bedroom.

"Neighbors?" Dell asked.

"Zilch," said Kenmare.

Kenmare and Dell cruised the living room and small kitchen, studying everything again, until Garvan came back out of the bedroom and announced, "It's clean." Then the men sat back down at the kitchen table.

"Let's line up tomorrow," Kenmare said. "Dell, you and I will work together, and I'll have Garvan sit in on the autopsy; he can also work some of the names in the address book by phone before and after. You and I will go see Ronald Deever and Sally Simms at the ad agency, maybe interview some of the other employees there also. We need to track down this guy Pilcher, too. Let's meet at seven for breakfast and see if there's anything we need to do before that. Frank, there's a little diner called Wally's just off Thirteenth and State. We can eat, then walk over to headquarters and set up a temporary desk for you in our bullpen."

"Sounds good," Dell said.

Kenmare left a uniformed officer at the door of Edie Malone's apartment, one at each end of the sixth-floor hallway, one at the elevator, and two in the lobby. When the detectives parted outside, Dell drove back to the South Side, where he lived. When he got into his own apartment, a little after midnight, he called Mike Larne at home.

"It's Dell, Captain," he said when Larne answered sleepily.

"How's it look?" Larne asked.

"Not good," Dell told him. "Only one possible lead so far: an ex-boyfriend who threatened to slap her around. We'll start doing some deeper work on it tomorrow."

"Was she raped?"

"Didn't look like it."

"Thank God for that much."

"I'll let you know for sure after the autopsy."

"All right. How's it setting with Kenmare and Garvan? You getting any resistance?"

"No, it's fine. They're OK. They're giving me a temp desk downtown tomorrow. What's the word on Dan?"

"The poor man is completely undone. The chaplain and the parish priest managed to get him drunk and put him to bed. Jim Keenan and some of the other boys are staying at the house until Dan's sisters arrive from Florida. Listen, you get some sleep. I'll talk to you tomorrow."

"OK, Cap."

Dell hung up and went directly to the cabinet where he kept his bottle of gin.

At the Able, Bennett, and Crain advertising agency the next day, on the fortieth floor of a Loop building, Kenmare sat in Ronald Deever's private office to interview him while Dell talked with Sally Simms in a corner of the firm's coffee room. Sally was a pert blonde who wrote copy for a dental products account. She told Dell that Edie Malone had been employed by the agency for about eight months as a receptionist and was well liked by everyone she worked with. Sally had double-dated with her half a dozen times, twice with the man named Bob Pilcher.

"He's from North Carolina, a heavy smoker," she said. "That was the main reason Edie quit going out with him; she didn't like smokers. Said kissing them was like licking an ashtray."

"What's the name of the club where he works?" Dell asked.

"It's called Memphis City Limits. Kind of a hillbilly joint. Over on Fullerton near Halsted."

"What made you tell your boss that you were afraid Pilcher might rough Edie up?"

"That's what Edie told me. She said Bob told her he wasn't used to women dumping him, and maybe she just needed a little slapping around to get her act together. Edie wasn't sure he meant it, but I was. I mean, this is one of those guys that doesn't just walk, he *struts*. And he wears those real tight Wranglers to show off his package. Got real wavy hair with one little curl always down on his forehead. Ask me, he's definitely the kind would slap a woman around. I told Edie she was better off sticking with guys like Bart Mason."

"Who's he?" Dell asked.

"Bart? He's a nice young exec works for the home office of an insurance company down on twenty-two. They dated for a while, then broke up when Edie started seeing someone else."

"Who did she start seeing?"

Sally shrugged. "I don't know. She went out a lot."

"Have you told Bart Mason that Edie's dead?"

"Why, no. That detective in Ron Deever's office told both of us not to mention it."

"We appreciate that you didn't," Dell said. "Besides this Bart Mason, do you know of any other men in the building that Edie went out with?"

"No," Sally said, shaking her head.

Just then, Kenmare came into the room. He said nothing, not wishing to interrupt the flow of Dell's interview. But Dell rose, saying, "OK, thanks very much, Miss Simms. We'll be in touch if we need anything else."

"Do I still have to not talk about it?" Sally asked.

"No, you can talk about it now. It'll be in the afternoon papers anyway. But don't call Bart Mason yet. We want to talk to him first." When Sally left the room, Dell said to Kenmare. "Bart Mason, guy works for an insurance company down on twenty-two, used to date Edie. Supposedly doesn't know she's dead yet."

"Let's see," said Kenmare.

Going down in the elevator, Dell asked, "Anything with Deever?"

"Nothing interesting."

The insurance company occupied the entire twenty-second floor, and the detectives had a receptionist show them to Bart Mason's office without announcing them. Once there, Kenmare thanked her and closed the door behind them. They identified themselves and Kenmare said, "Mr. Mason, do you know a woman named Edie Malone?"

"Sure. She works for an ad agency up on forty," Mason said. "We used to date." He was a pleasant-looking young man, neat as a drill instructor. "Why, what's the matter?"

"She was found murdered in her apartment."

"*Edie?*" The color drained from Bart Mason's face, and his eyes widened almost to bulging. "I don't believe it—"

"Can you tell us your whereabouts for the last forty-eight hours, Mr. Mason?"

Mason was staring incredulously at them. "Edie—murdered—?"

"We need to know where you've been for the last couple of days," Kenmare said.

"What? Oh, sure—" Mason picked up his phone and dialed a three-number extension. When his call was answered, he said, "Jenny, will you come over to my office right away? It's important."

"Who's that?" Dell asked when Mason hung up.

"My fiancée. Jenny Paula. She works over in claims. We live together. We're together all the time: eat breakfast together, come to work together, eat lunch, go home, eat dinner, sleep together. We haven't been apart since a week ago Sunday when Jen went to spend the day with her mother." He took a deep breath. "My God, Edie—"

A pretty young woman, Italian-looking, came into the office. She looked curiously at the two detectives. Mason introduced them.

"They need to know my whereabouts for the last few days," he said.

"But why?" she asked.

"Just tell them where I've been, hon."

Jenny shrugged. "With me."

"All the time?" asked Kenmare.

"Yes, all the time."

"Like I said, we do everything together," Mason reiterated. "We work together, shop for groceries together, stay in or go out together, we even shower together."

"Bart!" Jenny Paula said, chagrined. "What's this all about anyway?"

"I'll explain later. Can she go now, Officers?"

"Sure," said Kenmare. "Thank you, Miss Paula." She left, somewhat piqued, and Kenmare said to Mason, "We may need to talk to her again, in a little more depth."

"We're both available anytime," Mason assured him.

"How long did you date Edie Malone?" Dell asked.

"About six months, I guess."

"Were you intimate?"

"Sure." Mason shrugged.

"When did you break up?"

"Late last summer sometime. Around Labor Day, I think."

"What caused you to break up?"

"Edie began seeing someone else. I didn't like it. So I split with her."

"Do you know who she started seeing?"

"Yeah. Ron Deever, her boss upstairs at the ad agency."

Dell and Kenmare exchanged quick glances. They continued to question Mason for several more minutes, then got his apartment address and left.

On the way back up to the fortieth floor, an annoyed Kenmare, referring to Ron Deever, said, "That son of a bitch. He never mentioned once that he went out with her. I think I'll haul his ass in and take a formal statement."

"He'll lawyer up on you," Dell predicted.

"Let him."

When they got back to Able, Bennett, and Crain, Kenmare went into Ron Deever's office again while Dell took Sally Simms back into the coffee room.

"Did you know that Edie Malone had dated Ron Deever?" he asked bluntly. Sally lowered her eyes.

"Yes."

"I asked you if you knew of any other men in the building that Edie had gone out with and you said no. Why did you lie?"

"I'm sorry," she said, her hands beginning to tremble. "Look, this guy is my boss. I'm a single parent with a little boy in day care. I didn't want to take a chance of losing my job." She started tearing up. "First thing he asked me after you left was whether I told you about him and Edie."

"Why was he so concerned?"

"He's married."

"Did Edie know that when she was seeing him?"

"Sure. It was no big thing for her."

Dell sighed quietly. Reaching out, he patted the young woman's trembling hands. "Okay. Relax. I'll make sure Deever knows it wasn't you who told us. But if I have to question you again, don't lie to me about anything. Understand?"

"Sure." Sally dabbed at her eyes with a paper napkin. "Listen, thanks."

Dell sent her back to work and went into Deever's office, where Kenmare was reading the riot act to him.

"What the hell do you think this is, a TV show? This is a *homicide* investigation, Mister! When you withhold relevant information, you're obstructing justice!" He turned to Dell. "He's married. That's why he didn't come clean."

"I just chewed out Miss Simms, too," Dell said. "Told her how much trouble she could get into covering for him."

"All right," said Kenmare, "we're going to start all over, Mr. Deever, and I want the full and complete truth this time."

A shaky Ron Deever nodded compliance.

When they got back to the squad room, Garvan was waiting for them and a spare desk had been set up for Dell.

"She wasn't raped or otherwise sexually assaulted," he reported. "Cause of death was strangulation—from behind. Coroner fixed time of death at between nine at night and one in the morning. Best bet: between eleven and midnight." He tossed Edie's address book onto the desk. "You were right about this, Dell: It's old. Some of these people haven't seen or heard from her in three or four years. The ones who have couldn't tell me anything about her personal life. You guys make out?"

"Not really," said Kenmare. "We've got one guy who could have slipped out while his fiancée was asleep and gone over and done it—but it's not likely. Another guy, married, was at his son's basketball game earlier in the evening, then at home with his family out in Arlington Heights the rest of the night. One of us will have to go out and interview his wife on that this afternoon."

"I'll do it," Garvan said. "I need the fresh air after that autopsy. Oh, I almost forgot." He tossed five telephone messages to Dell. "These were forwarded from Lakeside. Three are from you partner, two from your captain."

"If you need some privacy to return the calls," Kenmare said, "Garvan and I can go for coffee.

Dell shook his head. "Nothing I can't say in front of you guys. You both know the situation." He could tell by their expressions, as he dialed Mike Larne's number first, that they were pleased at not being excluded. "It's Dell, Captain," he said when Larne answered. "I told you I'd check in when I had the autopsy results. Edie wasn't raped or anything like that. Somebody strangled her from behind, between nine Tuesday night and one on Wednesday morning." He listened for a moment, then said, "Couple of soft leads, is all. Very soft." Then: "Yeah, he's called me three times. I guess I better get back to him."

When he finished his call to Larne, Dell dialed Dan Malone's home. The phone was answered on the third ring. "Hello."

"Yeah, who's this?" Dell asked.

"Who are *you*?" the voice asked back.

"Frank Dell. Is that you, Keenan?"

"Oh, Frank. Yeah, it's me. Sorry, I didn't recognize your voice. How's it going?"

"Very slow. Dan's been calling me, I guess. How is he?

"Thrashed, inside and out. But the boys and me have him under control. And his two sisters are here with him. He's sleeping right now. It means a lot to him that you're working the case, Frank. He's got a couple of names that he wants checked: old boyfriends of Edie's that he didn't like. Wasn't for you being on the case, he'd probably be out doing it hisself. Pistol-whipping them, maybe."

"You have the names?"

"Yeah, he wrote them down here by the phone." Dell took down the names and told Keenan to tell Dan that he'd see him tomorrow with a full report of the case's progress. After he hung up, he handed the names to Kenmare. "Old boyfriends," he said.

Kenmare gave them to Garvan. "Start a check on them before you go out to interview Deever's wife. Frank and I are going out to that line-dancing joint—it's called Memphis City Limits—to interview Bob Pilcher. We'll meet back here at end of shift."

Memphis City Limits did not have live music until after seven, but even in midafternoon there was a jukebox playing country-and-western and a few people on the dance floor around which the club was laid out. It was a big barn of a building that had once been a wholesale furniture outlet, then remained vacant for several years until some entrepreneurial mind decided there might be a profit in a club catering to the area's large influx of Southerners come north to find work.

Dell and Kenmare found Bob Pilcher drinking beer at a table with two cowgirl types and a beefy man in a lumberjack shirt. Identifying themselves, Kenmare asked if they could speak with Pilcher in private to ask him a few questions. Pilcher shook his head.

"Anything you want to ask me about Edie Malone, do it right here in front of witnesses."

"What makes you think it's about Edie Malone?" Kenmare asked.

"No other reason for you to be talking to me. Story's been on TV news all morning about her being murdered." Pilcher spoke with a heavily accented drawl that sounded purposefully exaggerated.

"When did you see her last?" Dell asked.

"'Bout a week ago." He winked at Dell. "She was alive, too."

"Can you account for your time during the past seventy-two hours?" Kenmare wanted to know, expanding the time period more than he had to because of Pilcher's attitude.

"Most of it, I reckon," Pilcher replied. "I'm here ever' day 'cept Sundays from no later than six of an evening to closing time at two A.M. Usually I'm here an hour or two *before* six, as you can see today. As for the rest of my time, you'd have to give me specific times and I'd see what I could come up with." His expression hardened a little. "Tell you one thing, though, boys, you wasting good po-lice time on me. I didn't off the gal."

"We have reason to believe you slapped her around now and then," Dell tried.

"So what if I did?" Pilcher challenged. "You can't arrest me for that: She's *dead*, fellers, hell!" He took a long swallow of beer. "Anyways, one of the reasons women like me is that I treat 'em rough. That one wasn't no different."

"So you did slap her around?"

"Yeah, I did," Pilcher defied, him, lighting a cigarette. "Go on and do something about it if you can."

"Where can we find your employer," Kenmare asked, "to verify that you've been here the last three nights?"

Pilcher smiled what was really a nasty half-smirk. "So she was offed at night, huh? For sure you'll have to pin it on somebody else." He nodded across the club. "Manager's office is that door to the right of the bar."

Pilcher blew smoke rings at the two detectives as they left him at the table with his friends and sought out the club manager. He confirmed that Pilcher had indeed been on duty from at least six until two every night since the club had been closed the previous Sunday.

"Brother, would I like to nail that hillbilly for this," Kenmare groused as they walked back to their car. "I'd plant evidence to get that son of a bitch."

"So would I," Dell admitted. "Only there's no evidence to plant. Anyway, the timeline doesn't jibe. A second-year law student could get him off."

When they got back to the squad room, Garvan had already returned. "Struck out," he announced. "Deever's wife puts him at home from about ten-thirty, after their son's basketball game, until the next morning about eight when he left for work." He turned to Dell. "And those two boyfriends your partner didn't like: One of them's in the navy stationed on Okinawa; the other's married, lives in Oregon, hasn't been out of that state since last July. You guys?"

"Pilcher's a scumbag, but his alibi's tight," Kenmare said. He looked at his watch. "Let's call it a day. Thursday's a big night for my wife and me," he told Dell. "We get a sitter, go out for Chinese, and see a movie."

Dell just nodded, but Garvan said, "Go see a good cop picture tonight. Something with Bruce Willis in it. Maybe you can pick up some tips on how to be a detective."

"Up yours, you perennial rookie," Kenmare said, and left.

Garvan turned to Dell. "Buy you a drink, Lakeside?"

"Why not?" said Dell. "Lead the way, Homicide."

At two o'clock the next morning, Dell was in his car, parked at the alley entrance to the rear parking lot of the Memphis City Limits club. He was wearing dark trousers and a black windbreaker, and had black Nikes on his feet. Both hands were gloved, and he wore a wool navy watch cap low on his forehead, and a dark scarf around his neck. The fuse for the interior lights on his car had been removed.

He had been there for half an hour, watching as the last patrons of the night exited the club, got into their vehicles, and left. By ten past two, there were only a few cars left, belonging to club employees who were straggling out to go home. The lot was not particularly well lit, but the rear door to the club was, so it was easy for Dell to distinguish people as they left.

It was a quarter past two when Bob Pilcher came out and swaggered across the parking lot toward a Dodge Ram pickup. Dell got out of his car without the light going on and, in his Nikes, walked briskly, silently toward him from the left rear, tying the scarf over his lower face as he went. When he was within arm's length of Pilcher, he said, "Hey, stud."

Pilcher turned, a half-smile starting, and Dell cracked him across the face with a leather-covered lead sap. He heard part of Pilcher's face crack. Catching him before he dropped to the ground, Dell dragged the unconscious man around the truck, out of sight of the club's back door. Dropping him, he rolled him over, face-down. Pulling both arms above his head, he pressed each of Pilcher's palms, in turn, against the asphalt, held each down at the wrist, and with the sap used short, snapping blows to systematically break the top four finger knuckles and top thumb knuckle of each hand. Then he walked quickly back to the alley, got into his car, and drove away. The whole thing had taken less than two minutes.

Be a long time before you slap another woman around, he thought grimly as he left. Or even hold a toothbrush.

Then he thought: That was for you, Edie.

The next day, Dell went to be with Dan Malone when he came to the funeral parlor to see Edie in her casket for the first time. The undertaker had picked up her body when the coroner was through with it, and one of Edie's aunts and two cousins had gone to Marshall Field's and bought her a simple mauve dress to be laid out in.

There were a number of aunts, uncles, cousins, and other collateral family members in attendance when the slumber room was opened, and groups of neighbors gathered outside, easily outnumbered by groups of police officers, in uniform and out, who had known Dan Malone for all or part of his thirty-two years on the force and had come from half the police districts in the city to offer their condolences.

Dell was shocked by the sight of Dan when the grieving man arrived. He looked as if he had aged ten years in the three days since Dell had seen him. A couple of male relatives helped him out of the car and were assisting him in an unsteady walk toward the entrance when Dan's eyes fell on Dell and he pulled away, insisting on a moment with his partner. Dell hurried to him, the two men embraced, then stepped up close to the building where people cleared a space for them to speak privately.

"Did you find those two bastards Keenan gave you the names of?" Dan asked hoarsely.

"Yeah, Dan, but they're clean," Dell told him. "They're not even around anymore."

"Are you sure? I never liked either one of 'em."

"They're clean, Dan. I promise you. Listen," Dell said to placate him, speaking close to his ear, "I did find one guy. He's clean for the killing, but he'd slapped Edie around a couple of times."

"The son of a bitch. Who is he?" The older man's teary eyes became fiery with rage.

"It's OK, Dan. I already took care of it."

"You did? What'd you do?"

"Fixed his hands. With a sap."

"Good, good." Malone wet his dry, whiskey-puffed lips. "I knew I could count on you, Frankie. Listen, come on inside and see my little girl."

"You go in with your family, Dan. I've already seen her," Dell lied. He had no intention of looking at Edie Malone's body again.

Dell gestured and several relatives hurried over to get Dan. Then Dell returned to a group of policemen that included Mike Larne, a couple of lieutenants, Keenan and other cronies of Dan's, and a deputy commissioner. Larne put an arm around Dell's shoulders.

"Whatever you said to him, Frank, it seemed to help."

"I hope so," Dell said. "Listen, Captain, I'm going to get back down to Homicide.

"By all means," said Larne. "Back to work, lad. Find the bastard that caused this heartache."

In the days immediately following the funeral and burial of Edie Malone, the three detectives on the case worked and reworked the old leads, as well as a few new ones. A deputy state's attorney, Ray Millard, was assigned to analyze and evaluate the evidence as they progressed. Disappointingly, there was little of a positive nature to analyze.

"It's too soft," Millard told them in their first meeting. He was a precise, intense young lawyer. "First, you've got the guy she worked for: older man, married, concealed the relationship when first questioned. Solid alibi for the hours just before, during, and after his son's basketball game which he attended on the night of the murder. Decent alibi for the rest of the night: a statement by his wife that he was at home. He *could* have slipped out of his suburban home when everyone was asleep, driven into the city, and committed the crime—but *why* would he have done that, and who's going to believe it?

"Second, you've got the good-guy ex-boyfriend. He's well set up with a new girlfriend, and the two of them are practically joined at the hip: live together, work together, play together. Again, he *could* have slipped out of their apartment around midnight when his fiancée was asleep, gone to the Malone woman's apartment, a relatively short distance away, and killed her. But again, *why?* Let's remember that *he* dumped *her*, not the other way around. Soft, very soft.

"Third, bad-guy ex-boyfriend. The hillbilly bouncer." Millard paused. "Incidentally, I understand that the night after you guys interviewed him, somebody jumped him outside the club and broke his nose, one cheekbone, and both hands. You guys heard anything about that?"

The detectives shrugged in unison, as if choreographed. "Doesn't surprise me," Kenmare said.

"Me either," Dell agreed. "Scumbags like that always have people who don't like them."

"Well, anyway," the young lawyer continued, "bad-guy boyfriend would be a beaut to get in court. I could try him in front of a jury of his *relatives* and probably get a death sentence—except for one thing: He's got a home-free alibi on his job. No way he could have been away from the club long enough to go do it without his absence being noticed. He's the bouncer; he's got to be visible all the time." Millard sat back and drummed his fingers. "Anything else cooking?"

Kenmare shook his head. "We're back canvassing the neighbors again, but nothing so far. We had one little piece of excitement day before yesterday when a little old retired lady in the victim's building said she'd heard that the building super had been fired from his last job for making lewd suggestions to female tenants. We checked it out and there was nothing to it. Turned out she was just ticked off at him for reporting her dog making a mess in the hallway a couple times."

"Too bad," Millard said. "The super would've made a good defendant. Had a key to her apartment, found the body, whole ball of wax. He alibied tight?"

"Very. Lives with his wife on two. They went to a movie, got home around eleven, went right to bed. He's got a good rep—except for the little old lady with the dog."

"Had to be somebody she knew," Millard said. "No forced entry, no lock picked. No rape, no robbery. This was a personal crime. She let the guy in." He tossed the file across the desk to Kenmare. "Find me that guy and we'll stick the needle in his arm."

The three detectives took off early and went to a small Loop bar, where they settled in a back booth. Dell could sense some tension but did not broach the subject. He knew Kenmare would get around to whatever it was.

"We've enjoyed having you work with us, Frank," the senior detective finally said. "We had our doubts about your assignment, but it's turned out OK."

"Yeah, we had our doubts," Garvan confirmed, "but it worked out fine."

"I tried not to get in the way," Dell said.

"Hey, you've been a lot of help," Garvan assured him. "Got me away from this nag for a while," he bobbed his chin at Kenmare.

"Listen to him," the older man said. "Wasn't for me, he'd be directing traffic at some school crossing."

"What's on your mind, boys?" Dell asked, deciding not to wait.

Kenmare sighed. "It's a bit delicate, Frank."

"I'm a big boy. Shoot."

They both leaned toward him to emphasize confidentiality. "That first night in the apartment, you commented that Dan Malone and his daughter hadn't been close for a while," Kenmare recalled.

Garvan nodded. "You said he didn't approve of her lifestyle."

"You said he didn't talk much about her after she quit college and went out on her own."

Dell's expression tightened and locked. "You're getting very close to stepping over the wrong line," he said evenly.

"I'm sorry you feel that way, Frank," said Kenmare. "It's a step that has to be taken." He sat back. "You know as well as I do that if he wasn't one of our own, he'd have been on the spot from day one. As soon as we decided there was no forced entry, no rape, no robbery, we would have included an estranged father in our investigation. But Garvan and me, we kept hoping that evidence would lead us to somebody else. Unfortunately, it hasn't."

"Look, Frank," Garvan said in a placating tone, "it doesn't have to be a complicated thing. It can be, like, informal."

"Of course," Kenmare agreed, his own voice also becoming appeasing. "Drop in on him. Have a drink. Engage him in casual conversation. And find out where he was during the critical hours, that's all."

"Sure," said Garvan, "that's all."

Dell grunted quietly. Like it would be a walk in the park to handle a thirty-two-year veteran cop like that. He took a long swallow of his drink. His eyes shifted from Kenmare to Garvan and back again, then looked down at the table, where the fingers of one hand drummed silently. He did not speak for what seemed like a very long time. Finally Kenmare broke the silence.

"It's either that way or it'll have to be us, Frank. But it's got to be done."

With a sigh that came from deep inside of him, Dell nodded. "All right."

The tension that permeated the booth should have dissipated with that, but it did not. Dell once again became, as he had been at the very beginning of the investigation, an outsider.

Dan Malone smiled when he opened the door and saw Dell.

"Ah, Frank. Come in, come in. Good to see you, partner. I've missed you."

"Missed you too, Dan."

They embraced briefly, and, Dell sensed, a little stiffly.

"I was just having a beer after supper," said Dan. "You want one?"

"Sure."

"Sit down there on the couch. I'll get you one." He turned off a network hockey game, picked up a plastic tray on which were the remains of a TV dinner, and went into the kitchen with it. In a moment, he returned with an open bottle of Budweiser. "So," he said, handing Dell the beer and sitting in his recliner, "how's it going?"

"It's not going, Dan. Not going anywhere," Dell replied quietly, almost dejectedly.

"Well, I figured as much. Else you'd have been in closer touch. Not getting anywhere on the case?"

"No. I've been meaning to drop by and talk to you about it, but I thought you probably still had family staying with you."

"My two sisters were here for a week," Dan said. "And there've been nieces and nephews running in and out like mice. Finally I had enough and ran them all off. Then my phone started ringing off the hook all day, so I finally unplugged that just to get some peace and quiet. I guess they all think I'm suicidal or something."

"Are you?" Dell asked.

Dan gave him a long look. "No. Any reason I should be?"

Dell shrugged. "Sometimes things like this are hard to get over. Some people want to do it quickly."

"That's not the case with me," the older man assured him. "I lost Edie a long time ago, Frank. I think I probably started losing her when she slept with her first man. Then every man after that, I lost her a little more. Until finally she was gone completely."

"Were there that many men?"

"You're working the case; you ought to know."

"We've only found three."

Malone grunted cynically. "You must not have gone back very far." He stared into space. "I used to follow her sometimes. She'd go into a bar and come out an hour later with a man. Night after night. Different bars, different men. It was like some kind of sickness with her."

They both fell silent and sat drinking for several minutes. Dell, who had always been so comfortable with his partner, felt peculiarly ill at ease, as if he had now become an outsider with Dan Malone as he had with the two homicide detectives. Finally he decided not to prolong the visit any more than necessary.

"How long have we known each other, Dan?" he asked.

"What's on your mind, Frank?" the older policeman asked knowingly. It had been he who taught Dell that reminiscing frequently led to other things.

"The night of Edie's murder."

"What about it?"

"I need to know where you were."

Malone nodded understandingly. "I wondered when they'd get around to it." He smiled a slight, cold smile. "Suppose I tell you I was right here at home, alone, all night. What then?"

"Tell me what you did all night."

"Watched the fights on television. Drank too much. Passed out here in my chair."

"Who was fighting in the main event?"

Malone shrugged. "Some Puerto Rican against some black guy, I think. I was sleepy by the time the main go came on; I don't remember their names."

"Neither do I," said Dell.

"What?" Dan Malone frowned.

"I don't remember their names either. But you weren't alone that night. That was the night I dropped over. We both drank too much. I fell asleep on the couch. Didn't wake up until after one o'clock. Then I put you to bed and went home. That was the night, wasn't it, Dan?"

The older man's frown faded and his face seemed to go slack. "Yes," he said quietly. "Yes, I do believe that was the night."

There was silence between them again. Neither of them seemed to know what to say next, and they could not look at each other. Malone stared into space, as he had done earlier; Dell stared at the television, as if it had not been turned off. Only after several minutes did Dell drink the rest of his beer and put the bottle down. He rose.

"I'll be going now. You won't be coming back to work, will you, Dan?"

Malone looked thoughtfully at him. "No," he replied. "I'm thinking of putting in for retirement. My sisters in Florida want me to move down there."

"Good idea. You'd probably enjoy yourself. Lots of retired cops in Florida." Dell walked to the door. "Goodnight, Dan."

"Goodnight, Frank."

Only when he got out into the night air did Dell realize how much he was sweating.

The next morning, Dell typed up a summary of Dan Malone's statement, along with his own corroboration of the alibi. After signing it, he handed the report to Kenmare. The lead homicide detective read it, then passed it to Garvan to read.

"You've thought this through, I guess," Kenmare said.

"Backwards and forward," Dell told him.

Garvan raised his eyebrows but said nothing as he handed the report back to Kenmare.

"I don't think the brass will buy this," Kenmare offered.

"What are they going to do?" Dell asked. "Suspend Dan *and* me? Open an internal investigation? On what evidence? And how would it look on the evening news?"

"The higher-ups might feel it was worth it," said Garvan.

"Worth it why?" pressed Dell. "What's the gain? The department's getting rid of Dan anyway; he'll be retiring."

"But you won't," Garvan pointed out.

"So? What have I done that the department would want to get rid of me?"

"Helped him get away with it, that's what," said Kenmare.

"*If* he did it," Dell challenged. "And we don't know that he did. All we know is that we can't find anybody else right now who *did* do it." He decided to throw down the gauntlet right then. "You guys going to let this report pass, or are you going to make an issue of it?"

"You didn't mention this alibi last night when we were talking," Kenmare accused.

"Maybe I had my days mixed up." Dell shrugged. "Maybe I thought it had been Monday night I had dropped in; maybe Dan had to remind me it was Tuesday."

"Maybe," Kenmare said. He looked inquiringly at his partner.

"Yeah, maybe," Garvan agreed.

"You're sure Malone's retiring?" Kenmare asked.

"Positive," Dell guaranteed.

Kenmare pulled open a desk drawer and filed the report. "See you around, Dell," he said.

"Yeah," said Garvan. "Take it easy, Dell."

Dell walked out of the squad room without looking back.

That night, when Dell came into the Three Corners Club and took his regular seat at the end of the bar, it was the owner, Tim Callan, who poured his drink and served him.

"I've missed you, Frankie," he said congenially. "How've you been?"

"I've seen better days," Dell allowed.

"Ah, haven't we all," Callan sympathized. He lowered his voice. "I'm really sorry about the young lady. Edie, was that her name?"

"Yeah, Edie." Dell felt the back of his neck go warm.

"I seen her picture in the paper and on the news. Took me a few looks to place her. Then I says to myself, why, that's the young lady Frankie used to bring in here. Always wanted the booth 'way in the back for privacy.'" Callan smiled artificially. "I remember that every time I loaned you the key to use the apartment upstairs I had to make you promise to be out by midnight so's I could get the poker game started. And you never let me down, Frank. Not once. 'Course, we go back a long ways, you and me." Now Callan's expression saddened, genuinely so. "I'm really sorry, Frank, that things didn't work out between you and Edie."

"Thank you, Tim. So am I." Dell's heart hurt when he said it.

"They still don't know who did it?"

Dell looked hard at him. "No."

They locked eyes for a long moment, two old friends, each of whom could read the other like scripture.

"What was the name of that brother-in-law of yours charged with receiving stolen property?" Dell finally asked.

"Nick Santore," said Callan. "Funny you should ask. His preliminary hearing's day after tomorrow."

"I'll talk to the assistant state's attorney," Dell said. "I'll tell him the guy's going to be a snitch for me, that I need him on the street. I'll get him to recommend probation."

"Ah, Frankie, you're a prince," Callan praised, clasping one of Dell's hands with both of his own. "I owe you, big time."

"No," Frank Dell said, "we're even, Timmy."

Both men knew it was so.

THE TURN OF THE TIDE

(1934)

C. S. Forester

Although it may be possible to conduct a perfect murder, it is not uncommon for a killer to make a mistake. Such an error may prove fatal, or it could be relatively inconsequential.

British author Cecil Scott Forester (1899–1966) studied to become a doctor but found he preferred writing. His novel *Payment Deferred* (1926) is a study of the disintegration of a murderer's mind. Forester is best known for a series of books based on the adventures of the British Royal Navy. *Captain Horatio Hornblower* (1937) was a best-selling novel, later made into a movie starring Gregory Peck and Virginia Mayo (1951). Forester promoted his star naval officer to higher rank, as shown in the titles *Commodore Hornblower* (1945) and *Lord Hornblower* (1946).

"What always beats them in the end," said Dr. Matthews, "is how to dispose of the body. But, of course, you know that as well as I do."

"Yes," said Slade. He had, in fact, been devoting far more thought to what Dr. Matthews believed to be this accidental subject of conversation than Dr. Matthews could ever guess.

"As a matter of fact," went on Dr. Matthews, warming to the subject to which Slade had so tactfully led him, "it's a terribly knotty problem. It's so difficult, in fact, that I always wonder why anyone is fool enough to commit murder."

"All very well for you," thought Slade, but he did not allow his thoughts to alter his expression. "You smug, self-satisfied old ass! You don't know the sort of difficulties a man can be up against."

"I've often thought the same," he said.

"Yes," went on Dr. Matthews, "it's the body that does it, every time. To use poison calls for special facilities, which are good enough to hang you as soon as suspicion is roused. And that suspicion—well, of course, part of my job is to detect poisoning. I don't think anyone can get away with it, nowadays, even with the most dunderheaded general practitioner."

"I quite agree with you," said Slade. He had no intention of using poison.

"Well," went on Dr. Matthews, developing his logical argument, "if you rule out poison, you rule out the chance of getting the body disposed of under the impression that the victim died a natural death. The only other way, if a man cares to stand the racket of having the body to give evidence against him, is to fake things to look like suicide. But you know, and I know, that it just can't be done. The mere fact of suicide calls for a close examination, and no one has ever been able to fix things so well as to get away with it.

You're a lawyer. You've probably read a lot of reports of trials where the murderer has tried it on. And you know what's happened to them."

"Yes," said Slade.

He certainly had given a great deal of consideration to the matter. It was only after long thought that he had, finally, put aside the notion of disposing of young Spalding and concealing his guilt by a sham suicide.

"That brings us to where we started, then," said Dr. Matthews. "The only other thing left is to try and conceal the body. And that's more difficult still."

"Yes," said Slade, once more. But he had a perfect plan for disposing of the body.

"A human body," said Dr. Matthews, "is a most difficult thing to get rid of. That chap Oscar Wilde, in that book of his—'Dorian Grey,' isn't it?—gets rid of one by the use of chemicals. Well, I'm a chemist as well as a doctor, and *I* wouldn't like the job."

"No?" said Slade, politely.

Dr. Matthews was not nearly as clever a man as himself, he thought.

"There's altogether too much of it," said Dr. Matthews. "It's heavy, and it's bulky, and it's bound to undergo corruption. Think of all those poor devils who've tried it. Bodies in trunks, and bodies in coal-cellars, and bodies in chicken-runs. You can't hide the thing, try as you will."

"Can't I? That's all you know," thought Slade, but aloud he said: "You're quite right. I've never thought about it before."

"Of course, you haven't," agreed Dr. Matthews. "Sensible people don't, unless it's an incident of their profession, as in my case."

Dr. Matthews rubbed his chin as the conversation tended to lapse.

"And yet, you know," he went on, meditatively, "there's one decided advantage about getting rid of the body altogether. You're much safer, then. It's a point which ought to interest you, as a lawyer, more than me. It's rather an obscure point of law, but I fancy there are very definite rulings on it. You know what I'm referring to?"

"No, I don't," said Slade, genuinely puzzled.

"You can't have a trial for murder unless you can prove there's a victim," said Dr. Matthews. "There's got to be a corpus delicti, as you lawyers say in your horrible dog-Latin. A corpse, in other words, even if it's only a bit of one, like that which hanged Crippen. No corpse, no trial. I think that's good law, isn't it?"

"By Jove, you're right!" said Slade. "I wonder why that hadn't occurred to me before?"

No sooner were the words out of his mouth than he regretted having said them. He did his best to make his face immobile again; he was afraid lest his expression might have hinted at his pleasure in discovering another very reassuring factor in this problem of killing young Spalding. But Dr. Matthews had noticed nothing.

"Well, as I said, people only think about these things if they're incidental to their profession," he said. "And, all the same, it's only a theoretical piece of law. The entire destruction of a body is practically impossible. But, I suppose, if a man could achieve it, he would be all right. However strong the suspicion was against him, the police couldn't get him without a corpse. There might be a story in that, Slade, if you or I were writers."

"Yes," assented Slade, and laughed harshly.

There never would be any story about the killing of young Spalding, the insolent pup.

"Well," said Dr. Matthews, "we've had a pretty gruesome conversation, haven't we? And I seem to have done all the talking, somehow. That's the result, I suppose, Slade, of the very excellent dinner you gave me. I'd better push off now. Not that the weather is very inviting."

Nor was it. As Slade saw Dr. Matthews into his car, the rain was driving down in a real winter storm, and there was a bitter wind blowing.

"Shouldn't be surprised if this turned to snow before morning," were Dr. Matthew's last words before he drove off.

Slade was glad it was such a tempestuous night. It meant that more certainly than ever, there would be no one out in the lanes, no one out on the sands when he disposed of young Spalding's body.

Back in his drawing-room, Slade looked at the clock. There was still an hour to spare; he could spend it in making sure that his plans were all correct.

He looked up the tide tables. Yes, that was right enough. Spring tides. The lowest of low water on the sands. There was not so much luck about that; young Spalding came back on the midnight train every Wednesday night, and it was not surprising that, sooner or later, the Wednesday night would coincide with a spring tide. But it was lucky that this particular Wednesday night should be one of tempest: luckier still that low water should be at one-thirty, the most convenient time for him.

He opened the drawing-room door and listened carefully. He could not hear a sound. Mrs. Dumbleton, his housekeeper, must have been in bed some time now. She was as deaf as a post, anyway, and would not hear his departure. Nor his return, when Spalding had been killed and disposed of.

The hands of the clock seemed to be moving very fast. He must make sure everything was correct. The plough chain and the other iron weights were already in the back seat of the car; he had put them there before old Matthews arrived to dine. He slipped on his overcoat.

From his desk, Slade took a curious little bit of apparatus: eighteen inches of strong cord, tied at each end to a six-inch length of wood so as to make a ring. He made a last close examination to see that the knots were quite firm, and then he put it in his pocket; as he did so, he ran through, in his mind, the words—he knew them by heart—of the passage in the book about the Thugs of India, describing the method of strangulation employed by them.

He could think quite coldly about all this. Young Spalding was a pestilent busybody. A word from him, now, could bring ruin upon Slade, could send him to prison, could have him struck off the rolls.

Slade thought of other defaulting solicitors he had heard of, even one or two with whom he had come into contact professionally. He remembered his brother-solicitors' remarks about them, pitying or contemptuous. He thought of having to beg his bread in the streets on his release from prison, of cold and misery and starvation. The shudder which shook him was succeeded by a hot wave of resentment. Never, never, would he endure it.

What right had young Spalding, who had barely been qualified two years, to condemn a grey-haired man twenty years his senior to such a fate? If nothing but death would stop him, then he deserved to die. He clenched his hand on the cord in his pocket.

A glance at the clock told him he had better be moving. He turned out the lights and tiptoed out of the house, shutting the door quietly behind him. The bitter wind flung icy rain into his face, but he did not notice it.

He pushed the car out of the garage by hand, and, contrary to his wont, he locked the garage doors, as a precaution against the infinitesimal chance that, on a night like this, someone should notice that his car was out.

He drove cautiously down the road. Of course, there was not a soul about in a quiet place like this. The few street-lamps were already extinguished.

There were lights in the station as he drove over the bridge; they were awaiting, there, the arrival of the twelve-thirty train. Spalding would be on that. Every Wednesday he went over to his subsidiary office, sixty miles away. Slade turned into the lane a quarter of a mile beyond the station, and then reversed his car so that it pointed towards the road. He put out the sidelights, and settled himself to wait; his hand fumbled with the cord in his pocket.

The train was a little late. Slade had been waiting a quarter of an hour when he saw the lights of the train emerge from the cutting and come to a standstill in the station. So wild was the night that he could hear nothing of it. Then the train moved slowly out again. As soon as it was gone, the lights in the station began to go out, one by one; Hobson, the porter, was making ready to go home, now that his turn of duty was completed.

Next, Slade's straining ears heard footsteps.

Young Spalding was striding down the road. With his head bent before the storm, he did not notice the dark mass of the motor-car in the lane, and he walked past it.

Slade counted up to two hundred, slowly, and then he switched on his lights, started the engine, and drove the car out into the road in pursuit. He saw Spalding in the light of the headlamps—the rain making silver streaks in the beam—and drew up alongside.

"Is that Spalding?" he said, striving to make the tone of his voice as natural as possible. "I'd better give you a lift, old man, hadn't I?"

"Thanks very much," said Spalding. "This isn't the sort of night to walk two miles in."

He climbed in and shut the door. No one had seen. No one would know. Slade let in his clutch and drove slowly down the road.

"Bit of luck, seeing you," he said. "I was just on my way home from bridge at Mrs. Clay's when I saw the train come in and remembered it was Wednesday and you'd be walking home. So I thought I'd turn a bit out of my way to take you along."

"Very good of you, I'm sure," said Spalding.

"As a matter of fact," said Slade, speaking slowly and driving slowly, "it wasn't altogether disinterested. I wanted to talk business to you, as it happened."

"Rather an odd time to talk business," said Spalding. "Can't it wait till to-morrow?"

"No, it cannot," said Slade. "It's about the Lady Vere trust."

"Oh, yes. I wrote to remind you last week that you had to make delivery."

"Yes, you did. And I told you, long before that, that it would be inconvenient, with Hammond abroad, and so on."

"I don't see that," said Spalding. "I don't see that Hammond's got anything to do with it. Why can't you just hand over and have done with it? I can't do anything to straighten things up until you do."

"As I said, it would be inconvenient."

Slade brought the car to a standstill at the side of the road.

"Look here, Spalding," he said, desperately, "I've never asked a favour of you before. But now I ask you, as a favour, to forego delivery for a bit. Just for three months, Spalding."

But Slade had small hope that his request would be granted. So little hope, in fact, that he brought his left hand out of his pocket holding the piece of wood, with the loop of cord dangling from its ends. He put his arm round the back of Spalding's seat.

"No, I can't, really I can't," said Spalding. "I've got my duty to my clients to consider. I'm sorry to insist, but you're quite well aware of what my duty is."

"Yes," said Slade. "But I beg you to wait. I implore you to wait, Spalding. There! Perhaps you can guess why, now."

"I see," said Spalding, after a long pause.

"I only want three months," pressed Slade. "Just three months. I can get straight again in three months."

Spalding had known of other men who had had the same belief in their ability to get straight in three months. It was unfortunate for Slade—and for Spalding—that Slade had used those words. Spalding hardened his heart.

"No," he said. "I can't promise anything like that. I don't think it's any use continuing this discussion. Perhaps I'd better walk home from here."

He put out his hand to the latch of the door, and, as he did so, Slade jerked the loop of cord over his head. A single turn of Slade's wrist—a thin, bony, old man's wrist, but as strong as steel in that wild moment—tightened the cord about Spalding's throat. Slade swung round in his seat, getting both hands to the piece of wood, twisting madly. His breath hissed between his teeth with the effort, but Spalding never drew breath at all. He lost consciousness long before he was dead. Only Slade's grip of the cord round his throat prevented the dead body from falling forward, doubled up.

Nobody had seen, nobody would know. And what that book had stated about the method of assassination practised by Thugs was perfectly correct.

Slade had gained, now, the time in which he could get his affairs into order. With all the promise of his current speculations, with all his financial ability, he would be able to recoup himself for his past losses. It only remained to dispose of Spalding's body, and he had planned to do that very satisfactorily. Just for a moment Slade felt as if all this were only some heated dream, some nightmare, but then he came back to reality and went on with the plan he had in mind.

He pulled the dead man's knees forward so that the corpse lay back in the seat, against the side of the car. He put the car in gear, let in his clutch, and drove rapidly down the road—much faster than when he had been arguing with Spalding. Low water was in three-quarters of an hour's time, and the sands were ten miles away.

Slade drove fast through the wild night. There was not a soul about in those lonely lanes. He knew the way by heart—he had driven repeatedly over that route recently in order to memorize it.

The car bumped down the last bit of lane, and Slade drew up on the edge of the sands.

It was pitch dark, and the bitter wind was howling about him, under the black sky. Despite the noise of the wind, he could hear the surf breaking far away, two miles away, across the level sands. He climbed out of the driver's seat and walked round to the other door. When he opened it the dead man fell sideways, into his arms.

With an effort, Slade held him up, while he groped into the back of the car for the plough chain and the iron weights. He crammed the weights into the dead man's pockets, and he wound the chain round and round the dead man's body, tucking in the ends to make it all secure. With that mass of iron to hold it down, the body would never be found again when dropped into the sea at the lowest ebb of spring tide.

Slade tried now to lift the body in his arms, to carry it over the sands. He reeled and strained, but he was not strong enough—Slade was a man of slight figure, and past his prime. The sweat on his forehead was icy in the icy wind.

For a second, doubt overwhelmed him, lest all his plans should fail for want of bodily strength. But he forced himself into thinking clearly; he forced his frail body into obeying the vehement commands of his brain.

He turned round, still holding the dead man upright. Stooping, he got the heavy burden on his shoulders. He drew the arms round his neck, and, with a convulsive effort, he got the legs up round his hips. The dead man now rode him pick-a-back. Bending nearly double, he was able to carry the heavy weight in that fashion, the arms tight round his neck, the legs tight round his waist.

He set off, staggering, down the imperceptible slope of the sands towards the sound of the surf. The sands were soft beneath his feet—it was because of this softness that he had not driven the car down to the water's edge. He could afford to take no chances of being embogged.

The icy wind shrieked round him all that long way. The tide was nearly two miles out. That was why Slade had chosen this place. In the depth of winter, no one would go out to the water's edge at low tide for months to come.

He staggered on over the sands, clasping the limbs of the body close about him. Desperately, he forced himself forward, not stopping to rest, for he only just had time now to reach the water's edge before the flow began. He went on and on, driving his exhausted body with fierce urgings from his frightened brain.

Then, at last, he saw it: a line of white in the darkness which indicated the water's edge. Farther out, the waves were breaking in an inferno of noise. Here, the fragments of the rollers were only just sufficient to move the surface a little.

He was going to make quite sure of things. Steadying himself, he stepped into the water, wading in farther and farther so as to be able to drop the body into comparatively deep water. He held to his resolve, staggering through the icy water, knee deep, thigh deep, until it was nearly at his waist. This was far enough. He stopped, gasping in the darkness.

He leaned over to one side, to roll the body off his back. It did not move. He pulled at its arms. They were obstinate. He could not loosen them. He shook himself, wildly. He tore at the legs round his waist. Still the thing clung to him. Wild with panic and fear, he flung himself about in a mad effort to rid himself of the burden. It clung on as though it were alive. He could not break its grip.

Then another breaker came in. It splashed about him, wetting him far above his waist. The tide had begun to turn now, and the tide on those sands comes in like a racehorse.

He made another effort to cast off the load, and, when it still held him fast, he lost his nerve and tried to struggle out of the sea. But it was too much for his exhausted body. The weight of the corpse and of the iron with which it was loaded overbore him. He fell.

He struggled up again in the foam-streaked, dark sea, staggered a few steps, fell again—and did not rise. The dead man's arms were round his neck, throttling him, strangling him. Rigor mortis had set in and Spalding's muscles had refused to relax.

H AS IN HOMICIDE

(1969)

Lawrence Treat

Here is another story that uses the police procedural method of mystery writing. A careful investigation into a murder is conducted, leaving no stone unturned. There is no finer literary exemplar of this style than Lawrence Treat (1903–1998). Treat was a graduate of Dartmouth College and Columbia Law School, although he never practiced law. His prolific output includes fifteen books and hundreds of short stories. Treat won three Edgar Awards and was one of four founding members of the Mystery Writers of America in 1945. Among his books are *D as in Dead* (1941), *Over the Edge* (1948), *Big Shot* (1951), and *Mystery Writer's Handbook* (1982). This Edgar-winning story is his best, from *Ellery Queen's Mystery Magazine*.

She came through the door of the Homicide Squad's outer office as if it were disgrace to be there, as if she didn't like it, as if she hadn't done anything wrong—and never could or would.

Still, here she was. About twenty-two years old and underweight. Wearing a pink, sleeveless dress. She had dark hair pulled back in a bun; her breasts were close together; and her eyes ate you up.

Mitch Taylor had just come back from lunch and was holding down the fort all alone. He nodded at her and said, "Anything I can do?"

"Yes. I—I—" Mitch put her down as a nervous stutterer and waited for her to settle down.

"They told me to come here," she said. "I went to the neighborhood police station and they said they couldn't do anything, that I had to come here."

"Yeah," Mitch said. It was the old run-around and he was willing to bet this was Pulasky's doing, up in the Third Precinct. He never took a complaint unless the rule book said, "You, Pulasky—you got to handle this or you'll lose your pension."

So Mitch said, "Sure. What's the trouble?"

"I don't like to bother you and I hope you don't think I'm silly, but—well, my friend left me. And I don't know where, or why."

"Boy friend?" Mitch said.

She blushed a deep crimson. "Oh, no! A real *friend*. We were traveling together and she took the car and went, without even leaving me a note. I can't understand it."

"Let's go inside and get the details," Mitch said.

He brought her into the Squad Room and sat her down at a desk. She looked up shyly, sort of impressed with him. He didn't know why, because he was only an average-looking guy, of medium height, on the cocky side, with stiff, wiry hair and a face nobody particularly remembered.

He sat down opposite her and took out a pad and pencil. "Your name?" he said.

"Prudence Gilford."

"Address?"

"New York City, but I gave up my apartment there."

"Where I come from, too. Quite a ways from home, aren't you?"

"I'm on my way to California—my sister lives out there. I answered an ad in the paper—just a moment, I think I still have it." She fumbled in a big, canvas bag, and the strap broke off and the whole business dropped. She picked it up awkwardly, blushing again, but she kept on talking. "Bella Tansey advertised for somebody to share the driving to California. She said she'd pay all expenses. It was a wonderful chance for me . . . Here, I have it."

She took out the clipping and handed it to Mitch. It was the usual thing: woman companion to share the driving, and a phone number.

"So you got in touch?" Mitch prodded.

"Yes. We liked each other immediately, and arranged to go the following week."

She was fiddling with the strap, trying to fix it, and she finally fitted the tab over some kind of button. Mitch, watching, wondered how long *that* was going to last.

Meanwhile she was still telling him about Bella Tansey. "We got along so well," Prudence said, "and last night we stopped at a motel—The Happy Inn, it's called—and we went to bed. When I woke up, she was gone."

"Why did you stop there?" Mitch asked sharply.

"We were tired and it had a Vacancy sign." She drew in her breath and asked anxiously, "Is there something wrong with it?"

"Not too good a reputation," Mitch said. "Did she take all her things with her? Her overnight stuff, I mean."

"Yes, I think so. Or at least, she took her bag."

Mitch got a description of the car: a dark blue Buick; 1968 or 1969, she wasn't sure; New York plates but she didn't know the number.

"Okay," Mitch said. "We'll check. We'll send out a flier and have her picked up and find out why she left in such a hurry."

Prudence Gilford's eyes got big. "Yes," she said. "And please, can you help me? I have only five dollars and the motel is expensive. I can't stay there and I don't know where to go."

"Leave it to me," Mitch said. "I'll fix it up at the motel and get you a place in town for a while. You can get some money, can't you?"

"Oh, yes. I'll write my sister for it."

"Better wire," Mitch said. "And will you wait here a couple of minutes? I'll be right back."

"Of course."

Lieutenant Decker had come in and was working on something in his tiny office which was jammed up with papers and stuff. Mitch reported on the Gilford business and the Lieutenant listened.

"Pulasky should have handled it," Mitch said, finishing up. "But what the hell—the kid's left high and dry, so maybe we could give her a little help."

"What do you think's behind this?" Decker asked.

"I don't know," Mitch said. "She's a clinger—scared of everything and leans on people. Maybe the Tansey woman got sick and tired of her, or maybe this is lesbian stuff. Hard to tell."

"Well, go ahead with an S-4 for the Buick. It ought to be on a main highway and within a five-hundred-mile radius. Somebody'll spot it. We'll see what cooks."

Mitch drove Prudence out to the motel and told her to get her things. While she was busy, he went into the office and spoke to Ed Hiller, who ran the joint. Hiller, a tall, stoop-shouldered guy who'd been in and out of jams most of his life, was interested in anything from a nickel up, but chiefly up. He rented cabins by the hour, day, or week, and you could get liquor if you paid the freight; but most of his trouble came from reports of cars that had been left unlocked and rifled. The police had never been able to pin anything on him.

He said, "Hello, Taylor. Anything wrong?"

"Just want to know about a couple of dames that stayed here last night—Bella Tansey and Prudence Gilford. Tansey pulled out during the night."

"Around midnight," Ed said. "She came into the office to make a phone call, and a little later I heard her car pull out."

Time for the missing girl to pack, Mitch decided. So far, everything checked. "Who'd she call?" he asked. "What did she say?"

Hiller shrugged. "I don't listen in," he said. "I saw her open the door and then I heard her go into the phone booth. I mind my own business. You know that."

"Yeah," Mitch said flatly. "You heard the coins drop, didn't you? Local call, or long distance?"

Hiller leaned over the counter. "Local," he said softly. "I think."

"Got their registration?" Mitch asked. Hiller nodded and handed Mitch the sheet, which had a record of the New York license plates.

That was about all there was to it. Nobody picked up Bella Tansey and her Buick, Prudence Gilford was socked away in a rooming house in town, and Mitch never expected to see her again.

When he got home that night, Amy kissed him and asked him about things, and then after he'd horsed around with the kids a little, she showed him a letter from her sister. Her sister's husband was on strike and what the union paid them took care of food and rent and that was about all; but they had to keep up their payments on the car and the new dishwasher, and the TV had broken down again, and could Mitch and Amy help out for a little while—they'd get it back soon.

So after the kids were in bed, Mitch and Amy sat down on the sofa to figure things out, which took about two seconds and came to fifty bucks out of his next pay check. It was always like that with the two of them: they saw things the same way and never had any arguments. Not many guys were as lucky as Mitch.

The next morning Decker had his usual conference with the Homicide Squad and went over all the cases they had in the shop. The only thing he said about the Gilford business was, the next time Pulasky tried to sucker them, figure it out so he had to come down here, personally, and then make him sweat.

Mitch drew a couple of minor assault cases to investigate, and he'd finished up with one and was on his way to the other when the call came in on his radio. Go out to French Woods, on East Road. They had a homicide and it looked like the missing Tansey woman.

He found a couple of police cars and an oil truck and the usual bunch of snoopers who had stopped out of curiosity. There was a kind of rough trail going into the woods. A couple of hundred yards in, the Lieutenant and a few of the boys and Jub Freeman, the lab technician, were grouped around a dark blue car. It didn't take any heavy brainwork to decide it was the Tansey Buick.

When Mitch got to the car, he saw Bella Tansey slumped in the front seat with her head resting against the window. The right hand door was open and so was the glove compartment, and Decker was looking at the stuff he'd found there.

He gave Mitch the main facts. "Truck driver spotted the car, went in to look, and then got in touch with us. We've been here about fifteen minutes, and the Medical Examiner ought to show up pretty soon. She was strangled—you can see the marks on her neck—and I'll bet a green hat that it happened the night before last, not long after she left the motel."

Mitch surveyed the position of the body with a practiced eye. "She wasn't driving, either. She was pushed in there, after she was dead."

"Check," Decker said. Very carefully, so that he wouldn't spoil any possible fingerprints, he slid the junk he'd been examining onto the front seat. He turned to Jub Freeman, who was delicately holding a handbag by the two ends and scrutinizing it for prints.

"Find anything?" the Lieutenant asked.

"Nothing," Jub said. "But the initials on it are B.T.W."

"Bella Tansey What?" the Lieutenant said. He didn't laugh and neither did anybody else. He stopped to put his hands on the door sill, leaned forward, and stared at the body. Mitch, standing behind him, peered over his head.

Bella had been around thirty and she'd been made for men. She was wearing a blue dress with a thing that Amy called a bolero top, and, except where the skirt had pulled up maybe from moving the body, her clothes were not disturbed. The door of the glove compartment and parts of the dashboard were splotched with fingerprint powder.

Mitch pulled back and waited. After about a minute the Lieutenant stood up.

"Doesn't look as if there was a sex angle," Decker said. "And this stuff"—he kicked at the dry leaves that covered the earth—"doesn't take footprints. If we're lucky, we'll find somebody who saw the killer somewhere around here." He made a sound with his thin, elastic lips and watched Jub.

Jub had taken off his coat and dumped the contents of the pocketbook onto it. Mitch spotted nothing unusual—just the junk women usually carried; but he didn't see any money. Jub was holding the purse and rummaging inside it.

"Empty?" the Lieutenant asked sharply.

Jub nodded. "Except for one nickel. She must have had money, so whoever went through this missed up on five cents."

"Couldn't be Ed Hiller, then," Mitch said, and the gang laughed.

"Let's say the motive was robbery," Decker said. "We got something of a head start on this, but brother, it's a bad one. Why does a woman on her way to California make a phone call and then sneak off in the middle of the night? Leaving her girl friend in the lurch, too. Doesn't sound like robbery now, does it?"

"Sounds like a guy," Mitch said. "She had a late date, and the guy robbed her, instead of—"

"We'll talk to Ed Hiller about that later," the Lieutenant said. "Taylor, you better get going on this. Call New York and get a line on her. Her friends, her background. If she was married. How much money she might have had with her. Her bank might help on that."

"Right," Mitch said.

"And then get hold of the Gilford dame and pump her," Decker said.

Mitch nodded. He glanced into the back of the car and saw the small overnight bag. "That," he said, pointing. "She packed, so she didn't expect to go back to the motel. But she didn't put her bag in the trunk compartment, so she must have expected to check in somewhere else, and pretty soon."

"She'd want to sleep somewhere, wouldn't she?" Decker asked.

"That packing and unpacking doesn't make sense," Mitch said.

Decker grunted. "Homicides never do," he said grimly.

Mitch drove back to headquarters thinking about that overnight bag, and it kept bothering him. He didn't know exactly why, but it was the sort of thing you kept in the back of your mind until something happened or you found something else, and then everything clicked and you got a pattern.

But, what with organizing the questions to ask New York, he couldn't do much doping out right now. Besides, there was a lot more information to come in.

He got New York on the phone and they said they'd move on it right away; so he hung up and went to see Prudence. He was lucky to find her in.

She was shocked at the news, but she had nothing much to contribute. "We didn't know each other very long," she said, "and I was asleep when she left. I was so tired. We'd been driving all day, and I'd done most of it."

"Did she mention knowing anybody around—anybody in town?" Mitch asked. Prudence shook her head, but he put her through the wringer anyhow—it was easy for people to hear things and then forget them. You had to jog their memories a little. And besides, how could he be sure she was telling all she knew?

He felt sorry for her, though—she looked kind of thin and played out, as if she hadn't been eating much. So he said, "That five bucks of yours isn't going to last too long, and if you need some dough—"

"Oh, thanks!" she said, sort of glowing and making him feel that Mitch Taylor, he was okay. "Oh, thanks! It's perfectly wonderful of you, but I have enough money for a while, and I'm sure my sister will send me the money I wired her for."

By that afternoon most of the basic information was in. Locally, the Medical Examiner said that Bella Tansey had been strangled with a towel or a handkerchief; he placed the time as not long after she'd left the motel. The Lieutenant had questioned Ed Hiller without being able to get anything. Hiller insisted he hadn't left the motel, but his statement depended only on his own word.

Jub had used a vacuum cleaner on the car and examined the findings with a microscope, and he'd shot enough pictures to fill a couple of albums.

"They stopped at a United Motel the first night," he recapitulated, "and they had dinner at a Howard Johnson place. They ate sandwiches in the car, probably for lunch, and they bought gas in Pennsylvania and Indiana, and the car ate up oil. There was a gray kitten on the rear seat sometime or other. They both drove. Bella Tansey had ear trouble and she bought her clothes at Saks Fifth Avenue. I can tell you a lot more about her, but I'm damned if I've uncovered anything that will help on the homicide. No trace in that car of anybody except the two women."

The New York police, however, came up with a bombshell. Bella Tansey had drawn $1800 from her bank, in cash, and she'd been married to Clyde Warhouse and they'd been divorced two years ago. She'd used her maiden name—Tansey.

"Warhouse!" the Lieutenant said.

Everybody knew that name. He ran a column in the local paper—he called it "Culture Corner"—and he covered art galleries, visiting orchestras, and egghead lecturers. Whenever he had nothing else to write about, he complained how archaic the civic architecture was.

"That's why she had the W on her bag," Mitch said. "Bella Tansey Warhouse. And Ed Hiller didn't lie about the phone call. She made it all right—to her ex-husband."

Decker nodded. "Let's say she hotfooted it out to see him. Let's say she still had a yen for him and they scrapped, that he got mad and lost his head and strangled her. But why would he take her dough? She must've had around seventeen hundred with her. Why would he rob her?"

"Why not?" Mitch said. "It was there wasn't it?"

"Let's think about this," Decker said. "Prudence says Bella unpacked. Did Bella start to go to bed, or what?"

"Prudence doesn't know," Mitch said. "I went into that for all it was worth, and Prudence *assumes* Bella unpacked—she can't actually remember. Says she was bushed and went right to sleep. Didn't even wash her face."

"Well," Decker said. "I guess Warhouse is wondering when we'll get around to him. I'll check on him while you go up there." The Lieutenant's jaw set firmly. "Bring him in."

Mitch rolled his shoulders, tugged on the lapels of his jacket, and went out. The first time you hit your suspect, it could make or break the case.

Clyde Warhouse lived in a red brick house with tall white columns on the front. Mitch found him at home, in his study. He was a little guy with big teeth, and he didn't really smile; he just pulled his lips back, and you could take it any way you pleased.

Warhouse came right to the point. "You're here about my former wife," he said. "I just heard about it on the radio, and I wish I could give you some information, but I can't. It's certainly not the end I wished for her."

"What kind of end were you hoping for?" Mitch asked.

"None." The Warhouse lips curled back, telling you how smart he was. "And certainly not one in this town."

"Let's not kid around," Mitch said. "You're coming back with me. You know that, don't you?"

The guy almost went down with the first punch. "You mean—you mean I'm being arrested?"

"What do *you* think?" Mitch said. "We know she phoned you and you met her. We know you saw her."

"But I didn't see her," Warhouse said. "She never showed up."

Mitch didn't even blink.

"How long did you wait?" he asked.

"Almost an hour. Maybe more."

"Where?"

"On the corner of Whitman and Cooper." Warhouse gasped, then put his head in his hands and said, "Oh, God!" And that was all Mitch could get out of him until they had him in the Squad Room, with Decker leading off on the interrogation.

The guy didn't back down from that first admission. He knew he'd been tricked, but he stuck to his guns and wouldn't give another inch. He said Bella had called him around midnight and said she must see him. He hadn't known she was in town, didn't want to see her, had no interest in her, but he couldn't turn her down. So he went, and he waited. And waited and waited. And then went home.

They kept hammering away at him. First, Mitch and Decker, then Bankhart and Balenky, then Mitch and Decker again.

In between, they consulted Jub. He'd been examining Warhouse's car for soil that might match samples from French Woods; for evidence of a struggle, of Bella's presence—of anything at all. The examination drew a blank. Warhouse grinned his toothy grin and kept saying no. And late that night they gave up on him, brought him across the courtyard to the city jail, and left him there for the night. He needed sleep—and so did the Homicide Squad.

At the conference the next morning, Decker was grim. "We have an ex-wife calling her ex-husband at midnight and making an appointment; we have his statement that he went and she never showed up; and we have a homicide and that's all."

"The dough," Bankhart said.

Decker nodded "When we find that seventeen hundred, then we might have a case. We'll get warrants and we'll look for it but let's assume we draw another blank. Then what?"

"Let's have another session with Ed Hiller," Mitch said.

They had it, and they had a longer one with Warhouse, and they were still nowhere. They'd gone into the Warhouse background thoroughly. He earned good money, paid his bills promptly, and got along well with his second wife. He liked women, they went for him, and he was a humdinger with them, although he was not involved in any scandal. But in Mitch's book, he'd humdinged once too often. Still, you had to prove it.

For a while they concentrated on The Happy Inn. But the motel guests either couldn't be found, because they'd registered under fake names with fake license numbers, or else they said they'd been asleep and had no idea what was going on outside.

The usual tips came in—crank stuff that had to be followed up. The killer had been seen, somebody had heard Bella scream for help, somebody else had had a vision. Warhouse had been spotted waiting on the corner, which proved nothing except he'd arrived there first. Every tip checked out either as useless or a phony. The missing $1700 didn't show up. Decker ran out of jokes, and Mitch came home tired and irritable.

The case was at full stop.

Then Decker had this wild idea, and he told it to Jub and Mitch. "My wife says I woke up last night and asked for a drink of water, and I don't remember it."

"So you were thirsty," Mitch remarked.

"Don't you get it?" Decker exclaimed. "People wake up, then go back to sleep, and in the morning they don't even know they were awake. Well, we know Bella packed her bag, and she was in that motel room with Prudence and must have made some noise and possibly even talked. I'll bet a pair of pink panties that Prudence woke up, and then forgot all about it. She has a clue buried deep in her mind."

"Granted," Jub said, "but how are you going to dig it up?"

"I'll hypnotize her," Decker said, with fire in his eyes. "I'll ask a psychiatrist to get her to free-associate. Taylor, ask her to come in tomorrow morning, when my mind is fresh. And hers, too."

Mitch dropped in on Prudence and gave her the message, but the way he saw things, the Lieutenant was sure reaching for it—far out. Mitch told Amy about this screwy idea of Decker's, but all she said was that tomorrow was payday and not to forget to send the fifty dollars to her sister.

That was why Mitch wasn't around when Prudence showed up. He took his money over to the Post Office and there, on account he liked to jaw a little, make friends, set up contacts—you never knew when you might need them—he got to gabbing with the postal clerk.

His name was Cornell and he was tired. Mitch figured the guy was born that way. Besides, there was something about a Post Office that dragged at you. No fun in it, nothing ever happened. All the stamps were the same (or looked the same) and all the clerks were the same (or looked the same) and if anything unusual came up, you checked it in the regulations and did what the rules said, exactly. And if the rules didn't tell you, then the thing couldn't be done, so you sent the customer away and went back to selling stamps.

Which people either wanted, or they didn't. There were no sales, no bargains. A damaged stamp was never marked down—it was worth what it said on its face, or nothing. There was nothing in between.

Still, the Post Office was a hell of a lot better than what Decker was doing over at the Homicide Squad, so Mitch handed in his fifty bucks for the money order and said, "It's not much dough, I guess. What's the most you ever handled?"

The clerk came alive. "Ten thousand dollars. Six years ago."

"The hell with six years ago. Say this week."

"Oh. That dame with seventeen hundred dollars. Seventeen money orders. That was the biggest."

Click.

Mitch said cautiously, "You mean Prudence Gilford?"

"No. Patsy Grant."

"P.G.—same thing," Mitch said with certainty. "Same girl. And I'll bet she sent the dough to herself care of General Delivery, somewhere in California."

Cornell looked as if he thought Mitch were some kind of magician. "That's right," he said. "How did you know?"

"Me?" Mitch said, seeing that it all fitted like a glove. Prudence—or whatever her name was—had strangled Bella for the dough, then packed Bella's bag, dragged her out to the car, driven it to the woods, and left it there. And probably walked all the way back. That's why Prudence had been so tired.

"Me?" Mitch said again, riding on a cloud. "I know those things. That's what makes me a cop. Ideas—I got bushels of 'em." He thought of how the Lieutenant would go bug-eyed. Mitch Taylor, Homicide Expert.

He walked over to the phone booth, gave his shield number to the operator so he could make the call free and save himself a dime, and got through to the Homicide Squad.

Decker answered. "Taylor?" he said. "Come on back. The Gilford dame just confessed."

"She—*what?*"

"Yeah, yeah, confessed. While she was in here, the strap on her bag broke and she dropped it. Everything fell out—including seventeen money orders for a hundred bucks each. We had her cold and she confessed. She knew all about Warhouse and planned it so we'd nail him."

There was a buzz on the wire and Lieutenant Decker's voice went fuzzy.

"Taylor," he said after a couple of seconds. "Can you hear me? Are you listening?"

"Sure," Mitch said. "But what for?"

And he hung up.

Yeah, Mitch Taylor, Homicide Expert.

THE ADVENTURE OF THE ABBEY GRANGE

(1904)

A. Conan Doyle

Here is another classic story about the quintessential detective, Sherlock Holmes. Along with his boon companion and narrator, Dr. Watson, he races off on a train to what proves to be "a most remarkable case." A. Conan Doyle has many imitators, but none quite measure up to the original, even after all these years. This story was first published in *Strand Magazine*.

It was on a bitterly cold and frosty morning during the winter of '97 that I was awakened by a tugging at my shoulder. It was Holmes. The candle in his hand shone upon his eager, stooping face and told me at a glance that something was amiss.

"Come, Watson, come!" he cried. "The game is afoot. Not a word! Into your clothes and come!"

Ten minutes later we were both in a cab and rattling through the silent streets on our way to Charing Cross Station. The first faint winter's dawn was beginning to appear, and we could dimly see the occasional figure of an early workman as he passed us, blurred and indistinct in the opalescent London reek. Holmes nestled in silence into his heavy coat, and I was glad to do the same, for the air was most bitter and neither of us had broken our fast. It was not until we had consumed some hot tea at the station, and taken our places in the Kentish train, that we were sufficiently thawed, he to speak and I to listen. Holmes drew a note from his pocket and read it aloud:—

"Abbey Grange, Marsham, Kent,

"3:30 a.m.

"My dear Mr. Holmes,—I should be very glad of your immediate assistance in what promises to be a most remarkable case. It is something quite in your line. Except for releasing the lady I will see that everything is kept exactly as I have found it, but I beg you not to lose an instant, as it is difficult to leave Sir Eustace there.

"Yours faithfully, STANLEY HOPKINS."

"Hopkins has called me in seven times and on each occasion his summons has been entirely justified," said Holmes. "I fancy that every one of his cases has found its way into your collection, and I must admit, Watson, that you have some power of selection which atones for much which I deplore in your narratives. Your fatal habit of looking at everything from the point of view of a story instead of as a scientific exercise has ruined what might have been an instructive and even classical series of demonstrations. You slur over work of the utmost finesse and delicacy in order to dwell upon sensational details which may excite, but cannot possibly instruct, the reader."

"Why do you not write them yourself?" I said, with some bitterness.

"I will, my dear Watson, I will. At present I am, as you know, fairly busy, but I propose to devote my declining years to the composition of a text-book which shall focus the whole art of detection into one volume. Our present research appears to be a case of murder."

"You think this Sir Eustace is dead, then?"

"I should say so. Hopkin's writing shows considerable agitation, and he is not an emotional man. Yes, I gather there had been violence, and that the body is left for our inspection. A mere suicide would not have caused him to send for me. As to the release of the lady, it would appear that she has been locked in her room during the tragedy. We are moving in high life, Watson; crackling paper, 'E.B.' monogram, coat-of-arms, picturesque address. I think that friend Hopkins will live up to his reputation and that we shall have an interesting morning. The crime was committed before twelve last night."

"How can you possibly tell?"

"By an inspection of the trains and by reckoning the time. The local police had to be called in, they had to communicate with Scotland Yard, Hopkins had to go out, and he in turn had to send for me. All that makes a fair night's work. Well, here we are at Chislehurst Station, and we shall soon set our doubts at rest."

A drive of a couple of miles through narrow country lanes brought us to a park gate, which was opened for us by an old lodge-keeper, whose haggard face bore the reflection of some great disaster. The avenue ran through a noble park, between lines of ancient elms, and ended in a low, widespread house, pillared in front after the fashion of Palladio. The central part was evidently of a great age and shrouded in ivy, but the large windows showed that modern changes had been carried out, and one wing of the house appeared to be entirely new. The youthful figure and alert, eager face of Inspector Stanley Hopkins confronted us in the open doorway.

"I'm very glad you have come, Mr. Holmes. And you too, Dr. Watson! But, indeed, if I had my time over again I should not have troubled you, for since the lady has come to herself she has given so clear an account of the affair that there is not much left for us to do. You remember that Lewisham gang of burglars?"

"What, the three Randalls?"

"Exactly; the father and two sons. It's their work. I have not a doubt of it. They did a job at Sydenham a fortnight ago, and were seen and described. Rather cool to do another so soon and so near, but it is they, beyond all doubt. It's a hanging matter this time."

"Sir Eustace is dead, then?"

"Yes; his head was knocked in with his own poker."

"Sir Eustace Brackenstall, the driver tells me."

"Exactly—one of the richest men in Kent. Lady Brackenstall is in the morning-room. Poor lady, she has had a most dreadful experience. She seemed half dead when I saw her first. I think you had best see her and hear her account of the facts. Then we will examine the dining-room together."

Lady Brackenstall was no ordinary person. Seldom have I seen so graceful a figure, so womanly a presence, and so beautiful a face. She was a blonde, golden-haired, blue-eyed, and would, no doubt, have had the perfect complexion which goes with such colouring had not her recent experience left her drawn and haggard. Her sufferings were physical as well as mental, for over one eye rose a hideous, plum-coloured swelling, which her maid, a tall, austere woman, was bathing assiduously with vinegar and water. The lady lay back exhausted upon a couch, but her quick, observant gaze as we entered the room, and the alert expression of her beautiful features, showed that neither her wits nor her courage had been shaken by her terrible experience. She was enveloped in a loose dressing-gown of blue and silver, but a black sequin-covered dinner-dress was hung upon the couch beside her.

"I have told you all that happened, Mr. Hopkins," she said, wearily; "could you not repeat it for me? Well, if you think it necessary, I will tell these gentlemen what occurred. Have they been in the dining-room yet?"

"I thought they had better hear your ladyship's story first."

"I shall be glad when you can arrange matters. It is horrible to me to think of him still lying there." She shuddered and buried her face for a moment in her hands. As she did so the loose gown fell back from her forearms. Holmes uttered an exclamation.

"You have other injuries, madam! What is this?" Two vivid red spots stood out on one of the white, round limbs. She hastily covered it.

"It is nothing. It has no connection with the hideous business of last night. If you and your friend will sit down I will tell you all I can.

"I am the wife of Sir Eustace Brackenstall. I have been married about a year. I suppose that it is no use my attempting to conceal that our marriage has not been a happy one. I fear that all our neighbours would tell you that, even if I were to attempt to deny it. Perhaps the fault may be partly mine. I was brought up in the freer, less conventional atmosphere of South Australia, and this English life, with its proprieties and its primness, is not congenial to me. But the main reason lies in the one fact which is notorious to everyone, and that is that Sir Eustace was a confirmed drunkard. To be with such a man for an hour is unpleasant. Can you imagine what it means for a sensitive and high-spirited woman to be tied to him for day and night? It is a sacrilege, a crime, villainy to hold that such a marriage is binding. I say that these monstrous laws of yours will bring a curse upon the land—Heaven will not let such wickedness endure." For an instant she sat up, her cheeks flushed, and her eyes blazing from under the terrible mark upon her brow. Then the strong, soothing hand of the austere maid drew her head down on to the cushion, and the wild anger died away into passionate sobbing. At last she continued:—

"I will tell you about last night. You are aware, perhaps, that in this house all servants sleep in the modern wing. This central block is made up of the dwelling-rooms, with the kitchen behind and our bedroom above. My maid Theresa sleeps above my room. There is no one else, and no sound could alarm those who are in the farther wing. This must have been well known to the robbers, or they would not have acted as they did.

"Sir Eustace retired about half-past ten. The servants had already gone to their quarters. Only my maid was up, and she had remained in her room at the top of the house until I needed her services. I sat until after eleven in this room, absorbed in a book. Then I walked round to see that all was right before I went upstairs. It was my custom to do this myself, for, as I have explained, Sir Eustace was not always to be trusted. I went into the kitchen, the butler's pantry, the gun-room, the billiard-room, the drawing room, and finally the dining-room. As I approached the window, which is covered with thick curtains, I suddenly felt the wind blow upon my face and realized that it was open. I flung the curtain aside and found myself face to face with a broad-shouldered, elderly man who had just stepped into the room. The window is a long French one, which really forms a door leading to the lawn. I held my bedroom candle lit in my hand, and, by its light, behind the first man I saw two others, who were in the act of entering. I stepped back, but the fellow was on me in an instant. He caught me first by the wrist and then by the throat. I opened my mouth to scream, but he struck me a savage blow with his fist over the eye, and felled me to the ground. I must have been unconscious for a few minutes, for when I came to myself I found that they had torn down the bell-rope and had secured me tightly to the oaken chair which stands at the head of the dining-room table. I was so firmly bound that I could not move, and a handkerchief round my mouth prevented me from uttering any sound. It was at this instant that my unfortunate husband entered the room. He had evidently heard some suspicious sounds, and he came prepared for such a scene as he found. He was dressed in his shirt and trousers, with his favourite blackthorn cudgel in his hand. He rushed at one of the burglars, but another—it was the elderly man—stooped, picked the poker out of the grate, and struck him a horrible blow as he passed. He fell without a groan, and never moved again. I fainted once more, but again it could only have been a very few minutes during which I was insensible. When I opened my eyes I found that they had collected the silver from the sideboard, and they had drawn a bottle of wine which stood there. Each of them had a glass in his hand. I have already told you, have I not, that one was elderly, with a beard, and the others young, hairless lads. They might have been a father with his two sons. They talked together in whispers. Then they came over and made sure that I was still securely bound. Finally they withdrew, closing the window after them. It was quite a quarter of an hour before I got my mouth free. When I did so my screams brought the maid to my assistance. The other servants were soon alarmed, and we sent for the local police, who instantly communicated with London. That is really all I can tell you, gentlemen, and I trust that it will not be necessary for me to go over so painful a story again."

"Any questions, Mr. Holmes?" asked Hopkins.

"I will not impose any further tax upon Lady Brackenstall's patience and time," said Holmes. "Before I go into the dining-room I should be glad to hear your experience." He looked at the maid.

"I saw the men before ever they came into the house," said she. "As I sat by my bedroom window I saw three men in the moonlight down by the lodge gate yonder, but I thought nothing of it at the time. It was more than an hour after that I heard my mistress scream, and down I ran, to find her, poor lamb, just as she says, and him on the floor with his blood and brains over the room. It was enough to drive a woman out of her wits, tied there, and her very dress spotted with him; but she never wanted courage, did Miss Mary Fraser of Adelaide, and Lady Brackenstall of Abbey Grange hasn't learned new ways. You've questioned her long enough, you gentlemen, and now she is coming to her own room, just with her old Theresa, to get the rest that she badly needs."

With a motherly tenderness the gaunt woman put her arm round her mistress and led her from the room.

"She has been with her all her life," said Hopkins. "Nursed her as a baby, and came with her to England when they first left Australia eighteen months ago. Theresa Wright is her name, and the kind of maid you don't pick up nowadays. This way, Mr. Holmes, if you please!"

The keen interest had passed out of Holmes's expressive face, and I knew that with the mystery all the charm of the case had departed. There still remained an arrest to be effected, but what were these commonplace rogues that he should soil his hands with them? An abstruse and learned specialist who finds that he has been called in for a case of measles would experience something of the annoyance which I read in my friend's eyes. Yet the scene in the dining-room of the Abbey Grange was sufficiently strange to arrest his attention and to recall his waning interest.

It was a very large and high chamber, with carved oak ceiling, oaken paneling, and a fine array of deer's heads and ancient weapons around the walls. At the farther end from the door was the high French window of which we had heard. Three smaller windows on the right-hand side filled the apartment with cold winter sunshine. On the left was a large, deep fireplace, with a massive overhanging oak mantelpiece. Beside the fireplace was a heavy oaken chair with arms and cross-bars at the bottom. In and out through the open woodwork was woven a crimson cord, which was secured at each side to the crosspiece below. In releasing the lady the cord had been slipped off her, but the knots with which it had been secured still remained. These details only struck our attention afterwards, for our thoughts were entirely absorbed by the terrible object which lay spread upon the tiger-skin hearthrug in front of the fire.

It was the body of a tall, well-made man, about forty years of age. He lay upon his back, his face upturned, with his white teeth grinning through his short black beard. His two clenched hands were raised above his head, and a heavy blackthorn stick lay across them. His dark, handsome, aquiline features were convulsed into a spasm of vindictive hatred, which had set his dead face in a terribly fiendish expression. He had evidently been in his bed when the alarm had broken out, for he wore a foppish embroidered night-shirt, and his bare feet projected from his trousers. His head was horribly injured, and the whole room bore witness to the savage ferocity of the blow which had struck him down. Beside him lay the heavy poker, bent into a curve by the concussion. Holmes examined both it and the indescribable wreck which it had wrought.

"He must be a powerful man, this elder Randall," he remarked.

"Yes," said Hopkins. "I have some record of the fellow, and he is a rough customer."

"You should have no difficulty in getting him."

"Not the slightest. We have been on the look-out for him, and there was some idea that he had got away to America. Now that we know the gang are here I don't see how they can escape. We have the news at every seaport already, and a reward will be offered before evening. What beats me is how they could have done so mad a thing, knowing that the lady could describe them, and that we could not fail to recognise the description."

"Exactly. One would have expected that they would have silenced Lady Brackenstall as well."

"They may not have realized," I suggested, "that she had recovered from her faint."

"That is likely enough. If she seemed to be senseless they would not take her life. What about this poor fellow, Hopkins? I seem to have heard some queer stories about him."

"He was a good-hearted man when he was sober, but a perfect fiend when he was drunk, or rather when he was half drunk, for he seldom really went the whole way. The devil seemed to be in him at such times, and he was capable of anything. From what I hear, in spite of all his wealth and his title, he very nearly came our way once or twice. There was a scandal about his drenching a dog with petroleum and setting it on fire—her ladyship's dog, to make the matter worse—and that was only hushed up with difficulty. Then he threw a decanter at that maid, Theresa Wright; there was trouble about that. On the whole, and between ourselves, it will be a brighter house without him. What are you looking at now?"

Holmes was down on his knees examining with great attention the knots upon the red cord with which the lady had been secured. Then he carefully scrutinized the broken and frayed end where it had snapped off when the burglar had dragged it down.

"When this was pulled down the bell in the kitchen must have rung loudly," he remarked.

"No one could hear it. The kitchen stands right at the back of the house."

"How did the burglar know no one would hear it? How dared he pull at a bell-rope in that reckless fashion?"

"Exactly, Mr. Holmes, exactly. You put the very question which I have asked myself again and again. There can be no doubt that this fellow must have known the house and its habits. He must have perfectly understood that the servants would all be in bed at that comparatively early hour, and that no one could possibly hear a bell ring in the kitchen. Therefore he must have been in close league with one of the servants. Surely that is evident. But there are eight servants, and all of good character.

"Other things being equal," said Holmes, "one would suspect the one at whose head the master threw a decanter. And yet that would involve treachery towards the mistress to whom this woman seems devoted. Well, well, the point is a minor one, and when you have Randall you will probably find no difficulty in securing his accomplice. The lady's story certainly seems to be corroborated, if it needed corroboration, by every detail which we see before us." He walked to the French window and threw it open. "There are no signs here, but the ground is iron hard, and one would not expect them. I see that these candles on the mantelpiece have been lighted."

"Yes; it was by their light and that of the lady's bedroom candle that the burglars saw their way about."

"And what did they take?"

"Well, they did not take much—only half-a-dozen articles of plate off the sideboard. Lady Brackenstall thinks that they were themselves so disturbed by the death of Sir Eustace that they did not ransack the house as they would otherwise have done."

"No doubt that is true. And yet they drank some wine, I understand."

"To steady their own nerves."

"Exactly. These three glasses upon the sideboard have been untouched, I suppose?"

"Yes; and the bottle stands as they left it."

"Let us look at it. Halloa! halloa! what is this?"

The three glasses were grouped together, all of them tinged with wine, and one of them containing some dregs of bees-wing. The bottle stood near them, two-thirds full, and beside it lay a long, deeply-stained cork. Its appearance and the dust upon the bottle showed that it was no common vintage which the murderers had enjoyed.

A change had come over Holmes's manner. He had lost his listless expression, and again I saw an alert light of interest in his keen, deep-set eyes. He raised the cork and examined it minutely.

"How did they draw it?" he asked.

Hopkins pointed to a half-opened drawer. In it lay some table linen and a large corkscrew.

"Did Lady Brackenstall say that screw was used?"

"No; you remember that she was senseless at the moment when the bottle was opened."

"Quite so. As a matter of fact that screw was *not* used. This bottle was opened by a pocket-screw, probably contained in a knife, and not more than an inch and a half long. If you examine the top of the cork you will observe that the screw was driven in three times before the cork was extracted. It has never been transfixed. This long screw would have transfixed it and drawn it with a single pull. When you catch this fellow you will find that he has one of these multiplex knives in his possession."

"Excellent!" said Hopkins.

"But these glasses do puzzle me, I confess. Lady Brackenstall actually *saw* the three men drinking, did she not?"

"Yes; she was clear about that."

"Then there is an end of it. What more is to be said? And yet you must admit that the three glasses are very remarkable, Hopkins. What, you see nothing remarkable! Well, well, let it pass. Perhaps when a man has special knowledge and special powers like my own it rather encourages him to seek a complex explanation when a simpler one is a hand. Of course, it must be a mere chance about the glasses. Well, good morning, Hopkins. I don't see that I can be of any use to you, and you appear to have your case very clear. You will let me know when Randall is arrested, and any further developments which may occur. I trust that I shall soon have to congratulate you upon a successful conclusion. Come, Watson, I fancy that we may employ ourselves more profitably at home."

During our return journey I could see by Holmes's face that he was much puzzled by something which he had observed. Every now and then, by an effort, he would throw off the impression and talk as if the matter were clear, but then his doubts would settle down upon him again, and his knitted brows and abstracted eyes would show that his thoughts had gone back once more to the great dining-room of the Abbey Grange in which this midnight tragedy had been enacted. At last, by a sudden impulse, just as our train was crawling out of a suburban station, he sprang on to the platform and pulled me out after him.

"Excuse me, my dear fellow," said he, as we watched the rear carriages of our train disappearing round a curve; "I am sorry to make you the victim of what may seem a mere whim, but on my life, Watson, I simply *can't* leave that case in this condition. Every instinct that I possess cries out against it. It's wrong—it's all wrong—I'll swear that it's wrong. And yet the lady's story was complete, the maid's corroboration was sufficient, the detail was fairly exact. What have I to put against that? Three wine-glasses, that is all. But if I had not taken things for granted, if I had examined everything with the care which I would have shown had we approached the case *de novo* and had no cut-and-dried story to warp my mind, would I not then have found something more definite to go upon? Of course I should. Sit down on this bench, Watson, until a train for Chislehurst arrives, and allow me to lay the evidence before you, imploring you in the first instance to dismiss from your mind the idea that anything which the maid or her mistress may have said must necessarily be true. The lady's charming personality must not be permitted to warp our judgment.

"Surely there are details in her story which, if we looked at it in cold blood, would excite our suspicion. These burglars made a considerable haul at Sydenham a fortnight ago. Some account of them and of their appearance was in the papers, and would naturally occur to anyone who wished to invent a story in which imaginary robbers should play a part. As a matter of fact, burglars who have done a good stroke of business are, as a rule, only too glad to enjoy the proceeds in peace and quiet without embarking on another perilous undertaking. Again, it is unusual for burglars to operate at so early an hour; it is unusual for burglars to strike a lady to prevent her screaming, since one would imagine that was the sure way to make her scream; it is unusual for them to commit murder when their numbers are sufficient to overpower one man; it is unusual for them to be content with a limited plunder when there is much more within their reach; and finally I should say that it was very unusual for such men to leave a bottle half empty. How do all these unusuals strike you, Watson?"

"Their cumulative effect is certainly considerable, and yet each of them is quite possible in itself. The most unusual thing of all, as it seems to me, is that the lady should be tied to the chair."

"Well, I am not so clear about that, Watson; for it is evident that they must either kill her or else secure her in such a way that she could not give immediate notice of their escape. But at any rate I have shown, have I not, that there is a certain element of improbability about the lady's story? And now on the top of this comes the incident of the wine-glasses."

"What about the wine-glasses."

"Can you see them in your mind's eye?"

"I see them clearly."

"We are told that three men drank from them. Does that strike you as likely?"

"Why not? There was wine in each glass."

"Exactly; but there was bees-wing only in one glass. You must have noticed that fact. What does that suggest to your mind?"

"The last glass filled would be most likely to contain bees-wing."

"Not at all. The bottle was full of it, and it is inconceivable that the first two glasses were clear and the third heavily charged with it. There are two possible explanations, and only two. One is that after the second glass was filled the bottle was violently agitated, and so the third glass received the bees-wing. That does not appear probable. No, no; I am sure that I am right."

"What, then, do you suppose?"

"That only two glasses were used, and that the dregs of both were poured into a third glass, so as to give the false impression that three people had been here. In that way all the bees-wing would be in the last glass, would it not? Yes, I am convinced that this is so. But if I have hit upon the true explanation of this one small phenomenon, then in an instant the case rises from the commonplace to the exceedingly remarkable, for it can only mean that Lady Brackenstall and her maid have deliberately lied to us, that not one word of their story is to be believed, that they have some very strong reason for covering the real criminal, and that we must construct our case for ourselves without any help from them. That is the mission which now lies before us, and here, Watson, is the Chislehurst train."

The household of the Abbey Grange were much surprised at our return, but Sherlock Holmes, finding that Stanley Hopkins had gone off to report to head-quarters, took possession of the dining-room, locked the door upon the inside, and devoted himself for two hours to one of those minute and laborious investigations which formed the solid basis on which his brilliant edifices of deduction were reared. Seated in a corner like an interested student who observes the demonstration of his professor, I followed every step of that remarkable research. The window, the curtains, the carpet, the chair, the rope—each in turn was minutely examined and duly pondered. The body of the unfortunate baronet had been removed, but all else remained as we had seen it in the morning. Then, to my astonishment, Holmes climbed up on to the massive mantelpiece. Far above his head hung the few inches of red cord which were still attached to the wire. For a long time he gazed upwards at it, and then in an attempt to get nearer to it he rested his knee upon a wooden bracket on the wall. This brought his hand within a few inches of the broken end of the rope, but it was not this so much as the bracket itself which seemed to engage his attention. Finally he sprang down with an ejaculation of satisfaction.

"It's all right, Watson," said he. "We have got our case—one of the most remarkable in our collection. But, dear me, how slow-witted I have been, and how nearly I have committed the blunder of my lifetime! Now, I think that with a few missing links my chain is almost complete."

"You have got your men?"

"Man, Watson, man. Only one, but a very formidable person. Strong as a lion—witness the blow which bent that poker. Six foot three in height, active as a squirrel, dexterous with his fingers; finally, remarkably quick-witted, for this whole ingenious story is of his concoction. Yes, Watson, we have come upon the handiwork of a very remarkable individual. And yet in that bell-rope he has given us a clue which should not have left us a doubt."

"Where was the clue?"

"Well, if you were to pull down a bell-rope, Watson, where would you expect it to break? Surely at the spot where it is attached to the wire. Why should it break three inches from the top as this one has done?"

"Because it is frayed there?"

"Exactly. This end, which we can examine, is frayed. He was cunning enough to do that with his knife. But the other end is not frayed. You could not observe that from here, but if you were on the mantelpiece you would see that it is cut clean off without any mark of fraying whatever. You can reconstruct what occurred. The man needed the rope. He would not tear it down for fear of giving the alarm by ringing the bell. What did he do? He sprang up on the mantelpiece, could not quite reach it, put his knee on the bracket—you will see the impression in the dust—and so got his knife to bear upon the cord. I could not reach the place by at least three inches, from which I infer that he is at least three inches a bigger man than I. Look at that mark upon the seat of the oaken chair! What is it?"

"Blood."

"Undoubtedly it is blood. This alone puts the lady's story out of court. If she were seated on the chair when the crime was done, how comes that mark? No, no; she was placed in the chair *after* the death of her husband. I'll wager that the black dress shows a corresponding mark to this. We have not yet met our Waterloo, Watson, but this is our Marengo, for it begins in defeat and ends in victory. I should like now to have a few words with the nurse Theresa. We must be wary for awhile, if we are to get the information which we want."

She was an interesting person, this stern Australian nurse. Taciturn, suspicious, ungracious, it took some time before Holmes's pleasant manner and frank acceptance of all that she said thawed her into a corresponding amiability. She did not attempt to conceal her hatred for her late employer.

"Yes, sir, it is true that he threw the decanter at me. I heard him call my mistress a name, and I told him that he would not dare to speak so if her brother had been there. Then it was that he threw it at me. He might have thrown a dozen if he had but left my bonny bird alone. He was for ever ill-treating her, and she too proud to complain. She will not even tell me all that he has done to her. She never told me of those marks on her arm that you saw this morning, but I know very well that they come from a stab with a hat-pin.

The sly fiend—Heaven forgive me that I should speak of him so, now that he is dead, but a fiend he was if ever one walked the earth. He was all honey when first we met him, only eighteen months ago, and we both feel as if it were eighteen years. She had only just arrived in London. Yes, it was her first voyage—she had never been from home before. He won her with his title and his money and his false London ways. If she made a mistake she has paid for it, if ever a woman did. What month did we meet him? Well, I tell you it was just after we arrived. We arrived in June, and it was July. They were married in January of last year. Yes, she is down in the morning-room again, and I have no doubt she will see you, but you must not ask too much of her, for she has gone through all that flesh and blood will stand."

Lady Brackenstall was reclining on the same couch, but looked brighter than before. The maid had entered with us, and began once more to foment the bruise upon her mistress's brow.

"I hope," said the lady, "that you have not come to cross-examine me again?"

"No," Holmes answered, in his gentlest voice, "I will not cause you any unnecessary trouble, Lady Brackenstall, and my whole desire is to make things easy for you, for I am convinced that you are a much-tried woman. If you will treat me as a friend and trust me you may find that I will justify your trust."

"What do you want me to do?"

"To tell me the truth."

"Mr. Holmes!"

"No, no, Lady Brackenstall, it is no use. You may have heard of any little reputation which I possess. I will stake it all on the fact that your story is an absolute fabrication."

Mistress and maid were both staring at Holmes with pale faces and frightened eyes.

"You are an impudent fellow!" cried Theresa. "Do you mean to say that my mistress has told a lie?"

Holmes rose from his chair.

"Have you nothing to tell me?"

"I have told you everything."

"Think once more, Lady Brackenstall. Would it not be better to be frank?"

For an instant there was hesitation in her beautiful face. Then some new strong thought caused it to set like a mask.

"I have told you all I know."

Holmes took his hat and shrugged his shoulders. "I am sorry," he said, and without another word we left the room and the house. There was a pond in the park, and to this my friend led the way. It was frozen over, but a single hole was left for the convenience of a solitary swan. Holmes gazed at it and then passed on to the lodge gate. There he scribbled a short note for Stanley Hopkins and left it with the lodge-keeper.

"It may be a hit or it may be a miss, but we are bound to do something for friend Hopkins, just to justify this second visit," said he. "I will not quite take him into my confidence yet. I think our next scene of operations must be the shipping office of the Adelaide-Southampton line, which stands at the end of Pall Mall, if I remember right. There is a second line of steamers which connect South Australia with England, but we will draw the larger cover first."

Holmes's card sent in to the manager ensured instant attention, and he was not long in acquiring all the information which he needed. In June of '95 only one of their line had reached a home port. It was the *Rock of Gibraltar*, their largest and best boat. A reference to the passenger list showed that Miss Fraser of Adelaide, with her maid, had made the voyage in her. The boat was now on her way to Australia, somewhere to the south of the Suez Canal. Her officers were the same as in '95, with one exception. The first officer, Mr. Jack Croker, had been made a captain, and was to take charge of their new ship, the *Bass Rock*, sailing in two days' time from Southampton. He lived at Sydenham, but he was likely to be in that morning for instructions, if we cared to wait for him.

No; Mr. Holmes had no desire to see him, but would be glad to know more about his record and character.

His record was magnificent. There was not an officer in the fleet to touch him. As to his character, he was reliable on duty, but a wild, desperate fellow off the deck of his ship, hot-headed, excitable, but loyal, honest, and kind-hearted. That was the pith of the information with which Holmes left the office of the Adelaide-Southampton company. Thence he drove to Scotland Yard, but instead of entering he sat in his cab with his brows drawn down, lost in profound thought. Finally he drove round to the Charing Cross telegraph office, sent off a message, and then, at last, we made for Baker Street once more.

"No, I couldn't do it, Watson," said he, as we re-entered our room. "Once that warrant was made out nothing on earth would save him. Once or twice in my career I feel that I have done more real harm by my discovery of the criminal than ever he had done by his crime. I have learned caution now, and I had rather play tricks with the law of England than with my own conscience. Let us know a little more before we act."

Before evening we had a visit from Inspector Stanley Hopkins. Things were not going very well with him.

"I believe that you are a wizard, Mr. Holmes. I really do sometimes think that you have powers that are not human. Now, how on earth could you know that the stolen silver was at the bottom of that pond?"

"I didn't know it."

"But you told me to examine it."

"You got it, then?"

"Yes, I got it."

"I am very glad if I have helped you."

"But you haven't helped me. You have made the affair far more difficult. What sort of burglars are they who steal silver and then throw it into the nearest pond?"

"It was certainly rather eccentric behaviour. I was merely going on the idea that if the silver had been taken by persons who did not want it, who merely took it for a blind as it were, then they would naturally be anxious to get rid of it."

"But why should such an idea cross your mind?"

"Well, I thought it was possible. When they came out through the French window there was the pond, with one tempting little hole in the ice, right in front of their noses. Could there be a better hiding-place?"

"Ah, a hiding-place—that is better!" cried Stanley Hopkins. "Yes, yes, I see it all now! It was early, there were folk upon the roads, they were afraid of being seen with the silver, so they sank it in the pond, intending to return for it when the coast was clear. Excellent, Mr. Holmes—that is better than your idea of a blind."

"Quite so; you have got an admirable theory. I have no doubt that my own ideas were quite wild, but you must admit that they have ended in discovering the silver."

"Yes, sir, yes. It was all your doing. But I have had a bad set-back."

"A set-back?"

"Yes, Mr. Holmes. The Randall gang were arrested in New York this morning."

"Dear me, Hopkins. That is certainly rather against your theory that they committed a murder in Kent last night."

"It is fatal, Mr. Holmes, absolutely fatal. Still, there are other gangs of three besides the Randalls, or it may be some new gang of which the police have never heard."

"Quite so; it is perfectly possible. What, are you off?"

"Yes, Mr. Holmes; there is no rest for me until I have got to the bottom of the business. I suppose you have no hint to give me?"

"I have given you one."

"Which?"

"Well, I suggested a blind."

"But why, Mr. Holmes, why?"

"Ah, that's the question, of course. But I commend the idea to your mind. You might possibly find that there was something in it. You won't stop for dinner? Well, good-bye, and let us know how you get on."

Dinner was over and the table cleared before Holmes alluded to the matter again. He had lit his pipe and held his slippered feet to the cheerful blaze of the fire. Suddenly he looked at his watch.

"I expect developments, Watson."

"When?"

"Now—within a few minutes. I dare say you thought I acted rather badly to Stanley Hopkins just now?"

"I trust your judgment."

"A very sensible reply, Watson. You must look at it this way: what I know is unofficial; what he knows is official. I have the right to private judgment, but he has none. He must disclose all, or he is a traitor to his service. In a doubtful case I would not put him in so painful a position, and so I reserve my information until my own mind is clear upon the matter."

"But when will that be?"

"The time has come. You will now be present at the last scene of a remarkable little drama."

There was a sound upon the stairs, and our door was opened to admit as fine a specimen of manhood as ever passed through it. He was a very tall young man, golden-moustached, blue-eyed, with a skin which had been burned by tropical suns, and a springy step which showed that the huge frame was as active as it was strong. He closed the door behind him, and then he stood with clenched hands and heaving breast, choking down some overmastering emotion.

"Sit down, Captain Croker. You got my telegram?"

Our visitor sank into an arm-chair and looked from one to the other of us with questioning eyes.

"I got your telegram, and I came at the hour you said. I heard that you had been down to the office. There was no getting away from you. Let's hear the worst. What are you going to do with me? Arrest me? Speak out, man! You can't sit there and play with me like a cat with a mouse."

"Give him a cigar," said Holmes. "Bite on that, Captain Croker, and don't let your nerves run away with you. I should not sit here smoking with you if I thought that you were a common criminal, you may be sure of that. Be frank with me, and we may do some good. Play tricks with me, and I'll crush you."

"What do you wish me to do?"

"To give me a true account of all that happened at the Abbey Grange last night—a *true* account, mind you, with nothing added and nothing taken off. I know so much already that if you go one inch off the straight I'll blow this police whistle from my window and the affair goes out of my hands for ever."

The sailor thought for a little. Then he struck his leg with his great, sunburned hand.

"I'll chance it," he cried. "I believe you are a man of your word, and a white man, and I'll tell you the whole story. But one thing I will say first. So far as I am concerned I regret nothing and I fear nothing, and I would do it all again and be proud of the job. Curse the beast, if he had as many lives as a cat he would owe them all to me! But it's the lady, Mary—Mary Fraser—for never will I call her by that accursed name. When I think of getting her into trouble, I who would give my life just to bring one smile to her dear face, it's that that turns my soul into water. And yet—and yet—what less could I do? I'll tell you my story, gentlemen, and then I'll ask you as man to man what less could I do.

"I must go back a bit. You seem to know everything, so I expect that you know that I met her when she was a passenger and I was first officer of the *Rock of Gibraltar*. From the first day I met her she was the only woman to me. Every day of that voyage I loved her more, and many a time since have I kneeled down in the darkness of the night watch and kissed the deck of that ship because I knew her dear feet had trod it. She was never engaged to me. She treated me as fairly as ever a woman treated a man. I have no complaint to make. It was all love on my side, and all good comradeship and friendship on hers. When we parted she was a free woman, but I could never again be a free man.

"Next time I came back from sea I heard of her marriage. Well, why shouldn't she marry whom she liked? Title and money—who could carry them better than she? She was born for all that is beautiful and dainty. I didn't grieve over her marriage. I was not such a selfish hound as that. I just rejoiced that good luck had come her way, and that she had not thrown herself away on a penniless sailor. That's how I loved Mary Fraser.

"Well, I never thought to see her again; but last voyage I was promoted, and the new boat was not yet launched, so I had to wait for a couple of months with my people at Sydenham. One day out in a country lane I met Theresa Wright, her old maid. She told me about her, about him, about everything. I tell you, gentlemen, it nearly drove me mad. This drunken hound, that he should dare to raise his hand to her whose boots he was not worthy to lick! I met Theresa again. Then I met Mary herself—and met her again. Then she would meet me no more. But the other day I had a notice that I was to start on my voyage within a week, and I determined that I would see her once before I left. Theresa was always my friend, for she loved Mary and hated this villain almost as much as I did. From her I learned the ways of the house. Mary used to sit up reading in her own little room downstairs. I crept round there last night and scratched at the window. At first she would not open to me, but in her heart I know that now she loves me, and she could not leave me in the frosty night. She whispered to me to come round to the big front window, and I found it open before me so as to let me into the dining-room. Again I heard from her own lips things that made my blood boil, and again I cursed this brute who mishandled the woman that I loved. Well, gentlemen, I was standing with her just inside the window, in all innocence, as Heaven is my judge, when he rushed like a madman into the room, called her the vilest name that a man could use to a woman, and welted her across the face with the stick he had in his hand. I had sprung for the poker, and it was a fair fight between us. See here on my arm where his first blow fell. Then it was my turn, and I went through him as if he had been a rotten pumpkin. Do you think I was sorry? Not I! It was his life or mine, but far more than that it was his life or hers, for how could I leave her in the power of this madman? That was how I killed him. Was I wrong? Well, then, what would either of you gentlemen have done if you had been in my position?

"She had screamed when he struck her, and that brought old Theresa down from the room above. There was a bottle of wine on the sideboard, and I opened it and poured a little between Mary's lips, for she was half dead with the shock. Then I took a drop myself. Theresa was as cool as ice, and it was her plot as much as mine. We must make it appear that burglars had done the thing. Theresa kept on repeating our story to her mistress, while I swarmed up and cut the rope of the bell. Then I lashed her in her chair, and frayed out the end of the rope to make it look natural, else they would wonder how in the world a burglar could have got up there to cut it. Then I gathered up a few plates and pots of silver, to carry out the idea of a robbery, and there I left them with orders to give the alarm when I had a quarter of an hour's start. I dropped the silver into the pond and made off for Sydenham, feeling that for once in my life I had done a real good night's work. And that's the truth and the whole truth, Mr. Holmes, if it costs me my neck."

Holmes smoked for some time in silence. Then he crossed the room and shook our visitor by the hand.

"That's what I think," said he. "I know that every word is true, for you have hardly said a word which I did not know. No one but an acrobat or a sailor could have got up to that bell-rope from the bracket, and no one but a sailor could have made the knots with which the cord was fastened to the chair. Only once had this lady been brought into contact with sailors, and that was on her voyage, and it was someone of her own class of life, since she was trying hard to shield him and so showing that she loved him. You see how easy it was for me to lay my hands upon you when once I had started upon the right trail."

"I thought the police never could have seen through our dodge."

"And the police haven't; nor will they, to the best of my belief. No, look here, Captain Croker, this is a very serious matter, though I am willing to admit that you acted under the most extreme provocation to which any man could be subjected. I am not sure that in defence of your own life your action will not be pronounced legitimate. However, that is for a British jury to decide. Meanwhile I have so much sympathy for you that if you choose to disappear in the next twenty-four hours I will promise you that no one will hinder you."

"And then it will all come out?"

"Certainly it will come out."

The sailor flushed with anger.

"What sort of proposal is that to make to a man? I know enough of law to understand that Mary would be had as accomplice. Do you think I would leave her alone to face the music while I slunk away? No, sir; let them do their worst upon me, but for Heaven's sake, Mr. Holmes, find some way of keeping my poor Mary out of the courts."

Holmes for a second time held out his hand to the sailor.

"I was only testing you, and you ring true every time. Well, it is a great responsibility that I take upon myself, but I have given Hopkins an excellent hint, and if he can't avail himself of it I can do no more. See here, Captain Croker, we'll do this in due form of law. You are the prisoner. Watson, you are a British jury, and I never met a man who was more eminently fitted to represent one. I am the judge. Now, gentlemen of the jury, you have heard the evidence. Do you find the prisoner guilty or not guilty?"

"Not guilty, my lord," said I.

"Vox populi, vox Dei. You are acquitted, Captain Croker. So long as the law does not find some other victim you are safe from me. Come back to this lady in a year, and may her future and yours justify us in the judgment which we have pronounced this night."

PERMISSIONS ACKNOWLEDGMENTS

Grateful acknowledgment is extended to the following authors, publications, and agents.

Edgar Allan Poe, "The Black Cat," originally published in *Saturday Evening Post*, August 1843.

Roald Dahl, "Lamb to the Slaughter," from *Someone Like You*, 1954. Reprinted by permission of the Estate of Roald Dahl and Watkins/Loomis Agency.

Agatha Christie, "Philomel Cottage," originally published in 1927 and reprinted in *The Listerdale Mystery*, copyright 1934.

A. Conan Doyle, "The Adventure of the Speckled Band," originally published in *Strand Magazine* in 1905.

Thomas Burke, "The Hands of Mr. Ottermole," from *A Tea Shop in Limehouse*, 1931.

Ben Ray Redman, "The Perfect Crime," originally published in *Harper's Monthly Magazine* in 1928.

Anthony Berkeley, "The Avenging Chance," originally published in 1925.

Brendan DuBois, "The Dark Snow," originally published in *Playboy*, November 1996. Used by permission of the author.

Stanley Ellin, "The Specialty of the House." Copyright © 1948 by Stanley Ellin, renewed 1976. First published in *Ellery Queen's Mystery Magazine*. Reprinted by permission of Curtis Brown, Ltd.

Dorothy L. Sayers, "Suspicion," originally published in *Mystery League Magazine* in 1933.

Ellery Queen, "The Adventure of the Needle's Eye." Copyright © 1951 Mercury Publications, Inc. Copyright renewed by Ellery Queen. Reproduced here with the permission of the Frederic Dannay and Manfred B. Lee Literary Property Trusts and their agent, JackTime, 3 Erold Court, Allendale, NJ 07401.

John Updike, "Bech Noir," from *Bech at Bay: A Quasi-Novel*, copyright © 1998 by John Updike. Adapted from "Bech Noir" first published in *The New Yorker*. Used by permission of Alfred A. Knopf, a division of Random House, Inc.

Donald E. Westlake, "Never Shake a Family Tree," originally published in *Alfred Hitchcock's Mystery Magazine*, March 1961. Copyright 1961 by Donald E. Westlake. Reprinted by permission of the author.

Francis Iles, "Dark Journey," copyright 1934 by Anthony Berkeley Cox.

Ruth Rendell, "The Fall of a Coin," originally published in *Ellery Queen's Mystery Magazine*, 1975. Reprinted by permission of SLL/Sterling Lord Literistic, Inc. Copyright by Ruth Rendell.

Lord Dunsany, "The Two Bottles of Relish," originally published in 1922.

Vincent Starrett, "The Eleventh Juror," originally published in 1927.

James Holding, "The Inquisitive Butcher of Nice," originally published in *Ellery Queen's Mystery Magazine* and copyrighted in 1963 by Davis Publications, Inc.

Hugh Walpole, "The Silver Mask," from *All Soul's Night*, 1933.

Lawrence Block, "Keller on the Spot," originally published in *Playboy*, November 1997. Reprinted by permission of the author.

Permissions Acknowledgments

Anthony Gilbert, "The Invisible Witness," from *Ellery Queen's Mystery Magazine*, copyright 1973.

Clark Howard, "Under Suspicion," originally published in *Ellery Queen's Mystery Magazine*. Copyright 2000 by Clark Howard. Reprinted by permission of the author.

C. S. Forester, "The Turn of the Tide," copyright 1934 by C. S. Forester.

Lawrence Treat, "H as in Homicide." © 1964 by Davis Publications, Inc. Copyright renewed 1992 by Bantam Doubleday Dell Direct, Inc. The story first appeared in *Ellery Queen's Mystery Magazine*, published by Dell Magazines. Reprinted by permission of Rose Treat.

A. Conan Doyle, "The Adventure of the Abbey Grange," originally published in *Strand Magazine*, September 1904.